Bean in Love

Annie Hansen

To Jennifer —
Enjoy!
♡ Ann Hant

HF
Publishing

Also by Annie Hansen

Give Me Chocolate
A Kelly Clark Mystery

Dedication

This book is dedicated to my three angels:
Austin Hansen, Benjamin Hansen, and Aubrey Hansen.

Chapter 1

"Please, just take the money," I said.

My sister, Nikki, lounged on my living room couch with one of my gossip magazines like she didn't have a care in the world, though I knew different. She didn't even acknowledge my attempt to compensate her for allowing me to crash in her apartment above Chocolate Love, her specialty dessert shop in downtown Geneva, Illinois. I'd been living here rent free for almost a year now, and the guilt was killing me. I was starting to feel like a squatter.

"Do you think all of these photos are staged? I'm never this made up when I go to the grocery store. How could these people look like this? Kelly, see what I mean? Stars without make-up. Yeah, right. She's totally wearing make-up. And eyelash extensions! I have never even worn those, let alone worn them to a grocery store." Nikki's hand reached up and pinched at her eyelashes. "Maybe I should try them. Wow, do you smell that? They're making caramel brownies downstairs. Smells like it's going good, right? Or, wait, are they burning?" Nikki sat up and sniffed the air.

"Nikki," I said a little louder, interrupting her rant. "Will you at least look at me?"

Nikki let out an over the top sigh and tossed the magazine on the couch. She adjusted the sleeves on her pumpkin colored, zip-up fleece and finally swung her cocoa eyes in my direction.

"Please take this check," I said, holding the written check out to her. "It's time. It's *long* past time." The check shook slightly in my hand. I gripped it harder, trying to steady myself.

"We already did this two weeks ago. I'm not going to start taking money from you."

"Things have changed since then. I didn't know about your expansion project."

"The expansion has nothing to do with you, Kelly. We never planned on collecting rent for this apartment. I want you to spend that money paying down the debt you acquired from the divorce. Have you started that yet?" Nikki said, with a little more bite in her tone than I was used to.

Ouch. Automatically, my lips pulled up into a grimace. I fought to put them back in place.

"A little," I said, sinking down in my cushy office chair like a deflated balloon. There was no use lying to Nikki. It would be like lying to my own reflection. She knew me too well. It would take her less than a second to figure out I wasn't telling the truth. I pulled my long, brown hair out of its ponytail holder, allowing it to cascade around my shoulders like a shield from Nikki's words.

"But I don't understand. I had no idea the balance was that high. I don't even really remember opening that card to tell you the truth."

"It says right here that you did. We have your signature."

It would take me years to pay down what my lying, cheating ex-husband charged to credit cards in my name while he'd been wooing women behind my back. I hadn't even known some of the cards existed until he was sent to jail for attempted murder. Steve had been caught red-handed trying to kill a woman he impregnated while we were married. He got ten years, and I got all the debt. I also got stuck with the bills for our failed attempt at having a baby. Those IVF procedures were not cheap. With the recent sale of my new book, at least I finally had some money coming in. It wasn't enough though to cleanse me from my money woes. Still, I felt guilty living above Chocolate Love for free when Nikki could use my cash.

"I'm sorry to sound so harsh. I'm not trying to make you feel bad," Nikki said, shaking her head. "I'm so snappy today. Anyway, I'm just trying to help you get out of this hole. You're going to need all of the money you make on the sale of your books to pay off those cards and start fresh. If you start paying me, you'll be spinning your wheels. Just stick to the plan and start knocking off those high interest cards. Remember what the financial planner said?"

"I am doing those things. I just thought if I could give you a couple hundred dollars a month it would help. These are tough times," I said, referring to the struggling economy.

"Things are improving. Plus, coffee is booming during these tough times. It's where people are spending their money. If you're really serious about helping out, spend some time with me brainstorming on how we can do this. I want your brainpower, not your money," Nikki said, kicking her feet out onto my coffee table.

"Okay, then my brainpower you will get." I set the check on the table, somewhat relieved. As usual, Nikki was right. I still couldn't really afford to pay her rent.

Nikki smiled and lifted up her mug of hot chocolate. "Here's to making rent payments with your cranium," she said, lifting her mug in the air for a toast.

A knock on the door interrupted our toast. We studied each other as though we expected the other to know who it was.

"Who is it?" I called nervously.

I would never again open my apartment door without confirming who was on the other side. A few months ago, my older sister, Adelle, and I had been attacked by my ex-husband's psychotic girlfriend. She'd nearly killed us both.

So far, my experiences in life taught me you never knew what evil lurked inside of people. The ones you lived intimately day-to-day with, the strangers you passed on the street, and the ones that were on the other side of your apartment door. Everyone could turn on you. I'd become the most untrusting person on the planet. But who could blame me? Psychotic people seemed to run abundant in my life.

"It's me, Miguel."

Hearing his familiar voice, I reached for my hoodie on the back of my chair and put it on before opening the door. Miguel was Nikki's trusted right hand man at the store. He was welcome anytime, but nonetheless, I felt a bit naked in my yoga pants and skin tight, nearly see through tee-shirt I'd been hanging out in while working in my apartment. My newly added curves made me a little self-conscious. Not that I didn't love them. I'd just gotten used to life without them. I was happy to have them back. And excited to be in a place in my life where my body and my mind were healthy enough to allow them to come back. My weight loss post my divorce had not been an attractive thing. Skeleton was not a good look on me.

"I'm sorry to bother you ladies, but there is a problem. The cupcake order for Geneva High School is not right. The principal is on hold. She wants to talk to you, Nikki. I tried to work through it with her, but she keeps insisting on speaking directly to you," Miguel said, eyeballing Nikki for direction.

"No problem, Miguel. Melissa is an old friend of mine," Nikki said, bolting up from the couch.

"I'll come down with you and frost cupcakes for a bit. I need a break anyway."

"Okay, I'll run down and tell her you're coming," Miguel said.

"What about your book signing tonight?" Nikki asked as I locked up my apartment.

"I don't have to leave until five. It's an evening thing."

A small bookstore in Oak Park was hosting a book signing for me tonight. Since my book release last month, most of my time was spent promoting it and meeting fans. Because it was a Thursday in early October, I hoped the signing would go really well. In Chicago, fall was a great time to sell books and meet my target audience. The snow had not yet hit, and readers were still willing to venture outside of their homes. I had to do as many of these book signings as I could before the winter doldrums kept everyone locked inside next to their heaters.

Nikki and I walked together down the grand staircase leading from the second floor down to Chocolate Love. The smell of the caramel brownies got stronger and stronger as we descended the stairs, making me smile in anticipation. What a treat to live in a place like this. I grabbed onto the ornate, wooden railing with my right hand and ran my left along the wall. Nikki's in-laws had purchased this old Victorian home on Third Street in Geneva close to twenty years ago. Their hope had been to build a profitable business selling specialty chocolates to the wealthy citizens of Geneva. Today, the store was one of the main hangouts in the Historic District. It not only sold chocolates, but also ice cream, cupcakes, and toys for kids. The success of the store did not surprise me one bit. When Nikki went after something, she got it.

This afternoon, the store was filled with customers, mostly adults with small children inching up on their tip toes to get a glance at the delicious ice creams and fancy chocolates displayed in glass cases.

"What line is she on?" Nikki asked Miguel.

"Line one." We made our way through the crowd and slipped behind the glass counter to the back kitchen where Nikki kept a small office. Nikki had the store filled with pumpkins, gourds, and other fall décor to help put her customers in the mood for Halloween.

"What do you want me to start on?" I asked Nikki, before she grabbed the phone.

We had an agreement that whenever I was stalled on my writing, I helped by frosting cupcakes. Somehow it always got me past my writer's block and also made me feel like I was giving something back for living in the apartment rent free.

"Miguel will show you. I think we have a big order of vanilla cupcakes waiting in the kitchen," Nikki said before picking up the phone.

"Over here, Kelly." Miguel directed me to the counter where six trays of cupcakes sat.

"Wow, that's a big order," I said, nodding to the counter.

"It's for the Geneva History Museum. This month they're running the Haunted History Walking Tour every Thursday, Friday, and Saturday night. They want vanilla on vanilla and then the chocolate spiders placed on top."

"I can't believe it's already time for the ghost tours." My sisters, Nikki and Adelle, and I had gone on the haunted walk a couple of times. A member of the Geneva History Museum would lead a group of people around the town after dark while sharing urban legends. Some were based on true stories from the past, like the one about the two police officers killed while chasing a criminal down Third Street.

And some of the stories were just local Geneva folklore, like the one about the building that used to be a hospital and was now used as storefronts. Apparently, the lights flickered and merchandise moved around the store long after customers and shop owners had gone home for the night.

The town of Geneva was located right on the banks of the Fox River about thirty miles west of Chicago. In the early years, Native American tribes known as the Pottawatomi had ruled the land until the first settlers from Europe came over in the 1830s. When the railroad was laid through town in 1853, Geneva became connected to the city of Chicago, making it an illustrious location to visit or build summer homes. Although the town had grown significantly, things here were a lot slower and peaceful compared to city life.

My own parents moved here from Chicago over forty years ago when they were first married. They wanted to settle down in a nice suburban community before having children. My two sisters and I had been very happy growing up in Geneva and still lived here to this day.

After my divorce and harrowing escape from my life in San Francisco, Geneva was the first place I thought of to go. I needed a place to rebuild my life. Unfortunately, it quickly became apparent I couldn't hide from anything. Or anyone. Even in my beloved small town, evil lurked.

"What time do they need them?" I asked Miguel.

"The tour starts at seven. We should probably get them there by six for set-up."

I glanced up at the clock and saw it was inching near two in the afternoon. I threw on my apron and breathed out slowly. Time for some stress relief.

Just as I picked up my tools to start icing, the door leading from the store to the kitchen slammed shut with a bang. Startled, I dropped the icing onto the counter, causing it to splatter a couple of drops onto my pink apron that read, "Love Chocolate? Let it love you back. Give in to the craving."

My eyes jumped up to the door to see what could have caused it to slam. Normally, Nikki maintained an open door policy for the kitchen. She wanted curious shoppers to be able to look into the kitchen and see the work in progress.

"What was that?" I heard Nikki call out from around the corner.

Instead of answering her, my eyes locked on the man standing in front of the closed kitchen door. His complexion, though covered in scraggly facial hair, was a pale, milky shade of white, as though he had chosen to hide from the sun. His eyes swung frantically, searching for some unknown destination until finally landing on me.

A vampire, I answered Nikki silently in my head.

He looked familiar, but my fear blocked me from being able to grasp his name. On this warm autumn day, his sloppy, brown corduroys and wrinkled, tweed jacket seemed much too stuffy for the near seventy degree temperatures.

"I can't let them hear," he said in barely a whisper. He stayed glued to the door, but his anxious words filled the room with a nervous energy.

"Who?" I whispered back, wondering what Nikki's connection to this could possibly be. After all, he was here in her store. Although she always had the best intentions, she was a Clark sister. Trouble had the tendency to find us.

He jerked his head backward to the door.

It hit me then that this was Brian Sanders, the lead curator for the Geneva History Museum. He was nearly unrecognizable with his eyes blazing like he hadn't slept in days and his disheveled hair. What had happened to him? He'd been known to be eccentric, but right now he looked downright manic.

"What's going on?" Nikki asked, no longer on the phone. She came rushing into the room and stopped dead in her tracks next to me.

"She's back," he managed to get out. "And she wants revenge."

The sound of glass shattering on the other side of the closed door, combined with the intensity in the room, made me scream out in panic.

Chapter 2

"Sorry," I heard one of Nikki's employees call out. Patty pushed the door slightly open, sending Brian further into the room. His lip pulled up in annoyance as the door connected with his back. "Oh, sorry, Brian. Nikki, I just broke a few ice-cream glasses. No worries, I'll clean them up right now."

It registered then that Nikki was holding onto my arm tightly.

"Okay, thanks, Patty. No problem," Nikki said.

"Owww," I whispered to Nikki, causing her to release her death grip on my arm. Looking down, I noticed little half-moons had formed on my flesh from her fingernails.

"Brian, what's happened to you? You look like you've seen a ghost," Nikki said, making her way over to Brian.

Although clearly on edge like me, she didn't seem as frightened by Brian's appearance or comments. I, on the other hand, was ready to bolt out the back door.

"I think I have."

"Come in and have a cup of coffee. You look like you need one."

Nikki beckoned him to the little table set-up in the kitchen where employees took their break.

Without saying another word, Brian labored past me and plopped down hard on the chair. Instead of explaining himself, he simply dropped forward and put his head in his hands.

"I can't take any more of this. I think I need to go home. It's all too much," Brian whined.

"What is he talking about?" I whispered. My hand gripped Nikki's arm. "Is he okay?"

"I'll explain in a minute. Why don't you go grab him a black bottom cupcake from the front room? That's his favorite. Oh, and would you brew another pot of hazelnut coffee. We're running low."

I nodded my head yes to her request but grabbed her arm once more and narrowed my eyes at her.

Careful. He's unstable.

By the way Nikki held my gaze, I took it she understood my unspoken words. Her cocoa brown eyes blinked once as though sending code that she was okay to handle it alone.

This was why the community loved and embraced Nikki. She brought a personal touch to all of her clients. She wasn't afraid to get close to people. She was born with the skill. In that way, we differed so much. I'd always kept people at an arm's length. And now, after my life experiences, I wanted them even further away.

Reluctantly, I backed up toward the kitchen door and pushed through with my behind into the store. The last thing I saw was Nikki sit next to Brian and reach out to touch his arm. She murmured something to him, causing him to lift his head and stare at her. I allowed the door to close, shutting the moment off from the rest of the store. Poor Brian. He obviously needed some privacy. No one else needed to see his breakdown.

From what I knew of him, he took his job at Geneva History Museum very seriously, particularly at this time of the year when all of the fall activities and celebrations began. The Museum relied on him to be educated on all things Geneva for the Haunted History Walking Tour. The last time I went on the walk myself he told us it was his personal mission to teach people not only about the spooky stories of the area, but also the history of the Fox River valley and how it was settled. He wanted people to come back all year round rather than just the month of October.

There had been many times I thought of picking up the phone to schedule an interview with him. The main character in my Antique Murder Mystery Series, Mary, had just relocated to a suburb of Chicago from California. There were a million ways Brian's knowledge of the area could help my books.

Something had always stopped me from calling him though. Brian was so obsessed with his job it left me unsettled. Something about the vibe he gave off was too intense for me to be around. The energy threw me off. I knew he wouldn't let go of the ghosts of the past. He wanted them here with us now. That philosophy was the exact opposite of the way I was trying to live my life. I had to let the past go, so I could live again. Be present in the present. It was the only way for me to move on. Our mantras didn't seem to match up, and therefore we were incompatible.

"What can I get you, Kelly?" Patty asked, interrupting my deep thoughts. The glass had already been cleaned up. It must not have been as bad as it sounded.

I turned, startled by her words and adjusted my ponytail. When I didn't reply right away, Patty shot me a nervous smile.

Look, it's Nikki's crazy sister again, wandering through the store.

Patty was one of Nikki's employees responsible for working the front of the store. Her brunette, mid- length bob was streaked with strands of gray and her light blue, cotton shirt with Chocolate Love's logo on the front pocket was heavily starched. Every time I saw Patty, I was impressed by how well she presented herself. She was never messy or unkempt even after working a long shift behind the counter. I never understood how certain people were able to pull this off. My long, wavy hair was always falling loose out of my ponytail and my clothes were constantly getting full of flour or other various ingredients from the kitchen.

"I'm looking for a black bottom cupcake. Do we have any left?"

"Right here," she said, reaching her hand into the display case and pulling one out from the back of a tray.

"Thank you."

"Anything else?"

"No. I'm just going to brew another pot of coffee quick and get back to frosting."

"Let me do that for you. It will be my last task before heading home. What flavor do you want?"

"Hazelnut would be great. What time do you leave today, Patty?"

I glanced up at the clock above the coffee machine. The day had flown by and there was still so much to get done before heading out to the book signing.

"Nikki has me on 'mom hours.' I get to leave in a couple minutes, so I'll be home when Julie gets home from school."

Patty made quick work of fixing the coffee, efficient as ever. Technically, I could go back into the kitchen with the black bottom cupcake and come back and get the coffee when it finished brewing, but decided to wait instead with Patty.

After pressing a few buttons, she leaned back against the counter next to me. The store had emptied out from when Nikki and I came down. That was normal at this hour. One minute, the store was packed and then the next minute, no one. The crowds came back around three- thirty when school got out. Nikki called the hours between two and three-thirty "the dead zone" on weekdays.

"That's Brian from Geneva History Museum back there with Nikki, right?" Patty asked.

"Yep. Did you see him come in?"

"I did. He didn't ask if he could go back there. He just bolted past me into the kitchen. I hope Nikki won't be upset with me. Plus, I just broke two of the ice cream dishes. This has not been my day."

"She won't be upset with you, Patty. Nikki has an open door policy. She wants customers to come and talk to her. She's known Brian for years. The Geneva History Center has been a client for years."

"Oh, good. That's a relief. This is still my first month working here. It's been the perfect job so far. I don't want to blow it."

"Nikki's not like that, Patty. I'm sure you're going to do great here," I said lightly, trying to put her at ease.

"Thanks, Kelly. It's been a friendly environment so far. I think I'm just being paranoid. My husband recently lost his job."

Patty fiddled with a pen in her hand, and her eyes lingered on the floor.

"Oh, I'm so sorry to hear that. The economy has been tough on so many people."

"He's got a couple of interviews lined up, so I'm sure he'll be fine. It's just really stressful."

"I can imagine. How are you holding up?"

"Okay. It's tough living on one income. We've been pretty resourceful about our money, but, you know. When you get used to living a certain way and then you have to cut back, it's tough. We'll be okay." Patty pulled at the long sleeves of her shirt, straightening them out and clearing her throat. Her head bobbed up and down frantically as though in confirmation of something. I imagined she was telling herself they would be okay over and over.

I knew this loop way too well. How many times did I have to be my own cheerleader when things were looking bleak? My mind raced to think of something to pull her from the dark place I imagined her to be in.

The coffee machine beeped to signal its completion of the brewing process. Saved by the bell.

"Here, let me get you that cup of coffee. By the way, you referred to it as the Center. Did you know they are changing their name to Geneva History Museum?" Patty smiled and pushed herself forward to grab a mug from above the machine. I inferred by her crisp tone that she wanted to move on, so I chose not to say anything more about her husband's job loss. After all, she was talking to the queen of "can we move on already?!"

"That's right. I keep forgetting and using the old name," I said, watching Patty scan the mugs. She appeared to be having a tough time choosing. "Why did they do that?"

Nikki kept a collection of mugs on a corkboard hanging above the coffee machine. Some were gifts from friends, family members, and customers. She also had a few from childhood, college, and her early working years before taking over Chocolate Love. Patty finally picked a mug with a portrait of a Smurf on it. It brought back the memory of Nikki ripping open the packaging and yelling "Smurfette!" at the top of her lungs when she got it for Christmas from our parents years ago.

"I'm not sure, but I like it."

"So do I," I said.

"You want one as well?"

She must have seen the lustful expression on my face when she passed me Brian's mug. I was coveting the steaming, black coffee and the boost of energy that came with it. Coffee: my personal drug of choice, my addiction, my best friend, my loyal companion. I needed it tonight. It was going to take a lot for me to get motivated for this event.

Although I liked to dress up occasionally, this last month of promoting the book had been exhausting. It was not in my comfort zone to go out and speak to large crowds. As a writer though, it was part of the gig. I had to be able to go out and promote and market my work even though I wanted be home in a pair of sweats.

"Yes, I would. Thanks."

"I worked with Brian for a short period of time, you know," Patty said, surprising me.

"You did? When?"

"I was a volunteer docent for him up until a few months ago. I had to quit when my husband lost his job. There's no time to volunteer now that I'm working."

"What's he like?"

I regretted my question as soon as it escaped my mouth. The way I asked made me sound like I was digging for gossip, which was totally inappropriate, considering he was one of Nikki's clients. Yet, knowledge was power.

Patty paused before speaking. She reached up to straighten a coffee cup that was hung a little crooked on its hook. "He was really cool up until a few months ago. That was another reason why I quit. He changed."

Nikki popped her head in through the door.

"Hey guys. Did you find a black bottom?"

"Here you go," I said, passing her the cupcake.

"Awesome. Thanks."

"Oh, and here's the cup of coffee," I said, handing it to Nikki.

"Thanks."

"Is everything okay?" I asked Nikki quietly.

"Brian's just a little overwhelmed with his job. You should really talk to him sometime. He's so knowledgeable about Geneva. He'd be a great source for you, Kelly."

Nikki turned and headed back into the kitchen with Brian's cupcake and coffee in hand while I was left with my mouth open. What we just saw from Brian was clearly not just being overwhelmed. Was she in denial or was I being overdramatic?

She was right, of course, about one thing. He would be a good source of information. If only I weren't so freaked out by him. I'd learned to trust my inner voice, and right now that voice was screaming at me to keep my distance. My instincts did not have the greatest track record, yet still, they shaped my life. And at this moment, alarms were going off.

Patty wiped up the counter under the coffee machine and untied her apron.

"She's right. He does have a lot of good information. I learned a lot when I worked there as a docent. Just a word of advice. Take someone else with you."

"What do you mean?"

Patty diverted her eyes from mine as she made busy work of folding her apron into a small square, an unneeded task considering the apron would be hung on the employee hooks at the back of the store.

"Did he do something to you, Patty?" I asked, reaching out and touching her arm. Violence against women was a trigger button for me. It would be for anyone who had an ex-husband like mine.

"No, no, no. It's nothing like that. I really shouldn't be talking like this to you. I know you... Well, it's not like... He's not like..." Patty stopped talking as her face burned a crimson red.

He's not like your ex, Steve. It's not like what happened to you.

Was that what she was going to say? Ouch. Must I constantly be reminded that my story made national front page news? I was a labeled woman, no matter how far I moved on from the events of my past.

For a brief second, the image of Oprah pulling a wagon onto her stage with bags of lard in it popped into my head. She'd lost a ton of weight and was able to show the world what she'd shed. I was going to be pulling my wagon of lard for the rest of my life. And I would not shed a damn thing. No matter how far I went in life.

But it could have been worse, right? I thought to myself. I'd take my lard wagon over what could have happened any day. The woman and her unborn child had lived.

Coming back to the present, I focused again on Patty. She looked like she wanted to melt into the floorboards. "He's just a bit intense, if you know what I mean."

"I know exactly what you're talking about. You're right to trust those feelings. Thanks for the advice."

"Please don't tell your sister I told you this. I don't want to be the employee that gossips about clients."

"Of course."

"I've gotta go. Julie will be home soon. Can you hang up my apron for me?"

"Sure. See you tomorrow."

Patty passed me her apron and moved briskly around me to exit the store through the front door. I couldn't help but think handing me the apron and leaving that way was a sure way to avoid having to see Brian again. There was definitely something strange going on with Patty's behavior toward him.

In an effort to tidy up a bit for the three-thirty rush, I pulled out a broom and wiped up a few stray crumbs from under the glass display cases. Patty had left the place pretty immaculate, but I was still trying to avoid going back into that kitchen. Something shiny caught my eye under one of the cases, so I bent down to take a look. There appeared to be a gold backing of some sort lying on its side. Once in my hand, I guessed it to be some kind of pin backing. Perhaps it had fallen off of one of Nikki's employees? She sometimes had them wear pins on their aprons to promote new products or sales.

Suddenly my world went black when two large hands covered my eyes from behind. I dropped the gold backing to reach up and grasp at them.

"Give it to me," I heard an ominous voice whisper in my ear.

Chapter 3

"Jack, you scared me."

Jack released his hold of me and spun me around to face him. His green eyes lit up when they met mine, and his lips curled into a knock out smile. So many years we'd known each other, and so many years I'd loved him. Yet, still, his smile always made my heart melt. It was like coming home again and again. Being in his arms was my favorite place to be.

"Hi there," he said, bending his tall, athletic frame down to kiss me. He was 6'5", which was nice considering I was on the taller side for a girl. His law firm allowed him to work from home a few days a week if needed, hence his ability to drop in and see me in the middle of the day. Today he was dressed in casual, khaki slacks and a button down shirt, which I knew he preferred to the suit and tie he wore in the office.

"You look cute today. I like this little zip up thing you've got going on." He reached up and pulled the hood up onto my head playfully. "Sexy," he said, pulling me close to him.

I pushed him discreetly away. I was always on him to control his PDA at my sister's store. There was already enough talk about me here. Didn't need to add fuel to the fire.

"What are you doing here? I thought you were going to meet me at five?"

"I am. I mean, I was. Mom's not doing well today. I'm trying to coordinate with Mari to see if she can hang with her tonight, but I can't get a hold of her. I just wanted to give you a head's up in case I can't go. Maybe Nikki can go with you tonight?"

Jack and his sister, Mari, cared for their ailing mother, Peggy. She was still able to live on her own, but they took turns making sure she wasn't alone for too long a period of time. Lately, she'd taken a stumble or two while trying to move around her house. Luckily, the falls had not been too serious, but it was still enough to put Jack and Mari on high alert. They were trying to avoid the inevitable and stretch out the need for a nursing home as long as they could. Their mom was very verbal about wanting to stay home.

"I'm a big girl, Jack. I can go alone to these things. You guys have all been so supportive of these book signings. They must be getting old."

The truth was, I really wanted him there. He made everything fun in my life. The responsibility he felt for his mom though weighed on him heavily. Sometimes it was better to just go with the flow and get time with him later. Jack carried his own wagon of guilt for leaving his mom and living in London for a number of years before fleeing back to the states after a tumultuous divorce. There was a reason why we were together and why we worked. We got each other.

Taking a peek behind me, I moved closer and allowed myself to be swallowed into Jack's large arms. He raised his eyebrow at me in a teasing way and accepted my embrace.

"Come here, babe. I missed you," he said. He smelled of fresh soap and a tiny bit of after shave. As usual, Jack's smell was incredibly appealing and irresistible to me.

Despite the fact that we'd spent last night together, and pretty much every night for the last six months, I couldn't seem to get enough of this man. Our romance had begun when we were kids, and after an almost fifteen year separation post college, our spark had relit last summer. I made the mistake of letting him go once. I planned on doing everything in my power to keep him this time.

Luckily, he'd forgiven me for stupidly ending things years ago and seemed to feel the same way.

"I know you can handle it, but I like going to these things to watch you work. Plus, we were supposed to go to Winberries after your talk. Do you know how sad it makes me to think I'm not going to have a piece of their cheesecake tonight?"

I smiled up at Jack. He had a faraway look on his face. Jack loved me, but I'd never be able to compete with his love affair with food. It was the only mistress I would allow Jack to ever have. And what a sly mistress she was. There was never any evidence in his taught muscles and cut stomach that he liked to indulge. Quite unfair. A flash of Jack's strong chest ran through my head. Yes, I was a lucky woman indeed.

I reached up to play with his dark hair to get his attention back on me. He'd been wearing his hair a little longer this fall which gave me the ability to mess it up a bit. My plan worked. His eyes came back in focus and settled once again on me.

"I'll bring a piece home for you."

"Wait, you're still going to go without me?"

"Well…" I teased. At that moment, Nikki and Brian came through the kitchen door. Nikki took a second to place the stopper at the bottom of the door, so it would once again remain open.

"Thanks, Nikki. I'll see you around six," Brian said. Ignoring us completely, he shuffled past Jack and I in the direction of the front door.

"Sounds good, Brian. See you tonight," Nikki called.

"Is everything okay?" I asked when the store was empty except for the three of us.

"Kind of. It's a long story." Nikki stopped abruptly at the sound of the back door slamming shut.

Patty's replacement, Lisa, came in through the kitchen. She smiled at us while tying her apron behind her back. Her shoulder length, blond hair curled around her face, adding an angelic look to her young, pretty face.

"Hey guys. How's business today?" Lisa crouched down to check out the cupcake and chocolate displays in order to restock before the after school crowd piled in. Nikki had her scheduled to work the after school shift almost every day before she left for her evening classes at the local community college.

"Good," Nikki and I said in unison. Lisa stood up and raised an eyebrow at us.

"I have to finish my frosting," I said, hoping Nikki and Jack would follow me into the back kitchen, so I could ask about Brian.

"Wait!" I said, turning back around as I remembered the gold backing I dropped when Jack surprised me. "I dropped something. Just a second."

My knees cracked a bit when I bent down to look under the display case. The three miles I ran every morning were great for my psyche, but my knees were starting to protest as I aged. There had to be a way for me to ease up on them, but I needed that run in the morning. It was like a religion to me now. No run. No Kelly. My existence as a writer, sister, girlfriend, aunt, everything would cease. All would fall apart if I stopped.

The gold backing was nowhere to be found. I was starting to get grossed out crawling around on the floor and decided to give up. Why did I care about some dumb backing?

"Can I help you find something?" Lisa asked.

"Oh, sorry. I'm invading your personal space," I said, standing. When I did, my face was only a few inches away from hers. At this close proximity, I couldn't help but notice how few wrinkles she had compared to me. Her eyes didn't bear any of the laugh lines that were starting to find a home in the corners of my eyes. Oh, to be under thirty again.

I took a step back so as not to freak her out.

"I lost something a couple of minutes ago. It's a gold backing to a pin. If you find it, would you let me know?"

"Sure, Kelly."

"Okay, I'm going to frost. Wait, there it is," I said, bending down and picking up the shiny, gold pin backing under the counter where the coffee maker sat.

Tucking it in my hand, I stepped into the kitchen where Jack and Nikki appeared to be deep in conversation. Their talking came to an abrupt halt as soon as I walked in.

"What's going on?"

"We're just talking about tonight and how we can meet you at the book signing," Jack said innocently. He reached up and gave his head a quick scratch. It reminded me of something a dog would do when feeling anxious.

"Don't be silly. I can go by myself. You've both been to a zillion of these things. Nikki, you have an event, and Jack, your mom needs you. End of story."

"I would go, Kelly, but I have to set up at Geneva History Museum at six. I can send someone else to do it, but I promised Brian I would do the pumpkin thing with the cupcakes. No one else knows how to do it," Nikki said.

One thing that set Nikki apart from other local, specialty, dessert shops was her elaborate three-dimensional displays she made with her cupcakes and treats. Whatever a client wanted, she could accommodate. Around Halloween, she was famous for making a three-dimensional pumpkin with a cat coming out of the top.

"Are you still planning to take the train?" Jack asked, referring to the train that ran east or west out of Geneva. The stop was only a few blocks away from Chocolate Love, which was one of the reasons why the store was such a success.

"Yes. I'm going to grab the 5:05." My plan was to take the train eastbound into Oak Park, so as to avoid the horrendous traffic I would sit in if I drove.

"What time will you be home?" Nikki asked.

"I see where you are going with this. I will be fine. It's only a couple of blocks."

Geneva was not exactly a high crime area. It had a population of around nineteen thousand people, who were, for the most part, not hurting for money. I seemed to be the exception.

However, last summer, a chain of break-ins on Third Street rocked our community. A lot of the stores installed high-end security systems, and our small town was in a panic. In the end, it turned out to be just one person causing all of the trouble. Now that she was locked up, the town had relaxed, but the crime spree had left its mark.

"Don't worry. No one is going to mug me. In fact, when they see it's me, they'll run in the other direction because they'll know Kelly Clark doesn't have anything worth stealing."

Nikki and Jack didn't laugh.

"Why don't you drive instead," Jack suggested.

"That's crazy. It could take me close to two hours with the traffic. I would have to leave now in order to make it on time."

"Okay, just call me when you get in, and I'll meet you at the train," Jack said.

"But what about your mom?"

"She'll be asleep by then. I'm not planning on sleeping over there. We just want to make sure she has someone with her for dinner and to help her to bed. Mari is going over there early in the morning."

When we'd first started dating in high school, his mom was already a young widow raising two kids on her own. The stress had certainly taken a toll on her health. She was in good shape mentally, but after her stroke, her physical capabilities had declined.

"It won't be until about ten-thirty," I said, knowing Jack's penchant for going to sleep early. It was something the two of us had in common. We were both early to bed, early to rise types.

"I think I can make it," he laughed, flashing his bright white teeth. "Besides, this means I get to tuck you in."

"Oh, for heaven's sakes. I'm right here," Nikki laughed, making a gagging sound. "You know, at first when you guys got back together, all this cutesy talk was adorable. Now it's killing me. Get a room."

She was right. We were a bit over the top right now. It was just so nice to be together again. In some ways, it felt like there never really was a separation between us. Sometimes I wondered if we were meant to be apart after college, so when we got back together, we would appreciate what we had even more.

The issue now though was, what was next? Jack was hinting at getting engaged. I wanted that too, but the closer we got to it, the more I had to come to terms with the fact that there were trust issues I still had to overcome. Could I marry again? I did it once and it ended horribly. Steve was a cheat, a thief, a murderer. Could I have picked worse? It's not that I didn't trust Jack. I didn't trust myself.

"Watching you guys makes Bob and I look like an old married couple. It's only been five years!"

"You're lucky to have him and you know it. Don't complain," I said.

Nikki's husband, Bob, was one of the kindest, straightest arrows I'd ever met. When Nikki started dating him, I knew right away they were going to be a forever thing.

"It's fun to tease you. I'm a lucky girl. We both are. Wait, what is that?" she asked, pointing down at the gold backing I had in my hand.

"I was hoping you would know. I found it on the floor in the front room." Nikki shrugged.

"Not from one of your employees?"

"Not that I know of. We've worn pins on our uniforms in the past, but it's been a long time."

I tucked it into my pocket and got back to the matter at hand. "So, what was going on with Brian?"

"Yeah, he blazed out of here like he was on fire. That man is always in a hurry. He does give the best ghost tours though," Jack said.

"That's the problem. He's too good. He's actually starting to believe his own ghost tales. Right now he thinks he's being stalked by the ghost of Victoria Jacobs."

"Who is that again?" I asked.

"Don't you remember that story? It's on the ghost tour. Victoria was the young woman who was courted by the older gentleman. When she refused his advances, he killed her in her own house," Nikki said.

"I remember. My mom talks about it all the time. It's the house on First Street, right?" Jack asked.

Nikki nodded.

"What year did that happen? I vaguely remember the story but it's been so long since I did the tour." I moved a little closer to Jack, a slight shiver running through me. Although I didn't remember the exact details of the story, the untimely ending stuck in my head.

"It was somewhere around the turn of the century. Approximately 1910. Geneva's farmland was starting to be settled by wealthy Chicago families looking for a country retreat. Many of them were starting to settle here permanently. Victoria moved here with her family at the age of fifteen. By the time she was seventeen, she was the talk of the town. According to Brian, she had multiple male suitors anxious to become her betrothed. Her family was also anxious to get things settled for Victoria, so they put a lot of pressure on her to pick one to be her husband. Unfortunately, she wasn't that anxious to do so. She liked being the center of attention in town and took her time making her decision."

By the way Nikki retold the story with so much detail, I assumed Brian must have just recited it for her again.

"But she left the wrong man hanging," Jack interceded, flashing me a quick look before turning back to Nikki.

"Right, I remember it now. That old, rich guy killed her?" I said.

"He was never found guilty because it could not be proven he did it. But, old Mr. Weatherly was always considered to be her murderer by the people of Geneva. She was found strangled in her home right next to her beloved piano in the front window. The story is he became so enraged by her refusal to marry him, he strangled her and then simply dropped her body and stormed out of the house. No one else was home at the time, so there were no witnesses," Nikki explained.

"But her sisters told the police he was harassing her," Jack said. "They said she told him she was not interested, but he kept coming over and sending letters."

"How old was he at the time?" I asked.

"He was sixty-seven but she was only seventeen," Nikki said.

"Eww," I said.

"That poor girl," Jack said, putting his arm around my shoulders and pulling me closer.

"So, how does this all tie in with Brian?" I asked.

"The house is still one of the main attractions on the ghost tour. The family that lives there now still has a grand piano in the front window. Brian claims Victoria's ghost doesn't want him to have the house as part of the tour anymore. She doesn't want her story to be told over and over."

"Isn't that the opposite of how most ghosts work? Don't they want you to expose their killer, so they can have eternal rest?" I asked, thinking of all the silly television shows I'd seen on the spirit world.

"I don't know. I'm not an expert on hauntings. All I know is that Brian is completely freaked out. He said she keeps visiting Geneva History Museum late at night when he's working. She's wandering the archives in the basement, the upstairs apartment, the museum on the main floor. She's even calling him on the phone and leaving him messages. He's not sleeping well and feels like he's going a little kooky," Nikki said.

"Calling him? Ghosts use phones now? So, why is he telling you?" I asked.

"I don't know," Nikki mumbled. She looked away and fiddled with some pans on the countertop that suddenly held her interest.

Jack made eye contact with me. His green eyes squinted slightly, and he bit his lip.

"Nikki, come on. Out with it," I said.

"He wants me to help him."

"What do you mean 'help him'?" I asked.

"Not really just me. He wants *us* to help him."

"The three of us?" I twirled my finger in a circle to indicate Jack, Nikki, and myself.

"No. You and I. The Clark sisters. He wants us to do a séance to talk to Victoria."

"What?" I shrieked before breaking into a nervous laugh. "You told him no, right?"

Nikki's silence answered my question.

Chapter 4

"**N**ikki! I am *not* doing a séance with Brian. Are you crazy? Why would you think I would even consider something like that?" My hands immediately went to the zipper on my sweatshirt and ran it up as far as it would go as though signaling to Nikki just how closed I was on the matter.

"Okay, I think I better go. This looks like a matter between sisters. I have to get back to work anyway." Jack leaned over to kiss me. "Call me when you know what time your train will get in. I'll meet you at the station. And don't you dare agree to do this."

He leaned toward the tray of cupcakes I was working on and pointed to one. I was surprised it took him so long to ask.

"May I?"

"Of course, Jack. You know you don't need to ask," Nikki said. She always made plenty of extra when filling an order in case she needed them while assembling her three-dimensional creations.

Jack snatched it up from the tray and made a beeline for the door.

"Don't get into any trouble you two. And don't go knocking on the spirit world's door. They may just let you in."

"Nikki, don't you remember when we used that Ouija board as kids? I didn't sleep for a week."

"I know, I know. I'll tell him no. Seeing someone so desperate breaks my heart. You know what fear can do."

"Nope. Don't go there. Don't." I held my hand up in front of my face wishing there was something else on me I could zip up. Closed. Absolutely closed on the topic. Ghosts. Spirits. Hauntings. I knew all about them. They were everywhere in my life. And I didn't need more of it.

"He believes that Victoria's story should keep being told so other women who are harassed or stalked by men will remember her fate and go to the police. He wants us to convince her that her house and her story need to stay on the ghost tour."

"What? That is crazy. And why does he want me to help him? He barely knows me."

Nikki sighed and started rearranging cupcakes.

"So, I'm the poster child for abused women?"

"Sometimes God allows you to use the horrible things that have happened in life for good."

"Don't you dare bring God into this, Nikki. Especially when we're talking about Ouija boards." I put my hand down on the tray of cupcakes she was messing with and looked directly at her.

"Okay, let's just forget it. It's all pretty silly."

"I'm not doing it, and you're not either, right?"

Nikki didn't respond. She stared down at the cupcakes and moved her finger around as though counting.

"Right?" I asked again, with a little more edge to my voice.

"Right. No Ouija boards."

"Nikki, I'm not kidding. Jack's right, you know. We've had enough drama in our lives. Opening that door to the spirit world could only cause trouble."

"Let's just forget I brought this up. I don't know what I was thinking."

I shook my head at Nikki and picked up my bag of frosting. "I'm finishing these and then I have to get ready for my book signing."

"Okay, thanks. I have to head over to Geneva High School to meet with Melissa about her order. I'll see you tomorrow?"

"Sounds good."

"Good luck tonight. Don't forget to make sure to call Jack, so he can walk you home."

I smiled. "I won't. Don't worry about me. I'll be fine. Good luck with your pumpkin display."

"Thanks."

Nikki pulled a light jacket off of the antique coat rack she kept by the back door. The rack tipped slightly from side to side threatening to topple over. I watched to make sure I didn't need to go over and catch it.

Finally it settled on its base as I'd seen it do countless times before. The coat rack was one of the things Nikki took from the home we grew up in here in Geneva. My parents sold our childhood home a few years ago when they decided to downsize and move to a small condo in Florida. I'd stopped driving past it because it was just too painful to see another family occupying our home. They'd even painted it another color, light green, as opposed to the white it was when we lived in it. I didn't notice until now that Nikki had re-painted the coat rack a similar green from the white it used to be. That was a strange coincidence.

My parents visited a number of times each year, but it never seemed often enough. It was the right move for them, but I knew for a fact, all three of their children missed them very much.

Seeing the coat rack also made me think of the small storage unit I rented. It held all of the items I took from my home in California after the divorce, including the majority of things I had from my parents after they downsized. It was probably time to go through those things and decorate my apartment. I'd been putting it off for too long.

When I moved into the upstairs apartment above Chocolate Love, I was still in a daze from the divorce and kept thinking it would be more of a transitional thing. Now, the reality of the situation was that all the debt I still had was making me see the apartment might be more permanent.

"I thought the IVF treatments would be covered by your insurance."

"They would have been, but my insurance is being cut because my company is hurting. No worries, babe. We'll pay it off."

"No worries, babe," I whispered to myself. My hand wandered down over my flat stomach.

* * * * *

That evening at the book signing, I was pleasantly surprised by the amount of people who came out to hear me speak. The book store, Evil Things, specialized in mysteries and thrillers, so it was the perfect place to sell my books. Because Halloween was approaching, the store was decked out in hundreds of black, papier-mâché witches hanging from the ceiling. Their heads were tipped back in the air with mouths wide open. I could almost hear them cackling.

Although I was always nervous at these events, practice made perfect, and I'd had a lot of practice lately. My agent, Jackie Combs, was working like mad to get these signings booked for me. I even had to up my wardrobe a bit since the majority of my clothes were extremely casual. Tonight I wore a black, wool dress with three quarter length sleeves and a fitted waist. The heels I wore were killing my feet but worth it. With my hair loosely curled and half up, secured by a fancy comb my stylish sister, Nikki, gave me, I looked professional and hopefully, approachable.

Just as I was about to autograph a copy of my latest book, two little hands reached across the table and grabbed mine.

"Cindy!" I exclaimed. My five-year-old goddaughter smiled radiantly up at me. She was dressed in a bright red, taffeta dress with black polka dots all over it. She looked like a precious little ladybug.

"Hi, Aunt Kelly. Mom said we could surprise you tonight. I'm up past my bed time!"

"Hey, sis. Good crowd tonight," my older sister, Adelle, said.

"Sign, sign!" Cindy chanted enthusiastically. She handed me a copy of one of my books while simultaneously pushing her glasses further up on her nose.

"I didn't know you guys were coming tonight."

"Cindy can't resist these things. Once she got word that you had a signing tonight, she wouldn't let me rest until I agreed to take her. What time are you wrapping up here?" Adelle leaned forward to help straighten Cindy's crooked glasses.

"I think it's done at eight-thirty."

"Did you take the train?"

"I did." I nodded.

"Let us drive you home."

"You don't have to do that, Adelle. It will be so late for Cindy."

"I insist. Besides, I need to talk to you about something."

I stopped signing and looked up to observe my sister a little closer. As usual, she was dressed to the nines in a black turtle neck, suede skirt, and knee high boots. Her long, blond hair curled in soft waves around her shoulders. Adelle always looked like she had just come off a runway. Tonight was no exception. She was gorgeous as always. But she'd been dealing with a lot in her life, so regardless of how fantastic she looked on the outside, I knew there was a lot of stress harboring inside. The phrase "still waters run deep" popped in my head.

"Okay, sounds good." If Adelle was looking to talk, I was going to make myself available. She'd been quiet over the last couple of weeks. That made me nervous.

"Come on, Cindy. We need to let Aunt Kelly talk to her other customers. Let's go get a piece of cake." Adelle winked at me and headed in the direction of where Evil Things was serving a three-tiered, chocolate cake they always had at these kind of events. I wasn't sure if it was my books or the cakes that drew the crowd. It could easily have been the cakes. They were that good.

The rest of the night passed fairly quickly. It was tough to concentrate though because I kept stealing glances over in Adelle's direction, wondering what she needed to talk about. A few months ago, Adelle and her husband put their gargantuan Geneva home on the market. Adelle's husband, Mike, lost the majority of his home building business when the housing market burst and people stopped building new homes. The other half of his business, rental property, was keeping them afloat, but it wasn't enough to live the lavish lifestyle they once maintained.

With three kids to support, Mike and Adelle were actively downsizing. Things were changing in the Stefano home, and I knew it wasn't easy. So far, they'd been unable to sell their home.

By eight o'clock, the store was deserted.

"Well, looks like we're done," Francine, the owner of Evil Things, said, walking up to my table. "We just can't seem to maintain the crowd after that cake is gone," she joked.

"I don't blame them. Don't know what they put in those cakes, but they are irresistible."

I started collecting my bookmarks and pens from the table and packed them into my briefcase.

"I remember how you feel about those cakes, Kelly. I didn't forget you." Francine slid a piece of chocolate cake across the table.

The smell of the velvety chocolate hit me at once, making me realize how hungry I was. "Do you have a…?"

"Fork? Of course." Francine placed a fork on my plate. "Scoop that baby up and let's go finish our business, so we can get you out of here. I'm sure you want to go home."

Grabbing my cake, I followed her over to the small office she kept in the back of the store. Her long skirt swished from side to side, reminding me of the sound the brushes made in a car wash. She resembled a modern day gypsy and was quite the networker in the literary community of Chicago. People loved her passion, her honesty, and her wicked business skills. She knew how to draw a crowd and move books like no other. She'd developed quite the following of local mystery enthusiasts, for which I was grateful. I could write the greatest book, but unless I had a platform to market my books on, I'd be dead in the water.

I signaled to Adelle that I'd be just a minute. She and Cindy were still browsing through the store, but by the way Cindy pulled at her mom's skirt, I could tell they were anxious to get home.

While shoveling the cake in my mouth, Francine and I talked logistics about the book signing and set a date to visit the following month. She wanted to do another push of the book before the holiday sales began.

"Okay Francine, I'll see you right before Thanksgiving then. Have a great Halloween. What are you dressing up as?"

"Don't get me started. I want all of us to do a theme and dress alike here in the store. We can't seem to agree on anything. I may let everyone just do whatever they want. They're all such good ideas."

"Well, have fun," I said.

Francine and I did the air kiss thing, and I left to collect Adelle and Cindy.

"I'm tired, Mom," Cindy whined. "You have chocolate on your face, Aunt Kelly."

"I was saving that for you." I bent down and picked Cindy up. Setting her on my hip, I stuck my cheek out at her. "Go ahead. Eat it."

"Ewww," Cindy laughed. Adelle gave her a napkin from the bottomless supply in her purse. She wiped at my cheek tenderly and set her head down on my shoulder.

"Oh, you're tired, sweetheart," I cooed in her ear.

"Can I sleep over tonight?"

"Not tonight, honey," I said. "How about another night?"

"Okay. Let's go home."

The fact that she didn't fight me spoke to just how tired she really was.

A few minutes later, we were settled into Adelle's Cadillac SUV on our way back to Geneva. Cindy passed out shortly after being buckled into her car seat. Her soft snores filled the car in harmonious waves. They made me want to doze off as well.

"So, what did you want to talk to me about?" I glanced Adelle's way.

"I'm just going to be straight with you, Kelly. I have a huge favor to ask. It's a big one."

I could almost feel her hands on my back, remembering the night last summer when she pushed me to get me out of harm's way in order to take my place. She had a family; three kids and a husband, and she was still ready to sacrifice her own life for mine when Steve's psychotic girlfriend tried to kill us. Anything. She could have *anything* she wanted from me.

"Shoot."

"It's about the house."

"Oh, did you find a buyer?"

"We did. And we found a rental home until we are ready to buy again. The only problem is the dates don't match up. We need a place to live for a couple weeks."

Totally bewildered, I waited for her to go on. Where did I fit into all of this?

She pulled her eyes from the road for a quick second and gave me a sheepish smile. Her lips trembled slightly, the smile lasting only a quick second.

"Please, Kelly. I don't know what else to do."

Chapter 5

When Adelle dropped me in front of Chocolate Love, Jack was waiting for me. I'd alerted him via text about my change in plans. He was sitting on the front steps typing away on his phone. He put it away when he saw me and stood up to greet me.

"How did it go?" he asked as I approached him. Even though it was after nine, he still looked tidy and fresh in pressed khakis and a navy blue tee-shirt. I, on the other hand, felt like a wrinkled, worn-out mess. I couldn't wait to wash the make-up off my face, pull my hair free from the comb, kick off my heels, and get back into my comfortable clothes.

"Great. Are you sure you're okay with leaving your mom this early? I'm home so much earlier than I had planned."

"She's fine. She just wanted to lie in bed and watch television tonight. I'll call and check in on her in a little bit."

When Jack leaned in to kiss me hello, the bag over his shoulder dipped forward and knocked me back a bit.

"Geez, what have you got in there? A bowling ball?"

"Sorry. I have to head into the city tomorrow for a meeting and won't have time to go home and change. Well, I mean, I could have time, but I would rather spend more time with you in the morning, my little temptress."

He leaned in again to finish the kiss. I pulled my hand behind my back to remove the comb that was now irritating me beyond belief, but Jack beat me to it. My long, brown hair fell loosely around my shoulders.

"Better," Jack murmured into my ear.

"You don't like the comb?"

"I love it. I just like your hair down."

It was so easy to get lost in our own world even after all this time. It was probably inappropriate for two people our age to be making out in front of Chocolate Love, but I didn't care. Life had kept us apart for too long. I felt like I deserved every moment I got with Jack. It was my reward for getting out of my horrible marriage with Steve.

"Let's go inside," Jack said, pulling away from our embrace and grabbing my hand.

I let out a low moan and pulled back on his arm.

"These shoes are killing me."

"Take them off," he suggested.

"Once we're inside. I don't want to walk through…"

Suddenly, I was hoisted up and over Jack's shoulder. He reached and plucked my heels off before I could protest. We were up the front stairs of Chocolate Love in seconds.

"Jack, put me down. You're such a caveman. You're going to hurt your back."

He didn't answer or put me down.

Once we were up the stairs and in front of the door, he gently placed me down on my own feet.

"You're nuts," I laughed.

"Let us in, woman."

"Don't let me forget that I have to talk to you about something Adelle told me tonight."

"Later," Jack said simply. He leaned down and swiped the key from my hand. Jack was patient with my family drama and my stories, but now was not the time. A man had his needs, and I was more than happy to be the one to fulfill them tonight.

In the morning, Jack left early in order to retrieve a file he'd forgotten at his home. It worked out well for me. I needed to get in my run. It was essential to be able to deal with the news from last night in a calm manner.

After Jack left at six, my phone beeped, notifying me of a text message. I smiled, assuming it was Jack and thinking it was most likely something playful about our night last night. A few vivid images popped into my head making me laugh out loud.

Running? Meet you in front of the museum after run? Left my pumpkin stand there last night. Need your help.

I was a little disappointed the message was not Jack but was happy to help Nikki out. The stand was not the easiest thing to move. And besides, I needed to talk to her.

I wrote back:

Starting late this morning. Meet you at 6:45.

See you then, Nikki responded immediately.

I grabbed my iPod and dressed quickly in long, black, yoga pants and a light, North Face jacket. Just as I was about to head out, the phone beeped again. This time it was a text from Jack.

Please think about my offer, temptress.

Every time Jack used my pet name, it made me blush. Almost twenty years from its origination and it still worked. The offer he was referring to was attractive but definitely needed some thought. It was going to have quite an impact on the future of our relationship.

I will, I sent back.

It was time to put the heavy thoughts aside and go for a run. This morning, the temperature had dipped down to a cool fifty degrees. This was my favorite time of the year as a runner. The early mornings were still light, and the heat of the summer had subsided. The cruel winter temperatures would be held at bay for at least another month.

My plan was to head east through town until I hit the Fox River. Some of the geese were still flying south for the winter, and I'd become obsessed with checking how many were left.

A popular spot for the geese was Island Park, a local hangout for kids on the banks of the river. Adelle, Nikki, and I used to play there as kids. The park had been updated from the old jungle gym to a much more state-of-the-art playground for kids, but for the most part, it was exactly the same. It hosted many of Geneva's festivals including the Folk Festival that ran last month. It was the perfect location because of its proximity to the river and the local restaurants and hangouts.

In order to get to the park, I had to cross the river via a bike path that ran under the train tracks. This was by far the most exhilarating part of my run. If I timed it right, a train ran over head, which was frightening and consuming at the same time. The sound of the train zooming over head was so loud, it became impossible to hear my music.

Normally, I used my running time to think and work through what I wanted to accomplish for the day. In this lag of the run though, the outside sound was so consuming, it knocked me senseless. It was a mandatory mental break from all the to-do lists and worries that marched non-stop like soldiers through my head.

Unfortunately, due to my late start this morning, my timing did not coordinate with a train, and I remained consumed in my own thoughts. At the end of the bridge, I turned north.

My mind played a mental game of hopscotch through my lists and worries as I struggled to let go and take in my surroundings. The trees in this area of the park always drew me to the distant past. Thank goodness these trees had been spared when the settlers moved into this area.

All these thoughts about Geneva History Museum had me thinking of what I knew about the settlement of this area and how I could use it in my series. It had been a long time since I'd done any research. Nikki was right. Brian was an untapped resource for me. Although he was a little over the top, he knew his stuff when it came to the details of how Geneva came to be. I needed those details for my series. My next book was not developing the way I wanted it to right now. Perhaps meeting with him would point me in the right direction.

According to the little research I had done so far, I knew the surrounding towns of Geneva, now known as the Tri-cities; St. Charles, Geneva, and Batavia, were once settled by the Pottawatomie Indian tribe. The Pottawatomie were eventually forced off the land by warring enemy tribes. When the English settlers first came to the area from Boston, the rising tensions between the settlers and the native tribes caused them to form alliances and eventually turn against themselves.

I shuttered thinking what those years must have been like. The fact that it was less than two hundred years ago was staggering. To think that this area had come so far in so short of time was amazing. But the cost it had on many lives was sad and disturbing.

In my series, my main character, Mary, was always coming across an item that someone had either sold to her, or one she wanted to buy for her antique collection. Perhaps she could come across an old Indian warhead that was supposed to be very common in this area. Brian would know better about all of that.

Feeling better about having some direction for the book, I turned to head west, back toward the Historic District where Chocolate Love was located. Running across the bridge on Route 38, my thoughts raced back to my conversation with Adelle the night before.

My decision was made. I would accommodate her by giving her and her family my apartment for as long as they needed, with Nikki's permission, of course. It was her apartment. Wasn't there a belief somewhere that when someone saved your life, you owed them your own in repayment? The least I could do for Adelle was house her family while they were going through this transition. It would wreak havoc on my own structured schedule and the attempt at normalcy I'd worked so hard to achieve, but it was the right thing to do. Now what to do about Jack's offer?

Chapter 6

Running down Third Street, I noted the History Museum coming up in the distance. Apparently, my pace was faster than normal, or my calculations were off because I'd shaved five minutes off my three mile run. Nikki was not in front of the building, which surprised me because she was always ten minutes early to everything. Her rule in life was if she wasn't ten minutes early to something, she was late.

By the curb, I bent over and placed my hands at my waist to catch a breath and stretch.

The entire History Museum took up half a block and sat kiddy corner from Chocolate Love. Large plate glass windows facing Third Street allowed a nice view inside. From the angle I was standing, I was able to look in and see the gift shop and one of the large meeting rooms. The place looked deserted except for a light on near the back of the building where the museum was.

It hit me then that Nikki may have meant to meet at the back door rather than the front. From my past experience with helping Nikki, I recalled that the double doors in the museum around back were often used for loading and unloading of materials because of its direct access to the alley. It made more sense for Nikki to move the pumpkin decoration stand out those doors.

Glancing down at my watch, it read 6:48.

Perhaps it was my paranoia, but I was starting to get apprehensive. I needed to go around back, but the little voice inside my head was whispering ever so softly that something was off. If only I had my cell phone. I could just call Nikki rather than have to go search for her in the alley at this weird time of day.

Trying to look as inconspicuous as possible, I took a deep breath and made my way around to the back doors via the small alley on the side of the building. It was just wide enough for a car to drive through, but narrow enough to make me feel a bit claustrophobic.

Making my way around back, I found one of the double doors wide open. Seeing this made my blood go cold. Nikki would never leave the door open like it was now if she were in there.

Maybe she was cold from the low temperatures and just on the other side. Hoping she would peek out and look for me, I tiptoed slowly up to the door, taking my time.

No Nikki.

I was torn between going back home and getting my cell phone or rushing inside. If Nikki was in there, she might need my help.

"Nikki?"

I waited for a response. When I didn't get one, I peeked in.

"Nikki, are you in here?" I whispered urgently.

When I didn't get a response the second time, I stepped inside the museum. Allowing my eyes to adjust to the darkness, I turned slightly to my left in the direction of the light at the entrance to the museum.

"Oh my God!" I screamed, my heart nearly stopping at the sight in front of me.

Approximately fifty small beings, standing just below my knees surrounded me. Some of them stared directly up with glazed over expressions while the rest refused to acknowledge me, as though they were angry at my audacity to interrupt their private dance party. Their arms and legs were frozen at weird angles, sticking up in the air. It took a second to realize that one arm was actually touching my knee. I jumped back, knocking it to the floor. A weird smacking sound echoed in the dark room.

Dolls. Loads and loads of antique, horrible, wooden dolls. God, how I hated dolls. For a second, I thought Nikki may have been playing some sort of trick on me, but then it registered that I had walked directly into the display being featured this month in the museum. I remembered now that I saw an article in the paper earlier in the month talking about the dolls having some kind of link to the past hotels in the area. *Crap.* I moved quickly away from them and further into the museum, trying my best to forget what I had just seen. Sucking in air, I stopped in my tracks and turned back to pick up the one I had knocked over.

Grimacing, I turned it upright as best I could then released my hold, wiping my hands along my pants.

The museum consisted of multi-dimensional displays set-up throughout one large room. The set-up was sensational, allowing the guests to walk through a visual telling of how the land was first settled and eventually modernized by roads, electricity, and shops. A gleaming cement floor and high open ceilings added a modern loft-like feel. Normally, I appreciated the detail and the large space, but right now, I only wanted to find Nikki and fast. Those dolls had set me over the edge.

"Nikki?" I called out again a little louder this time. My voice echoed off the cement as I walked toward the front of the building.

As my eyes adjusted to the light, the pumpkin cupcake stand came into focus in the front entrance room. Natural light pouring in through the windows gave this area of the History Museum a warm, friendly vibe. The front reception desk sat empty. I noticed a phone atop the desk and briefly thought of calling Nikki.

Instead, I reached for the pumpkin stand to see how heavy it was without the cupcakes on it. My hope was to take it back myself. I wanted to get out of here as soon as possible.

As I was weighing my options, I heard a woman's voice coming from upstairs. I turned and looked behind me to see the door leading up to the apartment above the museum propped open. That was it. Nikki must have gone upstairs with Brian to have a cup of coffee. A wave of relief ran through me.

"Hello," I called out, making my way over to the door. Without waiting for a response, I climbed the cement stairs, anticipating enjoying a hot, steaming cup of coffee with Nikki and Brian. When I reached the top, a second door leading into the apartment was also wide open. Expecting to see Nikki, I was surprised when I found the apartment empty. A bathroom door to my right was open, and a small sitting room/kitchen to my left proved to be without guests. My eyes briefly focused on the coffee machine sitting empty on the counter. That meant that whoever was here was in the bedroom with Brian. The sound of a woman cackling on the other side of the door made me freeze. That was *definitely* not Nikki.

I turned on my heel and raced down the stairs as quickly and quietly as I could. Obviously there had been some kind of misunderstanding, and I was intruding on an intimate morning tête-à-tête.

At the bottom of the stairs, I stopped. It had taken a couple of seconds for it to register in my brain, but finally it became blatantly obvious that something was not right about the woman's voice. She began discussing the weather for the day like she was reading from a farmer's almanac.

Remaining at the bottom of the stairs, I forced myself to turn and listen again. Sure enough, she rambled on and on, but there never seemed to be a proper response time allowed for Brian. Where was the volley back and forth in the conversation?

Although I really didn't want to, I willed myself to climb the stairs slowly and investigate.

"Off. Off. Off," my mind kept repeating. "Something is off."

At the top of the stairs, I stepped into the apartment and knocked on the bedroom door.

"Brian?" I called out. The woman's voice never wavered. She continued to blabber on. Now she was talking about the use of Facebook in relationships.

"Nowadays, a relationship doesn't have time to even blossom before you're faced with having to label it and place it on Facebook. Are you in a relationship, or are you not? And how will you display that relationship? Will you post pictures? What kind of pictures will you post? Who decides which ones you will post?"

I finally recognized the voice to be that of a local radio DJ. I tested the doorknob and pushed while knocking. Sure enough, the room was empty except for a blaring radio and what I assumed to be a very tired Brian. There was no other explanation as to how he could possibly sleep through this loud chitter-chatter.

Unable to take it anymore, I made my way over to the clock radio on Brian's nightstand and un-plugged it from the wall.

"Brian, I think your alarm…"

I slammed my eyes shut, trying to erase the image I had seen when I looked down at the bed.

"No, no, no…"

When I opened them again, Brian's unmoving, frozen face was still there. It looked like the wax version of Brian rather than the real thing. His eyes were wide open, staring up at the ceiling and his skin had a weird gray/blue tint to it. My mind raced to the dolls downstairs in the museum. Maybe someone was playing some kind of sick joke on me? This couldn't be real. This was the doll version of Brian.

For the first time, the distinct smell of urine registered with me, and the stain on the bed cover confirmed what I assumed had happened. For absolute confirmation, I moved closer, reached my hand out and touched Brian's cheek to see if he was beyond help.

"Brian?" I managed to squeak out. The skin on his cheek sunk in to my touch, reminding me of a soft bread dough. His skin was cool to the touch. Too cool. My stomach began to rumble with the foretelling sign of what was to come, breaking my trance.

Desperate to control what had become a trend for me in stressful situations, I ran out of the apartment, through the museum, and out the back door. Once outside, I sucked fresh air into my lungs.

"Please don't vomit. Please don't vomit," I begged quietly.

"What are you saying? 'Please don't vomit'?" Nikki asked.

I was so distracted by trying to keep it together I didn't notice her approach.

"Oh my God, Nikki. He's dead," I managed to get out, sucking in more air.

"What? What are you talking about?"

Without waiting for an answer, Nikki dashed past me.

"Wait!" I reached out, grabbing onto her sweatshirt. "Don't go in there. Just call the police right now. Do you have a cell phone? Call 9-1-1 right now."

"Okay. Where is it?" She padded her body, feeling around for her phone. Her hands were shaking as she pulled it out of the right front pocket of her sweatshirt.

"Here it is. Here it is," she passed me the phone. "Is it Brian?"

I dialed 9-1-1 on the cell and nodded my head in confirmation.

Pulling the phone up to my ear, I checked for Nikki's reaction.

Gone.

"Nikki! Please stay out here with me," I begged.

Too late. When I looked inside, she was turning the corner to head upstairs to the apartment.

"9-1-1. What is your emergency?"

Before I could respond, the sound of a blood curdling scream from the upstairs apartment rang out.

* * * * *

Back at Chocolate Love, Nikki and I huddled next to the coffee machine in silence, both clutching mugs as though they were our lifelines. This morning, mine was a mug given to Nikki from my parents after a trip to Sanibel, Florida. It had a picture of a seagull flying across a sandy beach and the word SANIBEL splayed across the top. The serenity conveyed by the beach scene felt very out of place. I quickly reached up and replaced it with a cup that had the Chocolate Love logo on it. The last thing I needed was a coffee cup mocking me on a day like today.

Nikki clutched a mug that read, "Give me coffee. NOW."

"What time is he coming?" I asked.

"He said he would be here as soon as he could."

Nikki's eyes never left the machine while she spoke. "I think I might have to update this. It's taking longer than it used to, isn't it? Maybe when I buy the new stuff for the expansion, I'll get a new coffee maker for this location, too."

Nikki rattled on and on about the machine, but the way her hands shook as she fiddled with the coffee cups hanging from the board gave me fright. She kept changing her cup out after I did, like she was also unable to make a simple decision as to which cup to drink from. I finally reached out and pulled the original cup she chose and set it down on the counter. She simply stepped back and sighed, allowing her arms to finally rest at her side.

"Good morning, ladies. We meet again under sad circumstances," Detective Meyers said as he walked into the room. Nikki and I had worked with the detective last summer.

"Detective," Nikki said by way of greeting. The last time Nikki spoke to Detective Meyers, she accused him of wasting the tax payer's money. She had been frustrated by his lack of interest in some of her theories when last summer's crime spree was running rampant on Third Street. Nikki's fiery temperament and Detective Meyer's cool and calm demeanor were not a good mix.

"How are you guys holding up?" he asked kindly.

"Okay. We're just taking it all in," I said.

"Coffee?" Nikki offered.

"Actually, I'm not staying. I just came by to introduce you to my partner," Detective Meyers said. "John?" he called out behind him.

A gentleman dressed in an impeccable, dark blue suit came into the room, searching inquisitively with his light blue eyes. His gray hair was cut short in a military style and his friendly, confident smile was magnetic. He gave off a vibe much different than his partner's. Where Detective Meyers seemed to view us as either suspects, or at the very least, withholders of information, this new detective seemed to be asking with his eyes, "What happened to you today and how can I help?" He studied our faces with raised eyebrows that conveyed sympathy. It made me immediately want to confide in him the tragedy we walked into this morning. Whoever this was, he was clearly the proverbial "good cop."

"Wow. I've heard a lot about this place, but I've never been in here. This is something else. Hello, ladies. I'm Detective John Pavlik. I'm very sorry to hear about what happened. It's a pleasure to meet you," he said, reaching out his hand to shake mine, then Nikki's.

Nikki and I glanced at each other briefly. Because of our experience with Detective Meyers last summer, part of me had been waiting all morning to be accused of doing something wrong or somehow being involved in Brian's death.

"I need to talk to you two about what you found at the History Museum. Can we talk here, or should we go somewhere private?" Detective Pavlik asked.

I stole a glance at Meyers and caught him staring back at me, as though watching for my reaction. It made me want to shout, "I didn't do it, for God's sake!" Though I could understand his suspicions if he had any. Where there was trouble, there was Kelly Clark.

"We can stay here. I won't open the store until later this morning and my employees are in the back working on an order. Hold on," Nikki said. She moved to the door separating the front of the store from the back kitchen. "Miguel, we need to talk to the detective out here. I'm just going to close this door for a bit."

"Okay, no problem," Miguel called out.

Nikki closed the door and came back to where we were standing.

"I'm going to head out and let you talk. Call me if you need anything," Detective Meyers said, ghosting out of the room.

"Why don't we move to the front porch to talk?" Nikki suggested.

I knew what she was doing. The front porch was enclosed in glass and looked out onto Third Street. She wanted to be able to watch the comings and goings at Geneva History Museum while we spoke to Pavlik.

"Would you like a cup of coffee?" I offered Detective Pavlik.

"Sounds good to me," Pavlik said, accepting the cup of coffee I handed him. He pulled it up to his nose and sniffed at it briefly, his well-crafted moustache twitching slightly.

Grabbing our coffees, we made our way out onto the front porch. I could hear Pavlik behind me, commenting on the products Nikki sold in the store.

"I used to buy that kind of candy when I was a kid. I can't believe you have it here."

By the sound of Nikki's laughter, she was enjoying showing off the store and Pavlik's excitement for her hard work. "It's a big hit here. Help yourself to a sample if you like. We run a sale on those the last Wednesday of the month. Just in case you want to stop by."

"I'll remember that. My daughter will want to come with me. She's pregnant and can't get enough chocolate."

"Oh, that's nice. When is she…" Nikki stopped midsentence. We entered the front porch and were about to take a seat at one of the small tables set up for customers.

I turned my head to see what pulled Nikki's attention away from Pavlik. A large, white van marked "Coroner" was pulling down the alley on the side of Geneva History Museum. It turned right and drove away down Third Street.

"Oh my God." She pulled her hand up to her mouth and stumbled into a seated position at the table. When Nikki's eyes fell to the table, mine bounced to Pavlik. He was watching her closely, his moustache once again twitching slightly as though he was picking up the scent of something.

"Would it be better for us if we spoke inside?" Detective Pavlik asked.

"No, it's fine. I'm fine."

"Nikki, are you sure?" I asked.

"You were close to him," Pavlik observed.

I sucked in a breath quietly, trying to remain calm. I didn't want Nikki to incriminate herself in any way. Pavlik appeared innocent in his questioning, but this was another death in Geneva linked to Nikki and me. Did we need to have an attorney present?

Nikki nodded her head and buried her eyes in her coffee cup. "We were friends. He was having troubles. I was trying to help."

"I'm sure you were," Pavlik said, reaching over and patting her hand briefly. The gesture was so shocking to me that I couldn't help but gawk at the man. He actually touched her. Again, all I kept thinking was how different his M.O. was from Detective Meyers. He always physically recoiled from us like we were poison. How could these two men possibly work together? They were like polar opposites.

Pavlik looked over to me and pulled his lips into a sympathetic frown. Something in his look reminded me of a priest comforting a member of their congregation after the loss of a loved one.

"I'm very sorry for your loss. I can see this is painful for you. Sometimes these things happen and it's very hard to understand why. It's going to take you a long time."

No accusation. No suggestive comment. No damning implication. This *couldn't* be right. This wasn't what I was used to.

'So, you're telling us that your husband is going to kill someone tomorrow night. You have the location, the victim, and you even know the way it is going to happen, but you expect us to believe you're not involved in this at all?'

I wanted to trust Pavlik and be grateful for the way he was treating us, but I couldn't. The incident with my ex-husband in California had tainted me. It made me suspicious and jaded toward all police officers. They didn't believe me when I needed them to and a woman's life was in jeopardy. Thank God, they finally came around.

But with Pavlik, this was too easy. He believed us just like that?

"Do you know yet exactly how he died?" Nikki asked after we'd run through some details. Through the course of the conversation, I learned that her husband, Bob, had dropped her off at Chocolate Love before she met me at Geneva History Museum. That made me feel a little better knowing she had a strong alibi. I'd been with Jack the night before, so at least I had someone to speak for me. But I'd been alone on the run before I entered Geneva History Museum. It left a good hour of time where I didn't have an alibi. That made me a little nervous. Pavlik didn't seem to be bothered by that. He brushed over it quickly. Having seen Brian up close though, my guess was he had died much earlier than when I arrived, so I could see how Pavlik would not consider me a suspect.

"Not yet. We'll know more once the autopsy is performed," Pavlik offered.

"Detective Pavlik, Brian was in here yesterday. He was having a bit of a breakdown," I said.

"What do you mean?"

"He, well, did you know him at all?" Nikki asked.

"I met him once. My wife and I did one of the ghost tours a few years ago."

"So, you know how, um, eccentric he was?" she asked.

"I guess. He's not exactly a trouble maker, so he was kind of off my radar."

"When he was in here yesterday, he told me he thought a ghost was haunting him."

"Really? Interesting. So, he was dealing with a lot of anxiety?" Pavlik responded. He raised an eyebrow and turned his notebook to a new page. "And you think this haunting may have had something to do with his death? Tell me more."

Encouraged by his questions, Nikki went on to share all of the things Brian told her about his recent experiences at Geneva History Museum, including haunting voices heard late at night, objects inexplicably moved around in the museum, and his fear for his life. I kept waiting for Pavlik to silence Nikki by telling her this was all ridiculous, but he just continued to take notes.

"Do you believe these things were happening to him?" Pavlik asked simply when Nikki finished.

She opened her mouth to respond, but nothing came out. Instead, she sighed slowly and looked out the windows in the direction of the Geneva History Museum. Pavlik remained silent, waiting for her answer.

Nikki finally turned back, her eyes crinkled up in concern. "If you're asking me if I believe in ghosts, then I guess my answer is no. But something was certainly troubling him. I believe he was truly frightened."

"He was troubled?" Pavlik added.

"No, that's not what I said," Nikki said, looking at me, then back at Pavlik. "Being troubled and having trouble forced upon you are two different things. In Brian's case, I don't believe his issues were simply internal. Do you understand what I'm saying?"

Pavlik nodded his head and bent over his notes to write something down. I tried to lean in and peek at what he wrote. Unfortunately, he closed up his notepad and tucked it away before I had the chance. He met my gaze, and I sat back in my chair quickly.

"I do," he said somberly. "Unfortunately, I do from having so many years on the job. From what I saw though, no forced entry and the way he looked, it appears as though this was an unfortunate event, maybe an overdose of some kind. We'll know more soon though. I do my best to never make assumptions and let the facts speak for themselves."

Pavlik left shortly after that, promising to fill us in on any new information. The autopsy results were due in 24-48 hours and would give more light on the cause of death. Nikki appeared satisfied and calm after our talk with the detective.

After he left, we sat up in my apartment with coffee, watching the History Museum through my front windows. There were still a number of police cars and officers walking around, but the numbers were dwindling. It looked like they were wrapping things up.

"You liked him, huh?"

"I did. He was easy to talk to," Nikki said.

"You trust him?"

"Pavlik?" Nikki raised an eyebrow and gave me a smirk. I shot her one back.

"You don't?"

"I trust no one," I said.

"I know you don't, Kelly. I don't expect you to," Nikki said, reaching out and patting my knee.

"You knew Brian better than I did. How do you think he died? Do you think he took his own life? Pavlik seemed to be hinting at that. I didn't notice any pills near him. But, honestly, I was only looking at him."

"I'm not really sure. Maybe he got pushed too far with whomever or whatever was harassing him. I didn't notice pills either, but I wasn't looking. I was also completely focused on Brian. The police must have found something when they looked through the apartment. The door left open still bothers me though. Why was that back door open? I should have called someone. Maybe one of his family members. I didn't do enough yesterday. I knew he was frightened, but I didn't think he would kill himself. Maybe I didn't listen close enough."

"Nikki, breathe. It's okay." For a brief second, I thought of the scary dolls I ran into on the way into the Geneva History Museum. One of them? I shook my head, trying to get the image of one of those small bodies making its way up the stairs to the apartment out of my mind. "I've been wondering the same thing. Could he have been pushed that far? Do you know his family? Can you talk to them?" I asked.

"No. I remember him saying something about coming from Pennsylvania but wouldn't know anyone to contact. When he came in here yesterday, I should have spent more time with him and dug a little deeper. He said he was scared, but I thought he got off on the ghost stuff. I thought the whole thing was scary for him, but also thrilling. Not something that would make him kill himself."

"Tell me again exactly what Brian told you," I said, turning my body away from the window.

"He said that the ghost of Victoria Jacobs was haunting Geneva History Museum. He rents an apartment about thirty minutes north of here in Elgin, but when he's too tired to drive home at night or there's a snowstorm, he stays in the open apartment above the History Museum. In the last week, he spent a couple of nights there working on preparing his research."

"So, what was Victoria's ghost doing that scared him so much?" I asked, sitting forward in my chair.

"First, does that sound like someone about to commit suicide? Someone staying up late at night working on an upcoming event? And he even told me he was planning on putting a book together with all of the new research he was gathering."

"That's the thing about suicide. Many times you would never suspect it coming. People can seem so energized, and then they make the decision to end it all. We probably didn't know Brian as well as we thought. Perhaps, this Victoria Jacobs thing was the straw that broke the camel's back," I suggested.

"Maybe," Nikki said, pulling her one side of her lip up and shrugging her shoulders. "Anyway, Brian said lights he was sure he had turned off were turned back on. Objects in the museum were moved around, and windows would be open he was sure he never touched. Even the archives in the basement were disturbed."

"Well, that's strange, but that doesn't sound like a very vindictive ghost. Why would he be scared?"

"He said things would go missing that were linked to Victoria Jacobs. The night before he came to Chocolate Love, he woke up in the middle of the night to go to the bathroom. When he was walking back to his room, he tripped over a pile of books placed just outside his bedroom door. They were historical books from the downstairs gift shop with all of the pages regarding Victoria's story ripped out and strewn all over the floor."

"I don't understand. The Victoria Jacobs story has been part of the ghost tour for years. It was a part of the tour when we did it ten years ago. Why is it such a big deal now? If there really is such thing as ghosts, why didn't Victoria kick up a fuss when Brian first started the tours?"

"You don't really believe in ghosts, Kelly, do you?"

"Do you?"

A question in response to a question was never good. I didn't believe in ghosts, but sometimes I wasn't quite sure what to believe.

"I don't. Maybe I do. I don't know," Nikki sighed. "Brian was pretty freaked out when he came over yesterday. He'd just been to the old Jacobs' house. It's for sale now and vacant. Did you know that?"

"No, I had no idea," I said.

"I guess the family is out, but it's still somewhat furnished to help it sell.

Anyway, yesterday morning, Brian got curious, so he walked up the front porch to see if he could peer in through the windows. On the walking tour, he's not technically allowed to bring his group onto the grounds. He just keeps them on the sidewalk. So, he wanted to get a better look at the room she was killed in. But when he stepped up onto the front porch, he heard a woman's voice tell him to leave. He got scared and ran straight here. I told him the stress of his upcoming tours was getting to him, and he just needed more rest. Now I feel horrible. Maybe he just wanted someone to take him seriously.

"I owe it to him to figure out what was really going on over there," Nikki nodded her head in the direction of the Geneva History Museum.

We both turned to look out the window. The last police car was pulling away from the scene. That was it. Brian's life was over, cleaned up, and now the community would move on. But who would take Brian's place? Would the ghost walks continue?

When I looked down on the sidewalk leading up to Chocolate Love, a familiar form making her way up to the door caused all thoughts of Brian to halt. Time to make a decision.

Chapter 7

"Hey, that's Adelle. What time is it? Shouldn't she have the kids?" Nikki asked.

"Maybe Mike is with them this morning. Nikki, we have to talk about something. Adelle is coming here to talk to us about the apartment."

"What do you mean?"

"She and Mike have a buyer for their home, and they need a place to stay until their rental home is available."

"They want to stay here?" Nikki balked.

I nodded my head.

"But…"

A knock at the apartment door interrupted our conversation.

I walked over and let Adelle in. As usual, she was dressed well in a stylish tweed skirt over long, brown, leather boots. Her boots were probably worth more than my bank account.

"Good morning. Why did I see a police car leaving the Geneva History Museum? Do you know what happened?"

"Brian Sanders died last night. Nikki and I found him this morning."

Adelle pulled her hand up to her mouth in shock and sat down on my overstuffed couch.

"Oh, that's awful. Are you two okay?"

Nikki shook her head. "We're both still in shock. He came over yesterday to talk to me. I'm wishing I could have done a lot more for him."

"Why do you say that? Wait, do you think he, um…," Adelle stumbled on her words.

"We don't know yet. The autopsy will tell us more. We're not sure if it was self-induced or something else. We found the back door wide open," I said.

"The police?" Adelle added.

"We're working with them. They spoke to us this morning," Nikki confirmed.

"Do you two need an attorney?"

"No. Not at this time. We're not suspects," Nikki said, peering in my direction.

"I'm sure Jack would have a lead on a good criminal attorney, Kelly, if it turns out you do," Adelle said.

I nodded my head, hoping to God I would not need a criminal attorney.

Pavlik did not leave us with that impression. My stomach did a little flip at the thought of being in that situation again.

After that, a silence settled over the room like an ominous cloud. An odd moment for us Clark sisters. Usually we were all talking at the same time.

"Did you want to talk about the apartment?" I finally asked.

"Oh, this doesn't seem like the time. Maybe I should go. We can talk about this later. What you're dealing with is much bigger than this." Adelle stood up and flattened her skirt down with her hands.

"Where will Kelly go?" Nikki asked, ignoring Adelle's dismissal of the topic.

That made Adelle sit back down again slowly.

"Well, I have a couple of ideas I want to run by you. Also, I'm afraid there's been a change. The buyer wants to close quicker than we thought. It's a good deal for us. We won't be as financially strapped as we thought if we take their offer."

"How soon do they want you out?" My heart sank. Just when I was getting comfortable here, my little nest was going to be disturbed. I needed to look at the big picture though. It was only temporary.

Adelle sucked air into her lungs. I did the same trying to prepare for the bomb she was about to drop.

"In five days," Adelle said, rapidly blinking her eyelashes and refusing to look directly at me. She reached up and combed her fingers through her long, blond hair and pursed her lips together.

"What?" Nikki and I shrieked in unison.

"But the kids, your house, five days," I rattled.

"I know. I'm freaking out. The kids don't know yet, and we still have to sign the contract for our rental home. Mike says if we don't take this buyer, we may have to wait through the winter to sell. Also, the buyer is a friend of his father's with a lot of extra cash to spend. He's doing us a big favor by taking it off our hands at this price. He's going to use the property as a rental investment and has someone that needs to move in immediately. It's a client of his that is relocating his family to Chicago. We won't get an opportunity like this again. Not in this market."

"Oh, you have to take it," Nikki said. "Will you be able to buy another house with what you'll get?"

"Eventually, yes," she said, continuing to comb through and pick at her hair. "It will be much smaller than the one we live in, of course. And we're going to take our time shopping. We might be able to get a good deal the way the market has turned with so many foreclosures. I'm just glad that's not us. We will certainly be okay. Even comfortable." Adelle sniffed and looked down to the ground, allowing her long, blond hair to fall around her face in waves, shielding her eyes from us. Her hands finally settled away from her locks and on her lap. I could feel the defeat radiating off of her body. As well as the bit of denial she was clearly hanging onto.

"I just can't stand the thought of telling the kids. It's all so fast. What will it do to them?"

"Will the rental home allow them to stay in the same school?" Nikki asked.

"Yes," Adelle said, wiping at her eyes.

"That's great," I said, imagining my dear little Cindy having to make new friends and become accustomed to a new school. It would be a nightmare for her. Her older brother, Frank, would be fine, but Cindy was so sensitive.

Seeing Adelle tear up made me want to pack my bags and clear out immediately. She could have my home today. Right now even. But it wasn't even mine to give away. Nikki was the one that needed to make the call.

"Kelly, I thought about something. Why don't you stay at the vacation home in Michigan until we're out of here? It's on the market, but there's been no activity for months. No one seems to be in the mood to buy lake front property no matter how low we drop the price," Adelle said.

At the mention of the Michigan home, Adelle finally broke down sobbing.

Nikki and I swarmed around our sister, pulling her hair back from her face and hugging her.

"I'm sorry. We've been working with a therapist. She's really been helping us recognize our priorities. I know these homes are just things, and we should be grateful that we still have our family and our health. It's just the thought of losing that home in Michigan. We've had so many great times up there as a family. I'm going to miss it so much."

Adelle continued to sob despite our efforts to comfort her. Six months ago, she was a completely different person. She would never let anyone in and had a rather elitist attitude that drove me crazy. It was tough to hang out with someone who you felt thought they were better than you. The circumstances were certainly awful, but to be honest, I liked her so much more as a person now. She was no longer obsessed with material things and was easier to talk to. When Mike and Adelle were trying to hide their financial problems, she had a wall around her that no one could scale. She came off as haughty and self-centered. Now we knew she was just trying to protect her crumbling self-esteem.

"Maybe you won't have to sell the lake front property. Wouldn't the sale of your Geneva home be enough to turn things around for you?" Nikki asked.

Adelle sat up and wiped some of the tears off of her face. "We're just not sure yet. Selling Michigan would give us a better cushion for sure. It's nothing fancy, but it's been in Mike's family for a very long time. You know how great the location is, right on the Lake Michigan dune. It will probably be scooped up by a developer and torn down for someone to build a brand new home. That's the thing that breaks my heart."

"How much do you think it will go for?" I asked.

"Well, before the market burst, it was worth over a million."

"That thing?" I questioned, suddenly not feeling as bad for her. "Sorry, I don't mean to be rude, but it's just a little beach house."

In my mind, I saw the little miniature rooms and the tiny kitchen where Adelle and I made dinner the last time I was up there for a visit.

"I know. Can you believe it? It's the water front location. You've seen the houses being built all around it. It's the hot spot to be right now for people who can afford it."

"Oh no! I just remembered I have an appointment this morning in an hour. With all that's happened, I completely forgot about it," Nikki said, standing up.

"Where do you have to go?" I asked.

"Down the block, to look at the old Breakfast Bar location. They have an opening that might work for the coffee shop," Nikki said.

"So, you're definitely going through with opening up a coffee shop?" Adelle asked.

"I'm still thinking about it. I haven't made a decision or really made a big deal about it because you have a lot going on. I didn't want to transfer any of my stress onto you."

"That's great, Nikki. Trust me; feel free to unload on me. I'm happy for the distraction. But are you sure that opening another store is the best idea right now?" Adelle asked.

Nikki paused briefly before responding.

"Well, I've been doing some research. Despite the downturn in the economy, Chicago is the most caffeinated city in the country, and a lot of the major brands are expanding right now. Looks like caffeine is the one thing people don't want to let go of in these tough times. Plus, the two stores might balance each other out if Chocolate Love starts to suffer."

"Are you sure you can balance both?" Adelle asked.

"It's smart to keep expanding, and I think coffee is the place to be right now. I don't really have room to do it in Chocolate Love."

"It sounds great," I said, taking a sip of my own coffee. Nikki was right. Everyone was stressed out. People needed coffee to work extra hours to make ends meet.

"Want me to go with you?" I asked Nikki.

"Are you sure? Don't you need to work?"

"You know, after what happened with Brian this morning, I'm not going to be able to get much work done this morning. It would be nice to go with you just to get my mind off of things."

"Yeah, it's weighing on me as well. I keep thinking about the last thing he said to me," Nikki said.

"What?" Adelle and I said in unison.

"History repeats itself."

"What did he mean by that?" I asked.

"Don't know. But I'm going to be haunted by it."

Nikki leaned out the window to catch a glimpse of the front of the Geneva History Museum. Adelle and I both did the same. I noticed the wind had picked up and the sky darkened considerably from this morning. Dead leaves swirled in small tornados on the sidewalk.

Something wicked this way comes, I thought to myself.

"I would go too, but I'm volunteering in Cindy's class today," Adelle said.

"Thanks, Adelle." Nikki said.

An hour later, Nikki and I walked to the front of the old Breakfast Bar location. I'd showered and did a bit of organizing of what I wanted to get done for the day. With this being the start of a new book, it was always difficult to get into a routine. There wasn't really a definite path in the beginning. It always felt like I was just dog paddling, trying to figure out which direction to go. Although Adelle and her family moving in would be a complete disturbance of my routine, I was starting to think it wouldn't be the worst thing for me. I needed a little shake up. Jack's offer for me to move in with him while Adelle was staying at my apartment was tempting, but I was leaning more and more to heading up north to Adelle's vacation home in Michigan. It would do me good to get away from my comfort zone and spend a couple of weeks diving into the book to try and get into the zone.

I shook my head in disapproval. Why couldn't I just be honest with myself? It wasn't really about getting away to write the book. Maybe it was partially the motivation, but it wasn't the whole thing. I was really running away from a decision. I grabbed at my long, brown hair and pulled it into a messy ponytail.

"What's with you?" Nikki asked.

"What do you mean?"

"You're shaking your head back and forth. You're talking to yourself up there again, aren't you?"

Nikki could probably pinpoint exactly what was going on in my mind. She knew me way too well.

"Talk about it later?" she said when I didn't really answer her.

I nodded my head and smiled at her, knowing these were good problems to have. The man I loved wanted to start taking steps to further solidify our relationship. I'd been in love with him since I was a teenager. When I thought of us getting older, it was something I wanted to do together. That mental picture was so clear to me. So, why was I so distraught about us taking this next step? It should feel like a natural progression, but for some reason, I was stuck.

"Good morning," the real estate agent called out cheerfully as we approached the old Breakfast Bar.

Just like Chocolate Love, Breakfast Bar was another residential home from the turn of the century that had been converted into a restaurant when Third Street became commercial. It would be a nice addition to the Chocolate Love empire Nikki was building because of its location and similarities to the original Chocolate Love building.

"Hello, Tilly," Nikki said, climbing two small cement steps onto the front porch.

"Are you excited? I was just inside. It looks great. You're really going to be happy with it. It has all of the things on your checklist," an overly hyped Tilly said. She was vaguely familiar to me, but I couldn't place her.

"How come this one just became available this week? It's been vacant for two years. This is my sister, Kelly, by the way."

"Of course. Hi, Kelly. Tilly Dissert. Nice to see you again. Don't know if you remember, but we went to high school together. I was a senior when you were a freshman at Geneva High School."

I tried to get a mental picture of what Tilly looked like all those years ago, while she pumped my hand in greeting. Was she this enthusiastic back then? In present day, she was almost an identical twin to Adelle, tall with a great figure and long, beautiful, blond hair that fell in waves around her shoulders. She wore a well-tailored, gray suit that nipped in at the waist, showing off her curves in all the right places. Although they were similar in features, in my opinion she wasn't anywhere near the natural beauty Adelle was. Adelle could wake up and roll out of bed gorgeous. Tilly looked a little more made-up, like she had to put some effort into looking this way, but the end result was nice. I noted Tilly wore a much darker shade of lipstick than what Adelle normally wore. It gave her a more severe look than what my sister was able to carry off so well.

"It's nice to see you again."

"It's great to have you back in town. I've never left. I've been selling real estate in Geneva since I graduated from college, so I know the area well. When you're ready to move out of Chocolate Love, I'll be able to help you find a nice little place where you can write all of your masterpieces."

"Thanks."

I squirmed a little bit, wrapping my arms around my body, uncomfortable with the attention. She seemed to know a lot of information about me. Of course, this was a small town. Probably most people knew that I lived above Chocolate Love and was an author. That was no secret. Still, I hoped the spotlight would be taken from me quickly. Thankfully, Tilly seemed to pick up on my body language and changed direction.

"So, Nikki. In answer to your question. The owner of the building has been trying for two years to find another investor in order to re-open Breakfast Bar. He's finally stepping back and considering renting it out instead of re-opening."

"Are you saying he's been paying rent on this place for two years without bringing in any profit?" Nikki asked.

"He's the original owner of the building. It's been in his family for generations. He's not quite ready to give it up entirely, so he's looking to rent it out. If you ask me though, he might be looking for a rent-to-own, or even a sale in the near future. He's having a hard time giving it up because of the history of the building, but he might be more open to the right buyer. Since you're looking to turn this into a coffee house, he might be willing to sell it to you. He really wants to keep it in the food business."

Nikki nodded and turned to examine the building. She had not shared yet if she planned to rent or buy the place. I assumed her in-laws would be helping with the investment of opening up an addition to Chocolate Love since they'd been so active in the first business.

"Why don't we go in and see the place. I'm getting way ahead of myself. We have to know if you like it first before you can make any decisions, right?" Tilly laughed, making her way to the front door. "I don't mean to pressure you. It's just that this place seems perfect from what you described when we spoke. And now that he's finally put it on the market for rent, I think he'll find a tenant quick. This location is great."

I couldn't help but think Nikki was getting a hard sell here. If this location was so sought after, why hadn't the owner been able to get investors for Breakfast Bar?

The three of us entered the front of the house. It was similar to Chocolate Love in that the entrance was comprised of a small sunroom made up almost entirely of windows. Although empty now, I could visualize tables and chairs set up here for people to drink their coffee and gaze at the comings and goings on Third Street. Taking a step up, we entered the main room through French doors. The focal point was a large fireplace on the south wall with two windows on either side, allowing natural light to fill the room. The room was painted a dark red, a bad choice in my opinion, and was extremely dusty.

Even through the dust and the bad choice in paint color, I could recognize that this location had a lot of potential. Maybe Tilly was right and just genuinely excited about the find. Between the foot traffic on Third Street, the hype already established by Chocolate Love, and the economy's love of coffee, my gut instinct said Nikki should snatch this place up and move forward with her dream to expand. Not knowing any of the numbers though, I kept my mouth shut and waited for Nikki's reaction. Turning to observe her, I noted her taking it all in. I could almost see her mentally changing paint colors and knocking down walls to make it more open. If I was reading her body language correctly, she was in.

"What's upstairs?" Nikki asked, making her way across the main room to the flight of stairs at the far end of the floor. As well as stairs leading to a second floor, there was another flight leading down to a back door.

"The previous owner didn't use the upstairs for seating. The Breakfast Bar really only sat the downstairs. There's a small kitchen up there. Want to go take a look?"

"That's not a lot of seating at all. Could he have set tables upstairs if he wanted to?"

"I think so. Let's go look."

"Wait," Nikki said abruptly. "Is the bathroom upstairs?"

"The only bathroom is downstairs in the basement," Tilly said, pointing to the flight of stairs heading down. I assumed there had to be a second flight of stairs around the corner from the ones I could see from my viewpoint. From what I could tell, the stairs just led to a back door.

"It's kind of a strange place to put it, but that's how it's set up right now. You might be able to put one upstairs if you..."

Before Tilly could finish, Nikki ran down the stairs. The creaky wooden boards sounded in protest as though they were angered for being awoken from their slumber. She disappeared from view when she turned the corner to run down the second flight to the basement.

"What?" Tilly asked, looking at me as though I would have an explanation for my sister's strange behavior.

Rather than trying to explain, I ran after Nikki to figure out what caused her to bolt.

Chapter 8

"Nikki?"

Following her down the stairs, I was faced with three closed doors once I'd reached the basement. The sound of her vomiting confirmed which one I should open.

"Are you okay?" I maneuvered my body into the small bathroom and crouched down behind her. Her hair was cut in a short bob, so I reached up and tried to pull it back from her face as best I could while she emptied out the contents of her stomach.

Most people detested throwing up, but Nikki had an absolute aversion to it. I was the one with the weak stomach. It was an oddity to see Nikki sick like this. The times she had the stomach flu when we were kids were absolute hell in our house. Even now, I saw tears streaming down her face while her body spasmed in pain. It took a lot to make Nikki cry. My own eyes watered up at the sight of her in pain.

"Oh, Nikki, it's okay. I know that was tough to see," I murmured, assuming she was having a late reaction to finding her friend dead this morning. "This is too much too fast. We should have delayed the appointment. You're not ready for this right now."

When the vomiting subsided, Nikki plopped down on the bathroom floor and took a deep breath. Her skin was an ashen color, and her eyes appeared unable to focus on me. They floated around the room as though unable to rest. Seeing as the house upstairs was not in tip top shape, I could only imagine just how dirty this bathroom was. I followed Nikki's lead and didn't allow my eyes to focus on anything directly. She bent her legs up and wrapped her arms around them, shaking slightly.

"Feel better?" I asked, sitting down close to Nikki and rubbing her back.

Nikki nodded her head slowly before bending it to touch her knees.

"We've both been through a lot this morning. Your body is probably just reacting now."

Nikki lifted her head up to look at me. I waited for her to say something, but she remained quiet.

"Does this mean you don't like the place?" I joked, doing my best to try and lighten the mood. Nikki's silence was scaring me.

Nikki laughed and shook her head no. Finally, she seemed to be coming back. "I hate throwing up," she said in a hoarse voice.

"I know. Let's get you home and in bed."

A knock on the bathroom door startled us.

"Nikki? Are you okay?" Tilly asked kindly from the other side of the door. Unsure if Tilly knew what happened to us this morning, I tried to think of a way to diffuse the situation. Right now, I just wanted to get Nikki out of here.

"We're okay. We'll be out in one second," I called.

Nikki placed her hands on the floor to push herself up, making me cringe. She must really be out of it to touch the bathroom floor like that. I stood up quickly and did my best to help pull her off the ground. The small, white, porcelain sink had a liquid soap dispenser bolted next to it on the wall. I said a quick prayer that the previous owner left a few drops for us and motioned for Nikki to go first. When she pushed the dispenser, a small drop of soap dripped out. Praise the Lord.

After a quick goodbye, Nikki promised to go straight to bed. She was able to reschedule with Tilly for another day with little explanation. Thankfully, Tilly handled the whole thing with grace and professionalism, which I was grateful for. Tilly would hear the story eventually. I didn't want to put Nikki through having to retell it. She hadn't said much on the way home, but she also didn't put up a fight when I told her she needed to go home and get to bed. Although I offered to take care of her, she insisted I go back to work for the day. She wanted to be alone to sleep.

Back in my apartment, I struggled to regain my focus. My mind kept flashing back to the morning's events. The glazed, waxy appearance of Brian's face ran over and over like a bad horror movie in my mind. And the feel of his dough like skin was something I would not soon forget.

In an effort to distract myself, I did a couple loads of laundry and began the process of packing. Adelle told me it would only be a couple of weeks that she would need the apartment, so there really wouldn't be much to pack. I was pretty simple when it came to what I needed since I didn't get dressed up for work. Now it was just a matter of deciding where I would go. Jack and Adelle had both stepped up with great offers. Strangely enough, Nikki had not offered for me to stay with her. I found that odd, considering Nikki was always my go-to person.

Perhaps she thought if I wanted to stay anywhere in town, it would be with Jack? If that was her assumption it was correct, but still, it wasn't like her to not offer. And for that matter, she never offered to let Adelle and her family stay with her at the house. That would make the most sense, considering she had a four bedroom home. Her residence would be much more accommodating to Adelle and Mike's three kids than the apartment. I tried to think back to the conversation the three of us had about the living arrangements. The only thing I really remembered clearly was Nikki's concern as to where I was going to go if Adelle's family moved in to my apartment.

Maybe something more was going on with Nikki. Of us three sisters, she was always the one that needed the least and gave the most. We went to her with problems; she never had to come to us. It had to be true; I was missing something.

I heated myself a cup of tea and sat down at my desk to try and figure out my next move. Should I call Adelle and see what she knew? There had to be a reason why she didn't ask Nikki to stay there. My instincts told me to hold off. It didn't feel right to dig around and not go right to the source. If Nikki wanted me to know something, she would tell me. The three of us were working hard to support each other. Adelle was going through a major downsizing in her life, I was still recovering from my divorce and ex-husband's attempted murder conviction, and Nikki was spinning a million plates to keep a successful business going.

Suddenly, it hit me. I knew how I could get us all to communicate and talk about what was going on. Yes, I could spearhead this by getting us all together at a great location and creating the right environment for a talk. Ah, a plan. Having a sense of a plan always made me feel better.

I set my steaming cup of tea down on the small coaster I kept on my writing desk. It was one of the promotional coasters my agent made for my Antique Murder Mystery Series. The series name ran around the perimeter of the coaster and in the middle was the profile of a woman holding an antique lamp. The look was completed by a sinister profile lurking behind her.

"People get rid of bookmarks, but coasters are something they will keep!" Jackie had said when she ordered them. She was right. I held onto mine and Nikki proudly kept them in Chocolate Love for her customers. She also carried my books in her store and was pushing for more. She wanted tee-shirts, mugs, etc. All with the Antique Murder Mystery logo on it. Perhaps once she got the coffee shop up and running, I would expand my product line. My agent would love it. As far as Jackie was concerned, there was never enough time, money, or locations for properly launching and marketing a series.

I spent the next thirty minutes bouncing around on the Internet. Last summer, at the persistence of Nikki, I signed up for a few of the websites that offered the latest discounts and coupons for events in the area. Normally, I just deleted the emails because I couldn't afford too much of a social life, regardless of how good the coupon was. Plus, I had Jack now to keep me entertained. We were pretty much at the stage where all we wanted to do was stay home and be alone.

Finally, I found what I was looking for. Grabbing my cell phone, I made a few calls to confirm the offer listed last week was still good. Then I sent an email to both Nikki and Adelle to make my announcement. It read:

Dear Nikki and Adelle,

Life has been stressful lately. Let's go to a Hot Yoga class and burn

*the stress right off! How about Saturday morning at 8:00AM?
Hopefully, Nikki will be feeling better by then. I found a place in St.
Charles that offers a free trial with a coupon. I've attached a link.
Print one out from last week's email and we'll go! Let me know if
that sounds good, and I will call to make the reservation.*

Love, K.

I shot the email off and leaned back in my chair, feeling smug. This would do
the trick. Putting my feet up on the desk, I smiled and took a sip of my tea.
After my divorce, my sisters were there when I needed them most. Giving
Adelle a place to live, and Nikki a venue to relieve her stress finally made me
feel like I'd given them some payback. It was about time. It was true what
people said about feeling better when you helped other people. Finally, I was
in a position to do so.

Thinking back to the last yoga class Nikki and I took together brought
back a lot of memories. After I had moved to Geneva, she forced me to go
in order to get accustomed to being around people again. I pretty much went
into hiding after my ex-husband, Steve, was convicted of attempted murder.
It was just too much to bear to be looked at the way I was. Like a freak. The
ex-wife of a monster. The only thing I wanted to do was vanish from the
public eye.

There were still days I wished I had kept my mouth shut and not turned in
the information I found to the police. If I would have allowed him to follow
through with his deadly plans to kill his pregnant mistress, I wouldn't have
to live in fear of him getting out in seven years and finding me. He would
be on death row. But I wouldn't be able to live with myself knowing I let
someone die. It hadn't even registered as an option. I did the only thing I
could. Turned him in. As much as it hurt that the mistress, Mandy, existed,
especially because we had been trying for a baby of our own, she didn't
deserve to die.

But that day started a storm in me that raged on and on with no end in
sight. The fear I had for my future and for the return of Steve kept me from
finding peace. Lately, though, the winds had calmed a bit, and I was finally
able to allow myself to be happy. A little bit in denial possibly, but happy. I
felt alive again. That was what I kept coming back to. Regardless of what the
future would bring, I was alive today. And very much in love. I was finally
focusing on the here and now.

The yoga class Nikki had forced me to go to last summer turned out to
be a game changer for me. That was where Jack and I got the opportunity
to meet up again after being apart for so many years. The minute I laid eyes
on him in that yoga class, my life started to look up. He brought me so
much hope that I could feel again. Love again. These past few months had
been the best times of my life. Being with Jack was exciting, intellectually
stimulating, and fulfilling. So why then, was I unable to commit to moving

in with him for a couple of weeks while Adelle lived in my apartment?

It was difficult to determine if it was the idea of a commitment or the fear of change that held me back. My ex-husband was a cheat, a murderer, and a thief. The lowest of the low. And I picked him. Even wanted to have a family with him. What if I hadn't found that email? What if he had gotten away with murder, and I continued on living with him? How could I possibly trust my judgment again when it came to such a big decision? Choosing another partner in life was too much for me to handle right now. I was still healing.

I had to explain this to Jack. He needed to understand what was going on inside of me, so I didn't insult him. He had shared how much his pride was wounded when I ended our relationship so many years ago. It had been a foolish decision, and I didn't want to hurt him again. He was the right one for me back then, just like he still was now. I just needed more time.

The ringing phone interrupted my thoughts. Caller ID alerted me it was Nikki.

"Are you okay?" I asked.

"Can you come over?"

"Sure. Is everything okay? Is Bob home yet?" I asked panicked.

"Everything is fine, Kelly. I just want to talk to you. Can you come over?"

"Of course. I'll leave right now."

I hung up and brought my teacup over to the sink. While rinsing it out, I looked around my small kitchen and pondered leaving it in a couple of days. There really was no reason to pack anything up. Adelle's kitchen in Michigan was stocked with everything I would need in the way of dishes and such. I could keep everything here as is, so Adelle and her family would have what they needed.

I headed to my bedroom to grab a sweater before leaving. When I opened the white double doors to my closet, I sighed thinking of the work ahead of me. I needed to clear out some space for Adelle and Mike to hang up clothes. Mike wore a suit to work every day. He'd appreciate being able to store them properly rather than live out of a suitcase for a couple of weeks. Adelle would also have a tough time with all of her clothes. She had so many beautiful things. If I moved my queen bed out of my bedroom and turned the whole room into a closet, there still wouldn't be enough space for all of Adelle's elegant clothes and accessories.

Suddenly, the whole thing seemed like a logistical nightmare. What was Adelle thinking asking to move in here? The clothes were just the tip of the iceberg. What about the sleeping arrangements? There was only a queen bed here and a couch. Where would all of the children sleep?

I pulled out a long, navy, wool sweater and shut the doors quickly. This was not the time to try and figure it all out. Right now, Nikki needed me.

Ten minutes later, I pulled my bike up to the front of Nikki's house. The day had warmed into the low sixties. The combination of my wool sweater and the brisk ride had me in a full sweat. Ripping off my sweater, I tied it half-hazardly around my waist, and then parked my bike next to Nikki's front porch.

An older model black SUV that was unfamiliar to me was parked in the driveway. My first thought was that it must somehow be linked to Brian's death this morning. Last summer when an employee passed away, Nikki was adamant about helping with a memorial ceremony. It was only natural she would want to help with Brian's. My guess was perhaps this car belonged to someone from the Geneva History Museum here to help put the plans together.

I made my way up Nikki's front porch. Her American Four Square home was built almost one hundred years ago when the Tri-Cities: Geneva, St. Charles, and Batavia, where starting to boom. The block was filled with similar homes. Although they complained often that the rooms were too small, I loved coming over to Nikki's. Bob and Nikki had a very comfortable, loving relationship. Because of this, their home exuded a special kind of warmth that engulfed me upon entering.

I knocked lightly at the front door and waited for Nikki to answer. The front door was made up entirely of clear glass, so it was possible to see into the front foyer and on into the kitchen. The main level was basically a circle made up of a foyer, behind it a kitchen, a small dining room and a living room. From where I stood, it appeared as though all the rooms were empty. Finally, a set of feet came walking down the stairs from the second floor. Seeing them started a funny feeling in my stomach.

On the landing where the stairs split, Nikki's guest turned and looked directly at me, causing me to gasp.

Chapter 9

"What is going on? Whose car is that?" I asked when Adelle opened the door.

"Everything is fine. It's mine. We traded in the Cadillac this morning for something more affordable." Adelle nearly choked over the word affordable. My guess was she wasn't too happy about the trade.

"So, how is she?" I asked, pulling my sweater off and laying it on the small, brown bench in Nikki's foyer. I was feeling a little taken aback by the fact that Nikki called Adelle, but trying my best to hide it. We were changing. Things were changing. This was fine.

"Why don't you go up and talk to her? I'm going to make us some tea."

Adelle turned and made a bee line for the kitchen. Her swift departure from the foyer caused that tingling sensation in my gut to spike. This was something.

While climbing the stairs, things fell into place. I knew what was going on now. It was so clear in my head. But there had been no talk of it coming this quickly. Wouldn't Nikki have talked to me about it? But she wouldn't. She knew how hard it would be on me. If anyone knew, she would be the one to grasp the depth of my pain. The blow this would have on me.

"I'm sorry. You'll have to give yourself at least three months before you can try again. As your doctor, I'm ordering you to let your body recover. Unfortunately, this happens all the time. It doesn't mean it's not going to work. It just didn't work this time. Take a few months and talk to your husband. See if you want to try again. I recommend you do."

At the top of the stairs, I paused and leaned against the wall, trying to get a hold of my emotions,

"Calm," I whispered, desperate to keep myself in the here and now. This wasn't about the past. This was the now. And this was Nikki. She needed me.

From my position, I could see into the second floor bathroom. I'd helped Nikki lay the white tile floor last summer when she went on a remodeling spurt. Had she known then that she was going to try and get pregnant this fall? Was she already nesting?

"We can't afford to try again, Steve. How could we possibly do it without your insurance?" I asked.

"I can look for another job with better insurance. A better job that pays more. Something will come up. In the meantime, we'll charge the treatments

on your credit card and rack up some great miles so we can take the baby to Disney. Everything will work out. We want a baby and this is how it needs to happen. We just need to go for it," Steve said, smiling his over-confident grin.

He was always too sure about everything. Now those unsuccessful IVF treatments remained unpaid on my credit card while he sat in a California prison most likely plotting his revenge. And I remained childless. Empty.

Quickly, I pushed myself away from the wall and bolted down the stairs. God help me, I couldn't go into Nikki's room. Forgetting my sweater along with my manners, I flung open the front door and without looking back jumped on my bike. The last thing I heard was Adelle calling out my name from the front porch. The piteous sound of her voice confirmed everything.

When I got back to Chocolate Love, I left my bike on the side of the building not bothering to lock it up.

"Take it," I grumbled aloud to no one in particular.

Entering through the back door, I noticed right away that the kitchen seemed a bit hectic without Nikki's calming energy. Two of the girls from the front room were in a heated debate over which cake should go in the display case, and Miguel was struggling to pull two large pans out of the large industrial oven. I rushed over to him to help.

"Here, let me help you."

"Thank you. We're short today with Nikki out. I called in an extra pair of hands, but Denise won't be here for another thirty minutes. The pumpkin display is cancelled tonight for Geneva History Museum because of what happened, but we have a small display needed for the Batavia Mother's Club meeting."

"Do you want my help?"

"No, Kelly. Don't worry, we can handle this. You've got work to do."

After setting the pans down, Miguel turned to look at me. A fairly recent immigrant from an impoverished city in Mexico, Miguel took a lot of pride in his job and being able to support his growing family. I should have known he wouldn't ask for my help. Even though he was Nikki's right hand man, he never seemed sure about his job security. Nikki told me once that it was the combination of the troubled economy and his history of growing up in a place where there were never enough jobs for fathers to support their families that made him feel that way.

"Nikki is so lucky to have you. Call me upstairs if you need me." I turned to walk away.

"You spoke to Nikki then?"

I froze in place. He knew. Slowly, I turned to look at him. His dark brown eyes studied me. The skin around his eyes crinkled up in question. Would she really tell Miguel before me? Was I truly the last one to know? Shouldn't I have been the first? After her husband, Bob, of course.

"I did."

"She is okay then? She will be back tomorrow?"

Miguel reached up to adjust the hairnet he wore while baking. I took it to be a nervous gesture. How long had he known? Had Nikki been trying for a baby for a long time? It was all so confusing. She was so focused on her career and growing Chocolate Love, I thought she would wait for a few years.

Was there no bond in life that could be trusted? My best friend, my sister, didn't trust our relationship enough to confide in me on one of the biggest events of her life. Instead she went to Adelle and Miguel? Did she not think I could handle it? Didn't she need me?

Miguel cocked his head to the side and studied me. He pulled up one side of his face in a nervous half smile. He looked scared.

"Kelly, are you okay?"

In that instant, I realized what a ridiculous path I'd taken. He didn't know. There was no way.

"I am asking too many questions about Nikki?" He put his hands up in an apologetic gesture.

"No, it's not that, Miguel. Nikki is fine. She'll probably be back tomorrow. I…I have to go."

I turned on my heel quickly, desperate to keep my emotions in control at least until I got upstairs. *What the hell was wrong with me?*

In the front room, Patty was waiting for me with a cup of coffee in her hand. "Hey, Kelly. I thought that was you coming in. Want a cup of coffee?" she asked, extending the cup to me. She stepped back quickly when she saw how fast I was moving. Her quick movement splashed a bit of coffee onto her apron.

"Sorry for making you spill. Thanks," I mumbled, accepting it. "Have to get to work."

"Oh, sure. Is Nikki okay?" she asked. The whole staff seemed on edge with Nikki out.

"She'll be okay. Probably back tomorrow. Sorry, got to go." I could see Patty wanted to talk, but I wasn't up for it.

"Everyone, leave me alone!" I wanted to scream on the verge of a tantrum.

Upstairs, I set the coffee cup down on the little table next to my door where I kept my keys and bolted for my bedroom. The day had darkened early in typical fall fashion, making me want to dive under my covers and hide. Once I did, I allowed myself to surrender to my emotions. There was so much shame pumping through me for running out of Nikki's house like a coward. I'd ruined this beautiful, joyous moment for my sister by making it all about my emotions and my past. My god-awful, ill-ridden past.

"I need you to help me get rid of her. I can't let her burden me for the rest of my life," read the email.

"9-1-1, how can we assist you?"

"This is Kelly Clark. I need help. I just stumbled upon something on my husband's computer. I think he's planning on killing someone very soon. Possibly tonight."

During the trial, it was revealed that Steve's mistress, Mandy, had no clue he was married. He had deceived her just like he did me. She still sent an email once a year on the baby's birthday thanking me for what I'd done. Although painful, I looked forward to it in a way. It was a yearly confirmation that my life blowing up had at least one good outcome. A beautiful little girl, Caroline, who came into this world unharmed.

My cell phone buzzed, letting me know a text message had arrived. Without looking at it, I burrowed down deeper into my bed, allowing the tears to flow. Just like that, the storm was back. Would I ever have true happiness again? Or would I always be jaded? Would every step forward be a struggle? Every new life a reminder of what was taken from me?

This afternoon should have been a celebration of Nikki's news. Instead I felt myself building a wall to block out feeling any emotion for Nikki. I wasn't prepared to feel this. I was jealous. An ugly jealousy that made me sick. How many times had Nikki been there for me in my time of need? Given me a home when I needed it. Spent countless hours on the phone listening to me moan on and on about the divorce, and rejoiced with me when my life started to turn for the better.

This was how I was going to repay her? By running out the door when she wanted to share her good news? It made me feel like a monster. I wanted to curl deeper into a ball and shrink my body into nothing.

Wrapping my arms around my legs, I sobbed, allowing myself to hit rock bottom. As the tears finally subsided, my mind focused on one face. I thought I had been doing so well. So much for progress.

"I hate you, Steve," I whispered into my knees.

Feeling slightly better, I stretched my legs out and pulled back the blankets, hoping to gather the energy to shower. Despite the strenuous ride, I'd caught a chill on the bike ride home that I couldn't shake. I pulled my long, brown hair into a knot on the top of my head and turned on the water.

While waiting for the water to heat up, I stared at my reflection in the mirror. Dark lines of mascara ran down my face in messy streams, and my eyes burned a bright red. All signs of a major meltdown. My nose was aglow in a Rudolph the red nosed reindeer mess. The sight of it made me laugh out loud.

"Nice," I mumbled at my disheveled reflection. If my head spun all the way around on my head right now, I wouldn't be shocked. I was behaving like a lunatic. Shaking it in disapproval, I turned away from the mirror and into the sanctity of my warm shower.

While the hot water poured down my back, I made a decision to head over to Nikki's. This was ridiculous. I had to pull myself together and make this better. She deserved better from me. Hopefully, she'd forgive me.

While I was dressing, someone knocked on my apartment door. Quickly, I pulled a light, cotton sweater on over a pair of dark jeans and rushed to open it. Nikki stood on the other side, looking a bit green.

"Oh, Nikki. Thank God. I'm so sorry," I said, pulling her into the apartment. Her off-color complexion and the way she wouldn't meet my eyes caused me worry.

Without saying a word, she gently pushed me away and moved toward my bathroom. I sat down on my couch and waited patiently for her return. After a few minutes, she opened the bathroom door and shuffled her way over to the couch.

"Are you okay?" I asked quietly. Her expression was much more relaxed and her color was back to normal. She looked like a completely different person.

She smiled at me and stretched her legs out on the coffee table.

"Now I am," she said simply.

"How long have you known?"

"A few weeks. I've been fine up until this week. Something about the lunchtime hour. This goes on for about three hours every day and then it passes. No one told me it was going to be this fun."

"Nikki, I'm so sorry about the way I acted. I thought this was all about you reacting to finding Brian."

"It is. Finding Brian this morning like we did definitely kicked my nausea into full gear. You don't have to explain the way you acted, Kelly. Why do you think I didn't want to tell you? I wanted to spare you any pain as long as I could."

"That's awful. What kind of sister am I that I would make your baby news all about me?" I scratched at my scalp, hoping I could somehow pull my bad thoughts out of my brain.

"Stop, Kelly. We're not going to try and rationalize or explain away any of your feelings. They are all normal and expected. We knew this was going to happen."

"We never talked about it."

"No, we didn't. But we both knew this day would come, and we knew it was going to be tough to deal with when it did. Whether we talked about it or not, it was on both of our minds."

"God, I hate who I am. I hate these…feelings."

"Don't say that. You're on a journey of recovery and you're doing great." Nikki reached over and took my hand in hers.

"Running out of your house crying because I'm jealous of your good news is not 'great'. You call that great?"

"After what you've been through, I would call it normal."

As much as I didn't want to, I started to cry again.

Rubbing at my eyes, I tried to hold the dam before the levy broke entirely.

"Stupid," I whispered. "Stupid, crazy Kelly. At it again."

"No, Kelly, don't think…" Nikki cut her words off suddenly and abruptly sat back on the chair.

"Uh, oh," she mumbled. She reached her hand up to her mouth and took in three quick breaths.

"You okay?"

"Yep, just give me one second."

Nikki breathed in and out a few more times and then smiled slightly.

"Okay, I think it passed. One more hour and this will be gone." She took another breath. "Now stop beating yourself up. You have every right to go through this in your head. You wanted a baby. You found out you couldn't have a baby. Then went through hell and high water to try and have one. And now you're supposed to be happy for me when I'm getting what *you* wanted? Plus, it can't help that you think I didn't really want this."

I cringed when Nikki said that. As usual, she hit the nail on the head.

She leaned forward and took my hand in hers.

"But I do, Kelly. I know you think I'm obsessed with Chocolate Love and the new store, Bean in Love, but Bob and I have been talking about this for a long time now. I couldn't tell you because there never seemed to be the right time. I love you, Kelly. I didn't want to hurt you. We're going to figure out a way to make work and life balance and give this child everything we can."

"I know you will. I hate feeling this way. You have everything, Nikki. A loving husband, a booming business, and now a child. I'm so happy for you. But it does make me look at my life and feel…disappointed. I've made so many bad choices."

"That's why I came over here. I knew you would be thinking that way. But, Kelly, are you so blind that you don't see what's happened to you in the last couple of months? You have the chance to have everything you want. Your books are taking off, you're getting your finances in order, and most importantly, you are getting a second chance at love with a really good guy who wants to marry you and start a family. But, I can see the walls you're building to stop that. If you stay in this place of fear and self-protection, you won't continue to blossom like you have been. Don't blow this with Jack. He's not going to give you another chance if you do."

"But how can I give him a family? I'm not going to be able to provide children."

"You don't know that, Kelly. You weren't able to have kids with Steve, but things might be different with Jack. It just didn't happen. Maybe that was God's way of protecting you from birthing the devil's spawn."

"The devil's spawn?" I laughed, shaking my head. My reaction made Nikki break out into a big smile.

"That's why Adelle didn't move in with you. She knew," I said.

"She didn't want to disturb me in the first trimester. I'm sorry I told her first, but I needed someone to talk to. And she's had three children. This nausea has really rocked me. I didn't know what to do. She's been a big help. You understand, don't you?"

"Of course I do. There's a part of me that's hurt because you didn't tell me first, but now that you've explained everything, I see you were just looking out for me. Sorry about the way I acted. I need a little time for all of this to sink in. There are so many changes going on right now. For all of us."

"Tell me about it," Nikki said, leaning back on her chair and kicking her feet up onto the coffee table again. My eyes wandered over her petite frame, checking to see if I could pick up any signs of her pregnancy. She didn't have that glow that everyone talked about. In fact, if anything, her skin looked pale and light blue circles had formed under her eyes. It made me worry that she was taking on too much. I knew what Adelle went through trying to keep her three kids fed, dressed, and happy. How was Nikki going to do that while running Chocolate Love *and* opening a second store?

But, if anyone could do it, Nikki could. She was a powerhouse. Always had been. When she set her mind to something, she not only accomplished her goal, she went above and beyond expectations. And she had a very supportive, loving husband. I knew Bob would be an incredible father.

"You're not going to stay with Jack, are you? You're going to Michigan?" Nikki asked, interrupting my thoughts.

I rubbed my face with both hands.

"You're going to blow this, Kelly," Nikki said bluntly. "I'm only telling you because I love you."

Pulling my hands down from my face, I clasped them together on my lap. She was right, but I just couldn't get myself to accept his offer. If I wasn't ready, I wasn't ready. There was nothing I could do about it.

"Fine. I can see you are dead set against it. Break it to him gently at least. And, hear me out on something. If you're heading to St. Joe's then I am, too. I need you to be my partner in crime. We have some investigating to do up there."

Another one of Nikki's adventures. Now what did she have planned for us?

Chapter 10

"Investigating? What do you mean—investigating? Now what are you up to?" I asked.

"Do you remember when we went to Chocolate Café in downtown St. Joe's the last time we visited Adelle at the Michigan house?"

"Barely. It's been a couple of years since I've been up there."

"I remember really liking the way it was set up with the combination of coffee, treats, and sandwiches. Adelle said the company has done really well in the past couple of years and has expanded into Indiana and Ohio. They must be doing something right. Let's head up there and soak it in. I want to try and emulate what they are doing but on a smaller scale at Bean in Love."

"Are you sure you're up for this? I love the name Bean in Love by the way. When did you come up with that?"

"Bob did, actually. You know, like a coffee bean in Chocolate Love? Except, it's not actually going to be in Chocolate Love. It's going to have its own building. And it's also a play on words. People have *been in love*, meaning Chocolate Love, and now they can try something new. Get it? Bean? Like been?"

"Very creative," I laughed.

"And I think over the next week, things are going to get better for me. The last couple of days have been tough, but each day is slightly better. Look at me now. As I'm sitting here, the nausea has subsided. Maybe by the end of the week, it will be gone. Adelle said she had sickness for all of her pregnancies, but it was very brief and only in the beginning. Maybe I'll be the same."

"I haven't even asked you; how far along do you think you are?"

"I think I'm right around ten weeks."

That meant she got pregnant soon after our fiasco over the summer with my ex-husband's psychotic girlfriend.

"You're almost in your second trimester. Things are supposed to get a lot easier."

"It's been pretty easy so far. It's only these past two weeks that have been tough."

"Has Adelle heard anything more about when she'll need to move in?"

"She's waiting on pins and needles for the phone call. I think she plans to break the news to the kids tonight and then start packing. Can you imagine packing up that house? It's going to be a nightmare. All that expensive furniture and china. I would be a nervous wreck."

I nodded my head in agreement. The reality of how difficult it was going to be on Adelle's family was starting to sink in. Those poor kids. They'd never known anything but that house. They each came home from the hospital to their own beautifully made up custom nursery. It was going to be heartbreaking to take their rooms apart.

"Speaking of change, I made a few phone calls this afternoon," Nikki said. "I'm working with the Executive Director of the Geneva History Museum, Barbara Goila, to help plan Brian's memorial. All of his family is in Pennsylvania. They want his body sent back home. Barbara already spoke to his mother and mentioned they are planning a small memorial service for him on Sunday. His parents are not coming in. It's just his parents, who are elderly, and one other sibling who lives in L.A."

"What time on Sunday?"

"Barbara is still ironing out the details. But, here's the thing. I'm sure Adelle will want to do the majority of the move on the weekend, so her kids will be somewhat settled before heading to school on Monday. We'll have to go to the memorial service and then head right to packing."

It was all happening so fast. This meant I had to tell Jack what my plans were right now. And what my plans weren't.

"I have to call Jack. How would you suggest I go about doing this?"

"Maybe try and spin it that you are using this time for your writing and helping me look at Chocolate Café."

I shook my head. "No, I don't want to spin anything for Jack. If this relationship can't be straight truth, it's not going to work."

"You know what I mean. I'm not saying you should lie to him, I'm just saying, go easy. We both know you want a future with him. You just need a little more time. You've only been dating for what…four months?"

"I'll tell him tonight. We're supposed to see each other after work."

"This day has been such a whirlwind. I'm still so frazzled by Brian's death. Hopefully we hear the results from the autopsy soon. That back door. I can't stop thinking about it. What do you think?"

"I have no idea. Could he have just left it open by mistake?"

"No way. Not with the paranoia he's been experiencing. I'm having a hard time accepting that it was a suicide. I don't believe it."

"Maybe you didn't know Brian as well as you thought you did. When he was in Chocolate Love yesterday, he was completely unhinged," I said, widening my eyes.

"Well, he was scared, Kelly. No doubt Brian was an extremely passionate man. But he wasn't suicidal. He kept talking about going home. He was ready to take action to free himself from the fear. I thought he meant his apartment in Elgin, but maybe he was talking about going back to his parent's house in Pennsylvania? Do you think if I called them and talked to them, I would be able to find out more?"

"I don't know. What if it causes them more grief? Do you really want to do that to them? They just lost their son. I'd definitely wait for the results of the autopsy to come back so you at least know more."

Nikki shook her head and rubbed at her temples. "He was my friend. We weren't extremely close, but I feel like I owe it to him to at least find out more. Man, what I would do for a cup of coffee right now. How ironic is that? I'm opening my own coffee store, and yet, I have to limit my intake. Coffee, coffee everywhere and not a sip to drink," Nikki pulled her feet down from the glass coffee table and sat up straighter.

"You can't have any?" I asked.

"The doctor said I can have some…meaning a little. I've been having my cup in the morning, but sometimes it just makes me more nauseous. I think my afternoon headaches are partially linked to my withdrawal from the caffeine. Well, I should be going and let you get some work done. Let me know how tonight goes with Jack."

"I will."

When Nikki stood up, I studied her belly for any telltale bump. There didn't appear to be one yet.

"Oh, and no Hot Yoga for me," she said, sticking her index finger up in the air. "Doctor says it's a no-no. But Adelle expressed some interest, so check with her."

As if on cue, my cell phone rang.

"This is her."

"Okay, I'm off. I'll check in with you later."

Adelle and I agreed to meet for the 6:00 A.M. Saturday morning class. Although it was very early, it was the only time that would work for her. She planned to spend the weekend packing and chauffeuring kids around. She told me her family would live in my apartment for one week, shorter than I had initially thought, then move into the rental home. The move would primarily happen on Sunday, just like Nikki thought, so the kids could be somewhat settled for school on Monday.

"Are you okay, Kelly?" Adelle asked before we hung up.

Rather than give Adelle a quick answer, I paused before speaking. If someone told me I would be able to have true heart-to-heart talks with Adelle a year ago, I would have laughed. We just didn't have that kind of relationship. But I was learning how sibling relationships, or any relationship for that matter, could transform and grow as long as you were open to letting go of hurt feelings.

"No, Adelle, I'm not. I hate the way I feel. Instead of being happy for her, I can't stop thinking about my own loss. I'm disgusted with myself."

"That's so harsh. It's normal to feel this way with all you've gone through. At least you're honest with your feelings. That's a start."

I nodded my head in agreement but did not speak for fear I would start crying.

"It's going to be okay, Kelly. We'll get you through this. Nikki and I were trying to spare you the pain by holding off for a softer moment to tell you. The timing of your suggestion for Hot Yoga and then Nikki's illness kicking in just threw everything off."

"Do Mom and Dad know yet?" I asked.

"Mom was the first to know. Well, except for Bob of course," Adelle said, referring to Nikki's husband.

"I have to go. Wish I had more time to talk, but I have to take the kids to soccer. If we're late the coach gets angry. There's so much pressure on kids nowadays. I'm thinking of cutting back on their after school activities. But, that's a whole different story. I'll talk to you later."

After Adelle hung up, I shot Jack a text to see if he'd come over for dinner after work.

Come over to my place instead. You've been through a lot today. I don't want you to worry about cooking dinner, he wrote back.

I'd already updated Jack via text after we'd found Brian in the History Museum. He'd offered to come home, but he had an important meeting, so I insisted he stay there.

Are you sure? I wrote back.

Yes.

Jack enjoyed cooking and eating, so I never felt bad having him cook after a long day at work. If anything, it helped him relax and chill out. Considering we had a lot of complex issues to discuss tonight, it was probably better he was the one cooking. Maybe he'd take the news better if he was distracted.

What time? I wrote.

How about 8:00? I need to pick up a few things from the store when I get back to Geneva. How about chicken vesuvio, wine, and an arugula salad? You bring something sweet from Chocolate Love. Besides you, I mean.

Cheeseball! I shot back, laughing to myself. *Can't wait. I have a 6:00 A.M. Hot Yoga class with Adelle. Can't drink too much wine!*

Hot Yoga? You guys are nuts. See you tonight.

After signing off, I turned around to examine the apartment. It was a comfortable place for me, but I still couldn't imagine moving a family of five into it. If only there were another bedroom. That would make things a lot easier. The front of the apartment was made up of a large living room with a small kitchen. Both rooms faced east with windows looking out onto Third Street. The natural light streaming in could be a problem for the kids if they slept out here. Although, with it staying darker longer in the morning, it might not be an issue.

Maybe I would suggest to Adelle to set it up that way. I could even start to move some of the furniture, so she had a better picture of what I was thinking. She and Mike could take the queen bed in my bedroom and most likely keep their toddler, Craig, in there with them. She'd be most concerned with keeping Cindy, her kindergartner, and Frank, her third grader, on some kind of schedule.

It was time to get to it.

A few hours later, I plopped down on my living room couch and took it all in. The smell of fresh pine filled the room, making me smile. The place looked clean, organized, and inviting after all of the organizing and scrubbing I had done. My muscles were sore from rearranging furniture and moving things that were probably much too big for me to move on my own, but I didn't care. I wanted the place to be as inviting as possible for the weary bunch that would be settling in in just a few days.

I hadn't done any work on my book. It was just too hard to focus. The stress of the upcoming move was too pressing. The week I'd be staying in Michigan was looking more and more like it was meant to be. With all that was happening in Geneva between my sisters and my own life, it was next to impossible to get some quiet time nailed down for writing. Not to mention the disturbing sudden death of Brian. That alone still had me upset, though I could tell I wasn't allowing myself to really deal with it yet.

I forced myself to sit up and walk over to my bathroom for my third shower of the day. It was time to primp for my dinner with Jack. Knowing this might be one of the last nights I spent with Jack in a while, I wanted to look good.

While in the shower, my mind kicked into processing mode. Something about being isolated, surrounded on three sides by tiled walls and a shower curtain, allowed my brain to turn off the jibber jabber of everyday life and focus on the important things.

I thought of Jack. His strong chest, his big hands, and the way he laughed in bed. He didn't take himself too seriously in the bedroom, which in turn, made me relax. And when I relaxed, I had fun. I couldn't imagine wanting anyone else. So, what was the problem?

I wasn't ready. My recovery and rebirth from my divorce was still in progress.

Nikki was so right. I was going to blow it. And at our age, with us both wanting a family, a lot was at stake. With or without all the baby fever, it all came down to one thing: I wanted to spend the rest of my life with Jack. There was no one better for me.

But, I'd been married. I'd been in love. I chuckled quietly to myself thinking of Nikki's explanation of Bean in Love. I had truly "bean in love" and it almost destroyed me. My marriage to Steve shattered so many parts of me that I was still trying to put together. How could I promise myself to someone when I was still building myself back up? Jack deserved the whole of me, not the pieces.

"Damnit, this is hard," I said, pounding my fist lightly against the cold tile.

Giving up on my thoughts, I reached over and turned off the shower. With all of my processing, I was worried about being late for dinner. I reached for my white, fluffy towel and wrapped it around my head like a turban. Pulling back the shower curtain, I noticed a deep fog had settled, blocking my view of the bathroom door. A sure sign I'd been in the shower way too long.

I hustled into my bedroom and picked through my closet to find something to wear. A quick glance at the clock next to my bed confirmed I still had forty minutes to pull myself together and get packed for the night. Giving up on my closet, I walked over to my dresser and dug through my lingerie drawer. After my divorce from Steve, I threw out all of the expensive stuff I bought for our honeymoon. Seeing it disgusted me. It only made me think of the good times we had together. There were plenty, but because of the way things turned out, those memories haunted me. It was like watching an opera, starring me as the fool.

"What about this one? This will definitely get you pregnant!"

"Nikki! You're crazy," I laughed. *"Give that to me. I'm buying it."*

I dropped the black negligee I held in my hand to the ground and took a step back in disgust. Somehow this one had escaped my purging. I'd purchased it when Nikki came out to California for a visit. We'd spent the day shopping in the Marina District and wound up in an elegant women's lingerie shop. Taking a deep breath, I leaned over and picked it up to toss in the garbage. No matter how dire my financial situation was, I would never wear a piece of lingerie for Jack that I'd worn during my relationship with Steve. A girl had to have standards, and in my case, major superstitions.

Finally, I settled on a black lace bra with matching panties. Jack was pretty simple when it came to undergarments. I giggled thinking about the last time I tried to wow him with my choice of bedroom apparel. His reaction was "Wow" and then within twenty seconds, my expensive outfit had ended up on his living room floor. I still thought it was worth it though to put the effort in because I loved the expression on his face.

Forty-five minutes later, I was dressed in a wool skirt, long leather boots, and a fitted red sweater. This was much more dressed up than I would have normally been for a dinner date with Jack, but tonight was going to be our last together for a while.

Jack's condo was a five minute drive from Chocolate Love. The complex was just off of Geneva Golf Club, so the view from his living room balcony was spectacular. We'd spent many a night in the months we'd been dating drinking wine and chatting the night away on his balcony.

Tonight was a bit too chilly to be able to sit out there, but I found myself yearning for some balcony time with him. After the day I'd had, I yearned to kick back and spend time with the man I loved.

Pulling the car into one of his designated parking spots, I slammed my car door shut and glanced in the direction of his condo on the third level at the top of the building. His kitchen window, which faced the parking lot, appeared to be dark. Peering down at my watch, I saw it was almost eight. He should have been cooking by now. Perhaps his train was delayed or he was still at the grocery store. My stomach chose that moment to let out a loud growl. Luckily, Jack kept his place stocked with cheese and crackers for our nights out on the balcony, so I'd have something to snack on while I waited for him.

"Chill out," I said to my stomach. It was the running. It kept my metabolism on a constant burn, regardless of how much I ate. This was another reason Jack was the perfect man for me. His appetite could compete with mine, and he enjoyed keeping his woman fed. His constant attention to food had finally helped me put the weight back on that I desperately needed back after my divorce from Steve.

I climbed the three flights of stairs up to his condo and pulled out the spare key Jack gave me in case of situations like this. When I turned the key, it became clear that it was not locked. Slowly pushing it open, I felt a chill run up my spine. Finding this open door reminded me too much of the open door I found this morning at Geneva History Museum.

"Oh, no," I said quietly to myself, taking in the scene in front of me.

Chapter 11

"Hi, babe," I heard Jack murmur from somewhere in the darkness. The small entrance foyer had a small table and a mirror above it. Three small candles placed on the table shot rays of light up onto the mirror, allowing me to catch a glimpse of my reflection. The woman staring back at me looked shell shocked and a bit frightened. That probably wasn't the reaction Jack was going for.

While making a consorted effort to adjust my expression, I allowed myself to look around and take in the details Jack had obviously worked so hard on. Both the foyer and the adjacent living room were lit only in radiant candlelight. A sneak peek in the other direction revealed a trail of candles down the long hallway to the back bedrooms. This was quite a surprise. My body needed to know how much of a surprise it was. And quickly. I had broken out into an embarrassing sweat.

He couldn't possibly do this tonight?

"What did you do?" I laughed when I finally found my voice. I meant it to come off light but instead sounded accusatory.

Jack finally came into focus. He sat across the room on his sectional couch at an angle where he could see my reaction. Before walking over to me, he bent over to pick up a second glass of wine on the coffee table. As he made his way to me, I saw the look of panic on his face.

"What's wrong? If my memory serves me right, you like surprises." He raised his eyebrow as though to question.

Damn. He had picked up on my freak out.

Yes, the girl Jack knew years ago loved surprises. But that was also a very long time ago. When surprises were light and fun.

"I'm, um, just a little overwhelmed from the day I've had. Still coming down from it all."

Jack set the two glasses of wine down on the entrance table and pulled my overnight bag from my hand. After taking a second to place my things carefully on a bench he had near the door, he turned back to pull me into an embrace.

"Well, let me get you out of your funk," he said, before fixing his lips on mine. I couldn't help but laugh a little.

"Something funny?" he murmured. Instead of allowing me to answer, he bent down, pulled my legs out from under me and cradled me to his chest, walking with me in the direction of his bedroom.

"You have a one track mind," I said, giggling.

"Is that a complaint?" he questioned. He pulled his face away from mine and waited for me to answer. His green eyes, illuminated by the candlelight, searched mine. His fresh shower smell intoxicated me, leaving me in a daze. I tried to answer him with a kiss, but he pulled back further and raised an eyebrow at me in a joking manner.

He set me down in front of the doorway to his bedroom and stood up to his full height. Looking up at his 6'5" frame reminded me of just how big of a man Jack was.

"Do I look like I'm complaining?" I said, reaching up to unbutton his shirt.

To my surprise, he reached for my hands and held onto them instead of allowing me to continue.

"Now look who's got the one track mind," he laughed. He pushed his bedroom door open and turned my body toward the doorway.

Confused, I followed his lead and stepped into his bedroom filled with candles and roses. Soft music chimed in from the small stereo system in the back corner of his bedroom.

"What?"

Jack always made an effort to be romantic, but this was over-the-top, even for him. My first thought had been dead on. This was more than just a romantic night.

Without responding, he took my hand and pulled me over to sit down on his large king-size bed. The thick down duvet fluffed up when we sat down on it, cushioning our landing.

"I couldn't find tulips at this time of the year. Sorry, babe."

"It's okay," I stumbled. "This is beautiful."

"So, I've been thinking I need to up the ante on my offer to move in. If I'm to be a real gentleman, I need to go about this differently. And since you're a true lady…"

I laughed a bit when he said this, making him break out into a big smile. I could tell Jack was not reading my body language right. He was reading my level of nervousness as excitement. And I was excited at where I thought he was heading, but still, this didn't feel right. Especially with the conclusion I'd made this afternoon. If I was going to be Jack's partner in life, I was going to have to come to the relationship fully put back together.

One part. Kelly Clark as a whole, not fractured parts glued quickly back together. I wasn't there yet.

"Don't make me lose focus or I'll lose my nerve. Like I was saying, since you're a lady, you were probably thrown off by my offer to move in without a commitment from me. Don't want you to make the wrong assumption about my intentions. I want us to both be on the same page. So, really, what's the point in waiting? I…"

"Jack…"

"Got something for you to show you how serious I am."

Before I could say anything more, Jack reached into the nightstand drawer and pulled out a little black box. By this time, my heart was beating so fast I was afraid it was going to burst from my chest. Jack was like a train speeding into the station. I couldn't get him to stop.

He pulled the box open, revealing a gorgeous, square cut diamond engagement ring.

"Kelly Marie Clark, I know we haven't had the easiest path, but somehow fate brought us back together. We've both had bad experiences, but that doesn't need to stop us from making a fresh start. Will you marry me?"

My mouth dropped open while I ogled the ring, trying to buy time. I was at a loss for words. The fact that the ring was beyond what I would have expected was not helping me gain my focus or my sense of reality. I felt like I was dreaming. The man I loved was asking me to marry him.

"Kelly?" Jack's voice broke through the silence, making me wonder how much time had passed from when he asked the question.

"What?" I raised my head up and found him studying me with a puzzled expression.

He stared, rubbing his lips together while awaiting my response to his question. When I didn't give one, Jack set the open box down on the nightstand and reached out to me.

"Come here," he whispered. He pulled me into an embrace, and we laid down on his bed, spreading out over his soft down comforter. I didn't know what to say. My lack of response filled the room with my answer.

"Too soon?" he finally managed. The hurt I could hear in his voice was a dagger through my heart. My eyes filled with tears. Nikki's words ran through me "You're going to blow this, Kelly."

"Jack…"

He turned and unwound himself from me in order to face me.

"I just don't think I'm ready. I'm really scared to make a commitment like this."

"You don't think I'm scared? Look at my past. I'm still haunted by the thought of my ex-wife, Callie, trying to ruin my life again. But I know that I would rather face that bad time with you than be alone. And I don't want to waste anymore of my life running from my past. If it's going to come back for me someday, then let it come. There's nothing more I can do to stop it.

"But my fear is sure as hell not going to stop me from living the life I want now. Nor will it stop me from building the future I want. And I want a future with you," Jack said, reaching up and softly cupping my face.

Jack's ex-wife, Callie, still lived in London, the city where they had shared a home. After he'd married her, he found out she was a sociopath with many deep-seeded issues including, creating false identities and stealing. Like me, he still lived in fear of her trying to find him.

"And God forbid, Steve get out of prison and come looking for you. I want to be by your side when that happens. We'll face these demons together."

"And what if I can't give you a family, Jack? You know my history."

"What I know is that you were not able to get pregnant with Steve's baby. Do you honestly think the threat of not being able to have biological children with you would stop me from proposing? We don't know that we won't be able to have a child together. And if we can't, we'll look into other options. I don't have my heart set on having biological children. We could always adopt. I do have my heart set on marrying you, though. That's what I want, Kelly."

My mind swirled with conflicting responses, which was strange because I was never tongue-tied with Jack. Our conversations flowed naturally. Now, in this critical moment, I couldn't seem to find the words to express the way I was feeling. I wanted so badly to say yes, because truly, this *was* what I wanted. The thought of being Jack's wife and moving into this beautiful condo was a dream come true. My fairy tale.

Even the logistics made sense. With it being a three-bedroom condo, we would both be able to have our own home offices. And no more packing overnight bags and racing back and forth to each other's homes.

I could see us watching movies together at night, making dinner in our galley kitchen, working side by side in our offices, and then ending the day with a glass of wine on the balcony. The life we would have would be a perfect next chapter for me.

And then my thoughts projected further into a distant future. I held a small bundle with little green eyes staring back at me while Jack set up a white crib in the nursery of our new home. Further, Jack and I holding hands while our child smiled back at us and flashed a diploma. This future seemed attainable and beautiful. Something I so desperately wanted.

But then, we were answering the door to an unexpected caller. I saw the startled look on Jack's face when he opened the front door to a tall, angry-looking man with a smirk on his face and an ax to grind. Steve. Finally released from prison and looking for vengeance.

"Good evening, beautiful." In my mind, those words dripped sarcastically from his mouth before our unwelcomed guest crossed the threshold into our dream home.

"I'm not ready, Jack," I said quietly, putting my disturbing thoughts to an end.

Turning, I met Jack's pained expression. Seeing him look at me like that made my throat constrict and dry up.

"I'm so sorry. I'm just not ready," I managed to get out.

* * * * *

The next morning, I woke at five and rolled out of bed. Jack's large frame still faced the wall, as he had most of the night. I moved quietly from the room, collecting my things. Last night had been pretty tense after his marriage proposal. Although he said he understood and promised to wait until I was ready, things had been uncomfortable from that point on. I stayed over as planned, but instead of making love, we'd watched a movie together in silence and went to bed shortly afterward. Normally, we always fell asleep holding each other and talking about our days late into the night. But last night, those moments were filled with an awkward silence choking the room. There was just nothing left to say.

Pulling on my yoga gear in the bathroom, I decided to grab a cup of coffee on the road instead of making it at Jack's place. If I made a lot of noise in the kitchen, it would only risk waking him. I really wanted to sneak out and have time to think before class.

After brushing my teeth, I stared briefly at my reflection. Dark, purple circles pooled under my eyes. I hadn't slept barely a wink last night and it showed.

"Chicken," I said aloud to my scary reflection. Imagining Nikki behind me, I could almost hear her chant "Blowing it!"

"Shut up," I said to the imaginary Nikki.

After a couple minutes of prepping, I opened the bathroom door and peeked into the hallway. The bedroom door was still closed. It wasn't like Jack to pout, but then again, I'd never rejected a marriage proposal from him before. Maybe this was the thing that would finally push Jack over the edge and send him running. I hoped not.

On my way to the front door, I passed the kitchen on my right. From my peripheral vision, I noted that the kitchen lights were on. *Darn.*

"Good morning," Jack said in his husky morning voice.

"Crap," I said.

"Sorry. Did I scare you?"

He was dressed in long, flannel pants and a white Henley. His tall frame leaned against the counter with his arms folded into each other. I noticed his hair was sticking up as though he had slept, but the adorable sleep lines he always had from his pillow were missing.

"No. I didn't want to wake you. I thought I could sneak out without disturbing you."

My eyes studied him, trying to pick up what kind of mood he was in. His eyes turned down this morning in a gloomy way and their slight red tint made him look worn out,

"Let me make you some coffee before you go."

I stood for a moment debating on accepting his offer for coffee or telling him my plan to grab some on the way. Jack poured coffee beans into his grinder before I could give him an answer. I stepped into the kitchen, my decision made. Jack's coffee was better than anything I could buy anyway. And, perhaps the dawning of a new day would give us a new perspective on all of the things we discussed last night.

Moving closer to Jack, I got a whiff of the coffee and Jack's morning smell. It was a combination I wanted to keep waking up to. There had to be a way we could compromise. Perhaps if I gave Jack a timeline of what would work for me? No. That was impossible. Silly even. How did one know how much time it would take to heal a broken heart? There wasn't a mathematical equation to this type of thing.

"Jack," I began.

"Kelly." He turned his body to me and rubbed his left eye roughly. "I really don't want to talk anymore. I think I'm talked out for now."

"I was just going to tell you that I…"

Jack turned away from me again and pressed a few buttons on his fancy coffee maker. "This should be done in a few minutes. Help yourself. You know where the mugs are. I'm going to jump in the shower. Let's talk later, okay?" Jack brushed past me and left the room.

I stood alone in the kitchen, listening to the shower turn on. For a brief second, I considered following Jack into the bathroom to try and talk to him again. I was a bit put off by his coldness this morning. Wasn't a relationship based on compromise? He needed to hear that I was willing to make some compromises. He couldn't just storm off if he didn't get his way.

But there was something to be said for timing. And this morning didn't feel right. It was too early to have this conversation. He seemed frustrated, annoyed, and in need of some alone time. Maybe I'd stepped over the line this time. Even Jack, as patient as he had been with me, had limits. When we got back together last summer, he told me he had let go of any hurt he had been holding onto from our past and was ready to embrace a new start. Now, I just hoped that declining his proposal had not killed our chance to be together.

I turned and headed out the front door without filling a mug. I'd taken Jack's heart. Right now, it didn't seem right to take his coffee as well.

Chapter 12

On the drive over to St. Charles, I flipped on the radio to distract myself. If Adelle could escape her life and make time for Hot Yoga, I certainly should be able to.

I couldn't decide if I wanted to tell her about Jack's proposal. It would just have to be a decision I made upon seeing her. Right now, I really didn't feel like talking about it. The whole thing still seemed so surreal.

Driving along the Fox River, I spotted a few lone runners and walkers moving along the bicycle path. The water was calm this morning and the air had a slight fog to it. When my eyes wandered back to the road, I was shocked to see a rather large coyote dart across the street in front of me. I hit the brakes to allow it to pass unharmed. Rather than run into the safety of the trees that lined the bicycle path, it turned and gave me a menacing stare as though it was saying, "What are you looking at?"

I slowed my car to a stop in order to observe the mangy-looking mutt. I wasn't worried about offending other drivers because I was the only one on the road at this hour.

The coyote didn't look right. Its intestinal cavity was indented in a grotesque way, and the fur was flat and scraggily. A few weeks ago, the Kane County Chronicle published an article on the fact that the coyote population had spiked in recent years, but many of them carried heartworm. They were competing with the local fox population for food and were eating diseased road kill because they were desperate. The bad meat from the road kill caused them to develop heartworm, which made them very ill. The coyotes eventually became so sick that they were getting hit by automobiles due to making bad judgments as to when to cross the road. Luckily, I was not in a rush, or this coyote might have met his end this morning.

For a moment, I contemplated calling someone to tell them about the coyote. But who would I call? And what would happen? This coyote looked like it needed to be put out of its misery, but by the way it looked, that would happen naturally very soon.

The coyote finally gave me a farewell glare and trotted off into the trees. I eased my car back onto the road and continued on my way to Hot Yoga. What a strange morning it was shaping up to be so far.

Hot Yoga was located in a small strip mall just off of North Avenue, the main street that ran east and west through St. Charles. The SUV I noticed yesterday in Nikki's driveway was already parked in one of the spots closest to the building. I maneuvered my car next to it and put it in park. When I glanced into the car, Adelle waved at me. I noticed she was holding a travel mug. It hit me then that I forgot to stop for coffee. I had been so distracted by the coyote and thinking about Jack.

Stepping out of my car and locking my doors, I opened the passenger door to Adelle's car and hopped in.

"Good morning!" Adelle piped. From the perkiness of her voice, my guess was she'd been up for hours drinking coffee.

"Good morning. I was going to stop and get coffee on the way over but forgot. Where do you think I could grab a cup close by?"

"Right here. I brought one for you just the way you like it." She handed me a travel mug.

"Bless your heart."

A smile spread on my face as I snuggled into the toasty warm cocoon of her car with my newly acquired coffee.

"Did you just have the car cleaned? It smells good." The inside of her car was immaculate, as I knew it would be.

"Yesterday. You know me and my car."

Adelle's long, blond hair was pulled back into a ponytail, secured by a rubber band with a small, light pink, jeweled flower. I couldn't tell what she was wearing underneath her large coat but would have bet it somehow tied in with the flower.

"How is packing going?"

"Great," Adelle chirped.

Her mask was definitely on this morning.

I sighed and took a sip of my coffee.

"What's wrong?"

I stared out my window, allowing a few seconds to pass while I contemplated telling her what happened last night.

"Is everything okay with you and Jack?" she prodded.

"I don't really want to talk about it."

Adelle nodded her head. "I understand."

"So, what's the plan today? Where and when do I report for packing?"

Adelle sighed, mirroring mine, and took another sip of her coffee. When she didn't respond right away, I turned to look at her.

"I don't really want to talk about it, either."

Instead of grilling her, I held my travel mug up. She hit hers to mine quietly.

"Here's to not talking," I toasted.

We sat in silence, both lost in our own thoughts, waiting for the lights to go on in Hot Yoga. We were at least a half an hour early, and the studio appeared dark.

"This better be good," I said aloud.

"Tell me about it. I need an escape. The kids are so…" Adelle paused.

When I turned to look at her, her eyes had welled up with tears.

"Well, let's just say, they didn't take the news well."

"Oh, Adelle, I'm so sorry." I reached out and placed my hand on her shoulder.

"I can't get upset about this anymore. It's ridiculous. It's just a house, right? Home is where Mike and the kids are. We still have each other. It's just a stupid house."

Adelle's travel mug shook in her hands. I reached over to ease it out of her fingers.

"It's okay to get upset. That was your home. You worked really hard to make it perfect."

"I just don't want you to think I'm this materialistic witch that only cares about money and things. This is more than just a thing, Kelly. This is my home, my nest, being ripped apart. It's disturbing," Adelle said through a flood of tears. Her grief was so raw it gripped at my heart and made me tear up as well.

"I'm not judging you, Adelle. And I don't think you are a materialistic witch."

"But you and Nikki do. You think I'm this unfeeling rock, but I'm not. I'm hurting so much."

"You're wrong. We don't feel that way. I think we all have some built up anxiety about our relationship as sisters from years of not talking openly with each other. And we're also in such different places in our lives. You have three kids, Nikki's on the verge of motherhood, and I'm, well, me. You might think we feel that way, but we really don't. We're just learning to understand each other. But I understand why you might feel that way, and I take full responsibility for icing you out for a while. You were always so perfect and put together that Nikki and I felt you were unapproachable. We had a breakthrough this past summer though. Don't you think we're all in a better place now? I do."

Adelle grabbed a tissue from the car counsel and blew her nose a few times. "I don't know. I don't know anything anymore. Everything is changing."

"In the last few months, I've gotten to know you better than I ever have. You've built this incredible empire with Mike. You have your kids, his business, your homes, cars, etc. Maybe you need to make a few adjustments financially, but it's all still there. It's just changing forms during these tough times." I motioned around us with my arms to indicate the car we were in.

Adelle laughed suddenly.

"So, you're saying my beautiful horse drawn carriage has gone Cinderella on me and changed into a pumpkin, but will eventually change back?"

"All I'm saying is you've still got the empire. If you work hard and stay positive, it will all come back. And Nikki and I are not judging you. I can't imagine how hard it is to let go of what you're losing. You're accustomed to living a certain way, as are your kids. I think it's very healthy to look at it honestly and grieve."

"My therapist says the same thing. Surprisingly, Mike seems to be doing a lot better than me, which is odd because he grew up with money. You would think it would be harder for him. We didn't have all of this stuff when we were kids, and we were happy. I just thought we would always have the money.

"He said his father has gone through a reversal of fortune before but was able to get it all back. I just hope he's looking at this realistically. It's going to take time for the housing market to bounce. We're not going to be able to do it in a few months. It could take years and years to recover."

"At least you still have the Michigan home."

"For now. But our life is here. I could never move there."

"I'm just talking about as an investment. I know it's not worth what it was at the height of the market boom, but it must still be worth a pretty penny."

"Yeah," Adelle said quietly.

I decided to change direction. From the way Adelle responded, I could tell she did not want to talk about Michigan.

Just as I was about to tell Adelle about Jack's proposal, the lights in the yoga studio turned on. Adelle took a deep breath and pulled down the mirror above the driver seat to inspect her face. She rubbed under her eyes with a tissue in order to wipe away the mascara that had dripped down. "I look awful."

"Don't worry. It's a 6:00A.M. class. Most people will look awful."

"Alright. Let's do this."

It would have been great to tell Adelle about Jack, but the moment passed. That was the thing with Adelle. Her life was so busy. Even though we were a lot closer now, I still had to find the right moment with her when I wanted to share things. She had too many commitments and dependents to give me much time and attention. She just wasn't available.

A wave of worry ran through me thinking this was probably how Nikki would become. Soon she'd have a baby and two businesses to run. She wouldn't have much time for me, and I'd just have to accept that. It was the natural progression of life.

Still, it scared me. My family was moving on and nurturing their own families. Was this what it felt like to be an Old Maid? Was I a spinster?

I thought of my parents in Florida. I pictured them hanging out in their condo on the beach in Miami. If my books flopped and Nikki needed the apartment once her businesses took off, would they take me back in? Would they welcome me or would I be a burden? I pictured myself sitting with them at a game of bridge with their other retired friends. They'd built quite a life for themselves in Miami with a nice network. How foolish would I feel if I had nowhere to go but to run back into their nest? I shook my head to try and disperse the images from my thoughts.

"Are you okay? Do you still want to go in?" Adelle asked. She had already exited the car and was standing with her door open, staring at me.

"Yep," I said, pulling myself back into the present and stepping out of the car.

"Book stuff?"

"Uh, huh," I said, nodding my head.

As soon as we entered the yoga studio, I was impressed. I hadn't done any research, but my guess was they must have just opened. The paint smelled fresh, and the furniture was impeccably clean. I ran my hand along the back of a buttery leather couch in the waiting area as we approached the check-in counter.

"Good morning," the woman behind the counter called out to us. When we first walked in, I guessed her to be in her early twenties. As we got closer, I moved it up to more like late thirties, or maybe even forties. She had a glow about her that made it difficult to nail down her age. Good for her.

"Hi. I have a coupon for a free trial class," I said.

"Great. Let me take down some information, and we'll get you started. My name is Trisha. After we get you signed up, I'll take you back to show you where the lockers and the steam showers are."

"How long have you been here?" Adelle asked.

"We just opened last month. Are you ladies local to the area?" Trisha asked.

"We both live in Geneva," I responded.

"I'm surprised you didn't see one of our flyers on Third Street."

"Me, too. Our sister, Nikki, owns Chocolate Love on Third Street," Adelle added.

"Nikki! Of course. I met her when we were introducing ourselves to the shop owners there. She's so nice. Please tell her I said hello."

"How is business going?" Adelle asked.

"Pretty good, which I'm grateful for," Trish said. "We took a real chance opening, but so far we've been okay. I guess a lot of people are stressed out and need their yoga to relax. Have either of you done hot yoga in the past?"

"No," Adelle and I responded in unison.

"Regular yoga?"

"Yes," we responded again. We took a second to glance at each other and laugh.

"Then you'll be fine. The class runs an hour and a half long. The room is set at 105 degrees. Since this is your first class, all I want you to worry about is staying in the room. If you're too overwhelmed by the heat to keep up with the yoga poses, just lie down on your mat and rest until you feel better. This is all about getting accustomed to the heat. Did you bring water?"

"Yes," Adelle responded.

"No," I admitted.

"You're going to need it. There are water bottles in the women's locker room. Go ahead and grab one. Why don't you fill out the rest of this paperwork after you take a look at the locker room? I need to sign in the rest of the class, and then we'll finish up yours."

We took clipboards from Trisha and stepped away from the counter to allow the line that had formed behind us to move ahead. The group was a mix of ages and sexes, including a few that appeared to be well into their sixties. Most seemed to know each other and were chatting amiably.

"Let's go check out the locker room," Adelle suggested.

"This class is pretty packed for being so early," I commented.

"We also have a location in Glen Ellyn," another woman wearing the same outfit as the one behind the desk said. She was standing in the hallway on the way to the locker room.

"When we opened last month, we drew a lot of our students from that location because this one is actually closer for them. Hi, I'm Lucy. I'm the co-owner." Lucy was very tall and muscular with raven hair that fell down her back in long braids.

My mouth dropped open in awe when we entered the locker room. It wasn't at all what I was expecting. High-tech looking lockers and hair and make-up stations stocked with everything you might need to get ready for the day lined the walls in the front of the room. It reminded me of a glamorous spa.

"Wow," I said, gawking. "This is like a full blown spa back here."

"Wait till you see our showers."

Lucy waved us back toward the floor to ceiling shower stalls.

"We want our students to be able to check out from their daily grind. We installed these luxury shower stalls to help them do just that. And you'll be surprised how much you sweat in class. You'll be running for those showers when you're done. Trust me."

The back section of the locker room was lined with eight showers with glass doors closing each one off for privacy purposes.

"This is beautiful. How nice. We didn't realize there were showers though. I don't have anything with me," I said.

"No worries, we're stocked with towels and robes. We have everything you need to help make your visit with us enjoyable. I have to head up front now to help Trisha. Hope you enjoy your class," Lucy said, before making her way out of the locker room.

"This place is amazing. It's like a five star resort in here," Adelle said, reaching out to touch the arm of one of the robes hanging near the shower stalls. "I know this brand. They paid a pretty penny for these."

"They paid a pretty penny for all of this, if you ask me. They really did a good job, but what a big investment," I said.

"I was thinking the same thing. But she did say they have enough clients. There must be a real need for stress relief."

"Coffee and yoga. The two things that are going to get us through this hard time. Come on. Let's get to class and see what all this hype is about," I said.

The next hour and a half were a mixture of peace, pure panic, and more sweat than I'd ever imagined in my life. The peaceful moments came on when I allowed myself to let go and experience the healing powers of hot yoga. Panic kicked in when I couldn't hold my poses because my skin was too slick with sweat. There was so much liquid being released from my body it made me nervous. It began almost immediately upon entering the yoga room and stayed that way for the entire session. Trisha, serving as instructor, preached to the class about the benefits of sweating out the toxins. This sounded great, but I was losing so much fluid from my body, I was worried I might sweat out an organ.

My body was so hot, I followed the other student's lead and stripped down to the bare essentials: my sports bra and shorts. I really didn't care about showing a lot of skin, nor did anyone else in the class seem to. The class filled to close to thirty people, most of whom seemed to know not only Trisha, but each other.

When class ended, Adelle and I picked up our water bottles and made our way out of the classroom. Stepping from the yoga room into the main waiting room felt like walking into a refrigerator, allowing me to catch my breath for the first time in what felt like hours. Surprisingly though, my stress from Jack's surprise proposal had definitely subsided. It must have evaporated along with the gallons of sweat from my skin.

"Did you like it?" Adelle asked, as we made our way back to the locker room.

"I loved it. You?"

We'd not spoken to each other in class, part in respect to the instructor and part because we were both struggling so much with the heat.

Adelle nodded her head. "That was insane heat, but I have to say, I feel great."

Her hair was soaked as though she had just emerged from a pool, and the make-up she applied for class was completely melted away. A glow of optimism that wasn't there early this morning lit her face. She looked like Adelle, raw and exposed, and she was stunning. I smiled, thinking perhaps I had accomplished my mission by coming here this morning.

Adelle, being the mom she was, had some extra dry clothes for me to put on, so we both chose to indulge in a long, hot shower. It was nice to use the luxurious towels, soaps, and bathrobes provided by Hot Yoga. By the time we were ready to go, I felt like I had snuck away for a spa retreat rather than a short visit to our local yoga studio

"Wait. I want to get some information on the classes before we leave," I said, stopping at the front desk.

The front room was basically empty. Adelle and I had taken a really long time cleaning up, and peering into the yoga room, I could see the next class had already filled up. I shrugged and turned to leave, knowing I would have the ability to look up information on-line. Too bad. I wanted to thank Trisha and Lucy, but they were probably busy.

The sound of voices near the locker room made me pause.

"It's going to be short this month. The loan was more than I thought it would be and there won't be enough for rent," I heard someone say. I couldn't tell if it was Trisha or Lucy.

"We might have to close one."

"Don't say that. It will get better."

"You know how he is. He won't let us be late. He'll kick us out."

I motioned with a finger over my mouth to indicate we should keep quiet and leave.

When we were outside, Adelle said, "Darn. Just when we found something new."

"Don't say that. Just because they're struggling in the beginning doesn't mean they're not going to make it."

"Those robes," Adelle said, shaking her head. "They're in over their heads. Trust me. I would know."

Chapter 13

The rest of the day was a whirlwind of packing and organizing. My apartment was mostly done from my work the day before, so it didn't take too long.

When I finished with my place, I headed over to Adelle and Mike's house to help them. I rang the front doorbell and waited. Finally, the door opened very slowly, revealing Cindy on the other side. Her face was locked in a grimace as she struggled to pull open the gargantuan door.

"Guess what, Aunt Kelly?"

"What?" I asked, helping to push the door open.

"I get to paint my new room whatever color I want, isn't that great? Oh, and Jack is here!"

My stomach dropped at the mention of Jack's name. I still hadn't talked to him since early this morning when he left me alone in the kitchen. I tried calling when I got home from Hot Yoga, but there was no answer. We agreed earlier we would meet here to help Adelle and Mike pack but never set a time.

"Yes, Jack is here," a masculine voice from the right of me said.

I turned and saw Jack leaning in the doorframe of the formal dining room. His jeans had white paint splattered on them, and his shirt was filthy.

"How long have you been here?"

"I came early to help Mike take apart some of the furniture. How's the apartment?"

"Done," I said, moving closer to him. This wasn't the right time or place, but I was dying to talk to him. Cindy watched us like a hawk. She was slightly obsessed with my blossoming relationship. There seemed to be a mixture of approval and jealousy when it came to Jack. She had a hard time sharing me, but she also seemed to be very aware of how happy Jack made me.

"Where's your mom, Cindy?" I asked.

"Upstairs packing my clothes."

"Can you get her for me? I have to talk to her."

Cindy bolted up the grand, winding staircase in search of Adelle.

When we were alone, I turned to Jack.

"Are we okay?" I asked him.

I reached out to embrace him. He had not moved from his place in the doorway and that was making me uncomfortable. We were still pretty much in the honeymoon stage of our relationship, which meant we were usually all over each other regardless of who was around. I didn't like this new reserved Jack.

He allowed my arms to wind around him and pushed slightly away from the doorframe into my embrace. He took my face tenderly in his hands and rubbed my cheeks with his thumbs while gazing into my eyes. I studied him intently, trying to understand what was going on behind his guarded expression. His eyes were not connecting with mine like they normally did. I felt so disconnected from him.

"Jack, I figured out how to take apart the computer desk. Come and see," Mike called from behind us. "Oh, hi, Kelly. I didn't know you were here. Thanks so much for coming."

Mike turned and bolted back into the study where he came from.

Jack slowly unwound himself from me.

"We'll talk later, okay?" His voice was tender, but it didn't make up for the sting I felt. He never answered my question about us.

"Okay," I said, trying to sound positive.

Jack jogged across the entrance foyer and followed Mike into the study. By the way they were moving so quickly, both men appeared overly excited about dismantling the computer desk. I had a feeling Jack showed up early, not only to help, but also because there was something very thrilling about using tools and taking apart furniture for him. Boys would be boys.

I wound my way up the staircase in search of Adelle. When I found her in Cindy's room packing, Cindy was nowhere to be seen.

"How is it going? Where did Cindy run off to now?"

Adelle's back was to me. She didn't respond to my question, so I walked over to Cindy's dresser and sat down next to Adelle. Tears streamed down her face.

"I remember when I brought my little girl home to this room. We had the nursery stenciled with ballerinas on the walls. Do you remember that? Oh wait, I think you were still in California at that point. When she was three, I made it into her big girl room and that's when we put up this light purple on the walls over the stencils. The painting crew had to do it over three times because I didn't like the shade once it was up on the wall. It turned out great though in the end, didn't it?"

Adelle's eyes ran up the walls of the room. When I followed her gaze, for the first time, I noticed the miniscule ballerinas on the curtains. How many times had I been in Cindy's room and yet, some of the smallest details that were lovingly done by her mother had been lost on me. Adelle took so much pride in her family, her kids, and her home. This must be torture to watch it all be taken down. I knelt down next to her and fought the urge to sob. My heart was breaking for her, but I did my best to hold it together.

"Why don't we take a break, Adelle? You look like you could use it."

Adelle didn't even try to stop the tears. "No. I couldn't. There's so much to do."

"It looks like you guys are running ahead of schedule. The downstairs is almost done. I don't know how you have done it all so fast. Let's go downstairs and make some coffee. Did you pack the coffee maker yet?"

Adelle shook her head no.

"Come on. Let's go take a fifteen minute break. We can recharge and then we'll come back up and hit it hard. When is Nikki arriving?" I searched frantically around the room for tissue. Nothing.

"She's working on the display this morning for Brian's memorial and then she'll be over. She said she was going to let her staff do the finishing touches. What time is it?"

"It's near 11:00."

"She should be here any minute. Let me just go in the bathroom and freshen up before I come down. I don't want the kids to see me like this. Will you start the coffee?"

I openly cringed at her request, making Adelle laugh.

"Mike is down there. He can help you if you need it."

Adelle's coffeemaker was my arch nemesis. As much as I loved coffee, the fancy, high-end coffee maker they owned had a personal vendetta against me. Every time I thought I had it figured out, something went horribly wrong.

Helping Adelle up, I watched her head into Cindy's bathroom to freshen up. I bent down to pick up one of Cindy's dresses Adelle left lying on the floor. It was a checkered, light green and pink gingham pattern with butterflies on it in a cotton fabric. It looked like it had never been worn, even though I'd seen Cindy in it at least a dozen times. She loved this dress. It was a testament to how well Adelle took care of their clothes.

"This sucks," I sighed.

The rest of the day went fast. Jack and I were like two ships passing each other. He spent the majority of the day doing the heavy work with Mike while Nikki and I worked with Adelle. Finally, near ten o'clock, Adelle begged us all to go home. Mike and Jack, along with two movers, brought most of the furniture to a storage unit where it would stay until the rental home was ready.

It was disturbing to me how quickly you could take a life apart. In a matter of twelve hours, Adelle's custom designed home, which took years and years to put together, was stripped down to the bare bones.

Nikki and I stood in the foyer, getting ready to leave.

"Any news on the autopsy yet?" I asked her. Throughout the day, it was obvious Brian was on her mind because she kept checking her phone.

"Nothing yet. I thought we would have heard something by now, but no."

"That's okay. I'm sure you'll know something soon."

I knew Nikki would not let this go, but I was still hesitant to promise her my partnership in this investigation. The plan was to be in Michigan for at least the next week, so the most I could be was a sounding board to her.

That night, I ended up staying at my place because I still had a few loose ends to tie up before the move. Jack agreed to stay over, but after a quick shower, headed directly to the bedroom and fell into a deep slumber. The full day of manual labor had wiped him out, though I knew he enjoyed it.

It was probably best we didn't talk tonight anyway since we were both so worn out from the day. It wouldn't be a productive conversation, and we would probably end up frustrated.

By midnight, I had the majority of what I wanted to accomplish done and sat at my computer desk staring out onto Third Street, lost in thought. I should have been tired, but physically and mentally, I felt great, which I attributed to my early morning yoga session. Perhaps there really was something behind sweating out evil toxins.

I'd miss this apartment next week. It had become a little cocoon for me, yet I loved the fact that it was situated right in the hub of downtown Geneva. When I was in my own world writing my books, I still felt connected to the outside world because people were visible through my front window. Since I spent so much time with imaginary characters, it was healthy for me to see real people shopping, hanging out with their families, or running off to catch a train.

Just as I was about to shut down my computer for the night, my eye caught something in the direction of the Geneva History Museum. Although it looked like the lights were off in the building, I could have sworn I saw a flash in one of the upstairs windows. Scooting back my chair on the hardwood floor, I got up to turn off the lights in my living room, then moved back to the window to get a better look. With the lights off, it was easier to see the details of Third Street. It appeared completely deserted, even though it was a Saturday night and there were plenty of restaurants in this neighborhood.

After a few minutes of staring at the History Museum, I was sure I had imagined seeing the light in the upstairs. But all the windows remained dark and motionless. For a brief second, I thought of texting Nikki, but after looking at the time, knew it would be a huge mistake. Nikki would definitely be asleep and waking a pregnant woman was straight up cruel.

"Time for bed," I said to myself.

It was late and had been a long and stressful day. I needed to go to sleep and forget the silly ghost stories I'd heard lately.

Just before I turned to head back to my bedroom, the light flashed again. Who would be up at this time of the night, and what in the world would they want in that old apartment?

My mind raced to Victoria Jacobs, the ghost that had been supposedly haunting Brian. Was she back? If so, what was she searching for?

"What are you looking at?"

Jack's voice behind me made me jump.

"Christ, you scared me."

"Sorry. I didn't mean to do that." He put his arms around me and looked out onto Third Street. "I just came to collect you for bed and found you crouching over the window like you're about to leap out. What's going on?"

I pointed in the direction of the apartment.

"There, in the Geneva History Museum. I swear I just saw some flashes of light in Brian's old apartment. It looks like someone is in there."

"Really?"

Jack leaned closer to the window and stared out. I watched his face to see if he believed me or not, but his expression was unreadable.

"I swear it happened. I saw it twice."

"Why would someone be up there at this time of the night?"

"That's what I was thinking."

"So, a ghost has come back to haunt the History Museum?" Jack turned and crossed his eyes at me, lightening the mood. "Muhahahah," he said, releasing an evil laugh.

"Shut up," I said, playfully slapping his arm. "You're making fun of me. Brian did say that he thought the place was being haunted. It's possible it bothered him so much that he killed himself. Maybe he was telling the truth. It's not something to make fun of, Jack."

"You're right," Jack said, pulling me closer. "It's awful. I'm sorry."

We both turned back to glance one more time at the apartment windows.

Finally Jack sighed, released me, and rubbed at his face with his hands.

"Babe, we've had a long day. Can we go to bed and talk about this in the morning? I'm making jokes, but really, it's all so sad. I can't handle talking about ghosts right now."

"I agree," I said, turning my body back into Jack's and allowing him to embrace me again.

"But first, I need to know one thing."

"What's that?" Jack said, nuzzling his face into my neck. It felt good to be this close again. It seemed like ages since we touched. With last night's proposal fiasco, we'd slipped into this strange place. Right now though, in Jack's arms, I was secure and happy.

"Are we going to be okay?"

Jack sighed and slowly pulled his face away from my neck. He paused dramatically, but the small smirk that pulled at his lips eased my mind.

"I think so."

"That doesn't sound too confident."

"Kelly, you tell me. I'm ready to commit. You're the one with cold feet. Are we going to be okay?"

"I'm ready to commit, too. I am committed right now even without a ring. I don't need that to say we have a future together. As far as marriage, it's definitely on my mind. I'm just not there yet, but I'm getting close. We're getting close. When I think of the future, I see us together."

I paused briefly to gage Jack's reaction.

"Now why couldn't you say that last night?" Jack asked with a smile.

"Because I was in shock. The proposal was not something I saw coming."

"I know. But with all of the circumstances around us and the changes in the living situation, I did it on an impulse. You Clark girls come from a very traditional family. I got it in my head you wouldn't agree to live with me unless you had a ring. And when I thought of you actually living with me, all I could think of was how I could figure out a way to keep you there with me. The excitement of it all took over."

My laugh cut him off.

"What?" Jack said, widening his eyes and laughing with me. "Why are you laughing?"

"We spend almost every night together. I'm not exactly the poster child of tradition and purity. Did you forget?"

"I did not forget. I just got carried away at the thought of us taking the next step. I admit I rushed it a bit."

"And I love you for that. Please just wait a little bit longer. I want it as well."

"I will, babe. I'm sorry."

"I'm sorry, too."

Jack leaned in to kiss me. His lips brushed softly on mine at first and when I responded by running my hands through his hair, he pulled me to him and locked his body against mine.

"Now why don't we go to bed so you can remind me just how impure you really are, Ms. Clark."

"Lead the way, mister."

Chapter 14

The next morning when I rolled over, Jack was gone. Light filled the room, confirming I'd slept in. I spied a note on my nightstand and reached up to grab it. It read:

Temptress:

Left early to get some things done at home. I'll swing by in a few hours, so we can walk over to the memorial together. Last night was...

I love you—

Jack

I smiled and rolled over in bed not bothering to look at the clock. The memorial for Brian didn't start until ten. My guess was it was only about seven, which was much later than I normally woke, but still early enough to catch a few more winks. Now that the stress of packing had subsided and my worry about Jack's proposal was resolved, I felt a great sense of calm. I was really looking forward to a week at Adelle's home. It would be a mini-vacation for me. With that thought floating through my head, I drifted back to sleep.

Later, I awoke feeling refreshed and ready to start the day. From the way my apartment smelled, my guess was Nikki's employees were making blueberry muffins downstairs. The smells wafting up through the vents were something I was really going to miss while I was gone.

I climbed out of bed and headed directly to the coffee maker. In all the madness of last night, I forgot to pre-set the coffee, which actually worked out since I had slept in late. If it would have gone off at 5:15 like it normally did, the coffee would have been sitting for hours. Missing my run this morning would probably have consequences for me later in the day, but right now, I didn't care. It was so luxurious to sleep in and regroup. Today, everything looked brighter. I poured myself a cup of coffee and took it over to my computer desk.

Drawn to the sound of a small ruckus below my window, I glanced down and saw Miguel and two other employees of Chocolate Love struggling down the front stairs with the display Nikki made for the service. Once they made it down, the three turned in the direction of the History Museum. They appeared to be carrying a small replica of the building. Nikki had outdone herself once again.

I finally turned away, unable to watch. By the way they were struggling, there was a high probability they would drop Nikki's masterpiece. Normally, she was part of the team that carried the displays, but in her condition, I assumed she'd made a point to not be involved in that kind of manual labor.

The rest of the morning I spent getting ready for the service and organizing. At nine-thirty, I sat down to write, since I had a few extra minutes before Jack arrived. Unfortunately, the couple of days I'd spent away from my book had taken their toll. I found myself unable to connect, and once again, the whole project was very daunting. When I wrote every day, the book was cut down to a few pages a day, and that I could handle. But when I stepped away for a few days, I thought too much of the big picture, which was never good.

I focused on the thought of Adelle's home in Michigan. There I could see myself locked away, writing for hours and hours on end during the day and strolling on the beach at night to revive myself. No distractions, no temptations, just pure work. It would be heaven.

A knock on the door signaled Jack's arrival. I saved my story and shut down my computer. With Brian's memorial and Adelle's move, there was no chance of getting back to this today. It would be best to give up and wait till Michigan.

When Jack and I arrived at the memorial service, I was surprised by the amount of people in attendance. We spotted Nikki in the front lobby helping direct people into the main room where Brian used to hold his lectures. From what I could see, the chairs were filling up quickly.

"Wow," I said when we made our way over to Nikki. "I can't believe how many people are here."

"I know, right? Brian developed quite a following over these last couple of years. He started the Lunch and Learn program every Tuesday where he spoke for an hour about the history of Geneva. I think the majority of the people here are from that group. Turns out a lot of people are interested in the history of the town they live in. Who would have guessed?"

"Have you heard anything yet on the autopsy?"

"Still nothing," Nikki said, clearly frustrated. "I contacted Detective Pavlik this morning. Got his voice mail. Maybe they are making sure the family is notified first."

"Did any of his family come today?" Jack asked.

"We contacted his parents, but they said the drive would have been too much for them. I spoke with his father yesterday. I didn't want to ask him any pointed questions until I was sure he spoke to Detective Pavlik. They're having their own service for him back home tomorrow."

"Who's speaking today?" I asked.

"The Executive Director, Barbara Goila, and Alice Camden, the Administrative Assistant."

"I know Alice. She's been here since we were kids, right?" I asked.

"I think so," Nikki replied.

"I remember her from a research project I did in eighth grade. She helped me research the Native American tribes that first settled here," I said.

"Wow. I forgot about that until just now. I wonder if I still have that paper somewhere. I could use it for my book."

"Why don't you just ask Alice? I'm sure she would help you again," Jack laughed.

"I may just do that. She was so nice to me. Hey, by the way, Nikki, I want to talk to you about something I saw last night."

"What?" she asked.

"I'm going to go say hello to someone. See you guys in a minute. Just be careful what you get involved in," Jack said before walking away.

Nikki moved closer to me. "Okay, now you have my attention. Tell me quick because I have to go check on my cupcake display. I think one of my miniature streetlights is about to tumble over."

"Last night around midnight, I saw some lights on in Brian's old apartment." I pointed my index finger up in the direction of the apartment.

"Shut up," Nikki said, widening her eyes.

"I know. It's crazy. But I saw it more than once. It wasn't the overhead light on. More like flashes of light getting bounced around, like a flashlight. Is anyone staying up there?"

"Not that I know of. I could ask around. See! This is what I'm talking about. Don't you think there's something suspicious linked to…"

"Hello, ladies," a woman said behind us. We both jumped at the sound of her voice. We were so deep in conversation that we had not noticed Alice Camden approach us.

"Alice. Nice to see you. I'm so sorry about Brian," Nikki said, quickly recovering. She adjusted her black cardigan and cleared her throat quickly. "It's great that you're speaking today."

"He was a co-worker and a dear friend," she said, tearing up. Her graying hair was expertly weaved into a neat bun at the back of her head. She fiddled with it while she spoke. "I've been so disturbed these past couple of days. It won't be the same without him here. We've become close over the years. No one will be able to match the passion Brian had for the history of our town. Don't you girl's agree?" Alice moved her hands from her bun down to her well-fit pantsuit. She tugged at the bottom hem of the jacket to adjust it.

"Oh, Alice. I'm so sorry. You're right. There's no way the History Museum will ever be able to replace him. He was one in a million," Nikki said.

"I've spent the last couple of days trying to clean up the apartment. The police said they would, and they did their best, but they left that black fingerprint dust everywhere. Really, it was everywhere. Like an explosion of it. Oh well, if it's going to help figure out what happened, that's all that matters."

Hearing Alice's words, I wondered if they would still allow me to leave Geneva for my trip up north to Michigan. They must have found my prints in the room. But that didn't matter, right? They knew I had been in that room.

"Nikki, I know he tried to talk to you about the…" Alice stopped and looked around as if to check if anyone was listening to her conversation "…

ghost?"

"He did. He asked Kelly and I to try and figure out what was going on. Do you really believe in that kind of stuff, Alice? I kind of blew him off when he told me about it, but now I'm wondering if I should have taken him more seriously. Did you ever experience anything strange while you were working here?"

"Well, honestly, no. But, I am here most of the time during the day hours. He said most of the occurrences happened at night. Once and awhile I help out with the evening ghost walks, but Brian primarily relied on volunteers to help him with that.

"I had no idea how much all of this ghost nonsense was bothering him. I mean, sure, this place is filled with spooky old stories and relics from the past. But it's all harmless. Still, I should have taken his anxiety more seriously. I wasn't a very good friend to him at the end," Alice tugged at her jacket again and looked down at the ground.

"I feel the same way," Nikki responded.

"Do you know what haunts me the most? The fact that he was raised in a Catholic family. Catholics don't believe that a soul will go to heaven if someone commits suicide," Alice said, allowing a few tears to escape.

Nikki simply nodded her head and rubbed her arm.

"Why do you believe it was suicide?" Nikki asked.

"Well, because of the pills, of course."

"What pills?" Nikki asked.

Alice's eyes filled with alarm. I noticed her swallow a few times quickly before speaking.

"I'm sorry, ladies, I have to excuse myself. If I don't pull it together, I'll be a blubbering mess for my talk. I'm going to head to the ladies room."

Without another word, Alice darted away from us.

"That was weird. Should we go find a seat?" I asked Nikki.

Nikki's eyes followed Alice to the ladies room. "She was talking about the pills they think he overdosed on, right? I didn't see them in the room when we found him, but I was so distraught by the sight of Brian. I feel like she knows something that she's not telling us."

"What? Little old Alice? You think she was involved somehow? Come on, Nikki."

Nikki didn't say anything at first. But from the way her nostrils flared, I could tell her bloodhound instincts had picked up some kind of scent.

"I'm not sure she even knows she's involved, but she's got more information than she realizes. She's the key to figuring this whole thing out."

I turned my head in the direction of where Alice took off and saw her about to slip into the ladies' room. As though she knew she was being watched, she turned and gave the room one final scan before disappearing inside.

Chapter 15

By the time Monday morning came, I couldn't get out of town fast enough. It felt like I was unraveling. My home was upended, Nikki's anxiety about figuring out what really happened to Brian was growing by the minute, my work had been completely ignored, and to top it off, I'd been skipping my daily runs because things had been so hectic. Because I'd been up late at night packing, grabbing every moment of sleep I could in the morning became more important than exercising.

So, when I pulled out of Jack's parking lot with my car packed up for a week's stay, I practically squealed my tires. It was time for me to get the hell out of town for a couple of days and get some work done. The police hadn't called and said I couldn't, so I didn't bother calling them. They knew how to get a hold of me if they needed to. I had nothing to hide.

The drive took just over two and a half hours. Because I'd timed it to miss the bulk of the morning commuters, I never really hit any large pockets of traffic. Nikki still planned to come up at some point, but never nailed down an exact time. It would all depend on how she was feeling and when she could leave the store. While cruising along, I listened to a book on tape just released by one of my favorite mystery authors. Even this felt like a luxury. It had been a long time since I'd been in a car by myself for a long period of time. When my exit in Stevensville appeared, I was shocked by how quickly the time went.

As much as I loved the full life I'd created for myself in Geneva, it was nice to have some time to myself to think. Since I'd relocated from California, there was never a lot of alone time. I'd become much more social than I used to be. My sisters, my niece and nephews, Jack, and neighbors were all so much a part of my life now. I loved that, but there was still a part of me that loved the solidarity of being a writer. I'd lost some of that and needed to figure out a way to get it back. If I didn't, the quality of my work would suffer.

I glanced down at the directions I'd scribbled on a piece of paper. Even though I'd been coming here for over ten years now, I still had to confirm the exit, John Beers Road.

Adelle offered this home to me when I left California. As much as I was looking forward to staying here for a week, my gut told me I had made the right decision by taking Nikki up on her offer to live in the apartment above

Chocolate Love instead. I would have been so isolated out here. Although St. Joe's, the next town over from Stevensville, was a well-known tourist destination, overall this area seemed too quiet for me. Especially at a time when the thing I needed the most was human interaction to pull me back into the world. I just hadn't expected to be fully immersed.

I wound my car around the hilly dunes, making my way closer to the house and to Lake Michigan. As I drove, it hit me that it had been over three years since my last visit. I'd been so caught up in the divorce proceedings and the move to Geneva, I was never able to join Adelle and her family when she invited me.

I'd forgotten how curvy this road got as it approached the house. The neighboring homes were tucked either high up on the dunes or nestled close together at the bottom. The homes seemed to be set up at random, unlike the uniform lots in Chicago. It made me feel like I was driving into another time, when life was much simpler and people settled where the land best suited them, not where it was designated by property laws.

I thought of Mary, my main character in my Antique Murder Mystery Series, finding an arrowhead from the Pottawatomie Tribe. Something about the way these home plots were laid out spoke to me. Perhaps I would use that arrowhead as a way for Mary to look into the past settlements of the tribes and find out how it influenced the way Geneva was formed. I'd want to research more about how the land was divided and how property lines were drawn. It was interesting to think that land that was once open for the taking now went for a fortune. Even with the decline in real estate in recent years, Geneva was still a very expensive place to buy land or a home.

When I'd visited Adelle's Michigan home in the past, it had always been during the summer months. Things looked a lot different here in October. For one thing, the leaves on the trees had changed colors but not yet fallen. They waved down at me in welcome.

Normally, I had to make sure to drive very slowly on the roads because there were small children and dogs running along to get to the beach. Today, it looked like no one else was out but me. Instead of making me feel scared, this put a smile on my face. Alone time meant writing time. No interruptions.

Adelle's home loomed in front of me now. I pulled into the pebble driveway and peered at it through my windshield. Even though I couldn't see it from the driveway, behind the home was a tall sand dune and then a drop down to the Lake Michigan beach.

This was perfect.

Isolation, a beautiful beach to walk on, and motivation. All of the elements that would help me write my masterpiece. Now if only my Internet connection held. Adelle promised it would be okay, but from what I remembered, trying to use cell phones and Internet the last time I was here was rather difficult. Perhaps the area had become more connected to technology in recent years.

Deciding to leave all of my stuff in the car for now, I crawled out of my car and locked up. Adelle said this neighborhood had yet to experience much crime. In fact, most of the time the neighbors kept their doors unlocked. Living in Chicago for so much of my life, and then California, I didn't quite believe in that. And because of my past, I didn't care how isolated and small a town was, I knew better. I'd be locking the doors tonight.

As I approached the front of the house, I was struck again by the oddity of real estate values. This house was not large by any means, nor was it in mint condition. It was refreshing to think that Adelle and Mike owned a vacation home like this. It didn't bare the mark of Adelle's obsessive perfectionism, which was a good thing. It told me that when she did come up here, she really let go and relaxed.

My key fit smoothly into the front door, allowing me to enter without a problem. I turned back to examine it a bit closer. It looked old and the lock quite flimsy. Shaking my head, I refused to allow this to bother me. I couldn't obsess about the lack of security in the house. This was no Fort Knox, nor did it need to be. I was here to relax and work, not hide from something, or someone.

The first room I entered served as a sunroom. It was filled with various knick-knacks Mike and his family collected from over fifty years of vacationing here. From what I knew of its history, Mike's grandfather built this home. He had a vision of hosting his children's children someday and that was exactly what happened. He willed the home to Mike after he passed because Mike had the greatest connection to it. That was probably one of the reasons why Mike never sold it, regardless of how poor his business was doing. I wondered if he was kicking himself now with having to uproot his family back in Geneva. If he had sold this place a couple of years ago when the market was booming, he would have been sitting on some serious cash right now. Then again, maybe that was exactly why his grandfather left it to Mike. He knew he wouldn't give it up, no matter what.

I smiled at my favorite keepsake still hanging, after all of these years, on the wall of the sunroom. The red clay circle with the image of a squished face smiled back at me in welcome. It set the mood of the house. I always imagined it was trying to communicate something like, "Abandon all stress, ye who enter."

This beach community had a very strong artsy, almost hippy vibe. It poked fun at the stressed out, espresso drinking city dwellers. The downtown shops in St. Joe were a mecca of hand-made crafts, paintings, and sculptures. The combination of seclusion, the beach, and the laid back atmosphere set the tone for a perfect artist's retreat. This was exactly what I needed.

I made my way over to the small wicker couch on the far wall of the sunroom and plopped down to allow myself a quiet moment. The almost three hour drive, although refreshing, had taken its toll on me. My stomach growled from hunger, and I felt the slight twinge of a headache coming from the lack of caffeine. If I didn't get lunch and a coffee soon, I was going to collapse or become very crabby.

From the couch, I was able to see the entire front yard through the windows that enclosed the three front walls of this room. Considering this was where I remembered getting the best connection to the Internet the last time I was here, it might be the room where I would do the majority of my writing.

I stood up to examine the windows better. Upon inspection, they appeared as though they were rather new. Each and every window was locked up tight and secure. I chuckled at the irony of that. New windows, but a door that appeared so old the lock could be picked by a toddler. The sound of a car caught my attention. My head bolted up to try and identify exactly where it was coming from. The hilly roads running through the neighborhood made it nearly impossible to see a car until it was directly in front of the house. I could definitely hear it though because of it breaking through the otherwise peaceful silence.

Sure enough, a large SUV drove slowly down the road from the path to the left of the front yard. By the way it was moving, I assumed it to be a local. According to Adelle, the locals were careful and respectful of the neighborhood. They all knew each other and were cautious of the neighboring children, animals, and visitors that ran up and down the paths. It was the tourists that barreled up and down these roads, unaware of the danger they were putting themselves and the local residents in.

I didn't recognize the driver but noted right away it was a woman. She slowed down in front of Adelle's house, probably noticing my car. I waved to her from the sunroom, and after a second, I saw an arm sneak out the window and wave back at me. By the way she hesitated, it seemed like she was going to pull into the driveway. It wouldn't surprise me. Adelle's neighbors had all been here for a very long time. Most of the homes were handed down through generations, so the families not only knew each other, but were knowledgeable of guests. It was well communicated when there would be visitors. I assumed Adelle had alerted her neighbors that I would be here. When the car finally pulled away, I guessed Adelle also told them something like "My sister needs to write. Leave her alone!" I laughed at that thought.

Making my way into the house through double French doors off the sunroom, I walked through a small sitting room made up of two couches and a small television. Once in the kitchen, I searched around the countertops and cabinets, hoping Adelle had an old canister of coffee for me to brew. After a couple of seconds, I changed course. Adelle normally kept her coffee in the freezer or refrigerator at home. She and Mike were coffee snobs and only bought the high end stuff. Although I was sure Adelle allowed some things to slack in this setting, I couldn't see her lowering her coffee standards. That was one area of her life I didn't think she'd ever compromise on.

Sure enough, I hit pay dirt when I opened the freezer. Inside, three large bags of Starbucks coffee sat, as though strategically placed there by Adelle. I chose the Medium Roast Hazelnut Bean and filled up the grinder on the counter. Luckily, the coffee maker they had here was much less complicated than the one in their Geneva home. Within a couple of minutes, the hearty smell of fresh brewed coffee filled the kitchen, instantly re-energizing me. I pulled out a loaf of whole wheat bread from the freezer and popped two pieces into the toaster. This would have to do for now until I ran into town to pick up groceries. While the coffee brewed and the toast darkened, I ran out to the car to collect my bags. I dropped them in the sitting room and took a moment to enjoy my small lunch at the kitchen table.

Adelle had a magnetic notepad hanging on her refrigerator door. It had a picture of a cat sunning itself on the beach with the words "Just Hanging Out" on it. I reached up for it and grabbed a pencil from the counter. Munching on my toast, I jotted down a few things I'd need to pick up from the grocery store. I'd been so quick to get out of town, I forgot about essentials like food. It probably would have been easier to bring food from Geneva, but I was too rushed to leave.

I vaguely remembered how to get into St. Joe's where I'd be able to find a grocery store. Adelle could give me directions, but I didn't want to bother her right now. She was probably still getting settled in my apartment and figuring out how to work the kid's schedules from a new location.

With calling Adelle in mind, I glanced down at my cell phone. No bars.

"Great," I mumbled to myself. Perhaps technology had not moved that much ahead in this sleepy little town.

There was a house phone in the kitchen, so I wasn't totally disconnected from the world. It just made me uneasy to not have a working cell phone. A small shiver of panic ran through my body. I reached over to lift the phone from its base. Sure enough, a loud dial tone sounded in my ear.

"See, it's okay. Calm down," I whispered to myself.

Snatching up my grocery list, I grabbed my purse and headed out the front door, making sure to lock up. Now that I had my computer and belongings inside, I trusted that lock even less.

Going against my better judgment, I left my things in the house and headed to my car. If Adelle and Mike trusted this neighborhood, I needed to as well. What was I going to do, take my computer and bags with me everywhere I went while I was here? *Just Hanging Out.* The words of the cat on Adelle's notepad ran through my head. I smiled to myself and started my car. If he could figure out a way to relax, so could I.

* * * * *

A couple of hours later, I'd shopped, organized, and settled into the house. The majority of my stuff was unpacked and arranged in the master bedroom on the second floor. I'd set up my computer on a small desk in the master bedroom that looked out onto the front yard. Something about the light and the location of the desk pushed up against the windows reminded me of my writing desk in Geneva looking out onto Third Street.

Since I couldn't seem to get Internet no matter where I was in the house, I chose to write from the bedroom instead of the sunroom where I initially assumed I would be working.

Around four, I went for a walk on the beach before starting dinner, thinking it would clear my mind. I'd gotten a few paragraphs done, but things were not going as well as I had hoped. Too many distractions thinking about home.

In recent years, some of the older homes had been torn down to build new, modern mansions along the dunes. A walk to observe the progress of new wealth moving into the area would help pull me from my worries.

I took the steep wooden stairs to the top of the sand dune behind the house and looked down onto Lake Michigan. I gasped at the glory of the majestic view. It wasn't until I was up here that I could hear the sounds of the waves crashing in. The dune blocked all of that. This was why these homes were worth a fortune.

Closing my eyes, I breathed in the smell of the lake. It felt as though Mother Nature chose this moment to slap me in the face and say, "Wake up. The world is bigger than you and your little problems."

Opening my eyes, I carefully made my way down the steep dune onto the beach. Seeing how difficult it would be in my gym shoes, I slipped them off and left them on the top of the hill.

Getting to the beach was much more difficult than I remembered. A few times, I nearly stumbled and rolled down the dune but was able to remain upright. Perhaps the landscape had changed over the last couple of years. Become steeper. Or, ugh, my clumsiness was due to the fact that I was older and less agile than the last time I was up here.

By the time I reached the water, I was smiling and laughing. The thrill of a new experience, something out of my normal routine, had my heart pumping. Why hadn't I come up here more often? This was a perfect retreat. What could be more inspiring than a walk on the beach with gorgeous homes overlooking the water?

I spent the next hour walking up and down the beach in my bare feet, allowing the energy of the lake to rejuvenate me and inspire my story. By the time I was ready to climb the dune back up to Adelle's vacation house, I was practically giddy with excitement. With some of my major plot flaws now resolved in my mind, I could work through the entire night non-stop.

Somehow, I made it up the dunes, though my legs were tired from the walk. I picked up my shoes and walked bare foot across the little wooden deck that wound around the back of the house, ending at the back door. Before going in, I rinsed the sand from my feet with a small hose near the door and toweled off.

Forgetting about dinner, I raced into the house and up the steep staircase off the sitting room to my laptop in the master bedroom. It didn't take long for me to be swallowed up in my story.

Twenty minutes later, I was so in the zone the sound of a car door closing only slightly registered with me. Assuming it was one of the neighbors, I ignored it and continued my work. It was only when I sensed someone approaching the house that I stopped typing and glanced out the window.

This was the worst time for someone to stop in and say hello.

I wasn't comfortable letting someone in the home as dusk was approaching. And, getting away from constant interruptions was the main reason I came up here. A visitor was the last thing I needed.

I reached up and quickly switched off the small lamp on my desk. I hadn't left any lights on downstairs, so maybe if the house appeared dark, they would go away.

When my visitor glanced up to the bedroom, I knew I had turned off my light too late. They knew I was up here. I should have just left the light on and hid.

"Damn," I whispered out loud.

My eyes adjusted to the darkness in the room, allowing me to take in the details of who was walking up the stone driveway. The height of the man, as well as the shape of the head registered familiarity, but I couldn't figure out how I knew the person.

Suddenly, it kicked in.

"No," I said aloud. "Impossible."

My mind screamed at me to do something and do it fast, but my body was frozen in place.

Run! Run! I heard someone shouting. It took a second to register it was my own subconscious screaming at me.

Chapter 16

The wooden stairs creaked loudly as I rushed down them to the lower level. My eyes searched the sitting room frantically for my car keys, not giving a damn about leaving all of my belongings behind. He could have them all. At that moment, I could care less about earthly possessions. All I was worried about was getting out of the house and as far away as possible from here.

Unable to locate my keys, I gave up on the idea of driving away and decided my feet would do. In a panic, I realized too much time had passed. He would be at the front door by now. Sure enough, a quick peek out the windows confirmed he was making his way up the three small stairs to the front door. All I could think of was that flimsy lock on the door.

Frozen in horror, I watched as he dipped his head to peek in through the windows. His arm shot up in a quick wave.

Get out. Get out. Get out, I heard the little voice in my head screaming.

Turning on my heel, I ran through the kitchen to the back door. My hands shook violently, keeping me from being able to unlock the bolt.

"Come on!" I whispered in frustration when the bolt slipped from my clammy fingers for the third time. A quick glance behind me confirmed he had not yet entered the house. But a repetitive knocking at the front door told me he was still there and intent on getting in. A knock? He just *knocked?*

Finally, the bolt turned, and I was out the back door running as soon as my feet hit the wooded planks of the deck. When I turned the corner to head around the house and up the sand dune, I slammed straight into Nikki, knocking her to the ground.

"Kelly!" Nikki screamed as she fell. A small plate she was holding with some kind of aluminum wrapping on it fell to the deck.

Just barely hitting the ground herself, I crouched down beside her, pulling at her arms.

"Get up, get up, get up," I screamed so fast the words blurred together.

"What?" Nikki shook her head in confusion. She tried to make eye contact with me, but my head bounced frantically between her face and the back door.

"He's coming! Get up! We have to get out of here now!" I shrieked, pulling her to her feet.

"Kelly, it's okay!"

I was so frustrated with Nikki I thought of picking her up and throwing her over my shoulder. She wasn't getting it, and there was no time to explain.

"Just do it. Brian is at the front door," I growled at her through clenched teeth. "We have to get out of here."

Nikki allowed me to pull her up from the ground. She grabbed both of my arms and shook me. "He's here with me," she said.

"Brian?" I was totally confused at this point. Sweat ran down my face. Nikki's shaking was making me feel worse. My body had gone into full fight or flight mode.

"Kelly! Brian's twin brother is at the door. Brian is dead," Nikki said in a firm voice.

I shook my head in denial at first.

"*William*, Brian's *twin* brother from Los Angeles is here. Remember, Brian had a sibling? A brother." Her words were spoken in a slow, clear voice.

"William. Twin brother," I said in a shaky whisper. The mania raining down on me a few seconds ago came to an abrupt halt, but still lingered in the air. It was like someone had turned off a hot shower, leaving steamy drops of water in the air. The remnants of panic were still all around me.

"It's okay, Kelly. You're okay." Nikki squeezed my arm to try and get me back.

"Twin brother," I said again, releasing a manic laugh and wiping at the sweat on my brow.

"William is here to talk to us about Brian's death. The autopsy results came back."

Nikki pushed me backward on the deck and around the side of the house, so we could see into the front yard. William must have heard the debacle. He was standing only a few feet away from us by the back gate that separated the wooden deck from the front yard. The sight of him standing there with an apologetic look on his face made me gasp slightly. His mouth was open like he wanted to say something, but he closed it and watched me closely. "Twin brother," I said again.

"Hi," he said quietly, raising a hand in greeting. He looked just as spooked as I felt.

I wanted to ask Nikki, "Are you sure?" but remained quiet. My mind flashed to the waxy look on Brian's face when I found him lying in the upstairs bedroom of the Geneva History Museum. That was death. What I saw in front of me right now was most definitely alive.

"Hello," I managed to squeak out.

"William, can Kelly and I just have a minute to talk?" Nikki said.

"Sure. Of course. I'm so sorry for the scare." He fumbled briefly with his keys. "I'll just go wait by my car. Take your time."

When he spoke, I heard how different his voice sounded from Brian's. Although they were physically identical, I could see now they were very different.

I watched as he walked to his car and took in the details of his attire.

He wore well-tailored clothes that were out of place in this town, and his overall demeanor appeared much more confident than Brian's had been. I remembered the way Brian used to stoop and the sloppy way he dressed. The man in front of me now looked much more polished. He leaned back against his Mercedes and looked back at us briefly before turning away.

"You drove here with him?" I asked when I found my voice. Nikki walked back to pick up the plate she dropped in our collision. She held it now in her hand with a triumphant smile.

"Perfect. Landed right side up. Grandma's cinnamon cake is still intact. No, I met him here. I parked my car on the street for now. He's coming in from California and heading to Pennsylvania for the funeral. He wanted to meet us in Geneva, but I told him you were up here.

"Since I was planning to come up to look at the chocolate shop in St. Joe's, I told him to meet us here so we could talk. I've been trying to reach you, but you haven't been responding."

"I don't get a signal up here and the Internet connection is not working."

"Why haven't you been answering the house phone?"

"Because I didn't hear it. I've been out most of the day walking on the beach or shopping in town."

"I left a couple of messages on Adelle's house phone."

"I don't have a password for the voice mail. I wouldn't know how to check those messages if I tried."

"Well, we've all been worried about you. You should have called someone to tell us you got here safe. What were you thinking?"

"Nikki, what were you thinking, bringing a stranger to this house? We don't even know this guy?"

Nikki blew out a heavy breath.

As though both realizing we'd been squabbling in front of a complete stranger, we turned and glanced in William's direction. He was still leaning against his car and glancing down the street as though he was unable to hear us. From the way he was trying so hard, it was clear he'd heard every word.

"Let's go inside for a second," Nikki suggested. "I'm sorry I'm getting so heated. These pregnancy hormones are making me crazy. I hate being a drama queen, yet I can't stop myself."

"We'll be out in a minute," I called out to William. He turned and nodded in my direction.

I pulled Nikki in through the back door and took a second to catch my breath. "Man, that was really, really weird," I said, pulling one of the ancient kitchen chairs out to sit on.

"You didn't honestly think Brian's ghost was coming to haunt you? Did you?"

"I don't know what I thought," I sighed. "I was so deep in my writing, and I've been really stressed lately. This place is so cool, but it kind of gives me the creeps. No one told me Brian had a twin," I said, moving my hand in a rolling motion. "Didn't see it coming. I don't see a lot of things coming, I

106

guess."

"What are you referring to?"

"Everything," I said, thinking of her pregnancy, Brian's death, Jack's proposal, and now Adelle's move.

"And don't forget a murdering, cheating husband," a little voice in my head said.

"Just…everything," I said, sighing again.

"Let's make some coffee. We can't leave William out there forever. Coffee will make everything better, and we'll be able to think through this logically. Here, cut up Grandma Helen's cake. You'll love this one. We'll give some to William, too."

"Nikki, five minutes ago, I thought the living dead was walking up the driveway. You want me to think logically and break bread with him now? What does he think I'm going to be able to tell him anyway? Why didn't you just meet him in Geneva?"

"Well…" Nikki paused and wiped her hands together.

I sat up from my slumped position.

"Well what, Nikki?"

"Like I said, the results of the autopsy came back. The police spoke to William and he shared them with me. Brian overdosed, Kelly. Just like Pavlik was hinting at. There was a combination of anti-anxiety medication and sleeping pills in his system."

I gasped at this news. Poor Brian.

"Oh my, that's horrible. But, in a way it's good news. He wasn't murdered, and perhaps it was an accidental overdose. Maybe this means he didn't intentionally kill himself?"

"The police don't know yet. They're calling it an accidental overdose. It wasn't an exorbitant amount in his system, but still, they say he should have known better. They've confirmed with his doctor that he was prescribed the anti-anxiety medication recently, but not the sleeping pills that were found in his system."

"Probably because of all of the stress he was under. He did think he was being haunted. That would stress me out."

"Yes, but they don't have any record of prescribing him sleeping pills, Kelly. Don't you think that's odd?"

"You can get those anywhere. There's so many over-the-counter options. I tried some while I was going through my divorce and couldn't sleep."

"This was more of the heavy duty kind, the police said. There's a longer lasting version being prescribed now that when mixed with other meds, can be very deadly."

"So, that is what Alice was talking about yesterday when she mentioned the pills. Maybe she knew he was taking anti-anxiety pills. Oh my God, you don't think she gave him the sleeping pills, do you? Maybe that's why she was so weird to us yesterday at the memorial?"

"William spoke to Alice." Nikki said, putting plates out on the table.

"She told him she knew about the anti-anxiety meds but nothing about the sleeping pills. She felt horrible because she knew he had to take meds to calm himself. She thought they were helping him and didn't see any harm in it. Now she feels terrible that she didn't speak up more or try to get him off of them."

"How could she have known what would happen?" I said, shaking my head.

"So, this is horrible news, but I still don't understand something. What are you two doing up here? What do I have to do with any of this?"

"William wants our help. He's convinced there's foul play. He insisted he speak to both of us together. He is not accepting that his brother killed himself and wants to investigate. Can we call him in here now to talk with him?"

"Nikki, we don't even know this guy."

"But we knew Brian."

"Did you know he had a twin brother?"

"Let's call him in now. He's been out there so long."

"Nikki, you're avoiding the question."

"No, I didn't know," she said, sighing.

"Don't you think that's a little odd? This is supposed to be someone you knew pretty well, and he never told you he had a twin brother?"

"So, what are you saying? That he's a fake twin brother out there?"

I didn't respond. Nikki's tone was snippy. She was right. She wasn't herself right now.

"You're not saying you still think it's Brian. We saw him, Kelly. He's dead."

"No, that's not at all what I'm saying. I'm not *that* insane. I know he's dead. It's just being cautious about who we let into our lives."

Nikki nodded her head and sat down at the table. Her slightly red tinted eyes made her look haggard and stressed. I got up to finish prepping the coffee and coffee cake she was so intent on offering.

"I didn't hurt you out there when I knocked you down, did I?" I asked.

"No. I don't think my butt even hit the ground. You were pulling me up before it could make impact. I'm just worn out."

"Are you sure you can handle coffee?"

"I've been holding off on caffeine all day. This is me really needing a cup of coffee."

I prepped Nikki's coffee the way she liked it and placed it down in front of her.

"You're spending the night, right?" I asked, my voice soft with concern.

"You bet. There's no way I'm driving home this late. You're still planning on going with me to Chocolate Café tomorrow, right?"

"Of course," I said, aware this adventure would take away from my time to write. I'd just have to work something out. If anyone respected my work time, Nikki did. Besides, it was fun to have Nikki up here with me. We needed the bonding time. Plus, I knew I would have a hard time settling tonight if I were here alone.

"Okay, here's what I'm going to do," I said. "I'm going to invite William to have a cup of coffee and cake with us. You think he's legit, and I trust your opinion. Let's see what he has to say. I'm not going to play detective though. We're going to leave the hardcore investigative work to the police. And I'm not doing any of that weird Ouija board stuff you were talking about earlier to talk to the ghost of Victoria Jacobs. Got it?"

Nikki laughed into her cup of coffee.

"No Ouija boards," she promised, conveniently avoiding any comment about being involved in the investigative work.

I pushed the back door open and stepped out into the early evening air. In the last couple of minutes, we'd lost a lot of light. The sun had set, and the twilight sky was darkening quickly. I had to squint in the direction of William's car to spot him.

Sure enough, his shape took form against the side of his car just as we had left him.

"William?" I called out.

"Yes?" he responded, pushing himself away from the car.

"Would you like to come in for a cup of coffee?"

"I would love to." He turned and walked up the driveway to the gate that separated the driveway from the back porch. The wooden picket fence that surrounded the back deck hit him right at his midsection. "I appreciate you seeing me. Is there a lock on this?"

"No, just pull the metal latch up."

When he pulled on the metal latch with too much force, I worried he'd knock the whole thing over. The fence was rather fragile, like many of the things in this house. Perhaps it, too, was from the early 1900's.

"I'm afraid you and I got off to a rough start. My name is William Sanders. I apologize for scaring you earlier."

I reached my hand out to accept William's extended one. Even though it was dusk and we'd lost a lot of light, it was clear William was a very attractive man. Odd, considering I had not found his identical twin attractive at all. William was clean shaven, well-dressed, and stood tall and confident. His light brown hair was cut shorter than Brian wore his, and he appeared to have a good twenty pounds of muscle on his brother. William stood about six feet tall where Brian had always stooped over and seemed to fold into himself somehow. Brian's energy had exuded paranoia, while William's gave off a sense of focused energy and confidence. It added a level of calmness to the situation.

Nikki stood at the door, holding it open. She smiled briefly at me when he passed into the room as though saying, "See. I told you he was cool."

Once in the kitchen, William took a moment to look around. My guess was he didn't know what to do with himself in the tight proximity of the small kitchen.

"Wow. This is…" He paused as though searching for the proper word to describe the miniscule kitchen and all the knick-knacks. "…nice," he finally said.

From the corner of my eye, I watched William examine the chairs surrounding the kitchen table.

Nikki must have seen this as well because she said, "They're sturdier than you think."

William laughed and pulled one of the chairs back to take a seat. The chair made a loud, squeaking sound when he sat down but managed to remain intact. He looked very out of place here in his over-starched khakis, button down shirt, and get down to business attitude.

"You sure?" he said, flashing me a radiant smile.

"Don't worry, we won't bill you if you break it," Nikki joked.

"You said this is your sister's place?"

"Yes. Our brother-in-law inherited it from his grandfather when he passed. It used to be a hunting cabin before he turned it into a vacation home for his family," Nikki said.

"Really? What did they hunt?" William asked, looking around the kitchen.

"Bear and elk I think," Nikki said.

This was news to me. "I didn't know it used to be a hunting cabin," I interjected. "How did you know that?"

"Adelle told me the last time I was up here. There are over one thousand acres of woods and sand dunes in the local state park, Grand Mere. It's still a big attraction for hunting at certain times of the year."

"Really?" I asked horrified, thinking of my leisurely stroll on the beach earlier today. The thought of hunters in the area never crossed my mind. Perhaps I needed to be more mindful of where I wandered off to while I was up here. "What time of the year is that?"

Nikki shook her head. "I don't know exactly."

After I filled William's coffee and cut him a piece of cake, I set it on the table and stole a glance into the sitting room. Hunting cabin? I had no idea. Maybe that was why this place gave me the creeps. Bad vibes left over from the animal slaughters. I visualized a large, dead bear hanging from a hook in the sitting room. Hunting seemed so horrendously cruel to me. I couldn't understand why people enjoyed it so much. What kind of person would do that? And why hunt bear? We didn't need them for the survival of our species. It had to be for the thrill of the hunt.

"Kelly?" Nikki nudged me.

"What?" I asked, coming back to the conversation. Embarrassed, I worked to remove the look of horror from my face.

"William asked you how long you're staying here."

"Oh, sorry. I'll be here about a week. It all depends."

I chose not to give any more information because it was way too complicated and really none of his business. If all went smooth with Adelle's rental, I'd wrap my trip up by the end of the week. If not, I didn't even want to think about how long I'd be staying or what would happen.

"This is delicious," William said, digging into his cake. The way he ate his food reminded me of Jack. He sat scrunched over his plate, his large form devouring the cake in a few bites.

"Thanks. It's a family recipe passed on by our Grandma Helen. She used to make it for us when we'd sleep over at her house."

"Oh, that's what this is," I said.

"Yeah, don't you remember? She called it her Comfort Cake. It always made us feel better when we were sad or anxious. I think it might be the cinnamon she added. I thought it would be perfect for tonight. I'm even thinking about serving it at Bean in Love. It's exactly the kind of dessert I want to sell there."

"That would be perfect, Nikki. We should check out what cakes they sell tomorrow and see if…" I paused, sensing William's eyes on me. Nikki and I had gone off on a tangent.

"Go on," he said. The left side of his lip drew up into a smile as he watched me intently with his hazel eyes. He hadn't come up here to talk about cakes or Bean in Love. My cheeks flushed a bit at his attention. It was time to bring the conversation back to Brian.

"It's nothing. Just ideas about Nikki's new store. Why don't you tell us how we can help you, William? You've come such a long way."

"Yeah," William said, wiping his lips for errant crumbs. Even his large hands reminded me of Jack.

He paused for a second and sat back in his chair. By the way he took his time, I could see he was trying to gather his thoughts. "Again, I apologize for scaring you. I know your time is limited and you guys are busy, so I'll get right to it. I want to get more details on my brother's death. Has Nikki talked to you yet about what was found in the autopsy?"

I nodded my head in affirmation.

"I have my doubts it was a suicide."

William spoke in a calm manner. Yet, it was clear by the way he cringed a bit when he said Brian's name he was still in a lot of pain. He came across as very business-like and in control, but it didn't take a genius to figure out he was hurting. He met my eyes across the table for just a second, and then busied himself with tidying up his plate.

"You don't think he killed himself?" Nikki asked.

"It's not something he would do. Our parents raised us very strict Catholic. Regardless of how Brian felt about himself or his situation, he would never have done that to our parents."

"When was the last time you spoke to him?" Nikki asked.

"We used to speak every other day, but things tend to get so busy with my business. In the last couple of weeks, I haven't been as available." He paused, ran his hand through his brown hair, and leaned over the table, placing his elbows down upon it. "I knew something was going on with him by the way he was acting, but I was so distracted with work I didn't give him my attention."

"What did you guys talk about the last time you spoke?" Nikki asked.

Once again William's hand moved up to his hair, rubbing at the back of his head. "Ladies, I have to ask you something that may sound foolish."

Nikki shot me a look that said, "Here we go."

"Do you believe in ghosts?" William asked.

Chapter 17

Before either one of us could answer, a ringing sound blared through the awkward silence. I jumped slightly, making the table shake. It took a second to realize it was the kitchen phone ringing. The ancient phone was without any of the bells and whistles of modern phones, including caller ID.

"My God that scared me," Nikki commented.

I stood up to pick up the receiver.

"Hello?" I said into the mouthpiece. The bright red color of the phone made me think of fire trucks and Dalmatians.

"Kelly?" a male voice said.

"Yes?"

"Kelly, it's Jack. Are you okay?"

"Oh, Jack. I didn't recognize your voice. You caught us off guard."

"Us?"

"Nikki is here."

Nikki chose that moment to refill the mugs and cut more cake. I stretched the cord and walked around the corner into the sitting room so I could speak privately to Jack. I heard Nikki ask William how big of a slice he wanted. My guess was she was distracting him with mundane stuff, so he'd save his ghost story for when I came back to the table.

"Who is she talking to?" Jack asked me.

"Oh…" I said. "Brian's brother, William, is here."

"Brian from the Geneva History Museum?"

"Yes." I couldn't say too much without allowing Nikki and William to hear everything. The cord did not stretch far.

"Kelly, are you okay? You sound funny. Why didn't you call me when you got there?"

"I'm sorry, Jack. My cell phone and Internet aren't working up here. Do you think I can call you back later tonight? This isn't a good time."

"You're okay?" I could hear the concern in his voice.

"Yes, of course. I'm fine."

"Good. I had this really weird feeling earlier today that you were in some kind of danger. Do you want me to come up? I could try and switch some things around at work."

A huge part of me wanted Jack to come up, but I knew if he did I wouldn't get any work done. And he'd miss too much at the office. Plus, he'd have to make arrangements for his mom.

"It's okay, Jack. Maybe if I'm still here on the weekend you can come visit me."

"Deal," Jack chuckled. "I miss you. It's lonely here without you. Nothing is the same."

"I miss you, too. How's Peggy?"

"Mom's good. I'm heading over there in a few minutes to check on her, but I wanted to check in on you first."

While Jack spoke, my eyes were drawn to the front windows. I watched the trees in the yard bend and twist in a frantic dance.

"I sent you an email earlier today, Kelly, but never heard back. And then when you didn't call, I hunted down this number from Adelle."

"Yeah. I wish Internet and my cell worked here. It's starting to be a problem."

"Adelle said that might be the case. Something about the limit on the amount of cell towers they can put up. At least you have the landline."

Although I was listening to Jack, I couldn't help but overhear Nikki and William's conversation in the kitchen. They'd been talking about Brian, and I heard Nikki mention the name Victoria Jacobs. *Here we go.*

"Jack, can I call you back after William leaves?" From the way the trees were moving, I had a feeling a storm might be coming. I wanted to finish up our conversation with William, so he could be on his way before it hit. As nice as he seemed, I didn't want him stuck here all night due to a storm.

"Of course. Don't worry about calling me back, though. I know you'll have Nikki there tonight, and I'm going to be heading over to Mom's. Why don't you just call me in the morning, honey?"

"Okay."

"Just make sure it's Nikki tucking you in tonight and not your new house guest."

"Shut up, Jack," I chuckled.

I heard him laughing as he signed off with a "Love you."

I headed into the kitchen to hang up the phone and sat down at the table. William's new piece of cake sat untouched in front of him as he stared bug-eyed at Nikki. Her hands moved in a flurry while she spoke.

"Sorry," I mumbled.

"And when he left that day I never saw him again," Nikki finished up. "Kelly was with me at Chocolate Love. Do you remember how freaked out Brian was?"

"You're talking about Thursday afternoon, right? When he came in to talk to you?"

Nikki nodded.

"He called me that morning," William said, clutching his coffee cup. "I was in meetings most of the morning, so I couldn't take his call. He left a really weird message."

"What did he say exactly?" Nikki asked.

"Brian said, 'I think she's going to kill me,' and then he hung up."

At that moment, the wind knocked a tree branch against the kitchen window and I jumped. Finding an inner calm I didn't normally possess, I said, "Ghosts cannot kill."

I tried to be the voice of reason, but the look William shot me made me squirm. I raised my hands up in a sheepish shrug. My mind conjured an image of me running out the door just a few minutes prior to this conversation in order to avoid Brian's ghost. Wasn't I just in hysterics a few moments earlier about what I thought might be a ghost?

"I know that and you know that, but Brian was out of his mind with fear. You know how my brother was. He was that way all his life. Brian had this extreme passion for history and the spirits of the past. He thought he was offending this Victoria Jacobs night after night by keeping her house on the ghost tour and making a spectacle out of her death." He ran his hand through his hair. "Did he ever tell you about the things he thought the ghost was doing to him?"

"You mean about the lights being left on and things being moved," Nikki said.

Placing his hand back on the table, William shook his head. "I don't think he told you everything. Maybe he was embarrassed."

"I don't understand. Brian loved all of that ghost stuff. He devoted his whole life to digging around into the ghosts of the past. Why would he get so freaked?" I said.

"Because Victoria, or whoever this ghost was," William said, raising his hands up in the air to make quotations marks with his fingers "became violent."

"In what way?" I asked, sitting forward.

"A few nights before he died, Brian almost fell down the stairs at the History Museum. He tripped over some things that were left there. He told me he felt as if they were strategically placed there on purpose to trip him. Then later, he woke up to someone calling his name downstairs in the museum and almost fell to his death trying to investigate. You've seen those stairs. They're concrete. When he made it down to the museum, no one was there."

"Why didn't he go to the police?" Nikki asked.

"Because he didn't think they would believe him. He had a reputation for being obsessed with ghosts, which was true."

"No wonder why he was so scared," Nikki said.

"But we know this couldn't really be happening, right? This was Brian slipping deeper into delusional thoughts, don't you think? What about the pills? Could they have been causing paranoia?" I posed the questions quickly and as lightly as I could without being harsh.

"I'm scheduled to speak with his doctor tomorrow. But, he was only supposed to be taking anti-anxiety meds on an as-needed basis. Those shouldn't be causing delusions. In fact, I'm really surprised he was on them.

He tried taking anti-anxiety meds when he was having trouble as a kid, and he hated the way he felt when he was on them. He never would have mixed them with sleeping meds. He didn't like taking anything." He shook his head. "No, there's something we're missing. Something doesn't fit."

No one spoke for a moment as we took this new information in.

"He didn't tell you about the meds?"

We both shook our heads no.

His eyes widened as though surprised by this, but William continued on. "That's the million dollar question, isn't it? Was Brian imagining things or was there some credence to his fear? Was someone trying to scare him to get him out of there?"

"But why would anyone do that? What would Brian know or be doing that would be a threat?" I asked.

"That's what I want to figure out. Did somebody want his job? It's not like it was a high-paying gig. He was barely getting by. There's something more to this."

"And that's where you want our help?" Nikki said.

Before William could answer, rain began pelting the kitchen window. It sounded like large fingers tapping on the windowpane, trying to get our attention. From the way the storm had come in fast and furious, I had a feeling it was going to be a big one.

"Yes. Do you think you can spend some time in the Geneva History Museum? Maybe even spend an overnight there. See if you experience what Brian did."

"No way!" I said without filtering my response.

"Kelly," Nikki said, kicking me lightly under the table.

"What? You heard him. Falling down the stairs, calling out names. I don't want to get involved with that. Whoever or whatever is doing this is violent. It's best to stay far away from the whole thing."

"I would do it myself, but I have to get back to Pennsylvania for the wake and help my parents. I'll be back once my parents are settled to do some investigating of my own. I just thought that while the scene is active, you might be able to pick up some clues as to what happened."

"Wait a minute. You don't really believe there's an evil spirit behind this, do you?" I asked.

William lifted his coffee cup to his face and then set it back down on the table. His hand reached up to his head and at the last minute changed direction to rub his face. "I don't know," he sighed. "I loved my brother. My only brother. My twin."

His eyes moved around the table, finally settling on mine. He licked his lips and paused before going on. "And now I've lost him. Imagine what it would feel like to lose each other," he said, looking intently at Nikki, then at me.

His pain appeared so genuine, I felt myself falling apart a little bit inside for him. I nodded my head.

"Kelly, I don't mean to bring up the past to hurt you; I just want to make a point. I read about Steve's trial on-line. I know that at one point Steve tried to make it look like you set up the whole thing. He tried to convince the jury that you begged him to kill his mistress and her un-born child for you. I also know that his parents backed his story to make you take all the heat."

Ouch. I'd forced myself to bury that aspect of the trial. And somehow, I'd been successful. It's amazing what the human psyche can do to accomplish the number one goal: survival. Luckily the judge had shot down most of the material the defense put together to support this angle of their case.

"She asked me to kill her. She didn't want the other woman and my bastard child around to remind her of my mistake. We were going to start over together. She said we could have another shot if I would just get rid of Mandy and the baby. She even spoke to my mother about it."

My eyes fell to my hands on the kitchen table. It felt like William had just kicked me in the gut. He said he was trying to make a point. It had better be quick because he was losing me.

"In that moment, when Steve was trying to install doubt in the minds of the jury, how did you feel? If no one was going to believe your story anymore and no one had your back, where would you go? That's how I feel now. Brian only has me to defend him. He had no credibility in Geneva. Yes, people appreciated him and seemed to like him, but ultimately he was known as the crazy ghost tour guy. But what if there was a genuine threat to Brian's life?"

"But, William," Nikki said, "Brian most likely killed himself. Possibly accidently, but still, what are *we* going to find?"

"If Kelly had killed herself after what she went through with Steve, would you have wondered why and questioned if it was true? Suppose Steve had devised a plot to have Kelly disappear instead of Mandy, and then you found out he had another woman and a baby on the way. Wouldn't you have looked into it? Especially if you knew in your heart that Kelly attempting suicide was something she would never do? That's how I feel about Brian."

Nikki's response was to shift her eyes over to mine. I met them briefly and then my gaze dropped back to my hands, fearing she would be able to read what was on my mind. What if my family had not been there to speak on my behalf in court? Would the jury have believed I was involved in the attempted murder of Steve's mistress and unborn baby? They had my back when I needed them.

"She called me that night from the police station to tell me she came across an email of Steve's. She forwarded me the email. She was snooping because she was feeling uneasy at home and was suspicious of his late nights. What she found was shocking. It was Steve's plan to kill Mandy."

* * * * *

"Kelly."

"Kelly," Nikki said again, tapping one of my knees. She set a steaming mug of coffee down next to me.

"Where are you?"

"What?"

"You're gone. You've been staring at the same place on that wall for the past five minutes. What are you thinking about?"

I shook my head and wrapped my fingers around the mug she'd given me. I was thinking the same damn thing I'd been thinking for the past three years of my life. How did I get here? How did my life take this path, and what was I going to do next? I was lost. Still lost. As much as I wanted to fool myself into thinking I'd made progress and was finding my way after my divorce, I really wasn't. What I was really doing was just blanking things out to try and forget them, numb myself, and move on.

When I married Steve, my mother-in-law told me I was the daughter she never had. A couple years later, she wanted me to take the blame for her son's botched attempt at a double murder. How could she do that to me? And why had I not remembered that until tonight's conversation?

I took a sip of my coffee and met Nikki's gaze.

"I hope he made it to the bed & breakfast okay. I wish he would call and let us know," Nikki said.

"Yeah," I replied absently.

"This storm is bad. Did you know it was coming?"

What a question, I thought. No. I definitely did not.

I shook my head no and gazed from my seat on the couch to where William's car had been parked less than thirty minutes ago. After we agreed to think about what he was proposing, he'd left to check into his room at a local bed & breakfast in town. Apparently, he had known about the storm coming and made arrangements for shelter. Good thing, because it wouldn't be wise to be driving a long distance tonight.

"He said he'll meet us for breakfast tomorrow morning before we check out Chocolate Café's goodies. I'm not sure if you heard him say that."

"I didn't," I admitted.

"That's what I thought. We don't have to talk about this anymore tonight. I can see William's visit has disturbed you. I do think we should talk about flashlights and candles, though. I think the storm might knock out the power."

The fury of the storm outside had been lost on me ever since William's mention of the trial. I was battling an internal storm of my own as flashbacks dropped on me like bombs. My mother-in-law's betrayal had been completely wiped from my memory. Now her image taunted me. The way her tight eyes followed me around the courtroom like lasers haunted me once again. It was all coming back to me. Had her son been able to convince her that it was all my fault, or had she devised that theory herself to try and get him off? I'd never know. Either way, she became almost animalistic during the trial. It was spine-chilling to watch it happen.

"I'm going to go see what I can find in the kitchen," Nikki said.

I watched her make her way into the kitchen and pause as though contemplating where to begin the search. Suddenly, all the lights in the room went out. Nikki was no longer in my line of vision. I heard a violent crash in the direction I last saw her. My guess was she'd knocked over a kitchen chair.

"Are you okay?" I called out to her.

"Someone is here looking in the window!"

Chapter 18

"Crap!" I yelled as my left shin connected with the coffee table, sending a shooting pain up my leg. It was difficult to see a clear path to Nikki with the lights off as I continued to bang into things.

"Where are you?" Nikki shrieked.

"Damn, that hurt. I'm coming!" I managed.

I could hear Nikki stumbling around in the kitchen about ten feet away from me. By the sound of it, she was having as much luck as I was trying to find her way. Something crashed to the ground and shattered.

"What are you doing?" I called.

"The doors. Did we lock the door? He's heading to the back door," Nikki screamed back at me.

"Will you chill out? You're freaking me out. Who is it?"

Moving in the direction of Nikki's voice, I tripped over something and fell. My head grazed the side of the coffee table on the way down.

A low moan escaped my mouth while my hands moved around my head, feeling for any bumps and lumps. After confirming everything was still in place, I used the coffee table to pull back up to a standing position.

"He's at the door."

"Who is it?" I asked a little weaker this time. I made it to the kitchen and stood next to Nikki.

"I have no idea. He's…well, scary looking."

"Girls? Are you alright?" A voice called to us from the other side of the door.

A bolt of lightning illuminated the sky, revealing a better glimpse of our visitor.

"It's what's his name," I said.

"Who?"

"Adelle's neighbor. He's harmless," I whispered.

I pulled the door open to our straggly-haired, grungy-looking visitor. As I did so, a gust of wind and rain slapped me in the face, irritating the new scratch on my face from the fall.

"Mr. Morris, come in," I said through gritted teeth.

His first name escaped me even though I'd met him a few times. He'd owned the home next door to Adelle and Mike's for over forty years. From what I could remember about him, he was more of a recluse, so I was surprised to see him out and about, especially in this storm.

"I have a back-up generator, but I didn't think Adelle had one, so I knew you girls would be out of luck with this storm. Adelle emailed me to tell me you'd be coming up. Would you like some flashlights?"

He placed three flashlights in my hands before I had a chance to answer.

"Thank you. You have email access? How come I'm not able to get it?"

And who are you emailing? I wondered. Mr. Morris was over seventy-five years old and had lived alone for most of his life. From what I remembered from Adelle's stories, he came home from Vietnam and went into a seclusionary lifestyle he never came out of. She believed him to be harmless, and even trusted him with an extra key, but could never get him to come over for dinner or to socialize, hard as she tried. Looks like it took an emergency like this storm to make him come out of his hole.

"Yeah, all of these homes along the sand dune are in kind of a valley which can impede the signal. The towers are closer to the Interstate. I usually take my laptop closer to the road or in town if I want to go on-line."

My mouth dropped at the mention of him even *owning* a laptop. Who knew?

"Anyway, the power might be out for the rest of the night, so you girls sit tight. Phones are dead, too. You know where I am if you need me."

With that, he turned and zipped out of the room. That was the one thing I remembered very clearly about Mr. Morris. His entrances and exits were always awkward. You were never given a chance at a formal hello or goodbye.

I watched him as he snaked through the trees that separated Adelle's home from his. He opened his back door and disappeared into his tiny, unkempt, cabin-like house that ironically, was probably worth a fortune just because of the land it sat on.

I switched on all three flashlights and handed one to Nikki.

"You okay? You didn't say one word to him?"

"He never gave me a chance. That guy flies in and out like he's riding a broom or something."

"I was just thinking the same thing."

"He really freaked me out when I spotted him peering into the window. I forgot about him living next door. He really is a nice guy from what I remember, but he looks kind of like a scary bum."

"It's not like you to let appearances scare you. Who did you think it was at first?" I asked.

Instead of answering, Nikki shook her head and gave me a shrug.

"Come on, let's find something to eat and go to bed. This day is just getting stranger and stranger by the moment," I said.

* * * * *

Nikki and I turned in early. We were both exhausted from the adventures of the day. Nikki needed her rest more than ever. Even in the candlelight, dark circles were visible under her eyes like faint bruises. It made me worry, once again, how Nikki was going to take on opening a new coffee shop, running Chocolate Love, and carrying a baby. I was sure she underestimated the amount of energy it was going to take to do all that at the same time.

I tried to bring it up, but she changed the subject. Eventually, she said she was tired and excused herself to the bedroom across the hall from the master. The room was three times smaller than the master bedroom and faced the dunes. Since there were two small twin beds in there, I offered her the queen bed in the master bedroom, thinking it would be more comfortable for her. That, and the pregnant woman should automatically be entitled to the largest bed. She declined and headed into the guest bedroom, mumbling "So tired." Although I wanted to challenge her on choosing the smaller bed, the way she slurred her words made me hold back.

I stayed up for about an hour after Nikki went to bed, jotting down some things on a notepad and listening to the storm. My goal was to put down on paper everything we knew about Brian's death. The lights I saw in the apartment above the museum when Jack was over were really bothering me. I had assumed it was someone from Brian's family looking for some of his personal items. But now that we knew they had not been in town yet, that theory was blown.

Finally around ten, my eyes began to droop as my notebook kept falling onto my lap. I gave into my fatigue and blew out the candle next to my bed. My last thought before giving into sleep was a desperate prayer that tomorrow would be a better day.

* * * * *

Sometime during the night, I awoke to a shrieking sound. It made me bolt up in bed.

"Who's there?" I called out.

Twisting my head toward the window, I held my breath, trying to figure out what I heard. Had it come from outside or from in the house, I wondered.

"Nikki?"

Again the screech came from somewhere outside the window, making my heart stop. It sounded like a combination of an animal cry and a baby screaming. My first instinct was to crawl under the blanket and wait for whatever was out there to go away. My mind raced back to the comments about this house originally starting out as some kind of hunting cabin. I should have checked with Adelle about when the hunting season was. But surely she would have told me if this was the middle of hunting season. Besides, why would someone hunt in the middle of the night?

After a few seconds, the screech started up again, this time much closer to the house.

"Nikki!" I called out, hoping to draw her into my room. I didn't really want to go across the hallway to get her.

Slowly, I inched my way out of bed to the windows facing the front lawn. After a few seconds, I forced myself to peer out the window. By the way the lawn was lit with hazy, gray light, my guess was that it was nearing dawn. Still, I had to squint to make out any shapes. From my squat on the floor, only the far edge of the lawn and the street were visible. The short bushes that lined the street swayed back and forth in the early morning breeze in a mocking wave. I imagined them chanting "Good morning, Kelly. Wait till you see what's out here."

I shuddered, and leaned in closer to the window. In order to see the lawn in its entirety, I was going to have to move much closer to the window and stand up. That seemed like a bad idea though because if there was something or someone out there, I didn't want them to be able to see me.

Instead of standing, I leaned my face closer to the screen. When I did, the breeze kicked up, and the distinct smell of fire filled my nostrils. Someone out there was definitely burning something. Leaves?

My nose was pressed up to the screen, separating my face from the outside. Again I scanned the lawn, searching for the source of the screeching and the smell. My gag reflux kicked in as the smell became stronger. I knew the smell of leaves. This was definitely not that.

Still, the lawn looked empty, and the bushes continued on in their mocking dance. I gathered the courage to stand up straight and peer down directly beneath me onto the small walkway that lead up to the house.

"What?" I said, grabbing at my chest. Below me appeared to be a large, bird-like creature standing close to seven feet tall. Its height shocked me because it was unlike any type of bird I'd ever seen. Multi-colored feathers poured out from all angles at the tip of its head. The bird stood long and lean, its limbs tucked directly beneath it. More multi-colored feathers ran down its back and shot out from its body. I watched in horror as it leaned in closer to the house and looked in through the downstairs windows.

While trying to decide if I should let out a sound to scare it away or not, it turned its head 180 degrees to face back into the yard and let out another cry, this time more jagged. I raised my eyes up to the dancing bushes to see what it was signaling. Once the cry stopped, the bushes ceased moving and close to twenty other birds of similar shape and size stepped out from behind the bushes. They moved quickly toward the house in a fluid movement that brought them together into a group. They flowed so gracefully, it was like they were dancing to some unspoken song. My heart felt as if it was going to explode in my chest as they moved closer and closer to the house. They were *coming* for me.

I peered down again at the bird under the window and saw it had changed its position. The feathers on top of the head that had been pointing up to the window were now pointed back at the yard. It took me a second to put it together, but finally I figured out that I was looking directly into the eyes of the bird.

I shook my head, realizing my initial read was all wrong. This was no bird at all. Although covered in multi-colored stripes, it was clearly a human face. A *man's* face. And from the looks of it, a very angry man.

"Eeeeee-yaaawwwwww!!!!" he called out loudly, looking directly up at me. The twenty other men in feathered garb moved into a formation behind him and flipped their head dresses so they were also glaring up at me. A line of smoke that was not visible to me before registered in my peripheral vision. A quick glance to the right confirmed some kind of fire pit in Mr. Morris's yard. The smoke snaked up to the sky from what I gathered to be some kind of pig roast going on in his yard.

The size of the pig immediately registered as wrong. Whatever was roasting on the stick looked to be more the size of a human than that of a pig.

"Nikki!" I turned and screamed, heading to her room.

Before I could make it out of the bedroom, I ran directly into her in the bedroom doorway.

She wore a feathered headdress on her head, and her face was covered with multi-colored paint just like the Native American under my window. Her eyes were glazed over like she was in some kind of trance. Before I could say anything, she leaned into my bedroom and vomited onto the bedroom floor. It splashed onto my feet, making a sickening slapping sound.

"Nikki!" I screamed out.

Suddenly, I was alone in my room, sitting up in my sweat-drenched bed. The vomit, the headdress, the Native Americans—everything was gone. But the feelings from the nightmare were still there in my mind. I shivered.

"In here," Nikki called out. The sound of her retching followed.

I reached around on the bed in search of my robe. My body was shivering with sweat, and my head throbbed in pain. After wrapping myself in my robe, I rubbed at my eyes and slapped my cheeks a couple of times to gather my wits. My eyes rolled over to the window where the tribe had gathered in my nightmare. I turned away quickly and headed to the bathroom.

Nikki was hunched over the toilet quietly moaning to herself.

I made a beeline for the medicine cabinet and quickly swallowed pain killers to squash the headache that was setting in.

"Can I get you anything?"

"A shotgun," Nikki mumbled.

I sat down on the edge of the bathtub next to the toilet to rub Nikki's back. "It's getting worse, huh?"

"Ugh…" Nikki mumbled. "What the hell is happening to me?"

I rubbed her back, making sympathetic noises. This sure did not look fun. I was in California when Adelle carried her children, so I'd missed all this. I had no idea it was this bad. Adelle had never let on how bad the nausea was for her.

"What time is it?" Nikki asked.

"Umm…"

I twisted around to see if I could spot a clock in the bathroom. The upstairs bathroom was one of the rooms Adelle and Mike chose to renovate. It had a deep bathtub complete with whirlpool jets and a separate glass enclosed shower. The downstairs bathroom was also recently renovated. I remembered Adelle saying she could rough it, per say, in this house, but she'd be damned if she wasn't going to have nice bathrooms.

Unable to spot a clock, I gave up. There wasn't an abundance of them in this house. Time was not a priority here like it was in Geneva.

"Let me go check my cell phone."

I made my way back to my bedroom and was immediately struck by the memory of my nightmare. Those windows would never be the same. So much for this place being stress-free for me. My visit so far had turned into quite the nail biter.

My phone read 5:45A.M. Although there were still no bars, the clock on my phone had adjusted to the change in time zones.

Before heading back into the bathroom, I forced myself to peer out the windows into the yard. Those evil dancing bushes. Now, forever tools of concealment.

After confirming the yard was empty of anything suspicious, I shook my head. These nightmares. Would I ever escape them? They'd been with me for my entire life but escalated whenever I was under heavy stress.

Just as I was about to turn and head back to the bathroom, I stopped. Just like in my dream, the smell of something burning filtered into the room. Without being able to spot the source, I wasn't sure if I'd imagined it, or if I really smelled something. People built fires on the beach at night here all the time; so most likely, it was the aftermath of that. But I couldn't stop the image of a human form roasting on a stick when it popped into my head.

Shuddering, I turned back to the bathroom. Nikki was sitting on the toilet breathing in and out slowly.

"You okay?"

"I think so. I think it may have passed."

"It's quarter to six. Did you sleep okay last night? Do you want to crawl back in for a couple of hours?"

"Not really. I slept like a rock. I woke up to you screaming, and then was overwhelmed by a wave of nausea."

"I was screaming?"

Nikki nodded her head in affirmation, continuing her heavy breathing. "Nightmare?"

"Oh, God, yes. It was bad."

"Want to take a walk on the beach and talk about it?"

"You want to take a walk now?" I asked in disbelief. "Really?"

"Walking helps. Just be warned, I let out some massive belches when I walk or run now."

I hid a smile. "Do you want to run?"

"Maybe just a walk for now. It will help me think. Running seems too strenuous at this moment."

"Okay, let's go. Beach or street?"

"Definitely beach. We could walk on a street anytime at home. How often do we have a beach at our disposal?"

"Done. Meet you in five minutes. I'm just going to go change out of my pajamas."

While dressing, I tried to decide how much of my nightmare I was going to tell Nikki. She was so fragile now between the baby, the loss of Brian, and the launch of her new business. The last thing she needed was to take on her neurotic sister's problems.

My main focus was to talk her into staying up here another night. Suddenly my stress-free Michigan escape didn't seem so fun. It was starting to feel like I was losing my mind and my confidence up here. The house was beginning to frighten me. Who knew what was coming for me tonight?

Chapter 19

We pulled up in front of Chocolate Café just before nine. The walk on the beach had cleared my mind. With the storm passing and the sunshine beaming down, my nightmares and phobias were fading fast. By the time we pulled up in front of the store, I was in such a good mood, I'd forgotten we were meeting William for breakfast.

Nikki's nausea had passed as well. The walk did wonders for both of us.

"So, this is one of their multiple locations," Nikki explained. "The gentleman who created Chocolate Café happens to be in town this week and agreed to meet me. Adelle contacted him for me. They are up to sixteen stores now. I'm hoping some of his business ideas will rub off on me."

Seeing William's Mercedes parked in front of Chocolate Café gave me pause.

"What about William?"

Nikki glanced around, then at me. "The owner, Arnie, is not meeting me until ten, so we'll have plenty of time to spend with William before I meet with Arnie."

The café was located on a corner lot right in the heart of St. Joe's. The street appeared to be all commercial, made up of book stores, restaurants, salons, and souvenir shops. Even though it was a weekday, the café was bustling with a number of customers.

"They have a great location," I said, appraising the area. "It certainly catches my attention."

"For sure. Look at this corner lot. And look at the sign. Now that's great branding."

Above the café, a dark blue fluorescent sign read "Chocolate Café." The storefront was made up entirely of floor to ceiling windows, allowing foot traffic to see everything that was going on in the café.

"Shall we go in?"

"Wow, no wonder Adelle recommended checking this out. How can you resist going in? What a good job they did on the front of this store," Nikki commented. "Maybe I need to put in more windows in Chocolate Love."

The first thing that struck me upon entering was the immense size of the place. I estimated it to be at least four times the size of Chocolate Love. It was one large room with counter space and food product at the center of the store. Tables for customers to eat at were dispersed in a semi-circle all along the windows. The floor was cement, and the ceiling was unfinished, giving the whole store a cool lofty feel. Customers could order their food and then take a seat at the windows to people watch while they nibbled away.

"Look at that. They have a Chocolate Museum," Nikki commented.

"A what?"

"In the back. I read about it on-line. They give tours on the weekends in the back to show how the chocolates are made. It also gives a little history about chocolate and how Chocolate Café began."

"What a great idea! You should do something like that."

"I basically do, but I give it all away for free, where here they charge for it."

"What do you mean?" I asked.

"You know how I have my employees mold and dip the chocolate products in the front window."

"Oh, yeah. I see what you mean."

"It looks like one side is made up of the chocolates and the other side is hot food and coffee," Nikki observed.

"Looks like it. Wow. There is so much product. They do a great job with that, too."

Throughout the store, little kiosks about five feet tall were filled with souvenirs including mugs, bags of chocolates, tee-shirts, and stuffed animals. Bookshelves lined the far walls of the store with more products like the ones in the kiosks. Although there was a ton of product on the floor, the design kept it from being overwhelming and cluttered because everything was spaced out.

"This is basically the same concept as Chocolate Love but on a grander scale," Nikki commented.

"Mmmhmm. I love that they have the chocolates, coffee, and hot food combined. Would you ever think of doing that so you wouldn't have to take on another lease?"

"I wish I could. It's just that Chocolate Love is already cramped. We'd have to do a full renovation to the store. This store is so much bigger."

"You're right."

"Oh, look, there's William," Nikki pointed out.

William sat at one of the tables near the hot food side of the store. He was sipping coffee and reading a newspaper. When he spotted us walking over to him, he stood and flashed us a big grin.

"Good morning," he called to us.

He was dressed much more casually this morning in jeans, a long sleeve, cotton tee-shirt and a baseball cap. Maybe he'd finally caught on to the hippy vibe of the town and was trying to fit in. Somehow, he appeared much more approachable this way. Seeing him though only reminded me of what he brought up right before he left last night—ghosts. His hazel eyes watched me closely and his lips settled into a hesitant smile. I imagined he wanted to make amends for stepping over a line last night, but at that moment, another person joined our group.

"Nikki?"

A man in a dark blue suit and burgundy tie walked up to the table and addressed our group with a nod. Adelle must have given him a physical description of Nikki, because he barely glanced at me.

"Arnie?"

"Yes, I'm Arnie Tanner," he extended his hand, and Nikki shook it with vigor.

"So nice to meet you. Thank you so much for meeting me. This is my sister, Kelly Clark, and my friend, William Sanders."

"Nice to meet you all. Welcome to Chocolate Café," he said, flashing us a proud smile.

"It's absolutely beautiful. I'm floored by what you've done here," Nikki gushed.

"It's been quite an undertaking. This one was just renovated and so far is doing great. We're in sixteen locations now," he beamed.

"Nikki, I'm sorry," Arnie said, "but I've had a change in my schedule. I know we were planning to meet and talk at ten, but I have to head out in about forty minutes. Would it be okay if we had our meeting now?"

Nikki glanced back at us. Although I wasn't thrilled at the thought of eating breakfast alone with William, Nikki wasn't going to get another chance like this to sit down with someone who could mentor her as well as Arnie could.

"Go, go," I said. "Do you want me to order something for you?"

"I'll eat when I'm done. You guys go ahead. Don't wait for me."

"It was nice to meet you both," Arnie said. "Why don't you come in the back with me, Nikki. I have a small office where we can talk. First, I'll give you a quick tour though."

Nikki practically skipped behind him toward the back of the store. I smiled as I watched her go.

"So, should we go order?" William suggested.

My stomach chose that moment to let out a slight growl.

William chuckled and waved his hand in the direction of the hot food counter. "I guess that's a yes."

"Sorry. That was embarrassing." I covered my stomach.

"No need to apologize. I got up early and went for a run this morning. I'm so hungry I feel like if I don't eat soon, I'm going to start gnawing on my coffee cup. Let's see what they have to offer."

William stepped aside so I could walk ahead of him to place my order. I spent a few minutes looking at the choices listed on a large board above the cash register. Breakfast items were listed on one side, and the other side had items more appropriate for a lunch or evening meal. Below the counter was a large refrigerated glass case that displayed elaborately decorated cakes, pies, and cookies.

"This is tough to choose," I said.

William leaned in closer to me. "What did you say?"

"I said, I'm having a tough time choosing."

I turned and came face-to-face with William. My nose was nearly touching his, and from this close, I could see his eyes were freckled throughout with darker spots. He smiled and took a small step back to glance at the food selections. I pulled my hand up to my face to touch the scratch on it from last night's fiasco just to have something to do.

I tried my best to ignore the spark of electricity I'd felt between us when he was so close. There was no denying that William was quite an attractive man. Last night was too intense for me to grasp it, but here in this setting, it was hard to ignore those eyes, his full lips, and the way his cut physique pulled at his casual attire in all the right places.

You have a boyfriend. You are happily almost engaged, I silently repeated in my head.

"I agree," he said. "My intention was to get breakfast, but the sandwiches look so good. Did you see the portabella mushroom with roasted peppers on Focaccia bread? I know it's only nine, but do you think they would make that for me?"

"We can make that for you," an over-eager girl behind the counter suddenly called out.

William met my eyes for a second, and we shared a quick smile.

"Really? That would be okay?" he inquired, moving up to the counter. As he moved past me, I picked up just a hint of his cologne. I was unfamiliar with the smell, but it was appealing in its subtle presence.

"Sure. That happens a lot actually. People love the sandwiches here and can't wait till lunch. We aim to please. Are you a local?" she asked, blatantly hitting on William. She flipped her hair to one side in a dramatic way while simultaneously shooting her left shoulder forward so that the pin reading "Veronica" was visible to him.

"I'm not. I'm certainly enjoying my first experience here though. Kelly, ladies first. Why don't you go ahead and order."

William stepped back from Veronica, not taking the bait, and set his hand lightly on the small of my back in a gentleman-like gesture. He nodded his head, encouraging me to take my turn.

I finally settled on the breakfast quiche with spinach and mushrooms and a caramel latte. William insisted on paying, and Veronica promised our food would be delivered to the table. She gave a much less enthusiastic send-off, clearly catching on that William was not interested in her.

I couldn't help but wonder what his story was. I hadn't noticed a ring on his finger, and Nikki never mentioned there being a Mrs. William Sanders. Brian had always seemed so anti-relationship because of his obsessive personality. I just assumed his brother would be the same way. However, I was quickly learning the brothers were nothing alike. Although they shared identical genes, they seemed to be polar opposites.

When we sat back down at the table, I couldn't resist making a joke.

"She a little young for you?" I asked, sipping my delicious, caramel latte.

The rich, creamy beverage was so good; it sent an immediate jolt through my body. Hopefully, Nikki was wheedling this very recipe out of Arnie in their meeting.

"She's not my type," William said, smiling at me over his coffee cup.

Not his type. And what type would that be? Was she too young? Too blond? Too female? To ask would be showing way too much curiosity and that would be disrespectful to Jack. But God help me, I was curious.

An awkward silence followed where I could make another joke about the way the waitress was drooling over him, but I let it go.

"Kelly, I want to talk about something before the food gets here." He picked up a napkin from the table and wiped at his mouth quickly.

This was a good move considering there was a bit of froth on his lip leftover from sipping his coffee.

"I think I may have been out of line last night bringing up that stuff about your ex-husband and what you had to go through in court. I was trying to make a point, but I see now that it was too much. Sometimes, I'm so focused on my goal that I end up coming off as a total jerk. I hope you'll forgive me and give me a second chance. Please don't think I'm some horrible guy that does not consider a woman's feelings."

William's plea was so sincere, I couldn't help but appreciate his efforts.

"William, I…" I paused for a moment, trying to figure out exactly what I wanted to say.

The truth was, after last night, I had no intention of helping William. If Nikki stuck to her guns and decided to investigate, of course I would help her. But, I wasn't in it to help William. I barely knew him. And I barely knew his brother. I had no intention of becoming Geneva's investigator for hire. Even though it wasn't panning out this way for me, I still believed police work should be left to the professionals.

"I'm trying my best to move on from my past," I finally said.

"I see that now. When I read about your story, I created an image of who Kelly Clark was and see now that I was wrong. What you did and how you came off in your interaction with the press is very different than what I see in front of me. What you had to do was very tough. I didn't expect someone so," he paused, "vulnerable."

I struggled to keep eye contact with him, wishing to be swallowed by the floor.

"I did it again, didn't I?" William said. "I'm stepping where I shouldn't." He shook his head and looked down into his coffee cup. "I think I need to just stop talking."

William reached up and fiddled with his cap.

"It's just been such a bad week. I'm not myself. It's still so hard to believe he's gone," he said, meeting my gaze. William gripped at his napkin with both hands.

"I'm sure," I said softly.

"Sorry, I don't mean to dump this on you," William said, wiping his brow with his napkin. "We've been through so much with Brian. It's been…"

Veronica chose that moment to set our steaming plates down in front of us. My quiche bubbled with pieces of colorful vegetables bursting out from the creamy cheese and egg mixture.

"We're testing a new pop-over recipe in the store this morning. We're serving complimentary versions with all of our dishes. Enjoy! Oh, and by the way, here's a frequent flyer card we're giving out to all of our customers. If you visit us ten times in a year, we'll give you a complimentary sandwich. My name is on the back, so make sure to ask for me," Veronica said, throwing a wink in William's direction. She handed William the card and walked away from the table. Where was my card?

"And phone number," he laughed, flashing me the back side of the card.

"That girl is big time hot for you," I joked, happy that William's mood had lifted.

"She's relentless," he joked. "She's got to be almost twenty years younger than me."

"Doesn't seem to bother her. It probably wouldn't bother a lot of men."

"Well, it bothers me. She's a teenager, for God's sake. I prefer my women a little more mature," William said, reaching down and grabbing his sandwich. "Listen, let's enjoy our food. I need a break from heavy topics. I swear if I don't eat, I'm going to go crazy. My low blood sugar is half my problem right now."

William dug in, chewing off a large portion of his sandwich and closing his eyes.

"My God, this is good," he managed. The look of pure ecstasy on his face made me laugh.

"How far did you run this morning?" I asked.

"Too far. Six miles."

The way he ate his food once again reminded me of Jack. Almost as though he had been starved and was finally allowed to eat.

"So, I notice you don't wear a ring. You're not married?" The question came out before I could stop it. I ripped open my pop-over and stuck part of it in my mouth before any more nosy questions fell out.

"Nope. Never been. Work takes up most of my time. How about you?"

William's hand froze suddenly just before he was about to put a popover in his mouth.

"Crap," he mumbled quietly.

"It's okay. I know what you mean. We all know I was married."

Unfortunately, it seemed anyone who owned a television or had access to the Internet knew Kelly Clark was once married. And that it ended horribly.

"I believe what you are referring to is the present, right?"

"That is exactly what I meant."

"I'm engaged." I couldn't help but notice William's eyes fall on my empty ring finger.

"I'm about to get engaged, I should say. I'm in a serious relationship with someone back in Geneva. He's actually someone I dated in the past. My old sweetheart, I guess you would say."

"How nice. You guys found each other again?"

"He happened to move back to Geneva to take care of his mother when I moved back after my divorce. It's kind of crazy how it worked out."

"That's really sweet. Good for you," William said, ripping apart his popover.

"It's been really good," I said, choosing that moment to dig into my quiche.

"How is yours? This sandwich is delicious," William commented. "Too bad I don't live closer. I would definitely qualify for the frequent flyer free sandwich."

"You'd make Veronica happy," I joked. "Mine's really good, too. The cheese is amazing."

"Hey, did you and Nikki survive the storm okay? I never even asked about it."

"Oh, yeah. We were fine. We lost power but our neighbor came over with flashlights. The power was back on by morning. How about you? How was the bed and breakfast?"

"Great. The power stayed on the whole time. No issues there. It was really quite nice. I wish I would have found this little town under different circumstances. It's a nice vacation spot. Hell, I should have visited Brian and the town of Geneva when I had the chance. It's been nice getting to know the Clark sisters. Now I understand why Brian was so fond of you both. I wish I had gotten to know you and Nikki better before all of this."

I paused for a second before meeting his eyes over the table.

"Especially, you, Kelly," he said when I met his gaze. He shot me a cute smile and winked.

Chapter 20

I coughed up part of my quiche and spent a couple of seconds flailing about, trying to stop myself from choking. William simply lifted up my drink to my face, so I could take a sip. When his hands got close to my nose, I picked up the smell of fresh soap. Being this close also allowed me to notice tiny scars laced around his knuckles in strange spider like formations.

"Kelly, I'm not trying to freak you out. Just saying we could have become friends under normal circumstances. We have a lot in common."

I took a sip and composed myself. "I'm not freaking out. I just swallowed down the wrong pipe. I'm okay."

I felt foolish, but couldn't let go of the fact that I still felt William was bordering on flirting with me. Or perhaps, he was one of those people who came off super charming and flirtatious even when they didn't have other motives or intentions. Perhaps it was just his way. Still.

"Hey, we never talked about what you do for a living. I know you said that work takes up most of your time. What is it you do?" I asked, changing the subject so I could recover from my cough attack.

"I own a consulting business. My team works with companies to help grow their sales force. We step in and show them how to set-up a proper sales model and how to execute it."

"Is that your company? SC?" I asked, pointing up to the emblem on his hat.

"Sanders Consulting, that's right," he said, reaching up and pulling his hat off to glance quickly at the front. "This is an old one. We recently had the logo redesigned."

"How has it done with the changing economy? I imagine it's been tough since most companies are not expanding."

He shrugged. "The majority of businesses were scaling back for a while, but there's been a niche market that progressed during the recession and now that we seem to be rebounding, things have been great. The trick is to find the places in the market that grow during a recession, or because of the recession, and focus on those areas. Like what your sister is doing. She's figured out coffee sales have gone through the roof, and she's using that piece of market data to help open her next venture. She's very smart, that one. That's what I mean. I can see why Brian liked hanging out with you. Nikki's whip smart with her business skills and knowledge of the Geneva area, and you're just darn interesting."

"I'm darn interesting?" I laughed.

He mirrored my smile and nodded his head. He took a bite of his sandwich before continuing.

"You have to admit, you have an interesting past. And now what you've done with it and your stories. I've read your books. Did you know that Brian was a fan? He gave me an autographed copy of the very first Antique Murder Mystery for Christmas last year."

"He did? I had no idea."

"Yep. I enjoyed it. How many are you planning on writing?" He put his half-eaten sandwich down and sat back in his chair, watching me closely.

That was a good question. My agent was always pressuring me to give her an idea of what my plan was for the series. I was still at the point where I could see it going on for a long time.

"Honestly, I have no idea."

William laughed, exposing his perfect, bright, white teeth and a dimple on the right side of his face. He pulled his hand up to his lips and wiped briefly at them, once again exposing the small scars. I hadn't noticed them last night, but we weren't sitting this close at Adelle's house.

"It's nice to hear you say that. I always assume authors have everything figured out before they sit down to write a series. It's refreshing to know that you're thinking on your feet."

"Well, that's for sure. I'm definitely one that has to think on my feet. I can't see that far out in the future."

"Neither can I."

"Really? You seem so put together and organized. My read on you is that you have your plans laid out for the next fifty years."

"Like in what way?" he stared in my eyes, almost too intently for my liking.

"Like in business, financial…just…life."

"Kelly, no one has it all figured out, especially me. Life is full of surprises. You never know what or who is around the corner. And we're foolish to think we can control what life serves up for us."

There it was again. That hint of flirtation that could be taken as a totally innocent comment, or perhaps a suggestive innuendo. And by the way William watched me with his innocent, yet not so innocent stare, I couldn't help but take it as the latter.

"Can I ask you something?"

"Sure. Anything," William said, leaning back into the table.

"How did you get those little scars on your hands?"

William put his hands up on the table and smiled down at them. I was sure that wasn't where he thought the conversation was going, but I needed to change the path quickly.

"Boxing. It's a hobby of mine. I need all of the stress relief I can get," he laughed, pulling his hands into fists and shadowboxing. He flexed and shot me a goofy smile, showing off the large muscles in his arms.

"I get it. I use running for that purpose."

"Me, too. We should go for a jog sometime together."

I hadn't run with anyone but Nikki or Jack since I'd been back in town. My runs were a very sacred, quiet part of my day. The thought of bringing someone else into that time would imply they were an intimate, close relation to me. A trusted *compadre*. I wasn't sure if William would understand that. And I was sure Jack would *hate* the idea.

"I wish Brian would have found an outlet. He never did, even when we were kids. He just let things build up and build up. That's how he always got into trouble. And then he had to try meds. It didn't work then, and it didn't work now."

At that moment, Nikki danced up to the table from somewhere near the back of the store. William's comment hung in the air above us.

"That was awesome," Nikki said dreamily. "If I could sign the lease for Bean in Love at this very moment, I would."

"It went that well, huh?" William asked, pulling a chair out so Nikki could join us.

"Arnie is so motivating and positive about the whole thing. Do you know he started with nothing? He pulled together cash from family members for the first store eight years ago and has been blasting the market ever since."

"How is he doing so well with the downturn of the economy?" I asked.

"He's figured out a way. He's doing a really good job finding locations that are not saturated with other restaurants. Arnie feels location is the most important factor in figuring out if the store will be a success or not. Just like real estate. It's just like what we said when we were pulling up to this location. What do you think of the location we looked at in Geneva, Kelly? Do you think that has the same draw as this?"

"I do," I nodded.

"Okay, hold that thought. I have to go order something. I'm starving."

Nikki disappeared again in the direction of the food counter.

"What time is it?" William asked, patting his pants presumably for his cell phone.

"Near nine-thirty."

"Would it be weird to order chocolate cake at this time of the day? Did you see those cakes?" he asked, pulling his cell phone from his pants pocket and checking the screen. "I have to leave here in about an hour to head to Pennsylvania." Then he took a breath before he said, "I have another call scheduled with Alice from the Geneva History Museum. What do you know about her?"

"She's nice. She worked with Brian as the administrative assistant for Geneva History Museum. From what I gather, they were pretty close. She was very upset when he...," I paused, trying to find the right word. William was hard to read. One minute he seemed very emotional about his brother's death, and the next he was flirtatious and fun. He stared at me with his eyebrows raised.

"Killed himself? Is that what you were going to say? It's okay, Kelly. Right now all of the facts make it look that way. But sometimes the facts are skewed, and you need someone to make them right."

My mind raced back to the sight of Brian lying dead in his bed.

"What is that, by the way?" William asked, reaching out and touching the side of my face lightly.

I froze at the sensation of his warm hand on my face.

"It looks like a scratch. Right here."

He ran his index finger softly down my face from the tip of my right eye to my chin. Just like his spoken word, his touch gave off mixed signals. It was almost sensual the way he moved his finger slowly down my face.

"It's from last night's storm. I fell trying to make it to the kitchen and scratched it on the coffee table," I said, pulling back slightly. He took the hint and removed his hand.

"It's a strange little scratch. Did you treat it? Don't want it to get infected. You never know what could seep in through open wounds."

"Indeed," I thought to myself, mesmerized by the little freckles buried in the hazel irises of his eyes.

Before I could respond, Nikki was back at the table.

"Have you tried their lattes, Kelly? You're going to go crazy for those," Nikki said, plopping down at the table with a coffee mug bigger than her face.

"I'm going to order some cake. I'll be right back," William said, shooting up from the table when Nikki sat down. The movement reminded me of the Hungry Hippos game I played with my niece. One goes up, one goes down. I stifled a giggle.

"Kelly, where are you?" Nikki asked, finally reading something on my face.

"That William. He's, umm..."

"What?" Nikki asked, leaning in closer to me. "Is he bothering you?"

It was difficult to find the words to express what I was feeling right now. I was mainly taken aback by William. He was a bit too forward and playful for my taste. Yet, I was strangely intoxicated by the air of flirtation. I knew it was wrong, but I didn't hate the attention.

But there was no way I was going to share that with Nikki. Bottom line, I needed Jack here so I could snap out of this weird spell.

"No, it's not that," I combed my hands through my hair, trying to find the right words.

"He's cute, isn't he?" Nikki said. "Too bad we're both taken. There must be someone we can set him up with. Didn't see a ring on his finger. What's his story anyway? Did you learn more about him?"

Rather than say anything incriminating, I shrugged an indifference to her question.

"Okay, here we go," William said, placing a humongous piece of seven layer chocolate cake on the table. He set down three forks and sat back down in his chair.

"Are you crazy? I haven't even eaten my breakfast yet. It's nine in the morning," Nikki said.

I paused mid-air, fork already on path to dive into the cake.

"It's never too early for chocolate," William said.

"The man is right, Nikki," I said, allowing my fork to continue on its journey.

Nikki shrugged and picked up her fork. "Alright. What the hell. I'm here to do research for my business, right? If it means I need to eat chocolate cake before breakfast, so be it."

I forked a piece in my mouth and allowed it to melt into my taste buds. The chocolate was rich, velvety, and so moist, it nearly evaporated when it touched my tongue.

"Oh, my," I moaned.

"Do you guys sell stuff like this at Chocolate Love?" William asked.

"You betcha. Even better than this. Right, Kelly?" Nikki laughed.

"Better," I said, though this cake came close. There was a hint of coffee in this cake that I thought Nikki should consider adding to her seven layer chocolate cake recipe.

"Good, because I've made a decision. After I help my parents lay my brother to rest in Pennsylvania, I'm coming back to spend some time in Geneva. I wasn't thinking clearly last night when I asked you guys to look into Brian's death on your own. If you're going to spend the night in Brian's old apartment to get to the bottom of this, then I'm going to be sleeping right next to you."

I coughed and choked on my cake, causing pieces to land all over Nikki's place setting and her coffee mug.

* * * * *

Back at Adelle's Michigan house, my stomach flipped as we walked through the front lawn. This was how it was for me. My nightmares could ruin a perfectly good setting for quite some time. Some were so bad I never recovered. Others faded as time passed and things went back to normal. I hoped that would happen for this home. I didn't want to see angry Native Americans hunting me every time I walked through the yard. This time in Michigan was supposed to get me away from the drama of Geneva. Should have known it planned to follow me here.

As much as I wanted peace and quiet, I dreaded Nikki's departure. We still hadn't talked about her plans for the day.

"Are you going to hang around for a while, or do you have to head back?"

"I would love to hang around, but I have a meeting with Tilly, the real estate agent, later on this afternoon. We're going to do another walk through of Breakfast Bar since the last one ended so badly. Are you okay being here alone?"

"Yeah, for sure," I lied. After seeing her light up about her new store, I decided it was silly to ask her to stay over. I didn't want to delay her business deal, and it was time for me to get over my phobias and nightmares.

"I know there's not a huge rush on rentals right now, but I want to get things moving. I love the proximity to Chocolate Love. That factor alone will make running multiple businesses so much easier. If I can somehow transfer my customers over from Chocolate Love, we'll do okay."

"Are you worried about Chocolate Love's business declining if you open Bean in Love?" It was something we hadn't talked about and I wondered if it concerned her.

"No. I'm going to set it up so that they are not in direct competition to one another. Remember the way Chocolate Café was set up? It's going to be basically the same thing, but I'll split them in two completely. If my customers are in the mood for high end chocolates and ice cream, they'll go to Chocolate Love. If they have more time on their hands and want a coffee and a sandwich, they can go to Bean in Love. I'm also hoping to turn the upstairs of Bean in Love into a place where small groups can hold meetings. Casual book clubs with friends or maybe even fondue parties."

"Fondue parties. Now you're talking."

"I'm so excited. Before I go though, let's talk about one thing."

Nikki plopped down on the couch in the sitting room and waved her hand to motion me to sit down on the adjacent one. "What's going on with you and William?"

"What do you mean?" I asked, immediately flustered. *Damn.* She had caught on. I should have known she would.

"Come on. I might be completely distracted, but I'm not blind. He was obviously hitting on you."

"Do you think so?" I asked, feeling my face blush. "My read is so off right now. I thought he was a little forward, but I couldn't tell if it was just me reading the situation wrong. He's kind of got that charming businessman personality. That might just be the way he talks."

"I agree. He's polished. But he speaks to you much differently than he does to me."

"I told him about Jack. He knows I'm in a serious relationship," I said, fiddling with my jeans by pulling at the knees to straighten them.

"Okay, defensive! Relax. I didn't say you were acting inappropriately or anything. Just bringing attention to some vibes I was getting," Nikki said, putting her hands up like a shield.

"Wait a minute. Wait a minute. Are you blushing?" she asked, leaning forward to examine me.

"No!"

"You're not attracted to him, are you?"

"Don't be an idiot. I mean, don't get me wrong, he is an attractive man. He's really pulled together and nice. I'm being nice to a man who just lost his brother. We can both appreciate the emotions he must be going through right now." I coughed and looked away from Nikki's piercing examination.

"You're totally attracted to him."

"Aren't you? I mean, how can you not be? He's got those sexy freckled eyes and that confidence thing going. It's okay to say he's an attractive man, right? I would never act on it."

Nikki nodded, but her lips stayed locked in a straight line while she squinted her eyes at me.

I waited on pins and needles for her to respond. After a few tense seconds, she finally spoke.

"Yep, I was right. You're going to blow it."

Chapter 21

As much as I wanted her to stay, Nikki left shortly after our talk. Her comments about William reminded me of how much I needed to be alone with my thoughts.

Since my move to Geneva a few months ago, I'd embedded myself into my sisters' lives and they in mine. As much as I loved being so close to them, it was wise for me to take a step back every once and awhile.

When I divorced my husband three years ago, I developed a strong sense of independence in order to be able to function on a daily basis. I would not have been able to survive without the help of my sisters. But now that I was much stronger, I had to be careful not to use their love as a crutch.

That was exactly why I needed a little more time on my own rather than running into the arms of a new husband. I would be no good for Jack if I didn't have a strong backbone and a stable sense of self. I was almost there, but to exit the race without crossing the finish line would not be fair to anyone, most of all me.

After a short run on the beach, I spent the entire day writing. Around three o'clock I drove back into town with my laptop for a change of scenery and to work from Chocolate Café. Things were going great with my story, but I needed to do a little bit of research on the Native American tribes that settled Geneva. I wouldn't be able to go much further unless I had background on the pieces Mary found and sold in her store. For this, I needed the Internet, which I'd only be able to access from Chocolate Café.

The three o'clock lull in the café made me think of the one we always had at Chocolate Love about this time of the day. Kids were about to get home from school and the afternoon doldrums set in.

I ordered another one of their irresistible lattes and set up near the window so I could people watch. Since this was my first time checking my email in a couple of days, I wasn't surprised to find quite a few unread messages.

The majority of the emails were junk mail due to my address somehow getting passed to various stores and on-line catalogs I didn't remember signing up for. There were a few of interest though, namely one from my agent letting me know that one of the larger bookstore chains on the east coast had decided to carry my series.

"Yes!" I said, quietly to myself.

The influx of cash was much needed if I ever planned on getting out of debt. For a brief moment, I allowed myself to dream about having enough cash to actually buy a place of my own. It would be a great time to snatch up a home while the housing market was still down. I would need to get in soon though, because prices were already in recovery mode.

Would I really want to do that though, knowing Jack's intentions? Shouldn't we buy something larger than his three bedroom condo if we planned on moving in together and having children? But were the feelings I had in William's presence a sign I wasn't ready to make a serious commitment? Did the fact that his eyes made me squirm a bit hint of clear and present danger in my relationship with Jack?

"Would you like another?" a voice asked, disturbing my thoughts.

"What?" I jumped in my seat, knocking over my large, ceramic coffee cup. It fell to the floor shattering in a million pieces. My mind went immediately to Nikki's mugs at Chocolate Love. She got really upset anytime one broke since they all had sentimental value for her. Whenever someone broke one, Nikki tried to piece it back together with super glue. Judging by the amount of pieces skewed across the floor, there would be no gluing this mug.

"Oh, no. I'm so sorry," I said, bending down to pick up the shattered pieces of the mug. "Please don't worry about it. It's no big deal. Let me go get a broom," the young female employee said before walking away.

I searched for larger pieces on the floor even though they were clearly not as attached to their mugs here as we were at Nikki's store.

The young woman returned, and her shoes blocked me from picking up any more pieces. Crawling around like this while someone stood over me made me think back to last Thursday when I was searching for something in Chocolate Love. What had I been looking for again? I just remembered how inappropriately close I got to Nikki's employee, Lisa, because I had been so caught up in my search.

"Let me clean it up. No use saving the pieces. We're just going to throw them away."

"Please, let me pay for the mug. I feel horrible."

The girl shrugged it off and said, "Don't worry about it. We have like a gazillion of these in the back."

It made me a bit sad to watch her sweep up the fragmented pieces under my table. Perhaps this happened when multiple locations were opened. Sure, it was great to have the success, but maybe owners lost track of the little things that were once so important. I wondered if Nikki had thought about this. Would she loose some of the charm of Chocolate Love as her business grew? One thing for sure, I couldn't see her ever chilling out about her beloved mugs.

"Let me get you a refill on the latte. It was my fault for startling you. You looked really involved in your work," she said, walking away before I could confirm she was right.

I sat back down at my table and tapped at my keyboard, trying to remember what I was working on. To my surprise, there was a new email from an address containing the name William Sanders. How did he get my email address, I wondered?

It read:

Hey, Kelly-

Just wanted to tell you how great it was to meet you. Nikki gave me your email. Hope that's okay. When are you planning to come back to Geneva? Trying to make my plans with my parents to figure out when I'll head that way. Do you think you'll be back by Friday? That's the plan for me right now. If so, can I take you out to dinner on Friday night to brainstorm together? I really appreciate any time you can give me.

Hope to see you on Friday—
William

It was hard to ignore William's plea. I understood him wanting to get to the bottom of things but was still hesitant to dive into trouble. I had enough on my plate.

Then again, though it stung when he brought up the facts surrounding my scandalous court case, he had a point. What if my sisters had not been there as character witnesses? What if Steve and his parents were somehow able to sway the jury into believing I'd set up the attempted murder of my husband's mistress and unborn child? That was all William was trying to do, save his brother's reputation, like my sisters did for me.

Instead of responding, I pulled my cell phone from my purse with the intent to call Nikki to check if William had contacted her as well about dinner. He better have. If not, that meant he was asking me out to dinner solo on Friday night.

My cell phone alerted me that I had two unread text messages. The first one was from Nikki telling me she arrived home safely. The second one was from Jack and read:

Miss you. Can't wait to see you.

I smiled and sent back *Miss you, too.*

I contemplated asking him to come up and spend the night with me. He'd probably taken the train into Chicago though for work and would be without a car. My request meant asking him to take the train all the way back to Geneva and then drive out to Michigan.

Unless he could take a train here from downtown Chicago. I drummed my fingers on the table.

I knew one existed but had no idea how often it ran. The whole process would take way too long and was too much to ask, so I dropped the phone back in my purse. Instead of responding to William's email, I closed the page and got back to work. I didn't even know if I'd be back in town on Friday.

It would all depend on Adelle. My response could wait until the morning. Maybe by then, I'd know my schedule for the week.

After another two hours of work at Chocolate Café, I ordered a sandwich to go, and made my way home. It had been a productive day. Tonight, I was looking forward to starting a new book I'd checked out from the Geneva library before I left.

From the excerpt I read, *Devil in a White City* was based on a true story about a serial killer that struck the city of Chicago during the turn of the century. Because city officials were distracted by preparing for The World's Fair, a serial killer committed multiple brutal murders and walked free. I wasn't sure if this was really something I should be reading while alone in a strange house far from my home, but I was due a reward for all of my hard work.

By the time my car pulled into Adelle's driveway, the sky had already darkened significantly, making me regret staying at Chocolate Café for so long. It was getting darker much earlier with the fall season closing in, and I didn't feel comfortable walking into the house without any lights on. I should have been better prepared, but my story was going so well I didn't want to stop. Luckily, I carried a flashlight in my car, so at least there would be a little bit of light walking up the driveway.

Stepping out of the car, I was struck by how cold it was. It didn't feel this cold getting in my car after leaving the café. My guess was there was a significant drop in temperature due to the proximity of the house to Lake Michigan. The wind blew my hair, momentarily blinding me. I reached up and pulled my long, brown hair back into a knot with the hair band I always kept around wrist.

Behind me, the evil bushes danced in time with the wind.

"Welcome home, Kelly, you fool. Why didn't you leave any lights on?" I heard them sing to me. Shaking the crazy thought out of my head, I quickened my step to the house.

Tonight, I'd be better prepared if there was another storm. If the power did go out again, I had enough flashlights on hand to be able to function.

Those flashlights would have to be returned to Mr. Morris eventually, but not tonight. Hopefully, he wouldn't mind if I kept them for another night.

On first glance, it didn't look like he was home. All of the lights in his house were out. I imagined him sitting at one of the cafés in town updating his status on his Facebook page. After learning about his knowledge on Internet access, my guess was we may have misjudged him. He seemed more connected to the outside world than I thought.

By the time I reached the front door, my body was shaking from the cold. Just before placing my key in the door, the wind blew hard again, knocking me off balance and sending the key flying from my hand.

"Great," I mumbled, scanning the ground.

Luckily, the key had dropped right at my feet, allowing me to spot it easily. When I bent to retrieve it, the combination of the gold coloring of the key and the way my body was positioned sent my mind back a week ago to Chocolate Love. The gold backing. That was what I was looking for when I was crawling around last Thursday and nearly bumped into Nikki's employee, Julie. It was some kind of gold backing to a pin of some sort.

I shook my head and returned to opening the door. There was nothing significant about the gold backing, so I didn't know why it had popped into my head. I didn't even remember what I did with it after I found it.

Forget it. It was time to get inside and out of the wind.

Once inside, I locked up and made my way to the kitchen to deposit my turkey sandwich in the fridge. I wasn't really in the mood to eat just yet. After a hard day of work, what I really wanted to do was take a hot bath in Adelle's whirlpool tub upstairs so I could unwind.

While I filled the tub, I deposited my bag with my computer and purse in the master bedroom and undressed. Adelle had two luscious looking bathrobes hanging in the small closet inside the master. When I pulled one of the dark blue, fluffy robes off of the hanger, I thought about the robes we wore at Hot Yoga.

I hoped Adelle was interested in going back because I sure was. Plus, it would be nice to support the ladies running Hot Yoga, Trisha and Lucy. From what I had overheard, they were struggling to make ends meet, as most places in downtown Geneva were right now. It must be awful to live under the constant stress of having to make the rent on a downtown business. Nikki and her husband's family owned the building for Chocolate Love outright, so she didn't have that worry. Hopefully, she would be able to take the stress of paying rent for Bean in Love. At Hot Yoga, I had overheard the owners say, "You know how he is. He won't let us be late, or he'll kick us out." I hoped whoever "he" was they were referring to was not the same he that Nikki would be renting from. She didn't need that kind of stress in her life.

Once in the tub, my stress level dropped instantly and my troubles melted. Jack had a wonderful tub in his condo. It made me smile thinking of spending future evenings soaking there.

Now if only I had a glass of red wine. Adelle most likely had a bottle stocked somewhere, but at this point, it was too late. There was no way I was getting out of the tub to look.

Closing my eyes, I listened to the wind howl outside the window and glanced over at the flashlight I'd left on the rug next to the tub. Now that I was stocked with those, I wasn't as anxious about an impending storm. In fact, most of the things I'd been stressing about seemed fairly ridiculous in the cocoon of my warm bath. Adelle was working her way through her move, Nikki was expanding her business, the boyfriend of my dreams was committed to me, and to top it all off, my book sales were on the rise. There really was no need for me to get so worked up about the other things going on.

Yes, there was still sadness and confusion over the death of Brian, but maybe I could help William work through it. It would be the right thing to do. Someone had helped me when I needed it. Why shouldn't I help others now that I was in a better place? I'd stepped up for Adelle and Nikki, and it felt great. If I was feeling strong enough to help William, why shouldn't I? Plus, with the new information about the use of pills, it looked more and more like an accidental death. Nothing sinister. Just someone overwhelmed and confused, possibly making bad choices with their pharmaceuticals. That was a reasonable explanation for what happened to Brian.

As far as my strange read on William's possible innuendos? Ridiculous. That was probably my trust issues flaring up. William had been nothing but gentleman-like and appropriate. It was just me reading into his comments way too much.

Even the nightmares last night about the Native Americans in the backyard fell into perspective. Did I need to be so dramatic? It was surely all tied to the research I'd been doing for the Antique Murder Mysteries. It meant I was writing a great book if it was seeping into my subconscious.

After finishing my bath, I tucked myself in and read a few pages of *Devil in a White City*. Unable to keep my eyes open, I regretfully closed the book and turned in for the night. If I had the energy, I could have stayed up all night reading, but my fatigue took over.

Sometime after I shut my eyes, I was awoken to the sound of someone moving around downstairs. I heard the sound of the coffee table scratching across the hardwood floor in the family room. I knew that irritating sound well. It was familiar to me because I'd caused it when I knocked into it during the storm. It took me awhile to figure out what I was hearing because I'd fallen into such a deep sleep and thought I was dreaming.

Just as I was starting to put it all together, the sound of footsteps racing up the stairs registered with me. Heavy footsteps.

Chapter 22

Before I could move out of bed, a large, dark figure loomed in the bedroom doorway. It hesitated only a second then moved toward the bed before I could scream.

"Surprise," I heard a familiar voice whisper. Suddenly, Jack's intoxicating smell was all around me as he pulled me into an embrace.

"Jack, you scared me half to death," I said, clutching onto him and pulling him close.

"I'm sorry, babe. It was supposed to be a surprise."

Without turning on a light, his lips found mine. "I brought these for you."

"Flowers?" I guessed, smelling the fragrant bouquet he held near my face.

"Wait," he warned as I reached for them.

"They're roses. Be careful of the thorns. In fact, why don't I just set these down for now," he said, placing them on the night stand next to the bed. "So far, this is not going exactly as I had planned in my head," he laughed. "I've scared you half to death and then nearly punctured your hand with roses."

Jack crawled back toward me on the bed and nuzzled his head into my neck. "Sorry, babe. I just really wanted to see you."

"I'm glad you're here. I'm kind of in shock," I said, responding to his touch. It was still unclear to me if I was awake or dreaming. "How are you here? Don't you have to work?"

I ran my hand up and down his chest to make sure he was real. He responded by reaching down and pulling my knee over his body.

"Forget about work, I missed you," he said, kissing me passionately.

I kissed him back, overwhelmed with relief and passion. The feel of his hands running all over my body confirmed he was very real. This was no dream.

"I missed you, too," I said in between kisses.

"How much?" he asked.

"Too much."

"Show me," he teased.

"I will."

My time with Jack made the thoughts I had about William earlier seem ridiculous and unfounded. Being with him confirmed that this was where my heart and soul wanted to be. Any imaginary sparks with William were just me coming to terms with my decision. There was only one man for me—Jack.

Just before we fell asleep, Jack asked me a question.

"Are you doing okay up here?"

"I'm okay. I'm a little homesick to tell you the truth."

"Really?" Jack asked, snuggling me closer.

"Of course. Even though I've been able to get a lot of writing and research done, I miss my life in Geneva. It's a little spooky up here. There's a different kind of vibe when Adelle and her family are not around. Maybe it has something to do with being so close to the water. Feels like there are spirits floating about; some unsettled souls or something. It's kind of creepy."

"Ooo…" Jack made a ghost-like sound and laughed.

"Shut up," I said, slapping his arm playfully. "I'm serious. There's something other worldly here near the lake."

"Well, then I'm surprised. If you're that spooked up here, what are you doing leaving the door unlocked?"

"What?" I asked, unsure I'd heard him right.

"The door. It was unlocked. How do you think I got in? I don't have a key."

All the peace and tranquility I'd picked up from Jack's presence slipped out of my body in that instant. I was sure I'd locked the doors before going to bed. If the door was open, that meant someone had been in here and, for that matter, could still be.

* * * * *

The next morning, I packed my things up in my car and left with Jack to head back to Geneva. We parted ways when he directed his car east toward the city to head to work, and I continued mine west for his condo in Geneva. After my scare last night, staying with Jack suddenly seemed the better choice. I was a little upset with myself for not choosing that to begin with. It was stupid of me to pass up the opportunity.

What was the big deal? I wanted to be with Jack, I was happy with him, and I loved staying at his place.

After Jack's comment about the door being unlocked, we'd dressed and searched the home, but found no one and nothing suspicious. The door that he had been referring to was actually the back door, leading into the kitchen. When he mentioned the door had been open, I assumed he meant the front, which scared me half to death because I distinctly remembered making sure that one was locked when I returned from Chocolate Café.

When we'd examined the back door, he showed me how the top bolt had not been locked. There was no damage to the door, so I could only assume I had somehow accidentally left it open. After searching through my memory of the night, I could not remember locking it because I never looked at the door when I got home from the café. I had been in and out of it that morning because Nikki and I used it for our beach walk. I thought we'd locked up when we returned, so I hadn't bothered to check it again. The only explanation I could think of was that unbeknownst to me, Nikki snuck out one last time before she left to hose her feet off by the little spout next to the door and didn't lock the door, assuming I would.

Either way, whether it was a goof up on my part, or an actual break-in, I didn't plan on sticking around. My mojo was off in Michigan. I was making stupid choices like not double checking the locks on top of getting bad nightmares. It was time to go home to Geneva.

Jack and I chose not to report anything to the police, because nothing was missing and there was no sign of a break in. I didn't even want to tell Adelle about it because I didn't want to worry her. She loved that house.

When I reached Geneva, I smiled at the familiar site of Jack's condo, thinking of the last time I was here. The whole thing with the wine and the candles. Jack would probably never propose to me again, and I wouldn't blame him. When he did, I had acted like he was offering me poison.

My normal parking spot was open, so I pulled in and grabbed my bags out of the car. Leaves fell to the ground all around me in showers reminding me how quickly fall was passing through. That was how the season was in Geneva. One day there were tons of leaves on all of the trees and then suddenly they were all down. I wished fall would last a little bit longer here in the Midwest. It was such a beautiful time of the year, and the anticipation of the holidays added a current of excitement to the air. It wouldn't be long before the shops on Third Street were glowing with holiday lights and Christmas trees.

Thinking of Third Street made me wonder where Nikki was in the process. Had she signed the lease yet for Bean in Love? She left Michigan so fired up; she probably busted into Tilly's office yesterday and demanded ownership of the old Breakfast Bar.

On my way up to the condo entrance, a cold breeze slapped me in the face. This week had definitely turned colder than what I planned for. I needed to make it back to my apartment to pick up a few more things. I hadn't packed enough warm clothing.

Turning the key into the condo building's front door, I entered the foyer leading to Jack's place. The building's tenants shared a three-story front room made up primarily of a staircase leading up to Jack's place at the very top. The stairs were carpeted a dark khaki over a light, pine wood. As usual, the foyer smelled clean and inviting and was freshly vacuumed.

Because I'd decided to move in, at least on a short term basis, I was suddenly scrutinizing everything more intensely. Nikki had made my stay at Chocolate Love so nice. I liked the smells, the location of the apartment, the people that worked at Chocolate Love, and the guarantee that I would see Nikki every day. There was a big part of me that would miss that if I decided to move in here permanently.

It was silly though to even start thinking about that now. We were really only talking about a couple of days living with Jack. A week at tops. I wanted to soak it in and enjoy my time with him. Last night proved to me that this was where I needed to be.

Upon entering his apartment, I was hit by the scent of Jack's coffee still lingering in the air. He must have made a lot yesterday morning. Perhaps he had wanted extra caffeine to get through the work day and then the drive to come see me.

After dropping my bags on the bench by the front door, I made my way into the kitchen to fire up another pot of coffee. While it brewed, I headed straight for the shower. I was in such a hurry to get out of Michigan this morning, I hadn't bothered to shower at Adelle's. The combination of skipping my morning run and shower and then hitting rush hour traffic had left me feeling grimy and exhausted. All I really wanted to do was crawl into bed and sleep until Jack got home, but that wouldn't do me any good.

After the shower, I dressed in dark jeans and a red, long-sleeved, cotton tee-shirt, blow-dried my hair, and applied a little mascara and bronzer. Pouring my freshly brewed coffee into a to-go cup, I left Jack's apartment to head over to Chocolate Love.

By the time I reached downtown Geneva, Third Street was hopping with the lunch time crowd. I parked my car in my usual spot behind Chocolate Love and made my way inside.

Upon first inspection, it didn't appear as though Nikki was there when I entered the kitchen. Her staff buzzed around as usual preparing various baked goods and chocolates. When I spotted a tray of chocolate covered strawberries, my mouth curled into a huge grin.

"Have one!" Patty said to me, catching me gawking at the delectable treats. "I just made them. Nikki is training me on some of the chocolates."

"Are you sure?" I asked, even though I knew Nikki wouldn't mind. She was always pushing me to take treats from the store.

"You'd actually be doing me a favor. This is the first batch I've made on my own. I want to make sure they taste okay. Hey, what are you doing back here by the way? I thought Nikki said you were going to be out of town for a week?"

"I was supposed to be, but I had a change of plans," I said, not wanting to get into the whole story. "How have things been here?"

"Exciting."

"Really? How?"

"Just the talk of the new store opening. If my husband can't find a job, he said he might see if he can work for Nikki. He was a head chef downtown, but he's not having any luck with his applications right now. Bean in Love is not going to be as fancy as the menus he is used to, but I'm hoping Nikki would consider him while she's kicking things off."

"That's a great idea, Patty. Nikki loves to hire people she knows. I'm sure she'd love the referral. You should talk to her." I snatched two strawberries, popping one in my mouth at a time.

"I will. Just waiting for the right time."

As though she were summoned by our conversation, Nikki came whirling into the room.

"Awesome. Chocolate strawberries. I'm starving!" she said, snatching one. "Did you guys try one? What do you think?" she asked while making her way over to the small make-shift office around the corner from the kitchen.

"Wait a minute. What are you doing here?" she asked, turning back to look at me. Her eyes widened as though it just registered to her that I was here in Geneva instead of in Michigan.

"I decided to come home early after all. Wasn't getting enough work done up there," I lied.

Nikki pointed her finger at me and raised her eyebrow as though willing me to tell her more.

"Did Jack make it?"

I pointed my finger back at her.

"You called him, didn't you?"

My eyes darted to Patty, who watched our interaction closely. I didn't want this conversation gossiped about all over Chocolate Love. "Excuse me, Patty. Those are awesome," I said, pointing to the strawberries.

I made my way over to Nikki and pushed her into the little corner that served as her office. We were only about ten feet away from Patty and there was no door, so privacy was nearly nonexistent.

"I'm going to put these out if they're up to your standards, Nikki," Patty called.

Nikki gave her the thumbs up, and Patty left the kitchen, leaving us alone.

"You called Jack because you thought I was going to a weird place with William, didn't you? You sent him up there? Do you really have that little faith in me?"

Nikki grabbed a file from on top of her desk and motioned for me to follow her out the back door.

"Walk with me. I need to head back to Breakfast Bar. I have a lot of faith in your relationship, that's why I wanted Jack to get his behind up there to show you what you would mess up if you did anything foolish."

"Well, I didn't, and I wouldn't," I said adamantly.

"Okay, good. And for the record, when I called Jack, he was already planning on surprising you."

"What did you tell him?"

"I didn't tell him anything. I didn't have to. He had his bags packed for the overnight and brought them with him to work because, like I said, he planned on going to see you without any prompting from me."

"What reason did you give him for calling?"

"I said you wanted him to know how poor the cell service and Internet was and that's why you weren't calling as much."

While we spoke, we made our way through the side yard of Chocolate Love to the sidewalk on Third Street. Breakfast Bar was only two buildings down, so we were there in no time.

"I'm glad you're back. I didn't like leaving you up there all alone. It's got a different feel when Adelle and the kids are not up there, doesn't it?"

I contemplated telling her about last night's events with the unlocked door. Since I wasn't confident it wasn't my fault, I chose to remain silent. Didn't need any more lectures today. I nodded instead.

"Alright, change of topic. How do you feel about contracts? You review them all the time for your work. Tilly is inside with the rental agreement. I'm about to sign my life away in there. Do you think you could be another set of eyes for me?"

"Sure, but I would recommend getting an attorney instead of me."

"Already done. He said it looks good, but I still want you to look at it."

"What about Bob?" I asked, referring to her husband. "He's on board with all of this?"

"Of course, silly. Bob's dad is inside figuring out the renovations. Who do you think is funding this project?"

I let out a sigh of relief. Knowing Bob's family was going to be involved with Bean in Love made me feel so much better. Not that I didn't trust Nikki's abilities. Just knowing that Bob's parents, who had a successful track record of launching a retail business, would be helping guide the project made me more confident that all would go smoothly. Bob's father was the one that ran Chocolate Love with great success for over twenty years. When he handed it over to Nikki and Bob a few years ago, it experienced a surge of new business thanks to Nikki's efforts, but it wouldn't be where it was today without Bob Sr.

"Mr. Connors is okay with taking this project on?" I asked, referring to the health problems Bob's father had experienced a few years back. His heart attack was the main reason he gave up Chocolate Love. Plus, he had known a good thing when he saw it. He recognized Nikki's enthusiasm for the store and handed it over.

"He's been great. I think this will be a good thing for him. Bob's mom has been worried he's getting bored and feels this will keep him from going into a depression. It's hard to go from running something 24/7 and being busy all the time to nothing."

"I'm sure it is."

"Alright, come on then, let's go sign my life away," Nikki laughed.

Chapter 23

Bob Connors Sr. stood in the front room of the building that was to be the future home of Bean in Love. He was measuring the front windows with a tape measure and taking notes on a small notepad held by a string around his neck.

"Hi, Kelly. What are you doing back in town?" Bob, Nikki's husband, asked. He walked into the front room and handed his dad a drink of water.

"I decided to come back early."

"Good. We're glad you're back. And glad you are here. Another set of eyes always helps."

"Hello, Mr. Connors," I said, addressing Bob's dad.

"Kelly, so good to see you. Heard you gave up your apartment for your sister's family. That's awfully nice of you. Are you here to help us get this bad boy up and running?"

"I hope so. Looks like you've got some big plans?" I said, gesturing to the tape measure in his hand.

"Oh, we've got plans alright. I'm just happy to be back in the game. Nikki is the mastermind behind all of this. I'm here to follow orders."

This was exactly how I remembered Mr. Connors from when we were kids. Always very humble. Always ready to support others.

The sound of shoes clicking over the hard wood floor pulled my attention toward the main room. The real estate agent, Tilly Dissert, walked into the room with a gigantic smile spread across her face. She must have come in from the back door.

"Hi, everyone. Hi, Kelly, didn't expect to see you here as well. How are you?" she asked.

"Good, thanks."

"Great to see you again. Nikki, I have the paperwork for you. Is this a good time?"

"Actually, Tilly, I was hoping my sister could take a quick look at it this afternoon."

The smile on Tilly's face dimmed noticeably. It made me think she had a bottle of champagne chilling back at the office, assuming she would close the deal today.

"Of course," she said, recovering her smile. "Can we sit down for a second? I want to run over a couple of changes in the contract past you."

"Why don't we head in this side room? We can sit there and take a look at it."

Nikki and Tilly disappeared into the room off of the main room, which Nikki had mentioned would eventually be the home of the future kitchen.

"Now I remember where I've seen her before. She went to your high school, right, Kelly?"

"Apparently. I don't remember her. She was a few years older than me, and she graduated before Nikki went there."

"She was in the same class as Bob's older sister, Pat. Gave my daughter some trouble from what I can recall. Something about them both wanting to be the captain of the cheerleading squad. Tilly was a competitive one, all right. Probably makes her really good at her job now though. Oh well, that was a long time ago," Bob Sr. said, bending his head so he could peek into the side room.

"How do you remember all of those details, Dad?" Bob asked.

"When it comes to my children, I remember everything. Especially who messed with them," he smiled, knocking Bob on the shoulder in an affectionate punch. "You were my life. Still are."

Bob knocked him back with a light punch on his shoulder. Bob Sr. made a show of faking like he was having chest pains and then laughed when Bob's eyes widened.

"Gotcha," Bob Sr. said.

"That's not funny, Dad," Bob said disapprovingly. "You sure you're up for this?"

"Don't start that nonsense. Doctor approved it and everything. And your mother says I need to get out of the house. She's right. I'm going nuts. It's hard to go from working sixty hours a week to nothing. There's only so much television a man can watch. Besides, I'm in good with the boss. She'll go easy on me if I need to leave early."

"That's not true. She'll work you to the bone. You're going to wish you never said yes to this whole thing," Nikki said, walking back into the room. In her right hand, she held a thick file. Tilly called goodbye to us and left by the backdoor.

"And you better watch it too, Missy. That's my grandson you're carrying. I'll be sending you home."

"Nonsense. I'll have this kid scooping ice cream and serving coffee before he turns two. He's going to have to earn his keep."

Everyone laughed at Nikki's joke, then father and son turned back to whatever project they were working on before we stepped out. When they started speaking renovations, it all became a foreign language to me. From what I could tell, it sounded like they were considering possibly knocking down a wall. All the "do it yourself" handy work was way beyond my scope of understanding.

"Do you have some time now to look at these?"

The last thing I felt like doing was reading technical fine print of contracts.

I hadn't slept much last night with my late night visitor. And this morning, I was up and out the door early for the commute back to Geneva.

"I'll tell you what," Nikki said. "How about a quick two mile run to work out the crazies and then we can clean up and review these over a latte at Chocolate Love?"

"Now you're talking. I'm going over to Adelle's, I mean my place, I mean the apartment, to pick up some clothes then head back to Jack's to change. How about we meet for the run in a half hour in front of Chocolate Love?"

"Deal."

We walked back to Chocolate Love together then went our separate ways, Nikki into the kitchen, and I up the stairs to the apartment. I knocked hesitantly on the door, wishing I would have called first. If anyone was napping, I didn't want to disturb them. When no one answered, I turned to leave. It didn't feel right to just go in. But then I thought about my upcoming run with Nikki. It wouldn't be enjoyable unless I grabbed more layers.

As much as I needed my stuff, it felt wrong to just let myself in. I'd agreed to turn over the apartment for the week. Technically, it wasn't mine right now, and I didn't want to violate anyone's trust or privacy.

I whipped my cell phone out of my pocket and dialed Adelle's number. She answered on the first ring.

"Kelly?"

"Hi, Adelle."

"Is everything okay?"

It was then that I remembered I had not told her anything about Michigan. I never even contacted her to let her know I had arrived, let alone left.

"Everything's fine."

"I just got this weird feeling when I saw your number. It's good to hear your voice. We didn't hear from you, but I know the reception is touch and go up there. You're welcome to use my house phone if you like. How is the beach?"

"Actually, I'm back home in Geneva now."

"What? Why?"

"I…"

I stuttered, trying to come up with an answer. How did I communicate "your house creeped me out" without saying it?

"Kelly, are you okay?" Adelle asked, sounding frightened.

"I'm fine, Adelle. Completely fine. I just wanted to come back home. I missed Jack."

"Oh. That's great, Kelly. I'm relieved. Glad you're back in town. Jeez. For a second, I thought you were going to tell me something else."

"Like what?"

"No, it's nothing. I just can't take anymore scares right now. My mind is so maxed out with everything going on. I've just had trouble sleeping because of worrying about everything. I've got the creeps."

You too? I thought.

"Is everything okay with the contracts for the house?"

"Actually, that part is going great. This will sound funny, Kelly, but now that we are out, I'm relieved. It feels like a huge weight has been lifted off of us. I couldn't see how much the house debt was strangling us until I got away from it. Mike is like a new person. And the rental home will be much more affordable for us. By the way, it will be ready by Monday. Is it okay to wait that long?"

"Of course. That's fine. I'm so happy everything is working out. Hey, where are you right now?"

"I'm picking up a few groceries and then we're off to a playdate."

Darn. I was really hoping she was on her way home.

"Where are you?"

"I'm actually right outside the apartment door. I need to pick up a few things but feel funny about going in without you here."

"Don't be silly, Kelly. Go ahead and go. I won't be back until at least three. You don't want to wait around that long. Go ahead and go in."

"Are you sure?"

"Yes, I'm sure. It's still your apartment."

"Okay. I'm just going to run in and grab more clothes. I didn't pack warm enough for the weather change."

"We're dealing with the same thing. There's been a cold snap. I should have kept some of the kids' winter clothes from being packed away. Thank God we're getting this housing thing figured out before the winter. What if we would have been doing all of this in a snowstorm? What a nightmare that would have been."

"Alright, I'll talk to you later. Just going to run in and grab my stuff and then meet Nikki for a run."

"Okay, Kelly, I'll talk to you later."

I hit End Call on my phone then turned my key in the lock and headed into my apartment. As expected, Adelle had the place in tip top shape despite the fact that five people now lived in this tiny space. She'd rearranged the furniture in the front room to fit two small twin beds at the far end of the room for Frank and Cindy. A small Japanese screen separated the beds from the couches to create some privacy for her two eldest children. It also allowed the entertainment section of the front room to remain intact, so the family could still watch television together.

In my bedroom, she'd removed my comforter from the bed and placed her own there for her and Mike. A small toddler bed was tucked at the foot of the bed for her youngest son, Craig. Although there were only a few small changes made to the room, it looked completely different. Despite the fact that I was standing in my own bedroom, it felt like I was invading Adelle and Mike's privacy. I made my way quickly over to the closet, determined to pick out my stuff and get on with my day.

Adelle and Mike's clothing hung at the front of the closet, as I intended for them. Luckily, there was a second bar behind the front one where I stashed all of my clothing. Due to the fact that I worked from home and didn't need a lot of clothes, I'd been able to squish everything on the second bar and even leave some extra space there for Mike and Adelle, which I noticed she was utilizing.

I pushed Adelle's clothes to the side and pulled out a few of my things. At the very end of the bar was the warmest jacket I owned. It was a long, puffy, white down jacket I'd bought in Chicago more than ten years ago. It had traveled with me to California and then back home after my divorce. After contemplating for a second, I pulled it out and examined it closely. My mom and I bought this coat together eons ago at an Eddie Bauer end-of-the-season sale. Since I'd moved to California shortly after I bought it, it had almost never been worn. The only time I'd worn it was when I came back to Chicago for trips home to see my family during the winter months. Now it would become a staple in my wardrobe.

I sighed, thinking of the upcoming winter months. When Steve and I moved to California, I thought I had escaped Chicago winters once and for all. Now, here I was again, facing another cold winter. Oh, well. At least I had Jack to keep me warm. And possibly this coat if it still fit.

I slipped my arms into the jacket and zipped it all the way up. The coat hit me just under my knees and had a slight nip at the waist. Still fit. Should I bring it to Jack's? That seemed silly since it was only October and hovering somewhere between forty and sixty degrees this week. Some afternoons had reached up near the seventies.

While deciding what I should do with the coat, I reached my hands into the pockets. My hand closed around a cold metal object in the pocket on my right side. I pulled it out to examine it. It was a key of some sort. At first my stomach dropped, thinking somehow the key to my place in California had followed me to Geneva. But upon further inspection, I noted it was much too small to be that key. It was smaller than a key normally used to unlock a door, but had weight to it, like for a lock box, jewelry box, or maybe some kind of safe.

Puzzled, I slipped the key back into the coat and hung it up in the closet. It had to have something to do with my old life in California, because I'd not touched the coat since the move. As usual, just when I thought I'd closed a door to my past, there was always something sneaking up to pull me back in. Would I never be able to outrun the skeletons in my closet?

A chill ran up the back of my neck, forcing me to freeze in the moment and think more on what I had just discovered. Something in me was telling me to stop and take this in better. That key. What could it possibly be? We hadn't had a safe in our home. Or had I not known about it? That wouldn't surprise me. Who knew what Steve had hidden from me? And if there was a safe, I didn't want to know what was in it. But why was the key in my coat pocket? And my God, because I had the key, did it mean that whatever was in a safe years ago was still there? I didn't want to think about this right now. I needed to meet Nikki.

After I put the coat back, I pulled out what I needed and closed my closet door, leaning my back against it. Now I wished I'd never opened it. My mind raced as I looked up toward the ceiling.

"Please God, just let me forget about that key. Let's just pretend I never saw it," I said aloud. I scrunched my eyes closed, bracing for the flashbacks to hit me.

Nothing.

I truly had no memory of that key or what it was for. The image of Steve's face leering at me from his prison cell flooded my mind.

"Is it yours? What is it for?" I asked him in my mind.

"In time," he sneered, *laughing at me.*

My eyes flew open, searching the room for something…anything…to bring me back to reality. Sweat was beginning to form along my brow and I could feel my hands getting clammy. If only I hadn't reached into that pocket.

"Come back," I said aloud. "Back."

"Wait a second. Pocket," I whispered to myself, coming out of my crazy thoughts.

I turned around, opened the closet door and reached to the back of the closet, trying to find the sweatshirt I had on last Thursday morning. It was still in the laundry basket I kept tucked back there. Sure enough, in the pocket of that sweatshirt I found the gold backing I was looking for.

I held it up to my eye to look for any distinguishing features. Due to its shine, it looked newly made. No scratching or dulling of the gold. I popped it in my jeans pocket and got ready to leave. I couldn't really think of a reason why this pin backing should be important, but I was learning to never disregard a coincidence. The fact that I found it on the day Brian died might be inconsequential, but something was telling me not to ignore it. Anything could be a clue to figuring out the mysterious circumstances surrounding Brian's death.

Chapter 24

On Friday morning, I got a call bright and early on my cell phone. Because Jack was just about to head out the door for work, I let it to go to voicemail. It wasn't a number that I recognized. Slipping my cell phone in the pocket of my robe, I walked with Jack to the front door.

"So, I'll be home around six and then I have to take Mom over to her poker game. Are you still planning on seeing William for dinner tonight?"

"I think so."

"I wish I could go with you. Mom has had this on the calendar for weeks. It's so good for her to socialize with friends. She's becoming more and more isolated." Jack frowned, displaying the worry he must have been harboring for his mom.

Her poker game was at a friend's house about an hour away from Geneva. It wouldn't make sense for him to drive her there and then circle back to Geneva for dinner, only to turn around and pick her up.

"I know it's important to her. You can meet William another time."

Jack leaned in and pulled my face closer to his with both hands. I inhaled his fresh shower smell, wishing we could both take the day off from work. Things had been good for us over the past couple of days. Really good. I was enjoying playing house with Jack. Being here for an extended amount of time was making me appreciate the little things I missed when I wasn't here. Seeing him unwind after work, watching him get ready in the morning, doing laundry together. All of the domestic minutiae we didn't experience when we were living under two different roofs. In a way, it was romantic to live apart because it maintained an air of mystery for each other. We got to pick each other up to go on dates, etcetera. But, we were missing out on the bond couples formed when they made a commitment to live together, take care of each other, and be each other's spouse.

I wanted to be the one making Jack's coffee in the morning, cleaning his clothes, preparing his dinner. I wanted him to feel taken care of by me and vice versa.

"Do I need to be jealous?"

I leaned in close and lightly touched his lips with mine.

"I hope you will always feel a sense of possession when it comes to me."

Jack leaned his body even closer. "I thought I made it clear that I would like to possess you. Forever. You refused."

"I refused?" I giggled.

"Mmmhmm," Jack said, leaning in and kissing me. I pulled lightly on his tie, careful not to mess up his attire.

"I merely asked for a delay. I'm definitely warming to the idea," I said, stepping back a bit to stare into his smiling green eyes.

"Yeah, well, don't take too long to warm up."

"Why, are you cooling to the idea?"

"Winter is coming, baby," he joked, pulling me back to him.

He was clearly joking, but nevertheless, a chill ran down my spine. I needed to let him know my decision—and soon.

"What time will you be home tonight?" he asked, pulling away and picking up his briefcase. I knew he needed to go now or he would miss his train.

"I won't be late. Nikki and I will try to meet up with William early. She's having trouble staying up past seven anyways."

"Okay, I'll be home by ten. If you're still up, we can watch a movie."

"That sounds great."

"Okay, babe, be good," he said, planting one last kiss on my lips then turning to head out the door.

I stood for a couple of minutes staring at the closed door. My cell phone rang again in the pocket of my pink flannel robe.

I let out a sigh and reached in to grab it, wishing I could have another cup of Jack's coffee before dealing with my early morning caller. The area code struck me as being a familiar one, but I couldn't pinpoint why exactly. Then it hit me, this was coming from California.

Steve? Could he be calling me from jail in California? No way. He didn't know this number, nor was he supposed to be able to contact me.

"Hello?"

"Kelly? It's William. How are you?"

Considering what I was expecting, the sound of his voice was a great relief. Of course it was William. I should have known better. He was probably calling to firm up tonight's plans.

"Oh, William. Hi."

"I'm sorry. Am I calling too early? You sound like you were expecting someone else."

You have no idea, I thought. "I was, kind of."

"Do you want to call me back?"

"No, not at all. Sorry. I'm just…scrambled. Scrambling…"

"Scrambling eggs?" William asked, sounding confused.

"No, I'm just… Um, well. I thought you were my ex-husband calling after I saw the area code," I finally said. He didn't need to know this much detail, but I felt the need to justify my inability to form a complete sentence. "You just got me flustered for a minute."

There was a silence on the other end, and for a second, I assumed the call dropped or he hung up.

"My apologies. That must have been a shock. I'm calling way too early. It was inappropriate of me."

"No, you don't need to apologize. It's fine. I'm up early everyday anyway. Let me just grab a cup of coffee, so I don't sound like a complete idiot."

"I'm getting coffee, too. I got up early this morning and started the drive to Geneva."

William didn't ask me how or why I would expect Steve to be calling, which I appreciated. I was glad he didn't because the last thing I felt like doing was explaining any of my neurotic thoughts this morning.

"How did everything go back home?"

In the kitchen, I opened the cabinet above the coffee maker and reached for my favorite mug. There was only enough left in the pot to fill up my cup halfway. If I was going to be able to get myself going this morning, I would need more than that.

Normally, while I went out for my morning run, Jack woke up and drank the coffee I made before heading out. There was always plenty left over for me by the time he was off to work. That meant he must have had a lot more on his mind than he usually did.

"To be frank, it was awful," William said. He let out a long breath, then continued. "Mom and Dad are a wreck, and the rest of the family has put a ton of pressure on me to figure out what happened. No one believes Brian committed suicide. You should hear some of the theories they've come up with Kelly. Really out there. My dad even asked me if Brian could have been killed by autoerotic strangulation."

"What? Where would they come up with that? That is really out of left field."

"I have no idea. Probably the Internet. They're desperate. They're reaching for anything. Brian wasn't a freak. I don't even want to think about where my dad got that idea. They're all so shaken up. And now, so am I. I was handling everything so much better when I saw you in Michigan. Seeing Brian made it all so…"

I waited for William to continue.

"Real," he finally said after a pause.

"I'm sorry."

"My poor parents. They are devastated. Kelly…" He stopped before finishing his thought, and the line on his end was silent for a long time.

"Hello? Are you still there?"

"I'm here. I was going to beg you again to help me figure out what really happened, but I don't want to put more pressure on you. There's got to be something that will tell me the real story. Or hell, just more of an explanation. If I have to accept that my brother committed suicide, I will. I'll be in therapy for the rest of my life, but will work through it. Right now though, I won't. Something else happened there."

"Can you hold on for one second?" he asked.

"Sure."

I heard him order coffee and a scone. Clearly he was at some kind of drive through because I could hear the wind blowing and birds chirping in the background.

"It's cold this morning," he commented when he came back on the line.

"It is."

"Kelly, one more thing. I want to give you fair warning. My mom may have gotten your phone number from my cell phone. She asked if she could contact you or Nikki. I asked her not to, so you would not feel bombarded. But last night, I caught her scrolling through my phone contacts. You don't know my mom. She can be very determined. Especially when it comes to her kids."

"My mom is the same way. It's no problem."

"She wanted to come on this trip with me, but she would have trouble keeping up. She was older when she had us, and her health is not the best. Anyway, she might call you. I hope she lets me take care of this, but I'm not sure she will. I wanted you to be prepared."

"Okay, thanks." Perhaps she was my early morning call before Jack left. Whoever it was had left a message, so I could check after I got off the phone with William.

"So, here's my plan. I reserved a room at The Herrington Inn in Geneva. Are you familiar with that hotel? Is it nice?"

I heard skepticism in his voice and tried to reassure him. "Oh, yes. It's very nice. You'll love it."

"I understand it has a restaurant attached to it, Atwater?"

"Yes, that's right."

"Have you ever eaten there?"

"I have not, but my sisters and I have gone to the spa connected with The Herrington, which is wonderful."

"Would you like to have dinner there, or do you have another recommendation?"

"The Herrington will be great."

"It will take me the rest of the day to get to Geneva. Why don't we plan to meet there around six? If traffic is fair, I should make it to Geneva just in time for dinner. Does that work for you?"

"Yep, I'll be there."

"Will you call Nikki and let her know? Please invite Jack as well. I would love to meet him."

When he said Jack's name, it caught me off guard. I tried to recall if I had ever given William the name of my boyfriend. I didn't remember doing it. In fact, I distinctly remembered feeling guilty that Jack's name was absent from our last discussion.

"He would love to meet you as well, but unfortunately, he has a prior engagement, so he's not going to be able to make it. Nikki and I will definitely be there though."

"Great. I'll let you go. I'm cutting into your writing time. Isn't the morning your best time?"

"Uh, it is." Again, I didn't remember giving him that detail. We never talked about my writing habits. Maybe it was mentioned somewhere about me on my website or an article on my series. I had the distinct feeling he had done his research on me.

"Okay, six o'clock then at The Herrington Inn. I'll meet you in Atwater, reservation for three. Four if Nikki would like to bring her husband."

"I know Bob can't make it, so it will just be us three. See you then. Safe travels."

"Bye, Kelly."

After hanging up, I grabbed my cup of coffee and headed into the temporary office I'd set up in Jack's third bedroom. The desk he had for me in here was actually more comfortable than the one in my own apartment. The modern, large, glass tabletop allowed me to spread out better while working. Pulling up my website, I scrolled around a bit, and sure enough, there was a little blip about my theories on how to write a good story. In it, I mentioned what time of day was best for my writing and all of the tactics I used to keep myself motivated.

I googled myself, something I was scared of doing, and was pleasantly surprised when the articles about my writing came up before the articles about my connection to an attempted murder in California. Clicking around, I found pictures of me at book signings and other events related to my literary work. In one picture, the caption named Jack as my significant other and showed us at a black tie event for a book release party of a well-known author. It was a little spooky being able to find all of this information about me, but I'd gotten used to the media invading my life.

Shutting down the websites, I decided it best to stay clear of these. I didn't want to know what was written about me out there. I knew who I was. That was all that mattered.

And now William seemed to know a lot more about who I was, too.

Gathering knowledge about the people he was working with was probably second nature for him and what he needed to do in his business. Rule number one, know your clients.

But I was no client. Didn't he trust me? He must, if he wanted to work with me so closely on something as important as the death of his brother.

The next thing I searched for was autoerotic suicides. The main thing that popped up was autoerotic asphyxiation. I'd been too embarrassed to tell William I was only slightly knowledgeable about what he was talking about when he brought it up on the phone. From the tone of his voice though, I knew it was something he was ill at ease to talk about. The image that came up showed a picture of a man hanging from a doorknob dressed in women's clothing, his neck looped into some kind of rope.

"Oh my God," I said out loud.

I forced myself to read the rest of the description. According to the site, the act was normally practiced by young males who tended to be thrill seekers looking for a sexual adventure of some sort. In the case study I read, the victim was a twenty-one year old heterosexual man who was in a relationship with a woman at the time he was found dead. His grandmother had been the one to find him in the upstairs bedroom of her home. The case study read that apparently police figured out he had watched an erotic asphyxiation movie the night before and decided to experiment, killing himself accidentally in the process.

Scrolling down to the bottom summation paragraph, the author described how all findings indicated that the act was set up to stimulate the subject, but not necessarily kill them. If the subject was found dead, the police usually labeled it an accidental death rather than a suicide.

Why in the world would Brian's dad have brought this up? Did he know something we didn't about Brian's sexual orientation? Hell, this was not what I thought we would find out in the investigation of his death. It could only taint Brian's reputation even more. And that was not what his family needed.

But Brian had not been found hanging, so this theory wouldn't make sense. He'd looked peaceful and fully dressed in his own clothes from what I could tell. Plus, the thought of Brian in any type of sexual act was off the wall to me. Brian was not someone I would think of as being into erotic acts. Sure, he was quirky and obsessive and even a little bit socially awkward. Who wasn't? Everyone fell somewhere in the spectrum of social awkwardness. He had definitely been further out there than most, but not enough to do something like this. Especially with the mental state he was in—stressed and anxious.

Someone who did this had to be adventurous and a thrill seeker as the article described. Brian was a thrill seeker only to the degree in that he loved to push himself to learn more and more about the past and make his lectures exciting, but auto-eroticism? That just didn't fit the type of thrill he was into.

But then again, who knew what went on behind closed doors? One thing that no one ever questioned was Brian's private life. We all assumed he didn't have one. There was never any mention of a girlfriend. He wasn't a partner kind of guy. More of a loner. Almost like an asexual being that didn't need a mate. He had been too wrapped up in his stories and explorations of the past to seem to want a living partner in the present.

Was it possible, though? Could it be that Brian had no one special in his life? Or, had he been hiding someone?

I thought back to my ex-husband, Steve, and the women he'd been hiding from me. A part of me would always think that not only did a man need a mate; he might need multiple mates, like my ex thought he did. In recent months, I'd found out he was actually triple-timing me while we were married. I'd prepared myself for even more women to crawl out of the woodwork.

Could we all be missing something with Brian? I sat further back in my chair and looked up at the ceiling, lost in thought. In all of the crime books I'd read over the years in order to prep myself for writing my mystery series, a famous saying that came up frequently was *cherche la femme,* meaning, look for the woman. In most cases of murder, the crime was linked to passion gone wrong.

I remembered a few years back, I'd done a ride-along with a police officer while doing research for my first book. I got to follow him on a shift, observing how the dispatcher operated, and the way a team responded to a call. During that ride, I took the opportunity to pick his brain. He was an eighteen-year veteran and had spent nine of those years in investigations, which included homicides.

When I asked him what the biggest motivator for murder was, he replied in very simple terms, 'Love and greed.'

Love and greed. Could it be that simple in this story as well? I didn't think so, but still, it was worth contemplating. If this really wasn't a suicide, how did love and greed fit in to this equation? What or who did Brian love? As far as I could tell, his only passion was his work. The History Museum was his mistress, his partner. The thing he poured all of his time and energy into.

Greed. That was tough. To me, there hadn't appeared to be a greedy bone in Brian's body. The salary he made from the History Museum couldn't have been anything big. He'd lived a very modest lifestyle from what I could tell. Was there some kind of addiction or extravagant hobby Brian needed money for? For all intents and purposes, to me it seemed as if Brian did not chase money. In fact, he appeared to run the other way.

So, in simple terms, ruling out love, if there were two players in a murder, a victim and a perpetrator, who was the greedy one? Not Brian as far as I could tell. Then, what had been in Brian's possession that someone had killed for?

If I could figure that out, the real story would fall into place. But who was going to be able to tell me that story? There weren't a lot of players in Brian's life because he was such a loner. Who could take me into the depths of Brian's inner workings? William?

I got the feeling that the two brothers, although genetically identical, were driven by very different personalities and goals in life. With that in mind, would Brian have used William as a true confidant if he felt so different from him? If not, who would it have been? Everyone needed someone to talk to.

Because I'd been staring off in the distance for so long trying to organize my thoughts, my screensaver kicked in, revealing a picture of Nikki and me standing in front of the shark tank at The Shedd Aquarium in downtown Chicago. We'd taken Adelle's kids for the day last summer right before they were about to start school as an end-of-summer shindig.

Nikki and I both had our hands up in mock fins over our heads and were pretending to chase Craig and Cindy, like we were sharks ourselves. Nikki's eyes were closed and her lips puckered into a fish face. My eyes were wide and my mouth was stretched open as far as it could go. I remembered thinking sharks didn't actually scream but doing it to make the kids laugh.

I inched my face closer to the screen to get a better look at Nikki and the sharks swimming behind her in the tank.

"Nikki," I said, shaking my head. "What do you know?"

Chapter 25

After a quick shower, I hunkered down and spent the next few hours writing. It felt good to distract myself with something other than Brian's death. With William coming into town, I knew I would be busy with the amateur investigation we were about to conduct.

Around eleven o'clock, my stomach growled. Throwing together a couple of sandwiches, I decided to hunt down Nikki. We lunched together most days and shared a morning coffee break mid-morning. We'd been missing these pow-wows lately because I'd been out of town or away from the store at Jack's.

While packing up my backpack, it hit me that I'd never listened to the voice mail from this morning. I hunted down my cell phone in the office next to the computer. Normally while writing, I silenced my phone to keep from being distracted. Sure enough, there was a text message from Nikki asking if I was coming for lunch, and the voice mail from earlier remained, waiting to be heard.

I shot Nikki a text telling her I was on my way with sandwiches and then listened to the message. As William predicted, his mom had left a message asking me to call her back. Her voice sounded weak and shaky, as though she was having a hard time annunciating her words.

"Kelly Clark, this is Brian's mother, Delores Sanders. I was hoping you would give me a call back when you get a chance. Billy just left this morning. He's on his way to see you and your sister, Nikki."

I smiled at the mention of William's nickname, Billy. Just by the way she spoke his name so tenderly, I could tell in an instant that this was a mother that loved her children. A pit began to form in my stomach as it sunk in what I was about to get involved in. This woman was obviously deep in the depths of grief for a son she loved dearly.

"Kelly, please call me. I hope to speak to you before you see Brian...I mean Billy tonight."

A silence followed, leading me to believe she'd ended the call, but the sound of background noise kept me from disconnecting in case there was more. Just before hanging up, I heard her voice start up again.

"Kelly, I really need to talk to you. Please. Okay, I...goodbye."

The goodbye was so awkward, my eyes filled with tears. My mind imagined her working up the courage to find my phone number in William's phone and then calling me. Wherever I was before this message, I'd now crossed a line.

"Hello?" A man's voice answered after one ring when I called back.

"Is it her? Charlie, give me the phone," I heard a woman call out weakly in the background.

"Delores, let me talk. She might not be able to understand you," the man responded back, not in an unkind way. I assumed this to be William and Brian's father.

"No, I want to talk to her. I can do it better."

The phone jumbled around a bit, and I could hear them arguing. Although they whispered, they must not have realized how close the mouthpiece was because I heard every word. According to my screen, fifty-three seconds had passed since I'd made the call, and I'd yet to really talk to anyone.

The anxiety I sensed in the Sanders' home made me think back to the first couple of days after Steve was arrested and taken to jail. My entire family had come to stay with me in my home in California. Although they were trying to help, everyone was on their own personal mission to figure out why and how it had happened to me. They were there to help with the media, the food, the cleaning, and the general upkeep of a crisis.

I remembered at one point having a break-down and screaming at my mom for deciding to rearrange my closets while she was there. It was her way of trying to help, and at the same time manage her own stress level. Her actions had sent me over the edge. At my low, I'd screamed, "Throw it out! Throw it all out! Throw it on the reporters!" Afterwards, we'd been able to laugh at my reaction, but I'll never forget how scared my mom had looked at my outburst. I'd lost my mind.

Finally, Delores came on the line taking my thoughts back to the here and now.

"Ms. Clark?"

"Yes. Hello, Mrs. Sanders. This is Kelly. I'm returning your call." I kept my voice light and friendly, hoping it would bring her anxiety level down.

"Do you have a moment to talk about my son's death? I understand you were the one to find Billy, I mean Brian, last Friday morning?"

"Yes, that is true Mrs. Sanders. And please, call me Kelly."

The sounds on the other end made me think she was reading from a piece of paper. Not a bad idea considering how nervous she sounded. I'd been standing while waiting for her to come on the line and chose this moment to take a seat at my desk.

"Kelly, can you describe what you saw when you entered the building?" Her voice shook and slurred, almost as though she'd had a few too many drinks, which I wouldn't fault her for.

"Mrs. Sanders, are you sure you want to hear this?" I did my best not to come off condescending but felt like I failed miserably. The questions she was asking sounded like she'd pulled them right out of a book on police investigation, not a mother trying to find out what happened to her son. The last thing I wanted to do right now was describe in gory detail how I'd found her son's body. Especially with the state she was in.

I was shocked when I heard her swear quietly. After some time passed, another voice came on the phone.

"Kelly, this is Patrick Sanders, William and Brian's father. My wife just needs a minute. It's been a tough couple of days here."

"I can imagine, Mr. Sanders. I didn't mean to be dismissive of her question. It's hard to go into this."

"We know, Kelly. The police have already shared it with us. And William has done his best to tell us what he knows as well. Please, call me Patrick. You have to understand, Kelly, we're just trying to get to the bottom of what happened. I'm sure William has told you that we're having a very hard time accepting that Brian took his own life. It doesn't fit. The police have already described the scene for us. We feel the police have to be missing something. That's why my wife is asking."

"I understand, Patrick. Really, I do. It's a lot to take in. William will be here later this afternoon, and we'll look into things. Isn't it still possible though, that this was an accidental overdose? Possibly in response to the stress he was under?"

"No. We don't think so. Not by the amount of sleeping medication that was found in his system."

"Oh."

"According to what they found, they think he took three doses of sleeping pills at once. The new long-lasting ones on the market. It was too much for his system. He would never do that on purpose. We're…puzzled," he said.

"Wow. That is odd. I didn't know it was that much."

"My wife really wanted to come with William to meet you today, but I'm afraid the trip would have been too much for her. That's why she called. She wants to explain some things about Brian, just in case William does not remember to tell you. She'll be embarrassed I brought this up, but I have to explain something. Delores suffered from a stroke a few years ago, so her speech is…" There was a pause before he continued. "I'm just telling her, Delores, so she understands the situation better."

"Anyway, her mind is as sharp as a tack, but when her stress level rises, her speech slurs a bit. There is no one that knew Brian better though. She'll be able to, well, just a sec, here she is."

"Kelly? This is Delores again."

"Hello, Delores. I'm here."

"Can you understand me?" Her frustration was palpable. Jack's mom, Peggy, did not have any lasting effects on her speech from her stroke, but her mobility had forever changed. She did pretty well with it all, but there were times she'd been in tears from not being able to do the simple things that were once easy for her.

"I can understand you just fine. Patrick said you have some things about Brian you want to share. Please, go ahead, I'm ready."

"I've already told the police, but I want to share with you as well. Brian did not do this. He was a good boy. He didn't believe in suicide. All of his life, he struggled with his issues. He was very sens…" She paused.

I could feel her gearing up to try again.

"Always very sensitive and his imagination was beyond control most times. But it wasn't harmful or destructive. He was just a very curious boy."

I allowed her words to sink in. To me, it sounded like what most family members said when a loved one ended their own life. The whole thing was so unbelievable.

"Delores, do you know if Brian was dating anyone? Or if there was anyone special in his life? I'm just wondering if we're all missing something. There has to be an element we're overlooking."

"I don't think so. Pa…Pa…Patrick and I hoped for that, but he did not seem interested in anyone. Ever. He liked to be alone. He dated in college for a semester, but then nothing after that. He just didn't have in…in…interest."

I worried my questions were stressing her out, so I let her take the lead again.

"When Brian was in high school, he tried taking some anti-anxiety medication to help with his social anxiety. He didn't like the way it made him feel. He was embarrassed his friends would find out he was taking it. He stopped after a few months. We were surprised the pills were found in his system."

"What did the police say about that?"

"The police confirmed the prescription with his doctor."

I was having a hard time understanding her because her words were so slurred. Her frustration must have kicked into high gear. She seemed to sense this because once again the phone was jumbled about and suddenly Patrick was back on the line.

"Kelly, we've been thinking. When Brian tried the anti-anxiety medication as a kid, it made him different. The doctor told him to stay on it for a longer period of time, but he refused. I guess there is an acclimation period for those types of drugs you need to undergo before giving up on them. Our new theory is that maybe he was trying them again and it made him make poor choices."

"What do you mean by 'different'? Not suicidal?"

"No, not quite that. Just more paranoid than normal, and drowsy. In high school, one morning we came downstairs and found him asleep at the kitchen table on top of his homework. He was wearing all of his clothes from the day before and even had a half-eaten peanut butter and jelly sandwich in his mouth. It was like he just dropped onto his plate. His mom and I were so worried about the effects we encouraged him to stop. The sleeping pills are baffling to us. Brian never would have mixed sleeping pills with his anti-anxiety medication. He would have known it was too dangerous.

"We knew William would be able to fill you in, but my wife was insistent we talk to you as well."

"I want to help you. Really, I do. I'm just not sure how I can," I said, twirling my fingers in my hair.

What I wanted to tell him was that I didn't know his son that well, and that really, no one in Geneva did. Even Nikki, who was closer to him than I, hadn't known he had a twin brother. That was a pretty big piece of information to not know about someone. But, why put this couple through more pain? If their son had social issues growing up, they probably had an idea what his social status was here in Geneva. As off as he was, Brian had done a really good job managing his anxieties and finding a job that allowed him to work in an area he had a passion for. When he was giving his lectures and tours about the local history of the area, I'd never sensed anxiety. Over the top enthusiasm maybe, but not social anxiety or fear.

Brian had changed in the last couple of weeks. Even I, who didn't know him well, had picked up on that. He'd always been eccentric, but it was only in these past few weeks that he became anxious again. So what changed? Why the need for medication? The only thing I could think of was that stupid ghost he kept talking about.

"Kelly, we knew our son. He was different. He lived in the shadow of his twin brother, William, who is wonderful, but has always been successful in everything he does. Moving to Geneva was really good for Brian. It gave him his own spotlight. He seemed to have finally found his niche. There was no reason for him to overdose.

"Now, I understand you did not know Brian well and you don't feel qualified to take this on. But, from what we've learned about you and your sister from William, you two have a knack for this kind of thing. Please, will you help us? Help us get answers about our son. We don't want him to die in vain. We just want to find some peace."

Delores must have begun crying in the background, because I heard Patrick offering her quiet words of comfort while he waited for my answer.

I thought of my own mother and her reaction in California after Steve was arrested. After her cleaning and organizing frenzy, she'd finally come down from her roller coaster ride of grief and crashed right before my eyes. I'd found her one night in my living room at three in the morning. I could still see the mug of tea in her hand shaking while she sobbed uncontrollably and scratched at her eyes with a tissue. The only words I'd been able to make out in between her sobs were "Not this." I assumed she was trying to say something along the lines of, I wanted so much for you, Kelly, not this.

"I will do my best, Patrick. Nikki and I want to help you. We'll figure this out," I said, making a promise I wasn't sure I could keep.

"Let me ask you something," I said. "Did Brian ever talk to you about the ghost of Victoria Jacobs?"

* * * * *

After hanging up with the Sanders, I went over to Bean in Love to meet up with Nikki. The front door was open, so I walked in and found her about to send a sledge hammer through one of the walls. It crashed through, filling the room with a loud shudder.

"Whoa! Are you sure it's alright for you to be doing that in the condition you are in?" I said, holding out my arms toward her weapon of destruction.

Nikki grunted and pulled the sledgehammer out from the now battered wall.

"I'm fine. It's not like I'm eight months along. We're knocking this wall out to put a glass display cabinet here. It will really open up this porch and allow my customers to view the merchandise from multiple angles. How are you? You look like you've just seen a ghost. Want some coffee?"

"I would love some coffee. But Nikki, seriously, should you be doing that?"

"Here, sit down. I'm fine, really. I feel great."

Nikki led me into the main room where two men were prepping the walls for painting.

"Good morning, Kelly," I heard a male voice call out from somewhere behind me. When I glanced in the direction of the voice, I saw a rear-end sticking out of the doorway of the future Bean in Love kitchen.

"Busy day here," Bob Sr. said, turning and waving at me. "I was just going to take a quick break and grab a coffee. Let me get you ladies one as well."

"Wow, you really don't waste any time. How did you get approval to do all of this work so quickly?"

"It was written into the contract for the lease. He was even able to expedite the construction permit. Frankly, I think he's thrilled we're doing these updates. I'm sure he's happy to finally be paid rent. A part of me thinks he secretly hopes to re-open his beloved Breakfast Bar at the end of our lease."

"How long is it?"

"We signed a two-year contract with him. Which means the clock is ticking. We have to get the renovations going and start making sales."

"What's your goal?" I was curious. Nikki hadn't told me.

"Open in three weeks."

"Three weeks! Nikki, that's so fast. Are you sure you want to put all that pressure on yourself?" I asked.

"Nikki is her name, pressure is her game," Bob Sr. said. "Let me grab that coffee."

"Is this the same guy that owns the building of Hot Yoga, by chance?" I asked Nikki when Bob Sr. had left the room.

"What? No. I've heard of that guy though. He owns a few of the rentals in town. He's a real jerk. I wouldn't sign with him if my life depended on it."

I should have known Nikki would have done her research.

Bob Sr. walked back into the main room with two cups of coffee. He placed them down on the folding table Nikki had set-up next to the brick fireplace. A piece of old paint one of the workers scrapped off fell into one of the cups as soon as Bob Sr. set it down.

"Perhaps we should take our lunch outside?" Nikki suggested.

"Go take a break. In fact, why don't you take your sandwiches on the road? Go for a walk or something. You've been working all morning, Nikki. And no more sledgehammers for you. Leave that to me. That's my grandson you're carrying around in there."

"You're pretty sure it's a boy, aren't you?" I laughed.

"Well, a man can dream can't he? Let me get you another cup of coffee."

When he returned, he was carrying two coffees in "to go" cups. He sent us out the door and the second we were out, we heard music blasting from inside the building.

"Is that Paul McCartney?" I asked Nikki.

She rolled her eyes and smiled.

"He loves Wings."

"Live and Let Die?"

"Yep. It will be running in a constant loop until we get back. Those poor painters. At least it's not "Wanderlust". That one usually means something is bothering him."

"It's hard to picture that man in a bad mood," I said.

"He can get there. All of us have a dark side. Bob said starting the business was stressful on the family when he was growing up."

"I can imagine."

As we spoke, we sipped our coffees and headed in the direction of Chocolate Love.

"According to Bob, his dad is much different since the heart attack. He doesn't take everything so serious anymore. No more fear of failure. He's always been a very cautious businessman, and he still is, but he's much more relaxed. When we approached him about Bean in Love he never even hesitated. Even in this down market. I thought it would be more difficult to persuade him."

"Well, he's seen your success with Chocolate Love."

"Yeah, I guess," Nikki sighed.

For the first time, I picked up a note of caution from her. It was about time. She should be nervous about taking all of this on.

"What's wrong?" I asked, stopping and reaching out for her arm.

Nikki stared straight ahead and took a second before turning to look at me.

"Don't get me wrong. I'm still totally jacked about the store, the coffee, yada, yada. I just don't feel good," she said, emphasizing the word feel. "It's frustrating. I'm not used to being so handicapped. One minute I'm great and then the next minute, I'm crashing."

"Do you want to go to the hospital? Are you having cramps?" I asked, instinctively reaching out and touching her stomach.

"No, it's nothing like that. My doctor says I'm okay. Adelle says it's all perfectly normal. It feels like flu-like symptoms, but every day it gets worse. It used to be isolated to certain times of the day. But I've noticed the last few days it can be at any time."

I shook my head sympathetically and waited for her to continue. I was at a loss as far as words of wisdom.

"What else does Adelle say?"

"She said I will feel better once I get into the second trimester. She doesn't seem worried about me being able to handle all of this," she said, implying the two buildings we were now standing in between—Chocolate Love and Bean in Love.

"She keeps telling me to focus on the here and now in this first trimester and rest when I feel tired or nauseous because supposedly it will pass."

"How are you feeling right now?"

"Like crap. Ten minutes ago I was fine."

"Maybe you overdid it with the sledgehammer."

"Ha, ha," she laughed dryly.

"Are you trying to tell me what I think you're trying to tell me?"

She met my eyes and squinted. "What do you mean?"

"Remember, William will be back in town tonight. He wants to take us to dinner to discuss what happened to Brian. Are you thinking you're too ill to be a part of this investigation?"

"Oh no, definitely not. I'll be fine for that," Nikki said.

"So, you'll be at the dinner tonight?"

Nikki's lips curled up in disgust at the mention of dinner. She worked quickly to rearrange them into a smile, but there was no hiding her reaction. This could only mean one thing for me. Dinner alone with William.

Chapter 26

By five that evening, I was dressed for dinner and working at Jack's condo. When my phone rang, I cursed silently to myself, wishing for just twenty minutes more. I hadn't silenced my phone while I was waiting for William's call. When I glanced at the phone, my favorite number from Miami lit up the screen. I answered with a smile on my face.

"Hi, Mom."

"Hi, Kelly. How are you? I haven't spoken with you in days," my mom said on the other line.

We normally spoke at least every other day. The week had flown by with the move, my trip to Michigan, and Brian's death.

"I'm fine, Mom. Have you spoken to Nikki or Adelle? Do you know everything that's happening here?"

"I do. Just wanted to make sure you're okay. You're making a big sacrifice giving up your home for Adelle and her family. That was very nice of you."

"Well, I owe her," I chuckled.

"But how are you doing with the changes? Are you writing?"

"Trying."

"Oh, no. Am I interrupting you now?"

"Yes, but that's okay. I've been holed up here for the last couple of hours. We haven't spoken in so long and it's nice to hear your voice, Mom. Tell me, how are you guys? How's Dad?"

"Oh, he's fine. Sleeping a lot more than he ever did. And he's been watching a lot of football."

"Are you guys still walking every day?"

"You know, now that you mention it, we're not. He's glued to that television more than he ever has been. I need to make more of an effort to get him out."

When my parents relocated from Geneva to Miami a few years ago, it had been a good move. They were getting older, and the Chicago winters were too much for them. Also, some of their friends from the area were living there, so it had worked well. They came back often, but the thought of them slowing down stressed me out. If they were out there by themselves and something went wrong, who would take care of them?

"Everything is fine, Kelly. I swear. Your dad just needs to turn off that damn television once in a while. But enough about us. Nikki has been filling me in on your recent investigation. Tell me your point of view. What do you think happened?"

"It's not an investigation. Nikki thinks we are private investigators, or something."

"Well, you kind of are. You two are quite the sleuths of the area. I'm so proud of you girls."

"Gee, thanks. I got a disturbing phone call this morning from Brian's parents."

"What did they say?"

"They are so distraught, Mom."

"Do you think you can really help them?" she asked, concern in her voice.

Before I could answer, my phone beeped with another call coming in. I glanced down and saw it was William calling.

"Mom, can I call you back? This is William Sanders, the brother of the man who died."

"I heard all about him. Go. Call me later. And be careful, Kelly."

"Love you, Mom."

I clicked over to the other line and caught William in mid-conversation with someone.

"Hello?"

"Kelly?"

"Yes."

"Hey, it's William. I stopped by the History Museum on my way to dinner to see if I could see Alice. I was wondering if you would be able to meet me a little early and look around the apartment with me?"

"Sure. I'm ready. Let me check with Nikki."

"I just called and left her a message. Alice can only stay until five-thirty, so if you ladies are not able to make it, I can do it myself. Thought I would give it a shot and call you."

Something in the way William's voice shook told me to make my way over to the Geneva History Museum as soon as possible. He didn't sound like his normal, confident self.

"I'm on my way. I should be there in about ten minutes. I'll try getting a hold of Nikki."

"Thanks, Kelly."

After disconnecting, I rushed into the bathroom for one last check of my make-up. I reapplied my lip gloss and a little more bronzer, grabbed my trench coat, and headed out the door. I'd dressed in my new dark pair of skinny jeans, patent leather flats, and a fitted black sweater belted at the waist. The temperature had dropped throughout the day and was now in the high forties. I wanted to make sure I was dressed well enough for The Herrington but also appropriate for any sleuthing we might do afterwards.

Before starting up the car, I shot Nikki a text asking her to meet us at the History Museum.

When I pulled up, I parked my car on Third Street in front of William's. My old car looked even rattier than normal next to his gleaming Mercedes. For a second, I contemplated parking somewhere down the block and walking back to the building. I let out a sigh and decided against it. What was the point of that? This was me. I should just be happy I escaped California with my life. So what if I had a junky car? I closed my door quietly, hoping not to attract any attention to my absurd little vehicle.

No such luck. As soon as I got out of the car, Alice and William waved hello to me through the plate glass windows inside. They must have been waiting for me to arrive before going up to the apartment.

"Here we go," I said quietly to myself.

I raised my finger indicating I needed a minute and dialed Nikki's number. It went straight to voice mail.

"Nikki, William and I are at the Geneva History Museum with Alice. We're going to look around Brian's apartment before dinner. Don't know what you're in the middle of, but if you can, try and meet us here. Okay, hope you're feeling okay."

"Hey, Kelly. Thanks so much for coming."

William held the front door of the History Museum open for me. Dressed in a gray pair of pants and a light blue oxford shirt, he looked genuinely relieved and happy to see me. He glanced at my car and then back at me, his expression changing only slightly. He must have picked up on my hesitation because he stepped out onto the sidewalk and let the door shut behind him.

"Did you get a hold of Nikki?" he asked, taking a couple of steps closer. His eyes zeroed in on mine, making me squirm.

As he got closer, I noticed his hair was still wet, as though freshly washed. I caught a whiff of soap when he approached me.

"No, I haven't heard from her. She wasn't feeling well earlier today. I'm not sure if she's going to…" I stopped when William broke eye contact with me to look over my shoulder in the direction of Chocolate Love.

"Here she comes now," he said, smiling.

Sure enough, I spied Nikki walking down the front steps of Chocolate Love. When she saw we were watching her, she darted her right arm up in the air and waved. Even from this far away, I could tell the coloring in her face was off and her smile wasn't at full wattage.

"How are you?" William asked, pulling my attention back to him. He ran a hand through his hair and smiled. "It feels like I haven't seen you in so long. So much has happened since we parted ways in Michigan. You look great."

"Thank you. It's good to be back home."

"Have you been able to get work done on the book?"

"Here and there. I've come to accept that my schedule for writing is not set in stone. I just have to get things done when I can and when I'm inspired. Today was a good day. How are you?"

"Good. Or, I guess I should say, as well as can be expected under the circumstances. Nikki said your sister's family is still in your apartment, right?"

"Yes, I've moved in with my boyfriend for the time being."

"Wish he could have come tonight. I would have loved to meet Jack."

"Yeah."

"He's a lucky man," William smiled and folded his arms into one another. I didn't quite know how to respond, so I waited. "So, do you feel settled in?"

There it was again. That way about William and his mysterious questions. Was he asking me how long I planned to stay in Jack's home? If I was comfortable there? If by moving into Jack's place that it meant I'd made a commitment? Or had he messed with my perception of what he was asking.

I stalled with an "um" while trying to come up with an answer to his question. We stood like two animals encountering each other in the wild, examining each other. Was this an attack? An inquisition? A mating ritual? Or merely a friendly passing?

"Hi guys," Nikki called as she approached us on the sidewalk. "What did I miss?"

"Nothing yet. We were just waiting for you," William said. "Thank you so much for coming."

"Nikki, are you okay?" I whispered, horrified at her appearance. This close up, her eyes looked sunken into her head. The dark circles made her look like she'd been practicing her make-up for a Halloween costume. And the strange green glow that her skin gave off made her appearance almost alien.

"I'm fine," she snapped, obviously annoyed with me for asking in front of William. I couldn't stop myself. Surely William could see it as well. It would be like someone walking up with a unicorn horn on the top of their head and trying to ignore it. There was no hiding this.

"You should be home in bed," I snapped back at her. This was getting ridiculous. Nikki was obviously in no shape to be out and about snooping around. These symptoms were beyond the scope of normal now. A little bit of nausea was to be expected during this time of her pregnancy, but she was turning into Night of the Living Dead. This could not be okay.

"It's fine. It's just been a tough afternoon," she said.

"I think we should take you to see a doctor," I said.

"Kelly, leave me alone. Everything is fine."

William asked, "Nikki, are you ill?"

"I said I'm okay." Nikki charged past us both, shooting me the evil eye.

"What's going on?" William asked me.

It didn't feel right to share Nikki's news, so I shrugged my shoulders and followed her into the building. Inside, Nikki was already conversing with Alice at the reception desk and pointing to something up on the counter.

"So, like I was saying, this is a key to the apartment upstairs," Alice said.

"And, who had a key?"

"It was just Brian and myself. We were both given a key to the apartment upstairs, to be used at our discretion. It's really just a rudimentary kitchen, bathroom, and small bedroom. I never personally needed it because my home is just a couple of blocks away. Once and awhile I went up there on my break to make some tea, eat lunch, and find a couple of quiet moments to myself. I never used the bedroom. Brian used it all the time though. He loved to stay here late into the night to do his research. When he was too tired to drive back to his apartment in Elgin, he would crash upstairs. He even kept some spare clothes up there. Oh, that reminds me."

Alice took a step back and opened a closet behind the reception desk.

"I packed up his personal things he left up there for you, William."

She pushed the small cardboard box in his direction.

"Thank you, Alice," he said quietly. His eyes dropped to the floor as though it was too painful to look inside the box at Brian's belongings.

"You have not been up in the apartment yet, William?" Nikki asked.

"No."

"Will you go up with us, Alice?" Nikki asked.

Alice's face drooped slightly and the pink in her cheeks turned an ashy gray.

"Of course," she finally choked out.

I was waiting for William to give her an out since she clearly didn't want to go up, but he stayed quiet. Stealing a glance in his direction, I noticed his hands were in his pockets and his gaze was locked on Alice.

"Are you feeling well enough to do that?" Nikki asked.

"Yes," she said, finally meeting William's gaze. He was not going to let her off the hook.

"Great. Let's go," William said, turning and walking toward the museum.

"This way," Alice said, motioning directly behind the front reception desk to the door leading upstairs.

"Oh, I see. The way Brian described it, I thought the door was further in the back," William said.

"No, those are the doors to enter the museum. The ones Kelly entered the morning she found…" Alice stopped. Her lips continued to move, but no words came out. Eventually she continued, "Well, this is the door to upstairs. This is what we want right now."

"Okay, then let's go check it out," he said.

William grabbed for the doorknob and pulled the heavy metal door wide for the three of us to walk past him.

"Kelly, was this open the day you found Brian?" William asked.

I tried to think back to that morning. It had to have been. There was no way I would have heard the radio upstairs if it was closed. I closed my eyes, trying to recall the scene again.

"It was open. In fact, the door at the top of the stairs was as well. The only reason I went upstairs was because I could hear Brian's radio alarm going off. The voice on the radio was a woman's, and I initially thought it was Nikki."

By this time, Alice was at the top of the stairs, unlocking the door to enter into the apartment.

"Alice, the police found Brian's keys, right?" William asked.

179

"Yes," she said. "They found them in a pair of his pants."

"So, he left this door open at night? Why would he have left the door wide open?" Nikki asked.

"The police said they found a bunch of things from the museum downstairs up in the apartment. Like he was taking things up for his research and just gave up and went to bed," William said.

"He didn't normally do that," Alice said. "He'd been crazed over the past couple of weeks researching things for the ghost tours. They were about to hit high season. Brian was specifically obsessed with the Victoria Jacobs' house. He talked about that one non-stop with me. But the things that were found in his apartment that morning had nothing to do with the Jacobs' house."

"What do you mean?" Nikki asked.

We were standing in the front room of the small apartment which served as the kitchen. Two of the chairs at the kitchen table were pulled out. I could picture Brian leaned over in one of the chairs with his feet up on the other, pouring over his research late into the night. A wave of sadness ran through me. Being up here in this apartment made it sink in that Brian was really gone, and a life was cut short by tragedy.

As though thinking the same thing, William walked over to the chair and touched it gently. Finally, he pulled one away from the table and sat down. I could only imagine what he was going through. There was a big part of me that wanted to run over and give him a hug. I had to hold myself back. It wasn't appropriate.

"The items are all back in the museum now. We cleaned up this place. Well, we actually hired a cleaning service to clean up I should say. There was so much dust up here from the fingerprinting the police did. We needed to get professional help to make sure it was all cleaned right. I can show you the items in the museum downstairs if you want. He took a hat from the little model hat store they have set up from the early 1900s, an old-fashioned iron from the display of what homes looked like at the turn of the century, and one of the headdresses right off of the mannequin in the native American display," Alice said. "If you like, I can go show you what he took."

"Do you have any idea why he would have taken those particular items, Alice?" William asked.

Alice hesitated for a moment then pulled her lips together in a pucker. "I'm not sure. I guess for research, but I'm not quite sure why he took those items. It is a little strange. It's not clear to me how those items would be related to his research."

The comment about the headdress immediately brought back images of my nightmare in Michigan. Perhaps I had unknowingly seen it the morning I found Brian and my subconscious stored it to be used as ammunition.

"Do you have any idea, Nikki? Did he tell you anything?" William asked. He turned in his chair and looked at her. The three of us, Nikki, Alice, and I had remained standing. It didn't feel right to sit at the table with William.

"No, he didn't. I don't know why he picked those items. I didn't notice them when we found him that morning, but I was very distracted. Excuse me for a second. I'm just going to run into this bathroom quick," Nikki said, ghosting into the bathroom directly behind her. Perhaps that's why she didn't choose to sit down with William. Maybe she was just positioning herself closest to an escape route.

Before she could shut the door, I stuck my foot in the doorframe and blocked the door from closing.

"Just give us a second," I called out, muscling my way into the bathroom with her. Her green face was in stark contrast to the pure white tiles lining the floor and walls of the bathroom.

"What is going on? We've got to get you home," I demanded.

In answer to my question, she knelt down to lie her head down on the toilet seat.

"Oh my God," I said, cringing. Watching where her head landed was so disgusting, I was nervous it would start me puking.

"You are not going to dinner," I said, kneeling next to her and pulling her head back gently. My nose scrunched up in disgust as my hand grabbed the floor to balance myself. Touching other people's bathroom floors was becoming the norm for me with Nikki's nausea. At least this bathroom appeared fastidiously clean from what I could tell.

"I'm taking you home."

Nikki moaned but didn't vomit.

"What the hell is that?" I said.

"What?" she whispered.

Without letting go of her hair, I contorted my body so I could lean under the toilet seat and reach behind it with my free hand.

"This," I said, pulling out the small gleaming object that caught my eye. It would have been impossible to see unless squatted down at the angle we were now. It had been in what could only be deemed as a toilet seat blind spot, per say.

"What is that?" she asked through squinted eyes.

I didn't answer, but my mind began to race. Surely this must have been missed by the police. My instinct was to drop it, worried that I was damaging a print, if there was one to be found on it. But I didn't want to lose it or have it roll somewhere where I couldn't retrieve it.

"It's a backing for a pin of some sort," I said. "Now this is what I call a strange coincidence. Do you know what this is from? I found one in your store the other day. What is it doing here?" My stomach sank at the thought of Chocolate Love somehow being connected to Brian's death.

Chapter 27

"I don't know and I don't care," Nikki moaned.

"Okay. That's it. You're going home right now. Get up," I ordered Nikki, trying to pull her up off the floor. She pushed my hand away. "Leave me alone."

"Nikki, you can't stay here. You need to be home in bed. I'm calling Bob right now. You need to go to the hospital."

"No. Just give me a couple of minutes. This is how it works, the wave comes, the wave goes, and then I'm fine."

"Calling Bob."

"No. He's at Chocolate Love. Listen, fine, I will go home. Just leave me alone with my toilet for five minutes, okay? Then I swear I will walk straight back to Chocolate Love and make Bob take me home."

"You promise?"

"Yes. That's why I was late. I felt this coming on. This will pass in about ten minutes."

"Nikki," I began.

"Just give me a minute to work through this. Seriously, Kelly, get out."

"Okay," I said hesitantly.

Going over to the sink, I washed my hands and gave a quick check of my reflection in the glass. I could feel my neck tightening up and stress racing through my body. Nikki was acting so un-Nikki. It was upsetting. I wasn't used to her snapping at me and shutting me out like this. She normally filled my life with such joy and peace. Being around her right now was making me tense and panicked because I couldn't stand to see her in such pain.

On my way out the door, I looked back at her once more, wondering if I was doing the right thing leaving her alone. I tucked the backing in the pocket of my jeans and closed the door behind me to give Nikki privacy.

The kitchen was empty. At first I thought Alice and William had gone back downstairs, but then I heard the sound of voices behind the half open bedroom door.

Knocking lightly to make them aware of me, I opened the door all the way and made my way into the room. The bedroom was made up of a queen bed covered by a quilt in floral print. There were only a few other small pieces of furniture, including an antique night stand and a hope chest. An old-fashioned radio sat atop the hope chest. I could see why Brian liked staying in this room. It was clean, cozy, and simplistic. The perfect place to be left alone to organize one's thoughts. And even at this hour, the double window above the bed allowed a nice amount of natural light in.

Alice and William stood next to the bed peering down at the night stand. They both turned in my direction at the same time wearing identical looks of concern.

"Is she okay?" Alice asked.

"She's not feeling well. She's going to leave in a bit. I'm sorry, William, but I don't think she's going to make it to dinner."

"It's totally understandable. It's so difficult...," Alice said, stopping mid-sentence with a knowing smile on her face. "Well, please tell her we wish her the best." As far as I knew, Nikki had not shared her news, but as a woman, I was sure she was making an intuitive guess.

"She should definitely head home. It means a lot that she even came over here if she was not feeling well to begin with. Does she need our help?" William asked.

"No, she wants a few minutes alone, and then she will head out. What were you guys talking about before I came in?" I asked, intent on changing the subject.

"The pills. I was just showing William the nightstand where the police found his bottle of anti-anxiety meds," Alice said, pointing to the small nightstand next to the bed.

"They were here on the nightstand?"

"Yep. According to the police, no other prints but his own," William said.

"Speak up so I can hear you better," we heard Nikki call out from the bathroom. I should have known she wouldn't allow herself to be left out of the conversation.

"No extra prints on his medication bottle," I called out.

"Alice, how do you think he got the sleeping pills?" William asked.

"I didn't give them to him," Alice said defensively.

"I'm not accusing you, Alice," William said, reaching out and touching her arm in apology. "I apologize if it sounded like that. It wasn't my intention."

Alice nodded her head and brought her hand up to her face to wipe her brow. "I didn't mean to snap. It's just been a long week, and I'm tired myself. There's been so many questions. It feels like everyone thinks I have the answer to Brian's death, but I don't think I do. I know he was really stressed, he was obsessed about the research, and he was taking anti-anxiety meds. That's all I know. I swear."

"Okay, why don't we take a break?" William said. "We probably have everything we can from this apartment. The reason I ask, Alice, is because Brian's doctor told us he prescribed the anti-anxiety meds but not the sleeping pills. And what was found in his system was not the kind that could be bought over the counter, which means he got the meds from someone."

"Yes, but that still doesn't mean anyone killed him," I pointed out. "He may have taken them on purpose."

"I know," William agreed, nodding his head.

Alice and I glanced at each other. She gave me a small, sad smile and raised her eyebrows. It looked as though, to me, she was trying to figure out what to say next.

William kept quiet and studied the room. I imagined he was trying to memorize as many details as possible. I wasn't sure what he was looking for, but whatever it was, I chose not to say anything so he could concentrate.

"Okay, let's go," he said finally with his back to us, staring at the bed where his beloved brother had taken his last breath.

"Just give me a minute to collect Nikki."

When William turned around, his face was flushed and his eyes hard. "Okay, we'll meet you downstairs," he said roughly. His body language communicated very clearly to me that he had not found what he was hoping for on this visit. Perhaps it just confused him even more.

Alice and William made their way downstairs, allowing me a private moment with Nikki.

"Are you ready to go?" I asked, bending down and combing her dark hair away from her face.

"Yes."

"Did you get sick yet?"

"No. Just have to go home," she said weakly.

I slipped my arm around her waist and gently pulled her up to a standing position.

"Wait. Just one second," Nikki said, stabilizing herself.

"Are you dizzy?" I worried by the way she staggered back and forth that she would fall.

"Yep. Okay, now I'm ready. Don't hold me. I want to go down myself. I don't want to make a big scene on the way out."

Too late for that, I thought to myself. Alice and William had probably guessed what was going on by now. No one had uttered anything about the possibility of Nikki being contagious.

"I'm going to just bolt out of here, okay?" Nikki said. "Can you just explain to them? You know, without telling them."

"Of course, Nikki. I'll tell them you ate some bad chocolate."

"No, don't tell them that. They'll think I sell bad stuff at Chocolate Love," she said, attempting a smile.

"Bad chocolate at Chocolate Love? Never! Okay, get out of here. Go out the front door. They were heading into the museum in the back."

"Wait, one more thing. Those sleeping pills. Find the supplier, find the murderer."

"Really? You still think this was a murder? But what was the motive?"

The more and more I learned about Brian, the more I was inclined to think this was an accidental overdose. There was no motive for murder that we knew of, no women in the picture, no known enemies. As much as I wanted to help the Sanders' family find peace, my gut told me we were spinning our wheels. Why keep looking for a bad guy when there didn't appear to be one? In this equation, it was Brian's mental health. He was killed by his own demons as far as I was concerned.

"I don't know yet, but I'll find a motive. Sleeping pills. Find them." Nikki turned and bolted out of the bathroom. I heard her footsteps race down the stairs and then the front door opened and slammed shut. My hope was that she would make it across the street before getting sick. That was the last thing she needed the townspeople of Geneva to see. I glanced one more time around the bathroom and let out a sigh. There was nothing I could do here.

Downstairs in the museum, I found Alice and William examining the headdress of the life-size Native American Indian mannequin.

"Yikes," I said aloud.

"Do these scare you, Kelly?" William asked, turning to face me. "I think they are beautiful. Even when we were kids, Brian was obsessed with the history of the Native Americans. Only the most revered and powerful of the tribe were allowed to wear the headdress."

"That's right," Alice chimed in. "You've done your research. Each feather is supposed to represent something. Each time a warrior did something the tribe considered brave or courageous, he was awarded a feather."

"It is beautiful," I said. *And creepy.*

It was starting to get dark outside. All I wanted to do was get out of the museum. The thought of hanging out with the ghosts of the past may have been Brian's cup of tea, but I wasn't interested. Especially considering what happened to him.

"So, this is one of the items the police found up in the apartment when Brian was found?" William asked.

Alice nodded her head in confirmation.

"Any idea why?" I asked her.

"No. It doesn't really have anything to do with the Jacobs' house. Like I said, Brian did most of his research late at night. Maybe he was going to tie in this headdress to the upcoming ghost tours. I'm not sure."

"Speaking of, when will the ghost tours start up again? I really want to see this Jacobs' house myself," William said.

Alice let out a sigh. "I just don't know. We'll have to find a replacement for Brian. In the meantime, I will have to run them myself. Who am I kidding? There is no replacing Brian. I don't know half of what he did about the history of the area." She pointed her finger up in the air and broke into a grin. "You know. I just thought of something. We have another headdress in the archives downstairs. Maybe that's something. I just remembered it. The police never looked at that. Would you like me to show you the archives?"

I gulped. I didn't even know there was a downstairs to this building. My mind raced to the cellar under Chocolate Love. It was dark and creepy, not my favorite place. If their basement was anything like the one at Chocolate Love, I had no interest in checking it out, especially at this late hour of the day.

"The basement?" I squeaked out.

"We'd love to see it," William said.

My eyes shifted to the front windows. From where I stood in the museum, I could see the darkening sky.

Get out of here, Kelly, I heard the voice in my head say.

Before I could object, Alice and William started in the direction of the stairs leading to the basement.

"Follow me," she said. "Brian must have told you about the basement, William. It was his favorite part of this place. He could get lost there for hours."

Reluctantly, I forced myself to follow them. Just the words archive and basement on a darkening autumn night were enough to send goose bumps down my arms. I rolled my eyes and forced my legs down the stairs.

"How do I get myself into these things," I mumbled to myself.

"What's that, Kelly?" William turned and asked.

"Uh, nothing."

We followed Alice down two flights of stairs and down a long hallway. So far the basement appeared a lot cleaner and office-like than what my imagination had cooked up. By the way they kept the rest of the building in tip-top shape, I should have figured the basement would be just as clean and organized.

"Prepare yourself," Alice said, when we got to the end of the hall.

Holy hell. Prepare ourselves for what? What could she possibly be ready to show us? My mind raced to the evil little dolls I encountered in the upstairs museum the other night. Please, let there not be any more of those down here.

We stood in a doorway of what I assumed to be a very large room based on the way her voice echoed. Flipping on the lights, Alice stepped to the side for us to get a better view.

"Whoa," I said, my eyes widening, taking it all in.

"Wow. What is all of this?" William asked.

The room was filled with shelf after shelf of paperwork, file folders, artwork, statues, furniture, and other historical items of value.

"This is where we store all of the data and pieces we use in our museum. All of the important records of transactions that have taken place in the town of Geneva since the town was created are housed here. Real estate transactions, property developments, etcetera. And then over there, are all of the pieces we need for displays and exhibits."

The room was bigger than an entire floor of Adelle's old house. I just couldn't get over the mammoth size of the room. It was much needed though, considering everything they had stored in this room.

"What's behind those sheets over there by the wall?" I asked, glancing at the white curtain-like sheets hanging up.

"Come with me. That's what I wanted to show you," Alice said.

We walked to the west side of the room. An entire wall was covered in some type of high tech sheeting that blocked out whatever was behind it. My imagination got the better of me, and I couldn't help but brace myself, waiting for someone to pop out from behind them. What a great place for someone to hide.

"We put these up to try and cut down on the amount of dust settling on the historical valuables. Let's see, I think it's this one. No wait, this one." Alice pulled one sheet out then another.

I couldn't help but notice how excited she looked as she searched.

"Here it is. The other headdress," Alice said, pulling back a sheet, revealing a large Native American headdress. It was even grander and in better condition than the one upstairs in the museum. It must have had over five hundred feathers woven in place.

William and I both stood, staring at it. I knew what I wanted to ask but held back, waiting to see which direction William would go.

"Can I touch it?" William asked.

"Well, that's kind of why we didn't put this one up there. It might look really nice, but it's not as sturdy as the one upstairs. That's why we chose to put the other one on display."

"I was wondering the same thing," I said. "What are your thoughts, Alice? Does this make you think of anything related to Brian's death?"

"No. Not really. How about you, William?" Alice asked.

William shook his head no. "If anything, this just makes me more confused. This room is…overwhelming."

I couldn't help but notice Alice's face fall at his comment.

"But very interesting," William added.

"Should I tell the police about the second headdress?" Alice asked.

"I don't really see a reason to right now," William said. "Do you, Kelly?"

I shook my head no, already distracted by something that caught my attention across the room.

"What is that, Alice?" I asked, pointing to a small crib I'd spotted. Though cribs normally brought happy images to mind, for some reason this one was sending off alarm bells in my head.

Alice let the sheet she was holding fall back in place.

"That crib was from an exhibit we had last year. I never liked it. It's an original taken from the home for troubled girls set up in Geneva from 1850-1950."

"What do you mean by 'troubled girls'?" William asked.

"Well, you know, girls that were pregnant who were turned away by their own parents. The home was supposed to help these girls out and raise the babies. But, things were so different back then. The girls were basically shunned and hidden away. There wasn't a lot of funding and the community did not offer a lot of support, so the administrators and the girls did the best they could. A lot of them died because of lack of medicine and lack of care. Things were a lot different then as far as immunizations and safe birthing procedures. And doctors were not as available, either."

All of a sudden, I wanted to get out of the basement. The evil crib story was the last straw. I didn't have the stomach to hear about teenage girls and babies dying in some kind of horror house because no one cared about them. It was time to go.

"I think I'll meet you guys upstairs. I'm going to use the washroom."

"We'll go up as well. I'm sure Alice wants to get home. Thank you so much for the tour," William said.

"It was my pleasure. I'm so sorry it's under these circumstances. I just need to lock up the apartment upstairs, and we'll head out."

Once we were on the main floor, Alice checked the back doors of the museum to make sure they were all locked, then locked up the door leading up to the apartment.

"Did you want to look for a bathroom?" William asked me while watching Alice go through her routine. His hands were in his pockets in a casual stance, but by the way his eyes followed her every move, I could tell he was deep in thought.

"Bathroom? Oh, no. I'll wait for the restaurant. My hands are just dusty from touching all the artifacts." I'd completely forgotten about my excuse to get out of the basement and back to the main floor. Glancing outside, I noticed it was now fully dark outside. A couple walked past the large plate glass windows facing Third Street. The man looked inside, his head turned slightly to the side. I imagined he was thinking the same thing I was: What are those people doing in the History Museum this late at night?

Tell me about it, I thought.

"According to the police, both of those back doors were unlocked, right?" William asked me.

"Yes. They were both open the morning I found Brian."

"That's really strange. Why would Brian leave them open? It's like he left it open for someone to come in. Who was he expecting?"

"Well, he was expecting Nikki early Friday morning to pick up her cake stand."

William nodded his head and turned his gaze to me. "That's right. I remember her mentioning that to me."

"What are you thinking?"

"I honestly don't know," William said. "This visit has left me more confused than ever."

* * * * *

After we said goodbye to Alice, William and I stood on the sidewalk outside making plans.

"Why don't you jump in my car, and we'll ride over to the restaurant together?"

"Why?" I laughed. "You don't want to ride over in mine?"

"What?" William asked, looking genuinely confused.

"Nothing. I was just referring to what a junky car I have compared to yours. Just a joke."

"Kelly, I don't care what kind of car you have. Trust me, I didn't notice. You should have seen what I was driving when I started my company. The only way I could front the cash was to live frugally in other areas of my life. It's only in the last five years that things have started to take off for me. This car was a huge splurge. I'm still not completely comfortable with it."

William seemed relieved to be talking about something other than his brother's death. The tense mask he wore for Alice's tour had finally slipped. Maybe dinner would help us relax so we could actually think.

"Really? When I talked to your parents earlier today, they said you were always very driven and successful. I pictured you driving a car like this from the first day you got your license."

"Not exactly," he laughed playfully, pulling the passenger door of his car open for me. He reached in and grabbed a navy blue sweater off of the passenger seat. He stepped away, making a grand gesture for me to enter the car.

"We didn't have a lot of money growing up. And you know how proud parents are. They tend to overemphasize their children's success."

I stepped to the car and slid down onto the dark gray leather seat. Instant comfort.

"Ahh," I sighed, as William closed the door and walked around to the driver's seat. There was nothing like sitting in a luxury car. I felt my back curve into the soft leather like a baby settling into the comfort of its mother's arms.

"Heaven," I said aloud.

"Glad you like it. So, you said you had a chance to talk to my parents?" William asked, plopping down onto the driver's seat.

I couldn't help but notice the car fit him well and made him appear even more attractive. There was no denying there was something very sexy about a man with a nice car.

"This afternoon."

"How did they sound?"

I paused before answering. I didn't want to hurt him with how I really felt. William seemed to care for his parents just as much as I did mine.

"That great, huh?" He filled in the silence.

"They didn't sound good," I finally said. "I see what you mean about the theories and such. They sounded so disappointed not to be here looking into this themselves. I can't imagine how frustrated they must be."

"I don't want my mom to have another stroke. The stress of all this is very dangerous for her. Part of me is tempted to make up a story, but she's too smart for that. She'd figure it out. Plus, she's made friends with Detective Pavlik. They talk every day. He's done a good job keeping her filled in on the details."

William glanced into the rearview mirror, patting down his hair before turning to me.

"I like Pavlik," I said. "Nikki and I spoke to him after I found Brian. He's really easy to talk to."

"He's been great with my mom. Really patient. She's not easy to understand. I'm sure you picked up on that."

"Yeah, it seems like the more she gets stressed, the more her stutter worsens. Is that right?"

"Yeah. But Detective Pavlik never rushes her off the phone. It's when she feels time crunched that she stumbles."

"That's how Jack's mom is. She doesn't have the issue with the speech, but she stumbles and falls more when she feels she's under a time constraint. We have to work really hard at not making Jack's mom feel pressured. That's when she'll rush, and we run into problems."

"Jack's mom had a stroke?"

"Yes. Sorry, I should have told you that first. Jack's father passed away when he was young, so his mom raised two children on her own. I think the stress did her in. Although she initially recovered from her stroke, the last couple of years have been tough on her."

"He must have his hands full then, huh?"

"Luckily his younger sister lives in the area, so they are able to both step up and care for her. That's where he is tonight. His mom had a poker game."

"I'm lucky. My dad is able to care for my mom for the most part. I don't know what I will do if something happens to him, or if things get too hard on him. I don't see them moving out to California, and he would have a really tough time putting her in a home."

"That's the same thing Jack and his sister are dealing with. They don't want to put her in a home."

"It's a lot, isn't it? Brian and I dealt with so much guilt for not being closer to them. I'm sure it puts a lot of stress on your relationship."

"Yeah, I mean, no. It's fine." I stumbled over my words. It didn't seem right to be so brutally honest with William about my relationship. He had hit a soft spot. "I guess it is hard in that he's not always around when I would like to see him. Like tonight, for example. It would be great for him if he was able to go to dinner, but I understand he's made a commitment to his mom. Plus, we spend plenty of time together. We're adults. We both have our own lives."

It was time to change the subject. We didn't really know each other well enough to talk about my life with Jack and its ups and downs.

"Hey, what are these?" I asked, noticing for the first time a large plastic bag at my feet filled with some kind of small objects by the feel of it.

"Oh, here, let me move that for you. That's just some marketing paraphernalia for my company."

William reached down and grabbed the bag with his right hand. I noticed again the small white scars on his hand. His hand grazed my leg ever so lightly when he grabbed for the bag. I knew it was unintentional, but it still made me jump.

"Sorry," William said, plopping the bag in the backseat. He reached to place it on the seat behind me. When he did, his body moved even closer to mine. I noticed the muscles in his neck bulge a bit and the close proximity of his body near mine allowed me to take in the scent of his cologne. Tonight it was a sandalwood scent very similar to Jack's. I diverted my eyes and stared down at my feet. The car suddenly seemed a lot smaller than when I first got in. I glanced back and noticed a few other clear plastic bags filled with various items with his company's logo on it.

"All SC junk. Can I interest you in anything? Wait, I know what you would like."

He reached behind me again and pulled something out of one of the bags.

"How about a USB drive? You can use this to store your novels on. It's really best for Word. That's what you write in, right?"

I shook my head yes in response, too numb to say anything else.

"Kelly? What's wrong? You look like you've seen a ghost."

I braced myself, trying to gather up enough courage to ask him what was bothering me suddenly.

"Have you ever made SC pins? With gold backings?"

Chapter 27

"Pins with gold backings? No, not that I'm aware of."

"Are you sure?" I demanded. Bells were going off in my head. If I was going to jump out of the car, this would be the proper time to do it.

"No. What would I do with pins? We use pretty much all technical gadgets for marketing purposes. You know, USB drives, DVDs, etc. Pins are not exactly our forte."

My body relaxed a bit, sensing William was telling the truth. Still I reached into my pocket and pulled the small gold backing out.

"So, you've never seen this?" I asked, holding it up for him to see.

William grasped onto my wrist with both hands, steadying my shaking hand so he could better view what I was holding.

"No, what is it? Where did you get it?"

I pulled my hand away and took a few deep breaths. Did I dare tell him what I'd been thinking?

"Okay, you're going to think this is crazy but just hear me out. Motive. Still no motive. What would you gain?" I mumbled, reviewing all of the information one last time before verbalizing my theories.

"Kelly, are you low on blood sugar or something? You're not making any sense. Should I take you to the restaurant?"

"I found a similar backing in Chocolate Love last Thursday, the day before we found Brian. I just found another one in the apartment bathroom. It's a very strange coincidence. You said you had not been up there yet. If these were yours, that would mean you lied about not being up there. And it could mean you lied about when you arrived in Geneva. You could have been here as early as last Thursday. And for that matter, you could have been here during the time of Brian's death. Which means, you could have even been here a long time ago and been walking around, posing as Brian, since you are identical twins." Wow. I couldn't believe I said all that.

William's eyes widened and he sat back distancing himself from me. He blew out a slow breath through his nostrils, keeping his eyes on me the entire time. "Kelly," he growled. "I did not kill my brother."

My mouth opened to respond, but nothing came out. "William," I finally said.

"Hold on one second," William said, opening the driver's side door. He stepped out onto the street and walked behind the car. For a second, I assumed he was going to walk around to the passenger side and ask me to leave. But instead, he opened the trunk. I could hear him digging around, throwing items roughly around. He finally slammed it back down and re-opened the driver's side door. He held a small plastic bag in his hand.

"William, I'm sorry. My mind is a weird thing. You have to understand, I..."

"No need to explain. Yes, it threw me for a loop, but I like the way you think. Drop the pin backing in here before we get anymore prints on it. I'm not saying this is definitely tied to his death, but you're right. It is a weird coincidence. We shouldn't ignore anything."

I did as he said and released the pin backing into the clear, zip lock bag. He zipped it up and handed it back to me.

"Okay, let's go get the other one you found and compare the two."

He started the engine. "Where is it?"

"At Jack's."

"Okay. Wait, before we go, I have to say this." He killed the engine and turned his body toward me. Reaching out, he grabbed my hands into his, making my blood pressure spike.

"Kelly, we're on the same team. I did not kill my brother. I had nothing to do with his death. I am here to help figure out what happened to him and get some answers for the rest of my family. You understand that, right?"

He spoke firmly but compassionately. As distrusting as I was of most people, I believed him.

"William, I'm sorry," I paused, trying to find the right words. "Unfortunately, my...um...life has made me a very suspicious person."

"I expected that to a degree, but now I really see it. And I understand you better, Kelly. Someone you loved and built your life around betrayed you and now you can't trust anyone. But I *need* someone who questions everything, so we can dissect the situation until we figure this out. You're good for me right now."

I squirmed a bit in my seat. His eyes were intense and his grasp warm. Too warm. I pulled away, and he let go easily.

"But I loved my brother, Kelly. Like you love your sisters. I never would have hurt him. You understand that, right?"

I nodded my head and met his gaze again.

"And I do have people you can call in California that can confirm I was there last week. We can do that right now if you want. I won't be offended."

"No. That's ridiculous. Let's just forget that crazy theory."

"Okay, then let's figure out who did this to him. Someone was up in that apartment that shouldn't have been. And whoever it was, was probably in Chocolate Love as well."

* * * * *

I turned my key in the lock to Jack's place and swung the door open. I'd left one light on for myself, so we didn't step into complete darkness. It felt strange to have William inside of Jack's place without Jack present, but before I could ask him to wait in the car, he'd jumped out to open my car door. It felt rude not to ask him to come in.

"Give me a second, okay? I'm just going to run into the bedroom and find that backing." There was no way I was bringing him into Jack's bedroom.

"Sure, no problem."

William took a seat on the small bench near the entrance. His eyes moved around the room. "Nice place."

"Thank you," I responded before heading down the hallway. Once inside the bedroom, I opened the dresser drawer where I'd stashed the pin backing in a small, clear, ramekin snatched from Jack's kitchen. Inside the ramekin, the small key I'd found earlier in my winter jacket sat nestled beside it. After a moment's hesitation, I picked that up as well and headed back into the hallway.

"Here's the other pin backing," I said, opening one palm and presenting it to William.

"Can we turn on another light? I want to be able to see it better."

"Let's go in the kitchen."

Flipping on the overhead lights, I set the backing down on the granite counter and reached inside my jeans pocket for the plastic bag. Unzipping the seal, I dropped the other backing down on the counter.

"Huh, looks like an identical match, wouldn't you say?" William said.

I bent down to get closer to the pieces without touching them.

"Hold on." I reached into the utensil drawer and pulled out a fork. Turning both over a couple of times, I shook my head in affirmation. "Yes, I think they are."

"What a weird coincidence. What does it mean?"

"I have no idea."

At that moment, my stomach let out a loud, obnoxious growl. We were both huddled over the counter fairly close to one another, so I knew I was busted. This was the second time this happened to me in front of William.

His lips pulled up in a smile. "I'm starting to know that sound very well. I don't see any reason why we can't discuss this over dinner. Shall we go?"

"Sorry. It's been awhile since I've eaten. How embarrassing," I blushed.

"No need to be embarrassed. I'm hungry, too. Let's go."

"Wait, let me just put these in the bag together."

I set down the key on the counter and scraped the backings into my bag with the side of the fork.

"Why do you have a safety deposit key in your hand?"

"A what?"

"The key. That looks like a key to a safety deposit box," he pointed down on the counter.

I picked it up for a closer examination. A safety deposit key? I'd never even considered that. Having never rented one myself, I had no idea what one looked like.

"Are you sure?"

"Let me see," William said, motioning me to give him the key.

"Yeah, look here, it gives a box number on one side and the other side reads 'Do Not Duplicate.' I have one of these in California. The key looks just like this. Does this have something to do with Brian's death?"

I shook my head in confusion. "I don't think so. I found it the other day in one of my winter coats I haven't worn in years. I just brought it out because I thought the timing of me finding it was odd. I wanted to see if it struck any nerves with you."

William studied the key.

"I can't think of anything off hand. How would it have gotten in your coat? Was Brian ever up in your apartment?"

"Not that I can think of."

"Who has a key to your apartment?"

"Just my sisters, which means their husbands. And Jack, of course."

Maybe Steve had stashed the key to a safety deposit box in my coat. Perhaps this was what Steve's psychotic mistress, Sharon, was after last summer. Maybe I had the key to something valuable of his on me and didn't even realize it? But which bank? Back in California? And if so, what the hell was I supposed to do with it now?

"Kelly, what's wrong? You look pale all of a sudden."

"What?" I asked, coming out of my haze.

William stared at me and took a step closer.

"Hey, you okay?" he asked softly, placing his hand on my arm. "Where are you? What's going on?"

"Nothing, I'm fine. I don't believe this key has anything to do with Brian's death. Let me just go put this away and then can we head out."

"Sure," William said, eyeing me suspiciously. "Want me to wait here?"

"Yes, please. I'll be right back."

In Jack's bedroom I closed the door behind me and leaned back against it, trying to gather my wits. Damn, Steve. Always, always popping back up. Now I had this stupid key to contend with. It had to be linked to him somehow. What the hell should I do with it? If I sat on it that would mean his minions would keep coming after me. If I did investigate further though, I would be responsible for what I found. And who knows what I would find. It came out last summer that he had been laundering money while we were married. Is this the stash? If so, would I really want to find it? Did I even have energy to go hunt this down? Where would I even start?

I pushed myself away from the door and pulled open the drawer where I'd stored it. Dropping it back into the ramekin, I slammed the dresser drawer closed and squeezed my eyes shut. Talk about ghosts from the past.

"I feel your pain, Brian. And I'm going to help get to the bottom of this," I said quietly to myself.

By the time we arrived at The Herrington, my head was swimming with theories and half-baked plans. I couldn't stop thinking about my key and what to do with the contents of the box, should I find anything. Did I need to get the police involved? Detective Pavlik had been so easy to deal with. Perhaps I should call him and see if he'd talk to me. If Steve did steal money, I wanted to get it back to its rightful owner. Not that I couldn't use it myself.

Now that would be poetic justice. I could use the money Steve stole to pay back my debts he brought on me and start my life over. But that was like using blood money. Who knew how he got it in the first place, if there even was money? Maybe the fact that the key was still in my possession was the reason why I was having such a hard time moving on with my life. If I made things right, perhaps things would straighten out for me once and for all.

"I've lost you again, haven't I?"

"What?"

"You haven't said a word since we left Jack's apartment? Is everything alright? Do you still want to go to dinner?"

"Absolutely," I said, feeling bad that I'd checked out. "I'm sorry. Just have a lot on my mind."

"That key has something to do with your ex-husband, doesn't it?"

"No. Maybe," I sighed. "Honestly, I don't know."

"We don't have to talk about it. Let's go eat. It's been a long day. We're both hungry, right?"

"Yes."

William and I walked down a small flight of stairs into the lobby of The Herrington Inn. A beautiful limestone covered the floor, leading to the focal point of the room—a large winding staircase leading up to the second floor of the three story hotel overlooking the Fox River. All of the accents of the room were dark cherry wood from the railing on the elegant staircase to the wainscoting on the lower part of the walls. Everything from the can lighting set very low, to the Oriental rug looked as though it was purposefully selected to make the guests feel relaxed and at ease. Soft piano music piped in from speakers somewhere above our heads.

"My room looks right onto the river. Very peaceful. I checked in earlier before meeting you."

"It's got a great reputation," I added.

"I did a little research. I guess this building used to house a dairy and a water pumping house. It only became a boutique hotel as recently at 1993. I believe the restaurant is just through the lobby and to the left."

Sure enough a member of the wait staff stepped out into the lobby and smiled at us in welcome. After giving his name, William allowed me to step in front of him into the semi-circular room that housed the restaurant, Atwater.

"Gorgeous," I said, taking in the view of the river. Even though it was fully dark now, the lights along the river sparkled, allowing all of the guests of the restaurant a breath-taking view.

I made a mental decision to put the key aside and concentrate on William.

Regardless of how distracted I felt, or my initial thoughts on Brian's death, tonight I owed it to William to concentrate and keep an open mind.

"Oh, wow," William said. "This is amazing. You've never eaten here before?"

"No, but I've heard really good things."

"I'm surprised I'm able to delight you with this view. Don't you have this all the time?"

I laughed, taking a seat and spreading my napkin out on my lap. They seated us at the table closest to the river, which I was happy about.

"You know how it is. Sometimes you don't appreciate where you live or your surroundings when you're exposed to it all the time. It's when you sit down and allow yourself to take it in, or when you get the chance to show it off to a visitor that you appreciate it. Like for me right now."

"You know the only thing that could possibly make this better?"

"What?" I asked, suddenly alarmed. I'd forgotten about William's weird way of talking. It was back. That feeling that he was possibly, maybe, flirting with me.

"Wine," he laughed. "What did you think I was going to say?"

"Nothing," I laughed nervously, shaking my head and glancing down at the wine list placed before us. We both chose a Cabernet, which was swiftly delivered.

"Geez. That was fast," William commented.

"Tell me what else you know about this hotel," I said, folding my arms in front of me.

"Book material?" William laughed.

"Maybe," I smiled.

"What I know is from what I just read in the lobby today, and from Brian. But it's been a couple of years since I talked to Brian about it, so I might not have it right. Bear with me. From what I remember, this area was the site of Herrington and his wife's first log cabin. They came here from Philadelphia I believe somewhere around 1830, and settled here on Pottawatomie camping grounds. The draw was all of the fresh timber and a water source. Later, a creamery was built and then eventually they turned the creamery into a riverfront hotel and a few million dollars later, *voila!*"

William took a sip of his wine.

"I'm hearing so much about this Pottawatomie tribe. And now this head dress thing. Do you know anything about the Pottawatomie tribe and what ended up happening to them?"

"I'm doing some research on the tribe for my book. After this area was settled, they were eventually forced off the land and killed by enemy tribes," I said.

"How horrible."

"Yeah. Like most Native American tribes, their story ended badly. It was kill or be killed for the land. Feels like it's kind of like that right now here in Geneva. A lot of businesses are suffering so much and getting swallowed up because they can't make rent. People are losing their homes as well."

"Are you ready to order?" Our waitress was back and hovering near the table.

"Can we have another second?" William asked politely.

"Of course." After she left the table, we both hunkered down over our menus.

"Speaking of kill or be killed, I think we better order. She doesn't look like she'd be too happy if we only had drinks."

I nodded and scanned the menu, trying to make a decision. Finally, I chose sea bass with basil-scented jasmine rice. William ordered a prime beef tenderloin with jumbo crab in béarnaise sauce.

"So, let's talk about these pins while we're waiting for our dinner. Who wears pins and what were they doing in the apartment? And, why didn't the police find them?"

"It was nestled behind the toilet bowl at a really weird angle. I only found it because I was down on the ground trying to comfort Nikki."

"Eww."

"I know. Let's not talk about toilets at dinner. I swear I've washed up really good since then."

William laughed and his face lit up into a warm smile. "I believe you. Okay, so back to the pins. Who wears pins?" he said.

"Let's see. Policemen wear pins on their uniform. Docents of museums wear pins to notify patrons of their names. Wait staff. Librarians. Even Girl Scouts wear pins."

"Okay, I see your point. We have a lot of suspects. But what does this pin have to do with Brian, and why is it such a big deal?"

"Maybe it's not. Maybe it was Brian's pin. He wore one. That would make the most sense. He was in Chocolate Love the day I found it, and he was in the apartment bathroom. It doesn't have to mean anything malicious," I said.

"No, I guess not. We could ask Alice. Hers would be the same as Brian's. We could compare them. And maybe she could help us find his."

"But if it is something malicious, it places the owner at the scene of the crime," I said.

"Exactly."

"What about Brian's apartment in Elgin? We haven't even talked about that."

"I know," William released a sigh. "It's all so overwhelming. I have to head over there tomorrow to go through the rest of his stuff and talk to the landlord. It's not something I'm looking forward to."

"Well, maybe after tonight, you'll have better focus."

"God, I hope so. Honestly, I don't even know what I'm looking for anymore. It feels like we're on a wild goose chase."

William leaned forward over the table and glanced down into his glass of wine. The small candle on the table shot beams of light onto his face. Even in this darkened setting, I could see the lines of stress there.

Instead of offering words of comfort, I chose to remain quiet so he could process his thoughts. I couldn't imagine what he was going through and where his mind might be.

As though suddenly inspired, he looked up from his glass, eyes blazing.

"Do you think we can go see the old Jacobs' house after this?"

"What?" I stuttered.

"You know, the Victoria Jacobs' house from the ghost tour?"

"But it's dark out. We won't be able to see anything."

And it's haunted, I wanted to scream.

"I know. But it just keeps coming back to that for me. That was Brian's obsession right before his death and that's what eventually killed him. Can we at least just drive by it?" William begged. "We don't even have to get out of the car if you don't want to."

I nodded my head in agreement, though a voice inside was saying, *Don't go. Don't go. Don't go.*

Chapter 29

An hour later, we headed over to the Jacobs' house. Dinner had been delicious, but the stress of our upcoming house visit spoiled some of the joy I should have taken from the gourmet food.

"We're here," I pointed out.

The home loomed to the right of us. This particular street did not have the best lighting, giving me an uneasy feeling as William parked the car.

"Wow, that was fast."

"I told you, it's just a couple of blocks north of The Herrington Inn," I said.

"It's still really close to the river then."

"Yep, the river is just east of us," I said.

"What a great location. It's for sale, right? I'm surprised no one scooped it up yet. And what a great house. What's it like inside?"

"I have no idea. The ghost tours never took us inside the homes. We just walked around at night on the sidewalk surrounding it and Brian told the stories."

William stepped out of the car and I followed. I leaned back on the car, taking in the majestic home in front of me. It was a two story home, over one hundred years old, with two large front windows both upstairs and downstairs. The clapboard siding was painted a deep blue with red accents framing the windows. Currently all of the lights were out except for one left on in what I assumed to be an upstairs bedroom.

My favorite part of the house was the large wraparound porch painted white. It appeared as though the whole house had recently been given a fresh coat of paint, perhaps to attract more buyers.

"This is the haunted house everyone is talking about? It looks lovely. Maybe I should buy it."

I glanced in William's direction, thinking he was joking, but from the expression on his face it was obvious he was not. In a way, I couldn't blame him. Those who didn't know the sinister back-story would easily be taken in by the location and beauty of the old house.

At that moment my cell phone rang. Glancing at the screen, I saw it was Nikki calling.

"William, I have to take this," I called out. He'd already made his way up to the front sidewalk and looked dangerously close to opening the gate leading to the entrance walk.

"Okay, I'm just going to look around. I'll keep the car open for you," he said. Instead of going up the front walk, he walked around to view the side of the house. Being a corner lot, the home sat on a fairly large piece of land. I watched him go while pressing a button on my phone to pick up Nikki's call.

"Where are you?" she asked before I could even say hello.

"Uhh…" Did I really want to tell her? She would not be happy with my location. I opened the passenger door and sat back down in William's car.

"You wanted a motive. I think I found one."

"What?" I asked.

"A motive. In the bathroom you said there was no motive to kill Brian. That's not true. Did you know that the Geneva History Museum is owned by a private company?"

"No. I assumed it was owned by the city of Geneva. Wasn't Brian an employee of the city?"

"No, that's not what I'm saying. The museum, the employees, everything is supported by private donations, but the building itself is rented from a private owner. They're paying someone rent each month."

"Okay, I'm not following you. What do you mean, Nikki?"

"There's a possibility of the History Museum losing its place in that building. The owner is thinking of selling."

"So what? What does that have to do with Brian's death?"

"I'm not sure yet. But there are rumors the same person that owns the Jacobs' house is also the owner of the building that houses the History Museum."

While Nikki spoke, my eyes glanced up at the light left on in the house. Something was different from when we first pulled up. Nikki continued to chatter on about various theories, but I completely blocked her out when I figured out why. The reason the light looked different was because it was now blocked in part by what looked to be the profile of a woman's face. I gasped as the profile moved from one side of the window to the other. This building was supposed to be vacant. Who was the woman in the window?

For the love of God, Brian had been telling the truth. There was a woman haunting this house.

Suddenly, I heard a board creak. Glancing at the front door, I saw that William had climbed up the front steps and was now standing on the wraparound porch.

"Kelly? What's wrong? Are you listening?"

"Oh no, he's going in. Nikki, I have to go," I said before hanging up the phone. I had to warn William about what I had just seen.

I launched myself from the car, leaving my cell phone on the seat.

"William! William!" I called out in a whisper. Too late. He'd already entered the house through the front door, allowing it to close behind him.

Standing frozen at the front gate, I weighed my options. I needed to get him out of there. What was he thinking? He couldn't just walk onto private property uninvited. And certainly not when there was an angry ghost waiting upstairs. No, that was crazy thinking. There was no such thing as ghosts. I shook my head, trying to put together a plan. Ghost or no ghost, I needed to follow him and get him out of there. Whoever it was would not be happy to see him.

Sucking in a breath, I pushed open the gate and made my way up the front stone walk. I hesitated, contemplating if I should go back and get my cell phone. Just before I turned to head back to the car, I glanced up at the window and watched the shadow move from one end of the window to the other. Whatever or whoever was up there looked like it was getting agitated. No time for my phone. I needed to get William out of there.

Moving as stealth-like as possible, I climbed the front steps and reached for the door handle. Twisting it slowly, I pushed the door open and stuck my head in.

"William!" I called out. The downstairs was dark, except for the light spilling down from the upstairs bedroom. It ran down the stairs just to the left of the front door. When I stuck my head in further, I was treated to a view of the piano in the seating room to my far right. This was the piano room Brian spoke of on his ghost tour. The one where Victoria was found dead. *Damnit.* Why did they have to keep it there? Now I definitely didn't want to go in. I wished Nikki was here.

"William!" I called out again.

From somewhere in the back of the house, I heard him call out in a whisper, "In here."

"Get out here!" I said.

He didn't respond, but I didn't want to yell any louder for fear I'd entice whatever was upstairs to come down.

"What?" he finally said.

"Get..."

Oh, Christ. This wasn't working. I had to go in.

Maneuvering my body to slide through the crack I'd created, I entered the house, praying the door wouldn't squeak. Since I could barely see around me, I relied on my other senses to help me find William. I moved toward the back of the house where I could detect William's slight movement. It sounded like he was opening and closing drawers.

"William," I whispered.

"Here. In the kitchen. Keep coming. I can see you."

"I can't see you. And what the hell are you doing in here? You can't just walk in anywhere you want. This is private property."

I shuffled slowly toward the kitchen, feeling my way as I went. Spotting William's profile, I knew which direction to head.

When I got close, William pulled a finger up to his face to silence me. His hand reached out to pull me against his body in the darkness.

"I just heard someone upstairs," he whispered into my ear. I allowed him to lock my body up against his, too scared to consider pulling away.

"That's what I came in to tell you. I saw a woman walking around upstairs before you came in. We have to get out of here."

William gasped slightly, making me think he was considering the same thing I thought when I first saw the shadow in the window. Maybe Brian had been right. This house was haunted by an angry spirit belonging to Victoria Jacobs.

"This house is supposed to be empty, right?" he asked.

"Well, yes, but it's obviously not. Why did you come in?"

"The door was open."

"So?"

"I just wanted to get a better look at what had Brian in such a frenzy. I didn't think…"

William stopped speaking at the sound of a board creaking upstairs. Whatever was up there was moving around again. My mind tried desperately to grasp at the logic surrounding us. Ghosts didn't make boards creak, did they?

"Ghosts don't make boards creak," William said, reading my mind.

He wrapped his arm around me. I accepted his embrace willingly, feeling comforted by his hard, muscular body. Surely, he would be able to defend us if a demonic spirit or a mere crazy person came racing down those stairs.

"What should we do?" I whispered into his neck. "We need to get out of here."

Before I could answer, there was a whirlwind of movement upstairs, causing us both to freeze in place and wait. My initial response was to close my eyes tight and burrow my head further into William. As intimate as our embrace may have seemed, the only thing I saw when I closed my eyes was Jack, and his warm, green eyes.

Abruptly, I pulled away from William and searched for a back door. Suddenly, I didn't care if William decided to stay. I needed to get out of here and abandon this stupid investigation. This had been a huge mistake.

"Look," William called out. His hand pointed in the direction of the stairs. A woman raced down them with her back to us. Before I could get a better look at her, she pulled open the front door and fled from the house, her long, blond hair whipping behind her.

"What the hell?" William said before releasing me and chasing after her.

"Wait. Where are you going?" I called out.

Too late. He was already out the front door in hot pursuit.

Finally spotting the back door, I pulled at it with no success. I changed direction and felt the wall for a light switch and hit pay dirt. Once lit, it was easy for me to unlock the deadbolt and flee from the house. My feet raced down the porch into the backyard, intent on heading in the direction of where I thought our intruder was heading. If it was who I thought, I needed to get to her before William did.

At the bottom of the stairs, I turned to my left and ran headlong into someone, knocking us both to the ground. The force of our impact was so great, I was left sprawled on the ground, stunned.

"Kelly?" my companion on the grass called out.

"Bob?" I reached my hand out to grab him. Nikki's husband was moaning and rubbing his head at the same time.

"Are you okay? What are you doing here?" I asked, kneeling next to him.

"Nikki sent me. She had a feeling you'd be here. Are you okay? Christ, I hit my head. That's going to leave a mark."

"Bob, I've gotta leave you here for a second. I'll explain in a minute. Adelle needs my help."

Before I could say anything more, a figure ran in my direction from the far side of the yard. Blond hair cascaded out in all directions, and a panicked scream filled the yard that was most definitely not Adelle's. The animated crazy hair reminded me of Medusa and her head of snakes.

"Kelly! Oh my God, Kelly. You have to help me. He's after me. He knows I did it and he wants revenge. Oh my God, I did it, I did it, I did it. And I'm so sorry. He was going to expose the truth, and the sale would have been blown. He wasn't supposed to die."

Tilly Dissert, Nikki's real estate agent, ran toward me and pointed in the direction of the side of the house. William approached us slowly, a look of complete confusion on his face.

I was too shocked to respond. By this time, Bob was in an upright position rubbing his head.

"Kelly, come on, do you have a car? We have to get out of here," Tilly shrieked.

Suddenly the yard was filled with light. A combination of dogs barking and voices yelling out commands filled the air with pandemonium.

"What is happening?" I said to no one in particular.

"Nikki called the police," Bob said from his position on the ground.

"There!" Tilly screamed, pointing to the far side of the lawn. She clawed at my arms, trying best to position herself behind me. William stood next to an officer in uniform.

When they spotted us, the men began to approach us at a slow jog.

"No!" Tilly screamed again. "Don't let him come near me. Officer, take me in. Where's your car? I confess. I confess to the murder of Brian Sanders. It was an accident. Please, just get me out of here before he comes any closer. He's dead!"

Tilly took off in the direction of the three squad cars parked next to the house. We all watched as she pulled at the handle on the back door of a squad car. The three policemen on the scene glanced at each other in confusion and seemed to make a decision. Two of them turned back to make their way to the car to Tilly and the third addressed us.

"I'm going to call for an ambulance. You look like you got quite a bump on that head. Just stay put," he said to Bob, pulling for his radio.

"William, what happened?" I asked as he came to stand next to me.

"I don't know. I ran after her and when she turned around to see who was pursuing her, she went ballistic. I'm just as confused as you are. Who is that?"

"Kelly!" I heard a familiar voice call out.

"Jack!" Waves of relief shot through me at the sound of Jack's voice. All at once he was engulfing me in a hug.

Then he pulled me away to better examine me. "Are you alright? Bob, let me help you," he said, reaching his hand down to help him up.

"No, just leave him for now. He shouldn't be moved. He needs to be looked at," I said, snaking my arms back around Jack, finally feeling like everything was going to be okay.

"I'm okay, Jack. Just going to chill here for a second," Bob said smiling and rubbing his head. "Got in a little brawl with this grass here. She packs a mean punch."

"Are you okay? I got here as quick as I could," he said, pulling my face into his hands.

"How did you know?"

"Nikki called. She was worried. You're okay?"

"I'm fine, Jack. Just confused. This is William Sanders by the way," I offered.

William reached his hand out to Jack, but to my surprise, Jack declined and gave him a look of death instead.

"What the hell, man?" Jack said in an aggressive tone I'd never heard from him before. "She could have been hurt. What were you thinking bringing her here?"

"I'm very sorry," William responded quickly. "You're right. I shouldn't have brought her here. This night has gone really... Wait. Did that woman just confess to killing my brother?"

William turned in the direction of the car, trying to get a better look at Tilly. "I'm so confused. Who was she to him?"

He looked to me as though I might have the answers to all of his questions, but I didn't. I was just as confused as he was.

"She's our real estate agent," Bob said from his spot on the grass. "I think we need Nikki. She seems to have a better grasp of what's going on here. She might be able to shed some light. She should be here soon. Detective Pavlik is picking her up."

William looked down at Bob and then back at me, tucked tightly into Jack's embrace. Jack continued to snarl at William like an animal guarding his young.

"Who's that?" William mouthed to me, indicating Bob.

I shook my head and chuckled a bit. Too hard to explain to him right now. Bob was right. We needed Nikki. The only thing I cared about was that Adelle was never here and Nikki soon would be. It was all going to be okay.

"Are you okay, babe?" Jack whispered against my forehead.

"I just want to go home. Take me home, Jack. Our home."

Chapter 30

Two months later

"What do you know about stuffing? The last thing I want is dry stuffing. What time are they supposed to be here?" Jack asked, placing aluminum foil over his dish.

"Any minute," I said, pulling the turkey out of the oven.

"Here, let me help you with that. Oh yeah, that's done. Beautiful," Jack said, closely examining the turkey.

"Look at that. Not bad for our first one," he said, placing it on top of the stove. "Hey, before everyone gets here, let's do a toast to our first holiday as roommates."

Jack grabbed my glass of wine and handed it to me.

"Well, technically, Halloween was our first holiday together," I said. After the Tilly fiasco, I'd made quick work of moving into Jack's condo permanently. The apartment above Chocolate Love remained somewhat furnished with my stuff, but for the most part, I was out for good. There wasn't enough room or need in this condo for all of my furniture. Nikki was fine with me keeping it there until we made a decision on what our next move would be. No ring yet, but that was fine with me. As promised, Jack was waiting for me to give the green light and seemed perfectly happy with the set-up so far.

"Well, yes, technically, you're right. But Halloween was a pretty hectic time for us. I don't know how much we actually enjoyed it," he said, clinking his glass to mine.

After Tilly climbed into the backseat of the police car that night at the Jacobs' home, she had confessed to having a part in Brian's death and gave us the whole back story leading up to the events. Accident or not, she had given Brian the sleeping pills that did not mix well with the anti-anxiety meds that eventually led to his death. The night before I had found him, she met with Brian at the Geneva History Museum intent on discussing the Jacobs' house. Brian had approached her earlier that month and told her she had no right to sell the home because he'd discovered it was not in the hands of the rightful owner.

While doing his research, he'd uncovered some troubling paperwork. After Victoria Jacobs was murdered, her family went into a deep mourning. The primary suspect, Mr. Weatherly, was so angered, either at being fingered as the possible murderer or the fact that Victoria did not share his affections, that he had swindled the family out of their home. Brian found proof while going through old documents donated to the museum that the transaction was illegal, and he was going to out Weatherly. He may never have been proven as a murderer, but he was going to be exposed as a dirt bag. Because both the building that housed the History Museum and the Jacobs' house were passed on to Weatherly's grandson, both buildings were in question as to who was the rightful owner. Brian had been determined to make things right.

With the threat of her sales blowing up, Tilly was on a tear to find the documents and destroy them. The proof needed to vanish in order for the sale of both the building and the home to remain on her roster. She also wanted to mess with Brian's psyche, so he would give up and keep the information he'd found to himself. She worked to make him think the ghost of Victoria Jacobs didn't want him interfering with the sale by scaring him. She had a key to the History Museum, given to her by Weatherly's grandson because he wanted her to help make recommendations on how to best fix it up to sell it. Both Tilly and Weatherly's grandson did not share with the police that the building was about to go up for sale, because it was still in the initial talks. Only Brian had known what was really going on.

Tilly had used the key to enter late at night and mess with Brian by leaving things referencing Victoria or calling out to him while he was sleeping as though she were Victoria.

But Brian had been determined, and Tilly knew she had to step things up in order to accomplish her goal. So she visited Brian one evening, telling him she'd changed her mind and wanted to help him get the building back into the hands of the rightful owner. What she really wanted to do was drug him and remove the documents from Brian's possession in order to destroy them. She saw her window when Brian complained of a headache. She offered the sleeping pills as aspirin, which they closely resembled. Brian's judgment must have already been jeopardized by the anxiety he was dealing with as well as his inability to sleep well. He took them without any pushback. She was worried when he quickly downed three of the long acting sleeping pills but had no idea how damning they would be. He'd passed out shortly after taking them.

After a long night and a fruitless search, she'd checked on Brian to see if she had more time to continue and that's when she realized he wasn't breathing. Panicked, she'd fled from the building, leaving the back door open and the items she carried up from the museum left in the apartment.

Weatherly's grandson claimed to have no knowledge of any mishap involving the ownership of the two properties. He'd never pointed the police in Tilly's direction because he did not share that the properties were for sale because technically, they weren't yet. It was only later that his connection to Tilly came up. He'd wanted the best when searching for a real estate agent, and in these parts, that was Tilly. She was known for doing whatever it took to close a deal. I'd witnessed it firsthand when she closed on Nikki's rental for Bean in Love. What raised eyebrows though, was the fact that Weatherly's grandson was going to dump his property in Geneva and move out of the area right around the same time that the rumors about the documents started. He had a lot to gain from those documents disappearing. Without Tilly's confirmation that he was involved with trying to destroy the documents though, there was nothing to hold him on criminal charges.

I couldn't help but think he was cut from the same cloth as his great grandfather and was looking to grab his money and run. As of right now, things were still up in the air and being investigated. All real estate sales were placed on hold because the documents had eventually been found inside the old-fashioned radio in the apartment bedroom where Brian was found dead. Seemed as though Brian had been willing to listen to Tilly, but was still too suspicious of her to show her the real documents. If only that suspicion had been strong enough to hold him back from taking the pills from her, he would still be alive. My guess was he had a moment of weakness, and the pain from the headache clouded his judgment enough to make him accept her offering.

Luckily, the night we'd discovered Tilly running from the house, she already started to crack from the guilt and the worry that the documents would be found. When William chased her out of the house that night, Tilly had fallen apart completely. Like us, she'd had no idea Brian was a twin. So in her panicked state, she'd been convinced Brian's ghost was out for revenge. In the end she'd caved and started believing the same stuff she used to make Brian tip over the edge. Ironically, she had yelled 'He's out for revenge,' just like Brian had yelled out 'She wants revenge' when he first came looking for Nikki at Chocolate Love.

Because of the confession, the police didn't need proof, but we'd had it the whole time. The pin backings were hers, which placed her at the scene. They'd come from the pins she wore proudly announcing her as a Platinum Member of her real estate company, having sold the most properties in the area for the last two years in a row. Unfortunately, with the real estate market suffering, that didn't mean as much as it once did. Tilly had been struggling to make ends meet and was anxious for a sale in order to pay the mortgage on her own home.

Nikki put it together the night she'd gotten sick in Brian's old apartment. She'd seen the gold backing and remembered the one I found in Chocolate Love. When she was feeling better and thinking clearer, she remembered Tilly coming into Chocolate Love the same morning Brian did to drop off some information for Nikki on buildings to rent. She had been wearing her platinum pin and may have lost its backing on the way out. When she'd thought of Tilly, she started thinking real estate. She didn't have all the answers, but she had enough of an idea to start nosing around. That's when she'd found out the Geneva History Museum might be for sale and that it all might be linked to Tilly. She began calling some of the board members at the

History Museum. They didn't come right out and say it was for sure, but a few hinted that they had a feeling the location was in jeopardy based on the fact that the lease had not yet been renewed.

"And what about Alice? Have you heard from her?" Jack asked, bringing me back to the present. "What time is she due here?"

"Same as the others." I could tell Jack was getting anxious to eat. He was always a little antsy when he was hungry.

Alice had agreed to come partake in our little pre-Thanksgiving celebration. With Brian gone and her job in jeopardy, we thought she could use a little party. She had been unaware the History Museum was in jeopardy of being sold and was feeling naïve and vulnerable. Alice told us she thought she had known all the key holders to the building, so when she was told Tilly was in possession of one, she was not happy.

"It's scary to think people were coming and going as they pleased. I've worked there for over thirty years. It's my baby."

Alice confessed she was leaning more and more toward retiring. This last fiasco may have given her her fill of the past coming back.

"It really is true. I hate to sound cliché, but history repeats itself," she said when we explained to her what had happened. "The land. It was always about the land and it still is. Those headdresses were trying to tell us something."

I'd shivered when she said this, thinking about the nightmare I had in Michigan.

William and his family were, of course, horrified by the news that Brian had been murdered, but felt some justice that his death would not go unsolved. Mrs. Sanders sobbed openly when I got the chance to speak with her on the phone. William and I had called her together from the police station to give her the news after Tilly cracked. I sensed there was some peace she would take from the news though. At least she would not have to live with the idea that Brian had willingly ended his own life.

William had thanked me afterwards and said he would be forever grateful to the Clark sisters. He did point out how ironic it was that Brian spoke the truth a few days earlier; the ghost of Victoria Jacobs was indeed out for revenge and it looked like she was going to get it. Victoria's murder would remain unsolved, but at least now she might get her house back, or more clearly her descendants would.

When I'd asked William if he was still seriously considering buying the home if it remained for sale, he looked at me with a strange look and simply said, "Maybe."

My mind lingered on that as I opened the door to my family. Adelle, Mike, and the kids arrived, bringing the noise up to a new level in Jack's apartment.

"Welcome," I said, beaming at them. It was a joy to host my family in my new home. Just months earlier, I never would have dreamed this day would come. This Thanksgiving I had so much to be grateful for.

"Hi," Adelle said, ushering everyone inside and instructing them to take off their coats. "I brought a pumpkin pie for you. Made it myself."

"Wow," I said, genuinely impressed. "How in the world did you have time for this?"

"I'm enjoying my new kitchen, and Craig has been taking longer naps. The kids aren't always going to be little, you know. I've got to develop some hobbies of my own. Who knows? Maybe Nikki will be interested in selling these in one of the stores someday."

"Now you're thinking," Mike said, kissing his wife. "I like the idea of another business owner in our family."

Since they'd moved into their new house, both of them were less stressed and more laid back. The whole family in general seemed to be in a better, happier place. But there was definitely a fire that burned in both Adelle and Mike. I had a feeling they would always be chasing to get back what they'd lost.

It didn't necessarily feel like a bad thing though. I was starting to realize it wasn't about the money, the homes, or the cars. Ambition was something that lived in both of them. Wasn't I also chasing to get back what I'd lost? A partner? A hope for a family? Although different, my chase was just as intense as theirs. As long as we didn't let it gain control of all focus, it could be a good thing.

I was just happy that Adelle was happy.

And as I watched her proudly display her pie to Jack, I knew she was. She pushed back her long, blond hair playfully like a game show model and presented it. Watching her hair bounce off her back made me think of the night I'd seen Tilly run down the stairs in the Jacobs' house. How could I have ever thought it was Adelle?

"Hello? Is anyone home?" Nikki called out. She and Bob walked in, and the kids ran up to them in greeting. Nikki's face was much fuller now and the nausea had finally lifted. She'd put on a few pounds to make up for the ten she'd lost in her first trimester. Though scary at first, her body had stabilized for her and the baby.

She'd taken a major step back with the construction of Bean in Love and allowed Bob Jr. and Bob Sr. to make most of the decisions. Though she wasn't thrilled with every decision made, she'd done well with handing the reigns over to her father-in-law and husband for the time being. Bean in Love had opened with a bang and was doing great. Sales were through the roof, and Nikki had hired Patty's husband to take over as manager and chef so Bob Sr. could go back into retirement. Seems they were all finally willing to accept they needed help running their empire if it was going to stay successful.

After Alice arrived, we sat down to the table Jack and I had set for our feast. Because he didn't have a formal dining room, we'd borrowed tables Nikki kept for her catering business and arranged them in our living room. I was very happy with the autumn table clothes, plates, and cutlery we'd lovingly agonized over late into the night the previous evening. I wanted everything to be perfect. This meal meant a lot to me and our family.

"To family," Jack said, raising a glass. I'd seated myself just to the right of him at the head of the table.

"And to safe journeys," Adelle said, raising her glass in response.

"When do you leave again?" Nikki asked us.

"Monday. Remember we're driving them to the airport?" Bob said. He chuckled a bit, most likely in reference to Nikki's inability to remember anything lately. "Baby Brain," Adelle called it.

"And when will you be back?" Mike asked.

"Jack will be back on the following Monday. I'm going to stay a bit longer to help Mom and Dad set up the Christmas tree and such."

The whole reason we were having this early Thanksgiving meal was because Jack and I had decided to spend the holiday with my parents in Miami. Normally, they came to Geneva for Thanksgiving, but Dad was still under the weather and not wanting to travel. That fact loomed over all of us like a dark cloud. Not wanting to spoil the mood though, I chose not to discuss it. I was hoping my visit would allow me to get to the heart of what was really going on with Dad and maybe get him some medical attention. Mom had pushed as much as she could. It was time for one of his kids to nag him.

With me being the most mobile of his three daughters, I was the obvious choice, which I'd gladly accepted. It would be great to see my parents and possibly quell some of my anxiety about my dad's health.

"You'll be home before Christmas, though, right?" Cindy asked anxiously.

"Of course I will."

Hopefully, I thought to myself. My mind raced to my plane ticket tucked into my carry-on bag next to the small safety deposit key. So far, I'd only bought a one-way ticket to Miami. Once I got there, I'd buy another one, but it wasn't necessarily going to be back to Chicago. I had some business to take care of in California before heading back home. There was no telling how long that would take. I hadn't been able to share my plans with anyone, not even Jack. If I did, I knew they would try to stop me.

My sisters and I used to listen to a lot of Led Zeppelin when we were in high school and college. A line from one of their old songs ran through my head. Something about California and an aching heart. That line seemed appropriate for my upcoming trip.

"To family and safe journey," I said, raising my glass.

Everyone joined in, raising their own glass to my toast.

Then Jack stood, his carving knife poised to slice the turkey. I smiled, saying goodbye to the past, feeling satisfied with the present, and embracing my hope for the future.

Grandma Helen's
Cinnamon "Comfort" Cake

Ingredients:

1 box of yellow cake mix
1 small box of instant vanilla pudding
4 eggs
½ cup oil
1 cup cold water
¾-1 cup brown sugar
3-4 Tablespoons of cinnamon

Directions:

Combine cake mix, dry pudding, water, oil and eggs. Mix for 3-4 minutes on medium.

Mix brown sugar and cinnamon together.

Pour half of cake batter into a well-greased/floured pan, sprinkle half of brown sugar/cinnamon mixture on batter.

Pour remainder of batter in pan, and then remainder of brown sugar/cinnamon mixture on top.

Bake at 350 degrees for 45 minutes, or until a knife comes out clean.

Note: This recipe is for baking a single cake in a Bundt pan. It can also make 2 large loaf pan sized cakes (bake for ~40 minutes), or 3 small loaf cakes (bake for ~30 minutes).

Recipe by Helen Linkhart

Dear Reader,

I hope you've enjoyed **Bean in Love**. Now please enjoy an excerpt from Kelly's first adventure, **Give Me Chocolate**. I'd appreciate your review on it. Feel free to stop by my website to learn the latest news about Kelly's latest adventures and where to find me for book signings at www.kellyclarkmystery.com.

Thanks so much!
Annie Hansen
October 2014

Give Me Chocolate

Book 1 in the Kelly Clark Mystery Series

Late in the evening on a warm Tuesday night in early June, Nikki and I worked in the kitchen of her specialty dessert shop, Chocolate Love, as she finished up for the day. My sleeveless top and cotton shorts stuck to my body, and my long, brown, wavy hair hung limply down my back even though the air conditioning was on full blast. The heat in the kitchen was unbearable this late in the day, but it was better to be here in the company of my sister than up in my apartment.

Heat was nothing compared to the loneliness I faced up there. We sat at a small table in the old Victorian home Nikki's family converted into a chocolate shop years ago, off of the hustle and bustle of Third Street in Geneva, Illinois. Geneva was a beautiful, small town located about an hour west of Chicago nestled on the banks of the Fox River. Trees lined the streets, and large, bright pots filled with assorted flowers marked every corner.

The town was a high income community with a population of about nineteen thousand people. I was lucky to have the opportunity to live here. I didn't believe there was any real danger here, it wasn't a high crime city by any means, but after going through what I did three years ago, it was difficult to feel safe anywhere.

"You'll never know if you don't try it. Sometimes taking a risk can actually make your life better," my younger sister, Nikki, said while signing a time card for one of her employees at Chocolate Love.

"Yes, but speed dating is not just about taking a risk, it's a guaranteed disaster. And as far as I'm concerned, this girl is off the market for good. I'm never dating again. Period," I said, pulling my hair into a ponytail. It was time for me to give up on trying to wear my hair down in some sort of style. The day was just too hot for a hairstyle. Besides, I wasn't really looking to impress anyone.

The store was deserted because the majority of her staff had already gone home. Nikki signed off on some final paperwork for the day, so she could prepare to head home as well.

Chocolate Love had been in Nikki's husband's family for two decades. When her father-in-law, Bob Connors Sr., was diagnosed with heart disease, he retired. He wanted to pass the store on to a family member and was thrilled when Nikki had enthusiastically stepped up.

"Okay, you're right, Kelly," Nikki laughed. "Forget I brought it up. Just thought it might be time for you to get back out there. You're wasting away up there writing that damn book while all the fun passes you by. You're only thirty-three. You act like you're sixty-five, in bed every night at nine o'clock and up at the crack of dawn. Where's the fun? That's all I'm saying. Where's the fun in your life right now?"

"First of all, I'm hardly wasting away thanks to your desserts. Second, the crack of dawn works for me because I like to start writing first thing in the morning. It's when I'm the most productive. I thought I was making progress, and you were happy for me."

"Of course, I'm happy for you. I just want to see you, you know, *better*." She paused to fiddle with the pen she held in her right hand. "You know. Like you were before."

I grimaced as her comment hit me like a truck. It was too painful to talk about what Nikki was referring to. It was hard enough holding my head up back in my hometown after what happened three years ago. Divorcing a man who attempted to murder his pregnant mistress left me with a huge stigma. And having the whole event splattered all over the national news only made things worse for me. Being the ex-wife of a convict was not exactly the role I dreamed of when I was a little kid.

Instinctively, I wanted to shut Nikki out, but I knew she was just trying to be a good sister and good friend to me. She was a good friend to me. My *best* friend. She took me in and gave me an apartment to live in rent free above Chocolate Love after I was left penniless.

Living here these past few months had been great for me. It was a familiar place that gave me a lot of comfort and joy on a daily basis. Nikki had done amazing things for the store in the last two years. She gave the entire building a new coat of light blue paint with red accents, remodeled one of the kitchens, and added more windows to the front of the store for customers to watch the preparation of the chocolates. Being here amidst all of this excitement and development continually lifted my spirits during a rough transitional stage of my life. Not to mention all the free desserts. Plus, I couldn't help but think, if this store could resurrect itself, why couldn't I?

"Please, Nikki, can we just let it go for now?" I felt defeated when Nikki talked about getting "better." What was that supposed to mean? I was never going to be the same person I was before.

"Yes, of course, we can."

She brushed her hands over and over her apron. To a normal person, it might look like she did it to rub off excess flour or sugar left over on her hands from baking in the kitchen. But to me, it was a head's up to what was next.

"What?"

"What do you mean?" Nikki asked innocently.

"You're doing the hand thing on your apron again."

Nikki was five-foot, two-inches tall, but her firecracker personality made her appear larger than life. A dark, modern bob accentuated her eyes, which were the same color as the chocolate ganache she put on her fudge cupcakes.

"One last thing, and we'll drop it. Have you thought about going back to see Dr. Bruce?" she asked, referring to my psychiatrist.

I was trying my best to put my tragedy in the past. Rehashing it was not doing me any good. Why meet again and again with a shrink to repeat the same thing? I already knew I needed to put the past in the past and rebuild. Everyone just needed to shut up about it and let me do it my way.

"No. Not right now. I want to take a break and concentrate on my book. Writing is the only thing that makes me feel better."

Before I could say anything more, the back door opened and slammed shut.

"Here you are. Why haven't you answered my phone calls?" my older sister, Adelle, said. From her tone, it was obvious she wanted something. Which was nothing new. She always wanted something.

"I left my phone upstairs. We've been chatting."

"Is everything okay, Kelly?" she asked, pulling a chair out at the table to sit down next to me. Her form fitting yoga attire hugged her body and accentuated her large breasts. After popping out three children, she still had the body of a fit eighteen-year-old, even though she was a few years older than me.

"Everything is fine." As soon as I said it, I regretted it.

"Good. Mike and I want to know if you can baby-sit for us tomorrow night. We need a date night."

She sank lower in her chair and gave me her sad puppy look. Most of the time it was hard for me to say no to that face, but not now.

"I'm sorry, but I can't do it. You know how I feel about the weekday baby-sitting. I'm up so early in the morning to work."

"Oh, I know. I promise we won't be out late. We'll just grab a sandwich and talk for a bit. Please, Kelly? You know things have been tough for Mike and I lately." She pulled my hand into hers and pled with her eyes. They watered as though she was on the verge of tears. Her beautiful, long, blond hair fell forward, cascading around her shoulders. It wasn't what I wanted to do, but I chose to give in rather than deal with a nasty confrontation.

"Will you promise to be home by nine?" I could handle a couple of hours.

It would be nice to hang out with her kids.

"Absolutely. Like I said, just a sandwich. I'll see you at six." She bounced out the door and left before I could even confirm six would work for me.

"That one is unbelievable," Nikki said.

"I know. It would be great to hang out with the kids though. And if she and Mike are having problems, they probably need to have some alone time." I justified her behavior like I always did. It was easier.

"Then hire a baby-sitter for God's sake. They can afford it. You don't work for them. And the only problem Mike and Adelle are having is how to count all that money of theirs."

"Nikki, don't start. Please."

Nikki sighed and turned her back on me. It felt like a slap, but I knew it was only so she could shut down the computer and continue to close up the shop.

"She takes advantage of you, Kelly. You don't see her asking me to baby-sit."

"You? She doesn't ask you to baby-sit because you hate kids," I said with a note of humor in my voice.

"I do not!" Nikki laughed.

Nikki got up to turn off the lights. She locked the back door and walked with me to the front of the store.

The store was set up so customers could walk in through the front door, view the chocolates being made through a glass enclosed work room to their left and then continue down the hallway into the store. Once inside the grand foyer, there was a winding staircase on the right, a bathroom straight ahead, and the actual store on the left.

In the foyer, Nikki made sure things were locked up properly for the night. A number of break-ins had been reported in the last month from her neighboring shop owners. Chocolate Love remained untouched, but I understood Nikki's concerns.

"I'll see you in the morning?" she asked.

"Sounds good. I'll be here. Good night." I climbed up the curving staircase to my apartment.

My apartment door was located at the top of the landing. When I moved in, Nikki added another bolt lock to my door, per my request. The house was always locked up at night when the store closed, but being doubly secured made the space more livable.

After making a turkey sandwich, I sat down in front of my computer to check email. I was happy with the pages I had written today for my new book, so I made no plans to revise tonight. Usually, my evenings were filled with reading over what was written during the day and making changes. Some nights I skipped it because I needed a night to re-charge. Tonight was one of those nights.

I noticed right away the majority of my mail was junk mail and advertisements. That was easy. Delete. Delete. Delete.

But my heart stopped when I scrolled down to the one email of substance. I could see there was an attached photo thumbnail. My gut urged me to delete the email immediately, but I couldn't stop myself and opened it.

"Oh my God."

A picture of a two-year-old toddler with rosy, red cheeks and blond, curly hair appeared on the screen. She wore a white bathing suit with red cherries on it. Shining, blue eyes gazed into the camera, and the smile on her face lit everything up around her. She held on tightly to someone who was out of the frame of the picture.

I just wanted to let you know Caroline turned two today. You are the reason this little angel is here. I can never thank you enough. We'll never forget you.

Love Always—

Mandy and Caroline

My first reaction to the email was to back away quickly from the computer screen. My sudden movement caused me to knock over the chair. I ran to the bathroom, barely making it inside before vomiting into the toilet.

If you enjoyed reading **Bean In Love** by Annie Hansen, you may like these titles written by Helen Osterman and Mary Grace Murphy.

The Emma Winberry Mysteries
Helen Osterman

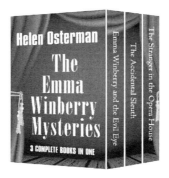

Praise for **Locked Within** by Helen Osterman:

"Locked Within is a simply wonderful story written by an author who clearly knows our craft. I had a great time with this book and recommend it to any reader who enjoys clever plotting and vivid characters. Osterman is a nurse who understands what it means to care and be cared for. Her writing is scalpel sharp and much more intelligent than some of the cozies I have read. Locked Within is fun and fascinating. Fans of my books will have a great time with it. Bravo, Helen Osterman!"

—Michael Palmer, MD,
New York Times Winning Author: *Political Suicide*

Emma Winberry and the Evil Eye

The first book in the Emma Winberry cozy mystery series, **Emma Winberry and the Evil Eye** combines mystery, suspense, humor, pathos and romance as the reader is introduced to amateur sleuth, Emma Winberry. When a world famous tenor, Marcantonio Speranza, a vendetta for a rival singer, and a boy named Angelo with a voice of an angel are all put together; it could be a plot for an opera. Emma's sixth sense tells her Speranza is in danger. To investigate she becomes a supernumerary (or extra) at the Midwest Opera Company. There she meets Nate Sandler, a fellow super, and they become romantically involved. But Emma has bizarre dreams and tries to warn the tenor he is in danger, but to no avail. In the exciting climax, during a performance of the opera, *A Masked Ball,* an unexpected sequence of events puts Emma in mortal danger as she tries to save Speranza's life. Will she succeed?

The Accidental Sleuth

Sixty-something Emma Winberry depends on her sixth sense and her Guardian Angel to get her through life. Nate Sandler, now her significant other, does his best to keep her out of trouble. *Most of the time.* When Emma leaves her house in the suburbs and moves into a posh condo in Chicago's lake front with Nate, she finds herself mixed up with a self-abusive, anorexic teenager, her cruel uncle, a couple of tough hoodlums who mistake Emma for someone else, and a cadre of homeless people. Emma feels the problems are somehow tied to the murder of an inventor found in a downtown alley. She calls on her Guardian Angel for help, but can her celestial guardian keep her out of harm's way as the complex puzzle unravels to a pulse-pounding climax involving treachery, deceit, and murder?

Stranger in the Opera House

Emma Winberry returns for another adventure in *The Stranger in the Opera House*. This time she and her significant other, Nate Sandler, are supernumeraries at the Midwest Opera for an upcoming production of *The Ghosts of Versailles*. This tile turns prophetic when the lead soprano screams that there is a strange man lurking in her dressing room. Although a police search turns up no evidence anyone was there, the cast and crew are left on edge. And nerves become more frayed as the 'stranger' is seen again and again, but never caught despite numerous attempts to apprehend him. Emma's sixth sense tells her he may be more than he seems. The rehearsals continue to be fraught with mishaps. When a large sum of money is stolen from the office and a guard seriously injured, everyone assumes it is the work of the mysterious 'stranger.' *Everyone except Emma.*

After finding an old trunk in a storeroom in the basement with documents dating back to the Underground Railroad, someone assaults the librarian in an attempt to steal them. The 'stranger' is again blamed, but Emma becomes convinced the apparition is a lost soul trapped between two worlds. Her Guardian Angel tells her she must help him cross over. But how? Adding to the mystery is a figure in black secretly leaving packages in a hidden niche. Can Emma solve this puzzle and release the 'stranger' at the same time? Determined to uncover the truth, Emma and friends are led on a life-threatening adventure that could very well be their last.

The Noshes Up North Culinary Mystery Series Mary Grace Murphy

Death Nell

Nell Bailey has always suspected food would be the death of her, but never did she consider her relationship with tempting treats would cause her to be a target for murder. After writing an extremely negative review and posting on her blog "Noshes Up North," a blog follower takes issue with her comments and won't let it go. The cyber bullying continues culminating in a gruesome murder. A fellow foodie, coincidentally also named Nell, has been slain in a most heinous manner. Could it be a case of mistaken identity and she was the intended victim?

As Nell wonders how to deal with the situation, her lifetime battle with weight and self image give her no relief. Then she gets help from an unexpected source. Sam, the owner of the restaurant she had torn to shreds in her review. As sparks ignite between them, a chilling question rears its ugly head in the back of Nell's mind. Could Sam possibly be the killer?

Death Knock

Retired teacher Nell Bailey loves her new career as a food blogger and restaurant reviewer. Her passion for food is good for the job, but plays havoc on her hips. As she tries to keep her life in balance, she learns that the new man in her life has a questionable past. Adding to her distress, there's a murder at Nell's new favorite local pub. She makes a disturbing discovery while investigating with her "partner in crime", Elena. Could one of their old friends be a murderer?

Acknowledgements

My deepest gratitude to my husband, Brent Hansen, who is always by biggest supporter. You inspire me to keep dreaming, keep writing, and keep going after my goals. I love sharing my life with you. Your love is my anchor.

Thank you, Mom and Dad (Tom & Gail McCarter), for always being there. You have taught me everything I know about the love of family. Thank you, Mom & Mary Koll, for always taking on first edits.

Thank you, Mike (Pop Pop) & Karen Hansen, for your encouragement and interest in my books. Our adventures in MI helped shape the plot for **Bean in Love** and get Kelly on the road. Here's to a shared love of the best things in life—coffee & chocolate.

Thank you to Geneva History Museum, especially, Terry Emma, Executive Director, for the private tour of your spooky archives and your excitement for my Kelly Clark Mystery Series.

A special thank you to the Kane County Sheriff's Office Citizens Police Academy run by Sgt. John Grimes. Your eight week class filled me with enough ideas to write for years and years to come. Thank you for your enthusiasm and genuine interest in sharing the behind the scenes with the public. Thank you, Deputy Thorgesen, for allowing me to spend the day with you on a ride-along. It gave me the opportunity to see first-hand just how well the citizens of Kane County are taken care of in times of trouble.

Thank you, Robert Reiner, RPh and Dr. Justin Hering, MD, for your medical expertise. I really appreciate you taking time out of your busy schedules to help with the clinical details of the book.

Thank you, Tom McCarter (Dad), Retired Special Agent in Charge, Department of the Treasury, Office of Inspector General and James McCarter (Uncle Jim), Retired Cook County State's Attorney for your help with the criminal aspect of the series. I love brainstorming with you both and coming up with the "why" behind the motives for my villains.

And finally, to my editor, Brittiany Koren, of Written Dreams. You have a true understanding of Kelly Clark. I appreciate all of the time and energy you put into making my stories come to life.

About the Author

Annie Hansen is a graduate of The University of Illinois with a B.S. in Biology. She is a partner with Hansen Search Group, a staffing firm she co-founded with her husband and business partner, Brent Hansen. She was named the winner of the Helen McCloy Mystery Writers of America Scholarship for her submission of her first novel, *Give Me Chocolate.* Annie is the author of The Kelly Clark Mystery Series and can be reached through her website: www.kellyclarkmystery.com. She lives with her family in the western suburbs of Chicago.

Made in the USA
San Bernardino, CA
18 October 2014